PRAISE FOR *THE INVISIL* TRIBULATION CULT BOOK 1

"SHOCKING!!! The first book in this series was riveting—great characters—I felt emotionally connected to them! Sitting on the edge of my seat, I couldn't stop reading!!! I felt empowered learning the enemy's historical tactics and knowing the enemy's weakness. We *can* be a threat for *good* and overcome the darkness that makes the Left's anti-America agenda seem stronger than it is."
— Sandra Guerra, Anaheim, California

"The first book in Michael Phillips's new series is all I hoped it would be: gripping, prophetic, hard-hitting. It's a winner."
— Nick Harrison, Eugene, Oregon

"*The Invisible War* by Michael Phillips, the first book in the Tribulation Cult series, is a powerful fictional interpretation of the transformation of America since the Vietnam era. It clearly and precisely portrays the methods used to attack the conservative, religious, and family structures in our country. When marching in the streets to protest the Vietnam War did not have the desired result, the teaching of Saul Alinsky opened the eyes of his followers to play the 'long game' to infiltrate and destroy religion, family, and our country as we know it.

"Having grown up during this era, reading this book has the 'hair on my arms standing up.' It is a powerful, well-written, fictional work that is a reminder to understand what has transpired, the need to be strong, and to put on The Full Armor of God."
— George Laman, BA political science and American history, firefighter/paramedic (Ret.)

5-STAR REVIEWS FROM AMAZON
FOR *THE INVISIBLE WAR*

Joseph Dindinger
Couldn't put it down!

"I've read Michael Phillips before, and this has a lot of the same heart, and depth of characters, but a whole new, and very relevant setting—our world today. Can't wait to see where the next volume, and the next, and the next, go!"

Cheryl Bussler
Michael Phillips books

"I love reading most everything from my all-time favorite writer/author Michael Phillips!"

Linda C. Livingston
Good read

"My favorite author, always a great story!"

Deanna Mosier
Great insight!

"The book starts in 1973 and goes to 2033, and follows four friends, two follow their faith and two go a different way. The author goes into society's changes through the years and has great insight into these years in America. I really enjoyed the depth of insight, the characters' growth, and listening to the excellent narrator. Looking forward to the next book!"

MICHAEL PHILLIPS

BIRTH OF A REMNANT

TRIBULATION CULT BOOK 2: A NOVEL

FIDELIS
PUBLISHING

Fidelis Publishing ®
Winchester, VA • Nashville, TN
www.fidelispublishing.com

ISBN: 9781956454499
ISBN: (eBook) 9781956454505
Birth of a Remnant:
Tribulation Cult Book 2: A Novel
Copyright © 2024 Michael Phillips

Order at www.faithfultext.com for a significant discount. Email info@fidelis publishing.com to inquire about bulk purchase discounts.

Scripture quotations are from the Revised Standard Version of the Bible, copyright © 1946, 1952, and 1971 the Division of Christian Education of the National Council of the Churches of Christ in the United States of America. Used by permission. All rights reserved. And from the Holy Bible, New International Version®, NIV® Copyright ©1973, 1978, 1984, 2011 by Biblica, Inc.® Used by permission. All rights reserved worldwide.

Author photos by Melanie Bogner, DuoParadigms Public Relations & Design
Cover design by Diana Lawrence
Interior layout design and typesetting by Lisa Parnell
Copyediting by Lisa Parnell

Manufactured in the United States of America

10 9 8 7 6 5 4 3 2 1

CONTENTS

CONTENTS

*When men differ in opinion, both sides ought equally
to have the advantage of being heard by the public;
when Truth and Error have fair play,
the former is always an overmatch for the latter.*

—BENJAMIN FRANKLIN

★ ★ ★

> "The kingdom of God . . . is like a grain of mustard seed,
> which, when sown upon the ground, is the smallest of all the
> seeds on earth; yet when it is sown it grows up and becomes
> the greatest of all shrubs, and puts forth large branches,
> so that the birds of the air can make nests in its shade."
>
> — MARK 4:30–32

PART 1

CONCEPTION

2032–2039

1

PΛLLΛDIUM
IN THE OVΛL OFFICE

OCTOBER 2033

WHEN NEW president Xavier Pérez named Akilah Samara, granddaughter of liberal financier Viktor Domokos, his new vice president in the second week of October of 2033, no one watching the televised announcement on the large screen at the Roswell estate in Mira Monte, California, was surprised. They had orchestrated the selection in highly confidential meetings with Pérez days after his swearing in.

The news media and entire country was still reeling from the events of the past ten days. No one was quite sure what to call the late president Adriana Carmella Hunt's death less than a year after her election. *Assassination* was the correct technical term. It had only been used previously, however, for the four US presidents who had died from gunshot wounds. It sounded peculiar to use the word for poisoning. *Murder* carried the subtle suggestion of organized crime or a gang hit. That didn't feel quite right either. But all three terms, used by pundits and commentators interchangeably, got the point across. She was dead, and after her state funeral, the country was trying to move on.

None of Palladium's members gathered at Mira Monte knew who had poisoned Pérez's predecessor. Even behind closed doors, they didn't allow themselves to go so far as to openly celebrate, though their toasts to the new president following his speech were buoyantly optimistic if not downright jovial.

Whoever was responsible had their undying gratitude. They could not have foreseen a more propitious series of events had they orchestrated ACH's demise themselves. Suddenly one of their own was sitting in the Oval Office. Pérez's most pressing immediate decision was whether to reinstate the name *White House* and repaint it and, while the painters were busy, strip off the hideous black paint and redo the Washington Monument according to its original design. That would also entail removing the Martin Luther King signs and shrine. BLM would probably instigate riots if he tried it.

One of their number, seeing events unfold, was not thinking of the crime so much as the potential opportunity. He and centuries of his forebears had been watching the West for signs of weakness. Though his grandfather had immigrated to the United States after the Second World War, and he and his father were natural born American citizens, their ancient loyalties were ever vigilant . . . watching . . . waiting. A moment would come. They could not predict when, but they must be ready. His father's bold and controversial vision to infiltrate the progressive movement was slowly and inexorably proving as prophetic as he had foreseen.

Sonrab Bahram realized that it was time he instituted more determined moves to get his son, Hamad, into Palladium's membership. Hamad was slowly making a name for himself at Harvard. But Sonrab must get him into this select circle where world events were secretly forged, just as his father, Nasim, one of Palladium's earliest members, had paved the way for his own elevation within the organization. It was the stepping stone. Who could tell? Perhaps it would be *his* son who would rise to the pinnacle.

He was sixty-five, thought Sonrab—old enough to think seriously about his legacy . . . and his son's. Hamad would carry the future of their cause on his shoulders. He needed the full weight of Palladium at his disposal to enable him to do so.

Sonrab reflected another moment. He would talk to Loring Bardolf at his earliest opportunity.

Meanwhile the FBI had no fewer than two hundred agents assigned to the assassination though they still had nothing solid to go on. Fingerprints, surveillance footage, a hot line fielding a thousand calls a day—nothing had turned up a single substantial lead. That the president was seen descending the stairs out of Air Force One with nothing in her hands but was seen holding the tainted water bottle when leaving the limousine, to walk through the crowd into the park, was the great unsolved mystery. Where had the bottle come from, and when? Never had such an insignificant item been the subject of such a thorough analysis. But every lab test known to man had revealed nothing other than the late president's fingerprints, and the presence of the rare poison homobatrachotoxin mixed with nondescript bottled water.

In the weeks that followed, FBI director Greg Telford, a Palladium voting member, said all the right things in nightly appearances on the network news programs—that whoever was responsible for the heinous crime, whether a single individual or a conspiracy, would be brought to justice, that the vast resources of the FBI would leave no stone unturned, that the manhunt for the perpetrator or perpetrators would not stop until the assassin, *or* murderer—he adjusted his terms as seemed appropriate—was apprehended.

Behind closed doors, though in public he maintained his stern and determined FBI persona, neither Telford nor his fellows among the seventy-two were especially anxious for the case to be solved. One never knew what worms might come to light if too many lids were pried off too many cans that lay comfortably hidden in darkness.

Palladium's League of Seven and their closest associates were discussing several misinformation options to make sure nothing pointed in *their* direction—though who could tell? Their concocted stories *might* be true. That hardly mattered. The public could easily be made to believe any of the three.

The simplest scenario was to let everything fade unsolved into the past, to be debated ever after along with the Kennedy assassination. The only drawback was that uncertainty left open the possibility of some ambitious reporter digging up something that might not be advantageous to the organization. Even if they had no hand in the thing, they didn't like surprises.

Better to control the narrative. A rumored foreign conspiracy involving the usual suspects—Russia, China, Iran, or North Korea—would fit the bill nicely. Better yet, all four countries together. The public would love that. The case would remain unsolved of course. But the rumor would keep conspiracy buffs looking offshore—assisted by a barrage of vague evidence they would set circulating in the conspiracy networks.

The third option might actually prove the most useful—killing two birds with one stone, as it were. That would be to pin it on right-wing Christians, some militia group, or the Trumpites. Or again, all three—a consortium of treasonous kooks. Advance the cause and solve ACH's murder in one fell swoop.

They could also set a match again to the 2018 Russian collusion scandal, implicating the next generation of Trumps in league with Vladimir Putin's daughter, Katerina, in an attempt to reinstate the rumored Trump/Putin alliance in Washington and Moscow. It was the kind of thing the public couldn't get enough of. They might even be able to orchestrate the arrest of Don Jr., Ivanka, Tiffany, Eric, and Barron in the bargain! The conspiracy of all conspiracies.

With his face suddenly one of the most recognized in America, the FBI director would not be visiting Mira Monte anytime soon. What Palladium feared more than anything was the spotlight. For the foreseeable future, Greg Telford's contacts with his clandestine colleagues, however their plans developed, would be carried out through multiple layers of secrecy.

His frequent meetings with Secret Service Director Erin Parva, understandable given her role in the events at Patterson Park, provided a natural conduit for information to flow in both directions through the Palladium pipeline without raising inquisitive eyebrows.

In spite of their affiliation, Telford's discussions with President Pérez in the Oval Office remained formal and detached. Listening ears were everywhere.

2

∧ Pastor Steps Down

2032

THE SMALL neighborhood church on the outskirts of Port Falls, Idaho, was not one that would ever come to the attention of the power-houses of evangelicalism. The attendance of approximately two dozen throughout the fall of 2032 was down significantly from the hundred or so who had been responsible for building the church a generation earlier.

In many circumstances, such a drop in numbers would doubtless have signaled something wrong either with the message or its deliv-ery. In the case of Truth Seekers Fellowship, that decline was actually proof that pastor Matthew Gardner was preaching his convictions with boldness.

On most Sundays, however, he had to remind himself that the mes-sage was God's, not his. Matthew Gardner was learning a principle that was being confirmed throughout Christ's body around the globe. The truths into which God was leading his discipleship believers were being spread like leaven through his eternal Church.

Mostly unseen. Truth perceived by the few not the many.

Perhaps God's highest truths could *only* be spread by small groups and small congregations.

The few, not the masses.

Ever since his wife, Sarah, had discovered the second of a series of biblical commentaries at a garage sale five years before and bought it for a quarter, Matthew's ministry to his flock—a dramatically reduced one now—had been transformed. Within weeks of reading the book, his entire outlook on the Bible had been turned upside down. Doctrine, theology, and analysis were gone from the calculus of his perspective, swept away as if by a hot wind. His new focus became living the life of Christ under the overarching Fatherhood of an eternally loving God.

The "church," or what he had always called *church*, receded far into the background of his thoughts.

Desperate to locate the other four volumes in the series, Matthew at last wrote to the author, whose son sent him signed copies of all five, which Matthew now treasured as among his most prized possessions.

By the time Matthew had been through the three New Testament volumes twice, his view on the church and its ministry had been entirely rebuilt on a different foundation than anything he had envisioned before—what he now considered a truer biblical model. Nowhere in his New Testament series did the author—a writer from the previous century, Dr. Stirling Marshall, whose name was now mostly forgotten in Christian circles—forcefully advocate for an alternate view of the afterlife than that of traditional evangelical theology. He only presented certain passages of Scripture that admitted to wider potential interpretations. Marshall's expansive view of the Fatherhood of God eventually led Matthew to the inescapable implication that infinite love and infinite forgiveness must surely take serious and open-minded Christians into realms of eternal possibility far beyond traditional doctrinal explanations.

In late summer of 2032, Matthew arrived at a turning point. Not a crisis, exactly, but a point of decision. He realized that he could not remain in the pulpit any longer while keeping his evolving and changing views to himself. His congregation must know.

After much soul searching and prayer with Sarah, he reached the decision to step down from the pulpit.

An impassioned yet quiet, thoughtful, deliberate sermon followed several Sundays later. In it Matthew explained his conviction that much of the theology of Christianity that had long consumed his interest no longer mattered alongside the life of true discipleship as laid out in the four Gospels. Such, he added, would henceforth be the focus and cornerstone of his life and whatever ministry God chose to give him.

"Finally," Matthew concluded, "the last of the major new convictions these recent months have forced upon me is my belief that God did not intend his church to be overseen by a paid clergy. I believe that the clerical hierarchy of pastors, ministers, and priests is an invention of men. I find not a hint of it in Jesus's words. And if he did not command it, why does the paid clergy sit at the root of every church and denomination in Christendom. Therefore, I am today tendering my resignation as your pastor—"

Gasps of whispered amazement rippled through the sanctuary.

"I will remain as long as necessary for you to find a replacement, though after today I will accept no more pay as your pastor. I will remain as long as you want me to but in the role of a layman. It has been a privilege and honor to serve you, as I hope I have. You remain good friends, dear to my heart. Sarah and I love you and will never cease thanking God that our lives have been intertwined with yours."

After a closing hymn and prayer, Matthew left by the side door amid a tumult of frenetic discussion. Thinking it best to leave their friends to respond on their own without the obligation to offer bland "Nice sermon, Pastor" comments, neither he nor Sarah appeared at the close of the service to greet the congregation.

Most of the Christian community of Port Falls got wind of the resignation of Reverend Gardner—as he continued to be called. It was the reasons for Matthew's resignation that kept the Christian gossip machine—which never needed much help—working overtime. The rumor mill was soon fueling reports that Pastor Gardner had lost his faith, accompanied by whispered speculation that either he or his wife was involved in an affair. There were also those quick to brand him a heretic who had succumbed to liberalism. A request for an interview with the local weekly newspaper followed. He declined the invitation.

On the following Sunday, the normal congregation of about seventy-five had swelled to over a hundred. The curious and ever-present controversy seekers would not miss this opportunity to hear something straight from the horse's mouth. Anyone who knew Matthew Gardner could have told them they would be disappointed. He preached nothing controversial, simply enumerating several New Testament commands to forgive, then offering a few words on the practicality of each. The service was concluded by ten till twelve, to the disgruntlement of those who had come expecting fireworks.

On the following Sunday, he preached to a congregation of about eighty on several other of the well-known commands from Matthew 6. By then, the skepticism among a certain quarter of the faithful about his "new views" was spreading. Weekly attendance continued to drop. Behind the scenes the board of elders was vigorously in search of a replacement. Two months later, Matthew was preaching to a mere twenty or twenty-five.

Eventually three of the elders appeared at the Gardner home, including two of Matthew's closest friends. Their mood was somber as they sat. At their meeting the previous evening, they began, the elders had decided to assume the pastoral duties of the church themselves pending the calling of a new minister. Matthew's services would no longer be needed on Sunday mornings, or for any other services.

As the matter had been decided, little discussion followed. The three left with forced smiles and handshakes that carried a tone of finality.

3

CLANDESTINE ASSIGNMENT

EARLY 2034

WHEN THE pouch from FBI headquarters arrived at Washington, DC's third police precinct with Lt. Court Masters's name on it, curiosity instantly ran high. It was delivered to his desk followed by six or eight uniforms with question marks all over their faces.

"What's it about, Masters?" asked his former partner. "You in trouble with the FBI?"

"No idea, Jeb. Not that I know of."

He opened the pouch and pulled out a single business envelope.

Expectant eyes clustered closer. Slowly he turned the envelope around. On it the others read the words "Eyes Only" stamped in red.

"Come on, open it!" said Jeb.

"Not with you all hanging around," said Court. "Can't you read? Beat it, guys."

Grumbling good-naturedly, the small gathering turned and sauntered slowly back to their desks.

Masters slit the envelope and pulled out a single sheet of paper. The message was brief:

Court,

I'd like to see you in private. Meet me Thursday, 6:15 A.M. at Oscar's Omelettes in Georgetown. Ask for his private room. Tell no one.

It was signed,

Erin Parva

He replaced the letter in the envelope and stuffed it into his brief-case. No one in the precinct ever heard a word about it.

Oscar's wasn't hard to find. By six every morning except Sunday, it was full with its regular breakfast crowd. Three days later, Court arrived at ten after six. A waitress met him as he walked through the door, beckoning with her head for him to follow. She led him through the noisy open seating area where every table was occupied, and into a small, almost cozily appointed dining room behind the kitchen. There she left him. A pot of coffee and platters of fresh fruit and breakfast rolls sat in the center of a clean linen tablecloth on a small table. Two cups and saucers, plates, and bowls had been placed on opposite sides of the simple but inviting spread.

He sat and had just poured himself a cup of coffee when another door across the room opened at the rear of the building. The Secret Service director walked in from outside. He rose.

"Hello, Court," she said. "I appreciate your coming."

"Madam Director," said Court as they shook hands.

"Please—Erin," she replied taking the chair opposite him. "I hope formalities won't be necessary between us."

"Coffee?"

"Yes, thank you."

Court poured a second cup.

"I'm sorry about the cloak and dagger," said Parva, dishing several fresh strawberries into the bowl in front of her. "I suppose they don't call us the *secret* service for nothing," she added, taking a sip at her coffee.

"Not a problem," rejoined Court. "Though I must say I am a little puzzled. I can't imagine what business the director of the Secret Service has with an insignificant former beat cop—that is, unless I'm a suspect in the assassination."

Parva laughed. "Not hardly! Though it *is* because of the assassination that I asked you here."

Court waited.

"I was watching you in Baltimore," the director went on. "I could see the alertness in your eyes, how you were paying attention to every little thing. Believe me, even some of my experienced agents don't exhibit that level of attentiveness."

"Just doing my job," nodded Court.

"I understand. Still—I noticed. Now I have an assignment I hope you will undertake for me—a top-secret one. For now, no one but the two of us will know about it."

Genuinely perplexed, Court stared across the table. "Why me?" he said. "You must have any number of people more qualified for whatever it is you have in mind."

"Perhaps. Let's just say I like what I saw."

"Well if there is some way I can be useful, I'm at your service."

"I was hoping you'd say that."

Parva paused, as if considering how to nuance what came next. However, when she spoke again, the words were without subtlety. "I want you to look into President Hunt's assassination," she said bluntly. "On your own. Quietly. Under the radar."

Again, Court Masters stared back at the Secret Service director, this time in astonishment.

"I understand your surprise," smiled Parva.

"Surprise hardly covers it! Director Telford is talking about the hundreds of FBI agents focused on the investigation. I'm not even a detective."

"I know, Court," said Parva. "I know more about you than you probably realize," she added, smiling again. "I've done my homework."

She had, in fact, thoroughly reviewed the lengthy file on Court Masters that had been compiled by Palladium's investigators and was the reason he had been earmarked for the assignment.

"You will be my personal eyes and ears," she went on. "I want you specifically to look into the Trump connection. No one has been able to uncover anything through the normal FBI investigations about the Trump cult. I am hoping you might be more successful."

"I'll do anything to help. But honestly, I'm hardly experienced in this kind of thing."

"Perhaps. But I have a feeling you're the man I want."

The director did not elaborate on her reasons.

"All right—fair enough. And my job at DC Metro—how will I—"

"You'll keep your job," replied Parva. "You will go to work as usual. Nothing will change. No one must know. Your investigations will have to be strictly on the QT. I will have a new laptop delivered to your home. Use it only for your investigations. Whatever you are able to squeeze in unnoticed during the day is fine, but most of your investigations will probably be during your off hours. I know it's a great deal to ask. But you will be compensated—*well* compensated. The computer will be set up with new email and internet accounts that will bypass police networks and be completely undetectable. Set up your own passwords and security measures. I will also have a new account to keep in touch. Everything will be loaded into the new computer. You and I will communicate with complete confidentiality. If you agree to join me in this, you can tell no one about it—not even your wife. If a conspiracy is involved, there may be danger. The fewer who know of your activities the better."

"I understand," nodded Masters. "And the current state of the investigation? I should know where things stand."

"The complete FBI files, current leads, all the crime scene data—everything will be uploaded onto the new computer dedicated to the investigation. As the probe is ongoing on multiple fronts, I will forward all new information to you as it becomes available."

4

NEW TESTAMENT CULT

FALL 2034

ON THE afternoon of one particularly painful Sunday in October of 2032, thinking about the church they loved but where they no longer felt welcome, Matthew and Sarah Gardner were working outside trying to take their minds off their troubles. Matthew was mowing their front lawn, while Sarah was planting two Daphne bushes in the border between the lawn and driveway. She glanced up to see three cars approaching along the street. They slowed then parked in front of the house.

Three couples from the church got out and approached. Matthew turned off the mower and walked toward them. Somewhat awkward greetings followed.

"Could we talk to the two of you?" asked one of the men.

"Of course," replied Matthew. "Let's go inside."

"I'll put on coffee," said Sarah, so hungry for fellowship that she could hardly keep from breaking out in smiles.

"I don't want to keep you guessing about why we're here," said one of the men as soon as they were seated. Harry Lawford and his wife, Jan, had only been in the church about a year and mostly remained in the background. Neither of the Gardners knew them well.

"We know it has been awkward for you at church," Lawford went on. "The treatment you have received has been, to put it mildly, less than Christlike. At least on behalf of the six of us, all we can do is apologize for the others who know no better. They are taking their cues from the elders, who *ought* to know better."

"Thank you," replied Matthew. "But really, we're doing fine."

"I am glad to hear it. But there is no excuse for their behavior. However, that is not why we have come. We still love the church and our friends. We have no desire to cause disunity or create a splinter group. But we—the six of us—we've been talking among ourselves. We want to learn and grow. We are not only curious. We are truly hungry to hear more about what you have discovered in the Scriptures about church and the afterlife—and about anything and everything. We believe that God has given you insight. Honestly, right now we're not being fed at church. We have no intention of leaving, but—well, we three couples want to ask if you would be willing to get together with us and teach us?"

Matthew stared across the room, hardly knowing what to say.

"You mean, start a Bible study group or something like that?" he said.

"I don't know. Call it anything you like. We would just like to learn from you what God is showing you, about deep things, not the first-grade spiritual milk the elders are dishing out with their incredibly boring sermons every week."

The other five who had come with him could not help chuckling and adding a few comments of their own.

"I would not want to do anything, as you say, to cause disunity," said Matthew.

"Nor do we. But neither do we want to stagnate."

"I understand," nodded Matthew. He drew in a deep breath and let it out slowly. "I appreciate what you are saying," he said after a moment. "Sarah and I will certainly pray earnestly. Of course, I would love to jump into an exploration of some of the things you mention. But we must walk carefully and prayerfully."

That had been two years before, immediately prior to President Hunt's election. The small Bible study that had begun, with the same four men and four women, had been meeting weekly ever since. Matthew suggested they progress through the books of the Bible, alternating every other week between the books of the New and Old Testaments, in the chronological order in which the books were written.

In the two years they had covered approximately thirty of the Bible's sixty-six books. They met on Saturday afternoons for a late barbecue when the weather permitted, or an indoor potluck if not, followed by a deep dive into the biblical book in question from about seven until nine-thirty or ten.

By 2034, the group had grown to two dozen, about half from their home church and half from around the community between Spokane and Coeur d'Alene. Whenever a prospective new individual or couple showed interest in the group, Matthew warned them of the possibility of criticism from those in their home churches.

"Many consider us a cult," he said. "Some of our former best friends no longer have anything to do with Sarah and me. People fear what they do not understand. Though Jesus often said to his disciples, 'Do not be afraid,' Christians are unbelievably afraid of new ideas. So count the cost. You may pay a price for delving into the Bible in the way we approach it."

Matthew's cautions were well founded. Everyone in the group had experienced exactly what he was talking about. Yet none would miss it. The Bible had never been more alive. The weekly gatherings were the highlight of their lives, and had invigorated not only their understanding of Scripture, but had also given them a new appreciation for God's expansive and eternal purposes for all his creation, as well as for their individual lives.

Upon his resignation, Matthew had gone to work as a laborer for one of the building contractors in the church. He was now the man's foreman overseeing commercial remodeling projects in Rathven and Coeur d'Alene. Most of the crew were members of the church, split about half and half between those who enjoyed seeing former "Pastor Matt" with his hands dirty and working alongside him as a hard-working regular guy and those who still viewed him with suspicion. More often than not the discussions at the worksite were not about the latest football games and coming week's prospects but were decidedly spiritual in nature.

Throughout the area many considered what came to be called the "Eyewitness Study" a cult, though obviously a thriving one. Those who were part of it called it their family.

5

Λ FELLOWSHIP BEGINS

THROUGH THE years, California rancher David Gordon had retained both membership and nominal attendance at Foothills Gospel Ministries, in Roseville, California, largely for his mother's sake. His spiritual center of gravity, however, had shifted almost entirely away from the mega-church his mother and father had helped start in the 1980s. He did not have many comrades in the Spirit. Neighboring rancher Robert Forster was a lifelong friend but not a man in whom coursed the deep currents whose ever-flowing, fluctuating, challenging, and life-giving waters occupied David's mind and soul.

David was ever on the lookout for hints of openness to higher things in those with whom his life brought him in contact. There were thus three or four in the church with whom the years had developed bonds that transcended what emanated from the pulpit or was found in the teachings then prevalent within the larger world of evangelicalism. Such fruitful companionships often grew among those with whom he had shared one or another of Stirling Marshall's books, and in whom the seeds of Stirling's challenge to bold-thinking faith had borne fruit.

Likewise, through the years, Timothy and Jaylene Marshall, the late author's son and daughter-in-law, found themselves less and less drawn to the frenetic round of activities, meetings, committees, ministries, and expectations of church life that had consumed their energies during their early married years. This process, too, had resulted in a handful of close relationships that invariably had the writings of Timothy's father at the heart of them. Nor had their daughter Heather, just turned twenty, ever fit in with most of those involved in the church's youth activities.

Prior to his parents' death, Timothy had resigned from the board of elders at Foothills. As he continued to make his father's vision of spirituality his own, gradually that mainstay of earthly worldwide Christendom—the weekly Sunday morning service—resembled to him a cacophony of noisy brass and tinkling cymbals rather than the worshipful and reverent quietude of Thomas à Kempis.

As the regular mail to his father from grateful readers now fell to Timothy and Jaylene to answer, Timothy saw ever more profoundly what an impact his father continued to have in lives. Answering the mail in a way that faithfully represented his father sent the roots of Timothy's own understanding yet deeper into the soil of his father's wisdom.

In speaking for his father, over time Timothy Marshall began also speaking for himself. Exactly as David Gordon had foreseen, gradually the mantle was passing to Timothy in more ways than he was aware of.

One of the first of what would become many long-distance relationships resulted from a lengthy and heartfelt letter from pastor Matthew Gardner in Port Falls, Idaho. No fewer than a half dozen letters had passed between the two men since. Initially thinking he was writing to Stirling Marshall, Matthew had no idea what a friend Stirling's son would become.

A letter from Matthew and Sarah Gardner had just come to Timothy as the Christmas season of 2034 approached.

Dear Timothy,

Sarah and I so enjoyed your last letter. Enjoyed is a poor word—it fed our spirits and uplifted our hearts. Thinking we were making contact with your father two years ago, we feel that even he could not have given us what you and your dear wife have since then. I have told you before that you need to write yourself and continue writing in the spirit with which your

*father's books and your own letters are infused. His life lives on
in you, my brother, and I exhort you not to take your calling
lightly . . .*

Timothy's heart was full as he continued to read Matthew's letter.
How remarkable it was that so often those very men and women who
wrote to him or to his father to seek their advice or counsel, God also
used to speak into his own life. It was truly an extraordinary circle into
which a gradually expanding community of life was being drawn.

It was not his father's books that bound them together, still less
him or Jaylene. It was the divine Fatherhood working in them all, setting chords in motion in hearts that vibrated in harmony with tens and
perhaps hundreds and soon thousands across the earth and around the
globe.

It was the beginning of a great symphony of interwoven hearts that
would prepare a people for its Bridegroom.

6

PROTÉGÉ

2033–2035

VIKTOR DOMOKOS was a true visionary, but his time was coming to an end. He had done his work. His efforts had succeeded in placing six hardcore liberals in what had formerly been called the White House and normalizing even more of the agenda spawned by the 1960s than Saul Alinsky and others of those times could have imagined. But the remainder of the twenty-first century would bring about even more sweeping changes than the early leaders of the movement had envisioned—global in scope. It was too soon to reach so high as to replace the term *democracy* with a different social and political model. He would leave that to those who came after him.

Domokos's final legacy, whose fulfillment he would not live to see, was a new US constitution. He envisioned it as the summit of his lifetime efforts to remake the country into a global federation. President Pérez's comprehensive new treaty with China was but the beginning. Its unprecedented inclusion of the Chinese premier in the US presidential cabinet was just a start. The changes he envisioned were so sweeping that he had not even shared them openly with Palladium's membership, though his "Final Declaration" now residing with its founding documents in the Mira Monte safe spelled out many of those ideas in general terms.

Viktor had always considered Slayton Bardolf a protégé. Slayton's premature death years before had affected him deeply. Though the boy did not see the aging Domokos often, ever afterward the affection

Viktor felt for Slayton had been transferred, not to his son, but to Slayton's grandson Mike.

Though nothing was ever said, Mike's father Loring noticed. Never a warm man, Loring grew yet more distant from his son, inwardly irritated by the attention shown him by Domokos. Though replacing his father as co-grand master of Palladium's League of Seven along with Talon Roswell, Loring was blatantly slow in grooming Mike to follow him into the cartel's leadership.

A brief conversation with Mike on the occasion of his address to Palladium two years earlier led to an invitation extended to the younger Bardolf by Domokos to spend a day at the latter's Maryland compound. Though Mike was no longer a boy, Viktor saw clearly that he was still young enough and full of the fire of idealism to be molded into a true disciple.

Within a month of that visit, at Viktor's request, Mike stepped away for a leave of absence from his father's company, taking up residence in one of the guest houses on the Domokos estate, to help put the older man's final papers in order, or so Mike explained to his father. No one expected the assignment to last more than a month or two. But it had continued, until gradually Viktor was dictating to and conferring with Mike several hours a day.

Viktor's goal was for those who continued his work to do as he had been instrumental in doing for decades, infiltrating new terms and motifs into the public discourse over the coming years. When the time came to talk openly about a new constitution, the terminology would not raise an eyebrow. The new blueprint for the nation, he was convinced, would face little opposition after a few initial flurries by the far right in its death throes. Once forty states were in their control, nothing could prevent its approval. The present congressional system would be abolished in favor of the new order, as spelled out in the draft taking shape at the hand of his young assistant. The changes would pave the way for unification with Mexico and the Central American countries, and Canada, if it wanted to be part of the future of America.

After a year together, the old man and his young protégé were in the process of hammering out a detailed text for the proposed document.

Mike Bardolf leaned back in his chair and closed his eyes, drew in a deep breath, then again glanced over the computer screen at what he had just written. It was enough for one day. Half his time was spent trying to decipher the dying man's nearly illegible handwriting and weak voice recordings, which sometimes drifted into lengthy reminiscing. It would be years before most of this came to fruition anyway. There was no need to rush. He would print out what he had entered today and pick it up again tomorrow. The original constitution had not been perfected all at once either.

In spite of their unusual bond, Mike was still curious—though delighted by his good fortune—why Viktor had requested him to act as his amanuensis on the project. In his early thirties, he was younger than dozens of others with more experience, his father included. But Viktor had taken him under his wing as if he were his own grandson, a fact which greatly annoyed Domokos's only progeny by blood—granddaughter and vice president Akilah Samara.

As a Bardolf, Mike's addition to the non-voting membership of Palladium had been taken as a matter of course long before now, as was Anson Roswell's. The two young men became non-voting members as soon after their graduation from college as vacancies appeared.

Talon and Storm Roswell, however, were eager for Anson to follow them into leadership, going so far as to submit Anson's name for consideration for the seventy-two at a mere twenty-three. Though young Anson was not voted in on that occasion, his rise in the organization was inevitable.

Loring, on the other hand, quashed the idea of adding Mike to the seventy-two whenever his name was put forward. His only reply was, "He's not ready." Whether he was trying to keep his son in his place or whether he feared that Mike, who had been a conniving rascal since his earliest days, might go so far as to replace his own father on the League one day, not even Loring Bardolf could have said.

After years of being snubbed by his father, Mike was elated to find himself in such an exalted position as Viktor Domokos's personal assistant—a claim no one in all the vast network of Palladium could make. Thomas Jefferson had been thirty-three when he wrote the Declaration of Independence. Had Domokos perhaps selected him in some subconscious way because he was close to the same age?

Would the future look back on the name Michael Bardolf as the third millennium's Thomas Jefferson, the architect of a new world order and the new document that would become a world constitution, a unifying secular global manifesto of equality, liberty, and freedom? Most of the ideas embodied in it, of course, were Viktor's. But the old man regularly encouraged Mike to add his own thoughts in marginal notes for consideration. Mike hoped his own stamp on the eventual text would be known to posterity to the same extent as Viktor's. Perhaps greater.

Whatever legacy the future bestowed on him would depend on the success of what he and Viktor were now engaged in at the Domokos compound. Though he was young and ambitious, Mike was a realist enough to know that he would never be president, probably never be in the public eye. That was both the fate and opportunity of those in Palladium's leadership. Their work would always be behind the scenes. He was not like Jefferson in that regard. The men and women in power depended on those like him who kept to the shadows. The masses would continue thinking that the Davos Economic Cartel and similar high-profile think tanks set the world's direction, with no inkling that Palladium completely controlled the Davos Cartel. No one got within a mile of influence at that level without Palladium's stamp of approval.

Palladium wielded the true power, though invisibly. His grandfather had prepared him for this time. Despite his father's disregard for his talents, his day would come. He was a Bardolf, and now Viktor Domokos's personal protégé.

The Clintons were gone. The nation's most famous black was in his dotage. Biden and Trump and Penskey were all dead. The era of Palladium's early battles against conservativism and the religious sentiment of the past were behind them. Progressivism had carried the day. The battles of the future would be launched by even more far-seeing visionaries. Like himself.

Still, there remained troubling pockets of resistance to the new order. Religion was a persistent menace to progress in all times.

Secularism always carried the future on its shoulders but not without determined efforts to discredit its adversaries as unthinking fools. *Atheism* was still a bit too strong a term even for progressive Americans. A little too communist in flavor for their tastes. Secular and humanist went down easier, though they meant the same thing. Separation of church and state was the thin edge of the wedge from which they had turned America, for all practical purposes, into an atheistic nation without using the word.

The recently inaugurated alliance between the US and China, ambiguously styled the Federation of Nations, avoided all such overtly communist pitfalls. The failed Russian union of republics of the previous century served as the test case for everything to avoid. The new federation would succeed in uniting the world's governments where Moscow had failed even to permanently unite Eastern Europe.

In spite of their success on this and many other fronts, however, Domokos had foreseen that the religious battle was far from over. The warnings in his speech at Mira Monte two years before, whose transcript Mike had read many times, were clear: "Do not relax your efforts. Christianity remains a powerful enemy. Do not underestimate it. Evil still lurks at its core. You must be vigilant and never let up your efforts to destroy it."

Mike had been at work at the Domokos compound in Maryland about a year when the slow-progressing Klebtridium 17 strain from the melted Greenland glacier swept through the country. Though the warming trend had been reversed and Greenland was now again under the same ice pack as in the 1980s, the ancient bacterial strain was like an evil genie that could not be put back in the bottle. It was particularly lethal on those of eastern European descent, and it seemed clear that it would probably claim Viktor before the cancer. In any event, together the two were a deadly mix.

His own son having passed many years before, Domokos's care ostensibly rested with his granddaughter Akilah to the extent her duties in the nation's capital would permit. She was, however, uninterested in either caregiving or listening to his stories of the past or his halting diatribes and exhortations. Her Saudi husband's wealth, not to mention her grandfather's, provided ample resources to hire round the clock medical staff to attend to her grandfather's final months. Publicly she said all the right things, played the role of compassionate granddaughter, making sure that "no expense was spared" to keep her grandfather comfortable while a team of doctors used "every means available" to bring her grandfather back to full health. But she was almost never seen at the compound.

Mike Bardolf filled the void. Delighted after their day's work was done to have someone to talk to who listened and who shared his vision for the future, Domokos hung on longer than anyone expected. He would have no one else beside him, finally insisting that Mike be given complete access to all parts of the compound and be allowed to come and go as he pleased.

7

Judgment on the Basis of Attendance

2035

FOR YEARS Geoffrey and Martha Powell had been immersed in Waco's largest evangelical mega-church—singing, teaching, serving on boards and committees, active in youth ministries. And of course they were both on the Sunday morning worship team, Geoffrey on drums and Martha at the mic. They were a young couple every pastor loves, the kind of man and woman who holds a church together.

Then their handicapped twins were born. Dramatically increased stresses—added to by financial and medical burdens and 24/7 time demands—suddenly inundated their lives like an emotional tsunami. Of necessity, their commitment shifted to their son and daughter. Never did a mother and father shower more love on two babies, then toddlers, and sacrifice so much of themselves for a needy boy and girl than Geoffrey and Martha Powell.

But there was no time for the same level of church activity as before. They tried to sustain it for a while, taking turns staying at home with the children. Eventually it became impossible. One by one they were forced to withdraw from the ceaseless round of activities, resigning from most of the boards, committees, and ministries they had been involved in. They also stepped down from co-leading the youth group.

Sunday morning worship services were perhaps the most difficult adjustment to make. Finally, they settled on a pattern of taking turns and attending in tandem every other Sunday.

It wasn't long before the questions began, mostly variations on the same theme: "Where's Geoffrey today? . . . I see Martha's not with you. Is everything all right at home? . . ." The slightly raised eyebrows suggesting doubt were clearly intended to invite elaboration about possible trouble in the marriage.

Many and varied were the cunning tactics of the gossipmongers, with which every church is afflicted, ever on the lookout to uncover some juicy tidbit that might be passed along to others as equally disobedient to James 3 as they. Truly were such the constant disuniters of the precious threads by which the fabric of the body of Christ is woven, and Geoffrey and Martha suffered much from their wagging tongues. Such schismatics go about, where not inventing evil, yet rejoicing in whatever taste of it they can unearth in others, even if imaginary—mishearing, misrepresenting, separating, dividing. Their self-appointed calling is that of the strife maker, and their work is indeed of the devil.

Geoffrey and Martha made no secret of their children's demanding needs. Nevertheless, rumors began circulating that all was not well in the Powell home. It is invariably true that parents of what might be termed more "normal" children are unable to grasp the challenges other parents face, almost without fail attributing perceived difficulties to parental shortcomings. In the case of the Powells, the advice from their Job's counselors at church was invariably the same: "That's what we have a nursery for, so you can come to church together."

Church was the solution to everything. Could they not see that the difficulties with their children would take care of themselves if they were in church every Sunday?

Martha's, "It would be impossible, their needs are too great," was usually met with furtive expressions of yet-deepening skepticism. Some of their closest friends suspected them of using their children as an excuse to withdraw from church.

A pastoral visit was perhaps inevitable. It was nonetheless painful to sit through—complete with predictable reminders of the injunction not to forsake the assembling of the saints, warnings against backsliding, and the importance of fellowship to sustain a vibrant faith. Not a word was said by their pastor, who had no children, about their years of service. Throughout the conversation, the pastor remained oblivious to the rising commotion in the next room, to attend to which now Geoffrey, now Martha excused themselves for a minute or two at a time.

Gradually the pastor's tone shifted from attempted concern to thinly disguised anger that they would presume to say that the care of their children was their primary responsibility. It was a cardinal sin to elevate family above church involvement, all the worse to consider their children more important than whether or not they were in church every Sunday.

The parting was awkward. There had been no meeting of the minds with the pastor who had married them, and whom they deeply loved. Geoffrey and Martha felt rebuked and condemned by the very man to whom they had been devoted for years.

The pastor's visit did nothing to quell the rumors. In an atmosphere where they knew they were being watched and subtly criticized, the incentive to continue making the effort to attend services was hardly strong. The pastor's greetings were cold and unsmiling. Former friends avoided them after church, and no longer called or visited.

Increasingly isolated and stunned at how quickly their friends abandoned them, gradually they stopped attending altogether.

It was about this time that Martha Powell received a book in the mail from a cousin, telling her it was like nothing she had ever read. Not that Martha had much time to read. The twins were now four and ran her ragged from morning till evening. She went to bed exhausted every night. Geoffrey helped when he could but had to take on extra work to keep up with their medical bills.

During the years of increasing isolation from former friends at church, Geoffrey and Martha found themselves reevaluating many of the teachings they had always taken for granted. So much of it now seemed empty. Was the Christian life really nothing more than going to church on Sundays and being involved in a breathless round of activities? Was fellowship on Sundays, as their pastor had emphasized, really a more important foundation to faith than how they lived the rest of the week? Was there no place for people like them whose lives and families didn't fit the comfortable evangelical mold?

They were lonely. They felt abandoned by their pastor and friends. They could not help being confused. Maybe the pastor was right—maybe their faith was slipping. But they couldn't help it. Life was hard. They were mentally, physically, and emotionally exhausted.

Into the midst of their spiritual quandaries, the book sent by Martha's cousin came as a gift from the hand of God. Though a novel about the English Civil War, it was far more. Its characters drew Martha into their lives and became true friends at a time when she needed to know she was not alone. She knew the characters were fictional. Somehow that didn't matter. They became real to her.

Devouring the book in moments snatched through the day, she ordered the sequel and told Geoffrey, "You have got to read this."

His reaction was much the same. The main character, a father, invigorated Geoffrey's commitment to his own fatherhood, reaffirming his dedication to be the best father in the world to his son and daughter, to give himself completely to them, and to support and encourage and share the heavy parental burden with Martha. Out of the renewed vision of his own fatherhood, the Fatherhood of God invisibly and quietly stole into Geoffrey's heart. The realization grew upon him that he, too, like his son and daughter, was in great need and required constant loving care—and that he had a good Father who was watching over him, who believed in him, and who loved him.

Halfway through the book, as suddenly the great truth of universal Fatherhood exploded into his consciousness, Geoffrey's eyes filled with tears.

"Oh, God, reveal to me the fullness of your Fatherhood!" he whispered. "Make me a son who delights to call you Father. Give me love and patience and humility to be a loving and sacrificial father to my two dear ones. May they grow up to know you as their heavenly Father because in tiny ways I have reflected the love of fatherhood to them."

His prayers stilled and he wept quietly.

Light began again to dawn in the lives of Martha and Geoffrey Powell—the light of hope, the knowledge that they were not alone. With hope, God grew in their hearts. His Fatherhood became precious to them. They knew their twins had been given to them to reveal the great truth that they needed the Fatherhood of God no less than their son and daughter needed them.

They knew they were loved!

The love flowing out of them to their dear young ones flowed into them from above. They were loved not because they went to church but because they were children of the Father. Their own inexhaustible love and dedication for their twins became a living image of God's care for them. They too were handicapped—trapped in the cocoon of their frail humanity. Yet they had a Father who would do anything for them, and who would bring good, and only good, to their lives.

One evening they were sitting quietly together after the children were asleep. Martha glanced up from the book she was reading.

"Do you suppose this man Marshall is still alive?" she asked. "We ought to write to tell him what his books have done for us."

"I don't know," replied Geoffrey. "This one was published—let me see," he said, flipping back to the front, "in the early 2000s. That's over thirty years—I suppose he could be. Depends on how old he was at the time. But, yes, I thought so—at the end of the introduction, here's his address."

"I'm going to write him a letter tomorrow."

Martha paused, then set aside the book and rose from her chair. "Better yet, I'll start it right now."

8

THE TORCH IS PASSED

2035

TO THE disbelief of his doctors, Viktor Domokos lived for another year, defying all the odds. By then Mike had become far more than secretary and scribe and assistant, but in every way his confidant. Viktor's trust in him was total. Sometimes confusing him with his grandfather Slayton, he saw Mike as successor to his own grandiose vision. Mike was by his side almost constantly as he poured what was left of his visionary lifeblood into Slayton's grandson. The hours spent at the dying man's bedside were amply rewarded. Slowly Viktor asked Mike for various things, papers, notes, files. Mike soon had full access to everything at the compound.

"Slayton, my boy," he said one day, "you must—"

"I'm Mike—remember, Viktor. Slayton was my grandfather."

"Of course, yes—I know that. You must write my biography, Michael," he went on. "No one understands me as you do. My colleagues from the past are gone. Even Barack has abandoned me. I made him. No one would have ever heard of him had it not been for me. I arranged it all, his speech at the convention—everything. He hasn't been to see me in fifteen years."

"He's not doing well, Viktor," said Mike. "He has lung cancer. All those years smoking."

"The young fool. I told him to give it up. People don't want their presidents to smoke—though he kept it secret, like he did everything about himself. Now only you are left, Mike. You must carry the torch

35

into the future. I am going to stipulate in my will that all my papers and personal documents and files be given to you. You must tell my story. You will don the mantle. It was yours from the day you heard me outline Saul's *Rules*—when was that, Slayton, my boy—'73, I think."

"I believe so, Viktor," said Mike. He did not object this time. Such lapses were becoming more and more frequent. Correcting them sometimes only added to the man's confusion.

"Now tell the doctor I want to see him," Domokos whispered at length. "And telephone my lawyer. He is one of us—Palladium, you know, though I know we're not supposed to say the name aloud. I'm only an honorary member, thanks to your, your . . . who is it, your father or your grandfather I think, though I get you all confused. Did he ever tell you how he got those Christians arrested and their house closed down?"

"Many times."

"I knew he was going places after that. A stroke of genius that was. And now you will do even greater things—which Bardolf are you again?"

"Mike."

"Of course. I know that. And you're a good friend, Michael. So tell my lawyer I want to make a new will."

His weak voice failed him, and he fell into a fit of coughing.

Still the end was not yet. More conversations followed, instructions about the disposition of some of his things, instructions about his secret files that, he said, Mike must guard with his life—they were worth their weight in gold—and persistent admonitions and instructions about the future of the country, and the constitution if he was not able to complete it. "You must finish it, Mike—you know my mind better than anyone—you must continue the work—it is all important—the cause must not die—fulfill my legacy, Mike—continue the vision . . ."

At length it was clear that the end was approaching. One evening Domokos awoke from a prolonged doze and glanced over. Mike was seated at the bedside reading. With a weak hand, Domokos motioned him closer.

"I have a final request to make of you, Mike," he said, his voice barely audible. "You have been a faithful friend and protégé. I am at peace. I know our dreams will be fulfilled."

Mike waited.

"Here—get this fool thing out of my nose! All these tubes and machines. They are enough to kill me if the virus and cancer don't."

Mike carefully removed the oxygen tube.

"I want to die on my own terms," said Domokos. "One of our goals is to legalize suicide. I want you to help me. All you need do, tonight after the doctor checks on me, is creep back in. Wait in the small study. Then we will unplug all the machines briefly, just long enough for my lungs to give up the ghost. I've been secretly keeping a little pill, which I'll take after the doctor leaves. It will put me to sleep. When I'm asleep, you unplug everything till you see my heart flatline. Then plug everything back in and leave. If they investigate, it will simply look like an electrical glitch of a minute or two. In my condition, no one's going to call for an autopsy. I've given the doctor a signed DNR note anyway that specifies no autopsy. I will be dead of lung failure, which they've been expecting for a year anyway."

He paused and looked up at Mike earnestly.

"Do you understand?"

"Yes, Viktor."

"Do you think you can do it?" asked Domokos, eyeing Mike with a penetrating stare.

"I would rather not."

"But you will," said Domokos, then paused briefly. "I think I have a good idea who took care of, shall we say, the situation with our former president," he went on after a second or two. "And probably why. Though I would love to know how it was managed," he added.

The flicker of a smile passed Mike's lips. He bent and whispered into the older man's ears for fifteen or twenty seconds. Gradually a smile spread over Viktor's lips.

"Amazing," he said. "So simple yet undetected. And no one, not even in the organization, knows?"

"Only you."

"Then I am privileged to be let in on the secret that will go down in history along with JFK. Now I am sure you will have no qualms about carrying out my final wish."

"I will do whatever you ask."

"Good. Now go. Return when the doctor leaves. That will be around ten. After it is done, leave the house by the back stairs. Come tomorrow at the usual time. By then the place will be in a hubbub. My grand-daughter will have been notified. She will be here—she's in Congress, you know, but she'll be able to get away."

"She is the vice president now, if you remember."

"Ah, yes—of course. Then she'll have nothing pressing—they never do. You will express suitable shock and condolences."

"I understand."

The following day every news outlet in the country ran stories through-out the day reporting the death of philanthropic legend and financier Viktor Domokos from lung failure after a long battle with the Green-land virus and subsequent cancer. His granddaughter, Vice President Akilah Samara issued the following statement:

> *"My grandfather was a pioneer of the New Left of this country. Though he will be missed, we who follow in his footsteps will take up the mantle and carry his vision into the future."*

Domokos's will left all his personal papers and files to his assis-tant of the previous two years, Michael Bardolf, who was also awarded a legacy of ten million dollars. It was a small sum given Domokos's estimated fortune of multiple billions. It yet caused more than a few eyebrows to lift when the news became public.

There were predictable accusations of opportunism. These were mostly quelled, however, once Domokos's desire for young Bardolf to write his biography became known. Suspicions were further mitigated by Bardolf's further commitment that all proceeds from the book and half the inheritance left him would go to the formation of a non-profit foundation under the auspices of the Davos Economic Cartel dedicated to furthering Viktor Domokos's vision for the transformation of the world into a global society.

There already was such an organization, of course, controlling the cartel and all its enterprises. The move was little more than classic Bardolf sleight of hand, adding another layer to Palladium's influence. The secrecy of Palladium would be even more carefully preserved with one more visibly public arm dedicated to the same purposes while the true power remained in the shadows. Many of Palladium's members acknowledged their approval and privately congratulated Mike on the move. His stature in the organization immediately took several strides forward.

Even his normally skeptical father had to hand it to the boy—it was a brilliant stroke.

9

UNDER BIG BROTHER'S RADAR

2035

TWO YEARS after she and Timothy and David first read Stirling Marshall's *Benedict Brief,* Jaylene suggested they invite a few select individuals who knew her father-in-law's work and considered him a mentor in the deeper things of God to meet at the Dorado Wood house.

Thus it was that nine individuals came together in October of 2035 for supper, followed by a discussion, ostensibly to share observations and experiences based on Stirling's *Unspoken Commandments.* Though not all David's closest associations overlapped with those of the Marshalls, most of those present knew one another. A newcomer from Reno—whom a letter about his father's book prompted Timothy to invite—was overjoyed at the invitation and joined them.

The discussion was lively, and the camaraderie of shared life and spiritual vision so universally felt, that well before the evening was over they were all looking at calendars and schedules to set a time and date to get together again. Some wanted to meet weekly. As word of the meetings slowly spread in the following months, however, out of respect for those who would be coming from greater distances, what came to be known as the Gold Country Gatherings gradually solidified into a twice yearly schedule every spring and fall.

There were usually fifteen to eighteen regulars. Recognizing the highly personal and almost selective nature of the group's perspectives, they took care to bring no one into the small fellowship who did not share a similar outlook. Invitations were extended only to those who were well familiar with Stirling Marshall's books.

Though Stirling's *Benedict Brief* was never mentioned, his cautions about the dissemination of his message guided Timothy, Jaylene, and David in establishing priorities for the group. They determined to invite only the spiritually mature and hungry. They were especially wary of church Christians who had not yet become commands Christians.

They had no interest in becoming one more tentacle of any church or denomination. If such an attempt was exclusivism, they said, so be it. It was the same exclusivism the Lord recognized as inherent in the four soils into which the seed of truth had been falling since the beginning of time. It was the exclusivism of Matthew 7:25–26. Some people hear the Lord's words and do them; others hear them and do not do them. Their group was committed to helping one another build on the rock, not coddle those building on the sand.

From the beginning, Timothy and Jaylene's daughter Heather was an integral, though obviously the youngest, member of the group. As a youngster she had been absolutely devoted to the two of her grandparents she knew most intimately. Entering college soon after their deaths, her spiritual roots continued to lengthen and, with the maturity of young adulthood, were soon extending down into the rich Marshall soil of her upbringing. She had always been a voracious devourer of books. Now a large portion of her reading diet was comprised of meaty spiritual fare. She was eager and hungry to grow as a Christian. The example of her grandparents and father and mother was one she desired to follow.

By the time of her graduation from Jessup University in 2036, she was as familiar with her grandfather's corpus as were her parents. It was not uncommon, when answering a letter from a reader, for Jaylene to ask her daughter, "Heather, where is that passage about such-and-such that Stirling wrote?" Often Heather was able to go right to it.

As an only child, Timothy and Jaylene always included Heather in their relationships. Around her parents' friends, she blossomed into an outgoing, friendly, engaging conversationalist. From an early age, Jaylene recognized that her daughter possessed a gift and love for hospitality. Whenever there were visitors in the home, she excitedly participated avidly in every discussion. It was natural by her college years, as the fellowship gradually began, that Heather was involved, fully stepping into the role of hostess with Jaylene—baking snacks or deserts ahead of time, arranging flowers or helping Timothy with the furniture, and warmly greeting guests as they arrived.

She never spoke in the meetings, however. She knew she was young and did not feel it her place. But she was listening, absorbing, gleaning, learning, and growing in the legacy of her grandparents.

When they met, discussions often ranged far afield from *Unspoken Commandments*, Timothy, David, and Jaylene occasionally finding opportunity to subtly inject elements of Stirling's ideas from the *Benedict Brief.*

"A caution has come to my mind," said David, a week after one such gathering when he and Jaylene and Timothy were together. "As I listened to the enthusiasm from those who had come, and when the two of you shared about the mail you receive, a strong sense came over me that being wise as serpents may require, in a sense, not only being circumspect with Christians, but also shielding our activities from the world."

He paused and chuckled.

"You know me," he said, "I am a dinosaur—my only adaptations to the world of technology are a cell phone and a computer. But I refuse to give in altogether. Everyone assumes that because technology comes up with some new thing—a new device, a new app, a new social media dynamo, AI, a new anything!—that it is a good thing and that everyone should embrace it with head-over-heels excitement. I do not agree. Most of those are bandwagons I refuse to jump on. How much better is the character, integrity, and moral and spiritual fiber of the world because of the internet or AI? Not an atom that I can see. The world has advanced technologically, but character and godliness have virtually disappeared as foundational priorities of our culture. If the internet were abolished and AI completely outlawed tomorrow, after some adjustments the world would eventually be better off. People would again have to rely on integrity, honesty, and dignity to think about what is true rather than relying on zeros and ones to do their thinking for them.

"I realize that because of your professions, the two of you are deeply connected to the technology of the times. You have to be. I realize that. However, I feel a caution is in order about how you handle your personal correspondence with readers, and how we proceed with this group that seems to be taking on a life of its own. It may be time that you consider separating the necessities of your professional duties from what God is doing in this alternate life in which we are involved. The world is watching. It is watching everything. Privacy disappeared in our country decades ago. With China now owning Amazon, Apple, and Microsoft and allied with our own government, everything in our lives is both being seen and manipulated by the Federation of Nations. We are living in Orwell's 1984. AI is Big Brother yet is so invisible that no one recognizes how thoroughly our lives are being monitored. It's another example of Christians going along with the world without considering the consequences. And as Christianity comes under increasing attack, we have to respond with God's wisdom."

Again he laughed lightly.

"I'm not a political man," he said. "Forgive what sounds like a cultural diatribe! But there is a practical aspect to what I am getting at. That is simply that the more we stand up for God's truth, the more persecution we should expect. I feel strongly that you should consider perhaps separating your spiritual communications and reader responses from your professional activities and in whatever ways possible disengage from technology altogether. All the social media and online platforms are open avenues into your lives that could be used against you. I would encourage you to communicate no more through the internet, asking readers to correspond with you by written letter. We must all be very circumspect in what we say openly. We may also want to say something like this to the group. In all ways possible, we must not allow our activities to raise suspicions. We must do so to protect the people who come to us, as well as to safeguard the truth. Christianity is under attack. We need to think of ourselves as part of an underground movement. If it is not such now, I am convinced it will become one."

Timothy and Jaylene listened attentively. They immediately realized that David's cautions were sound.

"We also need to be careful of hot-button words and phrases," David went on. "Not that we should be ruled by fear. But neither must we invite scrutiny. The tech companies are trolling everything. One careless word online could put a target on your back. The two of you are high profile individuals in your profession. Jaylene, you are no doubt still on academia's radar as a troublemaker. As much as possible I would prefer that you both flew under the radar."

"Most people contact us by email and social media without giving us a mailing address," said Jaylene.

"I realize that," nodded David. "But would it not be a simple matter to reply asking for an address, telling them that you conduct your correspondence by mail? I would feel more comfortable if you eventually discontinued email and social media altogether."

"How would people contact us? How would they even find us?"

"If they are intended to find you, God will make sure they do. If their correspondence is bounced back, they will find you another way. If God is in it, they will find you. God's purposes were being carried out long before the computer age. Your father's address is in most of his books. People can write letters. I would go even further and suggest using security envelopes. A day is coming when Big Brother will not only scrutinize electronic communications but even written communications that seem safe. There have been many times in its history when the Church was forced underground. I realize it may sound alarmist, but I believe perilous times are coming. With the proliferation of AI, 1984 is here and few realize it."

Jaylene and Timothy took in his words seriously.

"People can find you," David went on. "And your responses should be well guarded. Technology is not necessary for God to do his work. They open you up to being scrutinized by Big Brother in ways that may impede what God has for us to do."

"It would be hard to do what you suggest," said Timothy. "Yet you are right, we are far too accustomed to technology. What you say resonates with my father's warnings. I know he would agree with every word you say."

"If I know your father, he would say it even more strongly!" laughed Jaylene.

"You're right," nodded Timothy. "He hated what technology was doing to the world. If there was so much as a one-in-a-million chance that his *Benedict Brief* would ever be spread on the internet, or that a website would be set up to promote it, he would destroy every copy to prevent it."

"If Stirling would urge upon us the same cautions as David has," said Jaylene, "that decides it. Our objective is to further his vision and the teachings of Jesus. If he would not want that done through technology, that is reason enough for me. I will send out a blanket mailing to my personal contacts tomorrow saying that henceforth my personal correspondence will be conducted by physical mail. Then I will cancel my online and social accounts. What needs to be done for my work can be handled through the university accounts. It will be liberating!"

10

STALLED INVESTIGATION

2036

IT HAD been two years since Court Masters's clandestine meeting with Erin Parva. In what time he had been able to devote to his private investigation, he had discovered no hint of a conspiracy, nothing connected to any right-wing groups or lingering Trump faction.

He had interviewed Trump's two daughters and three sons and found them personable, intelligent, and engaging. They were aware of the rumors of an underground "Trumpite" group with sinister plans to disrupt the government. All five not only disavowed knowing anything about it; they insisted no such group existed but had been hatched by the Left. It was a useful ploy—invent a phantom enemy to blame for their own troubles, maintaining an undercurrent of accusation to keep the Right off balance.

If his investigator's nose was to be trusted, they were telling the truth. Theirs were not the expected knee-jerk denials of political hacks. They spoke with the confidence of knowing what they said was true. One of the sons let slip that they had looked into it themselves in the aftermath of the assassination. If there was a Trumpite group, it was in their interest to know it in order to preserve a positive legacy for their father. With the Trump billions at their disposal, they had the finances to uncover it. They had devoted considerable resources to the investigation but found nothing. The group was a mirage, brought back around into the news cycle every so often when the Democrats needed a foil.

Curiously, however, every time he spoke with Director Parva, which was once every two or three months, she seemed intent on beating the Trump drum in spite of the lack of evidence. Gradually the suspicion grew that she had enlisted him not so much to find what might have happened in Baltimore as to infiltrate whatever Trump faction might still be working in the deep underground. He saw her perk up noticeably when he mentioned the Trump interviews. To his insistence that there was no evidence such a group existed, she only said, "Keep digging. If it's not the Trumpites, find what you can on any secret right-wing groups. There are rumors of others. We need to know who these people are."

He also could not avoid the sensation that she was watching him with a wary eye, as if wondering if he might be hiding something. It was nothing he could put his finger on, but her tone and demeanor was definitely guarded. Yet as far as he knew, she was unaware of his political leanings. They never talked politics.

The Trump connection, which he was convinced was imaginary, represented but one of several aspects of interest in the case. Given Parva's role in the FBI, an arm of the executive under the Department of Justice, her anti-Trump bias was understandable. It was endemic throughout Washington. But despite his conservative perspectives, he could be objective. Even if Parva was obsessed with a potential Trump plot, until she took him off the case he would do his best to conduct a thorough investigation in spite of her prejudices.

He had been following two leads. Neither had turned up anything substantive. But they had as much potential as the Trump connection. The first was a thorough investigation of everyone who had been close enough to President Hunt to be involved, from the time she boarded Air Force One at Andrews until her collapse at Patterson Park. He was still not satisfied that his list was absolutely complete—though it now contained more than two hundred names, from the bevy of FBI and Secret Service agents to flight staff and Air Force personnel to various Baltimore dignitaries, and of course the contingents from the Baltimore and Washington police departments. Even his own name was on the list.

He had gone over every scrap of footage available, though the FBI had done so as well. It was doubtful he could find anything they hadn't. But he trusted his nose and preferred to draw his own conclusions. Nothing suspicious from the names on the list stood out. But somewhere in the film of the day's events, or on his list of names, an assassin was lurking. That the FBI had uncovered nothing raised the specter of a possible cover-up. Yet nothing pointed in that direction.

He had also been researching the mysterious poison homobatrachotoxin. Its extreme rarity, one would think, would make its scant supplies easy to trace. But he had not found it so. Originating in South America, every avenue he had explored led to dead ends and trails so murky he might as well have been traipsing blind through an Amazon jungle. How it had been procured, how it had been safely delivered to the States, when and by whom, he had no more idea than had anyone on the day of President Hunt's death.

But the poison and his list of names were the key, of that he was certain.

Then out of the blue a year later, Director Parva called and abruptly pulled him off the investigation.

As of that moment, she declared the case closed.

11

Faithful Wounded Parents

2036

THE LETTER Timothy opened one Sunday afternoon in 2036, though not lengthy, was poignant. On how many of its own, he thought, does the church inflict dreadful wounds from lack of support for those who need it most?

Dear Mr. Marshall,

I hope and pray this letter finds you. I realize the address is probably old, yet I must write and trust God to do the rest. My husband and I live in Texas and have been active Christians for many years. When our handicapped twin son and daughter were born, their care was so overwhelming that we had no choice but to scale back from our active round of church activities. We knew our family and the two young ones God had given us were our primary responsibility.

Our two dear ones have blessed our lives and we love them so much. At night my husband Geoffrey gets into bed with young Travis when he can't sleep or is afraid. Geoffrey puts on a quiet collection of harp music and it always helps Travis go to sleep. When I listen to them quietly talking, with the harp music playing, I cannot but think of heaven, and that God is acting as Father to us in the same way Geoffrey is to Travis.

Yet life is hard for us. How shocked we have been by the response of our pastor and friends at church who think we are backsliding because we aren't in church every Sunday. Our pastor called on us and quoted forsaking not the assembling together from Hebrews and warned us about falling away from the Lord. All the while he expressed no interest in our lives, our children, or in why we were not so involved as before. I admit his insensitivity made me angry.

In the midst of some very discouraging times we discovered your English Civil War series. I cannot tell you how it lifted our spirits. Not only did we learn about a historical period we knew nothing about—shocked at how similar to our own time was the hostility and division in the 17th century English church—we discovered an image of God's Fatherhood that was new to us. It transformed how we saw ourselves as Christians—as God's son and daughter. We saw that in God's eyes we were as precious to him as Travis and Kayla are to us. What a revelation! It brings tears to my eyes to think of it again.

We would love to read more of your books. Do you have a list? We are hungry to explore God's Fatherhood in depth. With all our hearts we desire to be Godly parents to our young ones, and to be a faithful son and daughter to our heavenly Father.

Thank you so much for being God's servant to deliver his message of Fatherhood into our hearts.

With much gratitude,
Martha (and Geoffrey) Powell

Timothy closed his eyes. *Oh, Father,* he prayed, *may I know your heart. Give me your words for this dear sister. Speak into her heart . . .*

He sighed and waited. When he began to write a minute later, his spirit was calm.

Dear Martha,

How wonderful it was to read your letter. My heart leapt to hear you speak of God's Fatherhood.

Next, I must tell you that I am Timothy Marshall, son of Stirling and Larke Marshall. My dear parents passed away some years ago, in 2031 and 2032. Yet my father's writings live on. Miraculously, it often seems, the mail addressed to him is forwarded to us. My wife and I do our best to respond in the spirit of my parents. I grew up watching them reply to readers. Inadequate as I feel, and though I know you were writing as if to him, God has privileged me with the opportunity to stand in my father's stead and try to speak from the wisdom his life imparted to me, or put another way, to speak what I think he would say if he were actually the one writing you this letter.

In that spirit, let me first encourage you to ignore the insensitive (dare I go so far as to call it absurd) counsel of your pastor, and any others who offer you similar perhaps well-meaning but opinionated advice that does not come from the heart of God. Christians can be far too quick to spout off foolish ideas without pausing to ask if those opinions originate with the Holy Spirit or their own immaturity. Ignore it. Seek and rest in the knowledge that you are in the Father's hands.

And you are!

Your heart for God, to be his daughter, radiates from the page as I read. Though you and I have never met, I know you in the Spirit because your spirit touched mine through your words.

Oh, and your dear husband! What an example of the Father's love he is giving to your son. He typifies everything my father's writing and life-passion was about—the revelation of the divine Fatherhood.

When we all are joined in the great "gathering" when all earthly limitations fall away, Travis will be suddenly revealed for the fully formed Godly man his heavenly Father has been fashioning within him all his life. Many will awaken to the life of beyond in confusion because they never made it their life's business to discover the character of God and know his heart.

One person who won't be confused is Travis Powell.

Travis will look around and be completely at home. He will wonder why there is any confusion about God at all. There will be no mystery about heaven to him.

"I know who the Father is," Travis will say. "My dad showed me God all my life. God is just like him."

A brochure of my father's books is enclosed. We've managed to get most of the titles back into print and will try to help you find anything you might like to read.

Many blessings to you and Geoffrey, and also to young Travis and Kayla. It would be a privilege to meet them some day.

Your brother in Christ,
Timothy Marshall

12

FAR TO THE NORTH

2036-2038

SEATTLE, WASHINGTON, had proven a hothouse for the four college friends from northern California's obscure state university. After only a few years in the King County DA's office, Linda, now married as Linda Hutchins Trent, had surpassed her older brother, Sawyer. Gaining a reputation as one of the top public minority rights activist ADAs in the state, she became the county's youngest ever district attorney. Almost instantly she was being talked about for one of Seattle's prize judgeships. Christian groups and leaders amassed enough money to wage a campaign against her. Their efforts, however, were unsuccessful. After Linda's victory in a special election in 2035, Sawyer replaced her as DA.

Linda's erstwhile law school lover had his sights set even higher. After being reelected to the House of Representatives in 2034, Jefferson Rhodes mounted a successful bid for the Senate, where he was elected in 2036 at the age of thirty-six.

Meanwhile, the two "religious" members of the Humboldt foursome, as Jeff and Linda called them, had done equally well in their respective spheres by the world's reckoning of success. Linda's brother Ward's first book became a huge bestseller. Three more followed. By the time Seattle's former mayor's son was moving from the lower chamber of Congress to join the nation's most elite political club, fully half of Ward's time was spent speaking to enthusiastic evangelical crowds nationwide. Though only a year older than his pastoral protégé Mark

Forster, Ward Hutchins was one of the best-known faces in American Christendom. Some were hailing him as the next Billy Graham.

Though nothing specific had been said, Mark sensed that Ward was grooming him as his replacement. As Ward devoted more and more time to travel, speaking, and writing, Mark was in many respects already the de facto head of Puget Sound Vine Ministries. Not as flashy as Ward, and more cerebral in his pulpit and teaching style, many in the congregation loved his warm and personable pastoring heart and would have wholeheartedly supported his elevation to the senior pastorate of the rapidly growing church and its wide range of ministries. Throughout the mid-2030s, Mark's name thus came to be associated with Ward's and was one of growing stature in and around Seattle.

Notwithstanding his national reputation, Ward was an embarrassment to his brother Sawyer and sister Linda. As his fame mounted, he became one of the Left's favorite targets, the epitome of the Neanderthal thinking that Seattle's political machine hated. Linda and Sawyer were outspoken in disavowing a connection to their right-wing brother. The division within such a high-profile Seattle family kept the Hutchins and Trent names constantly in the news.

Always looking ahead on the political chessboard, though not considered one of the intellectual heavyweights of the new senatorial class of 2036, Jefferson Rhodes shrewdly managed to insert his former friend, and more than a friend, who was rising rapidly in Seattle's legal community, into the judicial conversation at the highest levels.

The pieces on the chessboard were beginning to align themselves.

In the years following Viktor Domokos's death, progressivism in the United States flourished. It almost appeared that Domokos's vision of a global secular society would be achieved sooner than the 2050 date he had always envisioned.

Rankled that she had only received fifty million dollars from her grandfather's will alongside the unconscionably generous ten million given to Mike Bardolf, Akilah Samara yet dutifully pretended that she and the youngest Bardolf were as close as he had been to her grandfather. She glowingly endorsed his biography of her grandfather, which pundits hailed as one of the best biographies written in years. Though inwardly chafing that he had been privy to her grandfather's secrets that even she still knew nothing about, and that he continued to safeguard his papers from her, the vice president realized that nothing could be gained by feuding with him.

She knew that Palladium's political operatives were already talking about who would be their candidate in 2040, when recently reelected Xavier Pérez's two terms from 2032 to 2040 were up. Out of consideration for her grandfather, Palladium's higher-ups showed her begrudging respect. But she knew most of the top names of the seventy-two considered her a lightweight. Even holding presumably the second highest office in the land, she had never been considered for elevation to the voting membership, and probably never would be. As heir to the Domokos legacy, she should have been in the top leadership long before now.

Their rebuffs angered her. She was the obvious choice to succeed Pérez. She knew they were looking elsewhere, probably a man, a black . . . a black Muslim . . . or a black gay—either would be "acceptable" to the Left. In spite of its gender diversity, in some ways Palladium remained an old boys' club—no longer dominated by whites but nevertheless masculine in its underlying ethos.

However, she had no intention of fading into the sunset or suffering the ignominy of returning to Congress. If she made the first move, none of them would oppose her or dare run another Democrat against her.

That was exactly what she planned to do.

She intended to announce for the presidency in October, a month prior to the midterms. She anticipated no blowback from Palladium's powerful elite. If they didn't like her acting without their prior blessing, let them eat cake.

If they made unpleasant noises in her direction, or started throwing their weight around, she would remind them that she was in a position, even without being in the innermost circle, to take down the whole thing.

13

INTO A THIRD GENERATION

2038

HEATHER MARSHALL had lived at home throughout her years at Jessup, both because it made sense financially and because she loved being involved in her parents' lives. She also felt more and more integrally connected to the expanding correspondence related to her grandfather's legacy.

As the completion of her nursing degree approached, one Sunday afternoon she asked to talk to her parents. They could tell something serious was on her mind.

As they sat together, Heather drew in a deep breath.

"Mom, Dad," she began, "you know how much I love you—at least I hope you do. You are my best friends. There is a part of me that would like to stay here with you for the rest of my life. The little girl part, I guess you would say. But the grown-up woman part—which I'm not yet, but I'm getting there—that part of me wants . . ."

She hesitated and looked down.

"If what you were about to say," said Timothy, "is that you're thinking it is time to get a place of your own, please don't worry about it on our account."

"Thank you, Dad," smiled Heather, obviously relieved. "I didn't know what you would think."

"We love having you here, but we know what it's like to be young. We'll help you any way we can."

"What about you, Mom?" asked Heather, glancing toward Jaylene.

"I would say the same thing. We love your being with us, but if it's time for a change, we will support you completely. It might be good for you. I'm sure you would really enjoy it. I remember how exciting it was when I moved out on my own for the first time. Do you have any ideas?"

"Actually—yes," replied Heather. "One that involves you."

"We're intrigued," said Timothy. "Tell us more!"

"Well, you know I've been volunteering at Alpine Meadows in Dorado Wood. They've offered me a full-time job when I graduate."

"That's great. Congratulations!"

"Thank you. I like it there. I think I will enjoy it more than hospital work. But it's a long drive from here, and I would like to find a place closer. What I was wondering—what would you think of my renting one of the bedrooms of Grandma's and Grandpa's house in Dorado Wood—until you and Aunt Jane and Uncle Woody and the others decide to sell it?"

Timothy and Jaylene looked at one another in surprise.

"That's a fantastic idea!" said Timothy. "Though the others have been pestering me, wondering how long we're going to hang onto it. So long term—I'm not sure."

"I realize that," said Heather. "I've heard you talking about it. Uncle Woody and Uncle Graham seem especially anxious to make a decision."

"But it makes sense—imagine how economical it would be rather than having to set up an apartment on your own. It's completely furnished. The house is paid for. You could move right in, and it wouldn't cost a thing."

"The others think we've held onto it too long already," added Jaylene. "Fortunately, up till now they have respected our wishes about keeping it, though like you say, Tim, how much longer that will be true is anyone's guess."

"Actually—" Heather said slowly, "I had an idea about that too."

"Go on," said Timothy.

"What if—I know it sounds ridiculous. I'm still so young. But what if I could buy it?"

Again Timothy and Jaylene exchanged glances accompanied by raised eyebrows.

"That's quite a possibility!" said Timothy. "Obviously, you have no money so of course we would help, but . . ." His voice trailed off.

"I was thinking, once I'm making money from the job, that I could pay you and the others rent," Heather went on. "I could start helping more with the mail that comes, and I could keep the place up."

"It would be good to have someone living there, Tim," said Jaylene. "I've never been comfortable about the house sitting empty."

"I could make sure it's ready when we have meetings there so the two of you don't have to do everything."

"What if . . ." began Timothy. "Hmm—I'm just thinking aloud—but what if we offered to buy my brothers and sisters out—buy their shares of the ownership, and go in together, the three of us. Obviously, they would have to agree for us to make payments rather than a lump sum. Then we, and you, Heather, once you are working, we could make payments to them."

"You mean the three of us own the house together?" asked Heather.

"That's what I was thinking. You could buy us out in the future if you wanted to. For now it would make it affordable if we shared it."

"We could probably get a loan," suggested Jaylene. "If any of the others would rather be cashed out, I'm sure we could arrange it."

Timothy nodded. "Of course. That would easily be possible. Shall I talk to the others—see what they think?"

"Oh, I'm so excited!" said Heather. "I love that house. It's been one of my secret worries that you would sell it. I've dreamed about living there all my life."

"Why didn't you say something, honey?"

"I didn't want to presume. I didn't think it would be right until I was in a position to do something about it."

"And now you are. I love it!" said Timothy enthusiastically. "Your love for the house would make your grandparents very happy."

Heather moved into the house in Dorado Wood a month later and began work at Alpine Meadows Care Facility a week later. The transfer of ownership to Timothy, Jaylene, and Heather—to which Woody,

Graham, Cateline, and Jane all enthusiastically agreed, two opting for ongoing payments, the other two opting to be cashed out—was fully completed by the end of the year.

14

THE CHURCH QUANDARY

2038

As THE decade of the 2030s progressed, by ones and twos the number of those gathered periodically at the former home of Stirling and Larke in the foothills of California's gold country, now their granddaughter Heather's home, grew. None of the regulars would miss what they now called the GCG. The group's time together had become a vital and anchoring source of fellowship and spiritual refreshment, teaching, and unity in the bonds of the Spirit. Without actually identifying it succinctly, they had become a community of like-minded men and women dedicated to helping one another understand more deeply, and to practically live by, the spiritual principles that bound them together.

Letters from readers continued. Timothy, Jaylene, and Heather answered them all personally. They regularly noticed themes in the letters that dovetailed with the concerns those in their GCG "community" expressed. Nor did it seem coincidental that they were also topics Stirling had written about in his *Brief*.

Following Stirling and Larke's example, for years they had shared letters that had come around the family supper table. Now living in the house, Heather took a greater share in processing and answering the mail. Those who made contact by whatever means seemed equally grateful to hear from son or daughter-in-law or granddaughter as if they had received a letter from Stirling Marshall himself.

As the gatherings were occasionally mentioned in their correspondence, a few readers asked if they could attend. The fellowship continued to grow, some coming from great distances to spend a weekend with others facing similar issues.

There were usually thirty or more who also got together between the twice-yearly gatherings, Heather acting as hostess. Whenever they were together, everyone sensed that they were part of something that was slowly building, not merely in northern California but elsewhere.

"I've often mentioned the letters that come to us," said Timothy during their first gathering of 2038. "My dad put our address and the name of the university in his books. He wanted people to be able to contact him.

"So the letters keep coming. Most are forwarded to us either from the university or the people who live in the house I grew up in. My parents tried to arrange for their mail to be forwarded, but much of it slipped through the cracks at the post office. My folks had alerted the people who bought their house, and they were most cooperative. They began reading my dad's books and became avid fans themselves and have continued to forward the mail all these years, and are now retired. Much mail also comes here to the Dorado Wood house where my parents spent almost thirty years. People find ways to make contact. Most now know that my parents have passed, yet they seem just as eager to talk to us. They want to share their stories and tell us how much my dad's books have meant to them.

"Similar stories could be told about nearly every one of you here. You have contacted us, and now here you are carrying on my father's legacy as well. New generations are continually being raised up, from around the world—as you will see—as people discover the truths my father pointed to. What is happening is far bigger than my father or his books. It is God's work. A new era in his eternal plan is being birthed. I have the sense that what we are witnessing is only the beginning.

"The interlacing connections between brothers and sisters across the entire spectrum of Christianity, and from around the world, is the most amazing thing. All my life I have been privileged to witness this tapestry of unity and the deep bonds of life that are being woven. It is God's doing. Yet my father had a gift for recognizing very personal doors and windows into the heart of God and beckoned others to look through those windows and walk through those doors with him.

"That work continues, not merely through his writings but even in what we do here, in our coming together. God is stirring. I have no idea where it is going—but the Spirit is moving."

Timothy paused. The room was silent for ten or fifteen seconds. At length he laughed lightly.

"I didn't plan to say all that!" he said. "I just wanted to tell you why I occasionally feel led to read one or another letter that has come. It may be that one of them will be from a future David Gordon, one who will begin weaving this invisible tapestry of interconnected bonds of unity in his own community."

"So tonight," he went on, "I want to read a letter that came since we were last together that typifies exactly what I mean."

He paused again then picked up the letter from his lap and began to read.

Dear Mr. Marshall,

I have never written to an author before, but I had to write to tell you what an impact your book Unspoken Commandments has had in my life, and to thank you from the bottom of my heart for writing it.

My wife and I have long attended an evangelical church in Kansas. In recent years, as the world slides deeper into the moral abyss of relativism, we have had increasing misgivings as our church seems gradually more tolerant of what to us are flagrant violations of scriptural truth.

We find ourselves increasingly isolated even from those we have long considered close friends who seem blind to these trends. We never hear a challenge to stand strong for truth, only bland talk about inclusiveness and not appearing judgmental so that the world will be able to accept the Gospel. To ourselves we wonder, "What Gospel?" Such is not the strategy we see Jesus employing. It's come to feel more like a social club.

In your books we have discovered food for our spiritual souls. You continually keep our focus on the true Gospel, and of course on the Lord's words, which your book on the commandments emphasizes on every page. We read it daily to remind us where our true priorities lie. You challenge us to stand and live for truth.

But we are in a quandary about what to do about church. We detest church hopping. We're not really sure there's anything better out there. It seems that most of Christendom has given in to the world. We don't even know what to ask. What church do you attend? Have you faced this same sense that the church is in decline? How do you resolve these dilemmas?

We have stopped attending our own church regularly. It both depressed and angered us. We knew that wasn't good. Better to stay home than sit through an hour and a half with a judgmental attitude—not toward sin and the world, but toward our fellow Christians!

Your novels, too, have spoken to us. Through your characters you portray real life, how the principles in your other books are lived. Those who say that fiction doesn't reflect real life have never read your novels!

Also those you recommend by Mr. MacDonald. My favorite is the novel about the pastor who realized his faith was shallow and experienced an awakening. What a powerful story! My wife's favorite is the story of the young woman who dedicated her life as a single woman to ministry and music.

Your portrayal of the Father heart of God has revolutionized our entire outlook. I always thought of God as a tyrant. You helped me discover the true heart of God, and that I have a good Father. Through your writings I had to learn the difficult truth that God had aspects of his Fatherhood he wanted to teach me through my earthly father too. It was the most difficult lesson of my life, that God lived within my own father. I knew what you were saying was true, as hard as it was to accept at first. But at the end of a long road, I can now say that I love my father, and the process has deepened my relationship with my heavenly Father too.

I have rambled on long enough. Thank you for listening. I hope you get this and maybe you will find time to give us a few ideas about what we should do about church.

Sincerely and with much gratitude,
Gerald (and Rebecca) Stevens

The regular inquiries they received in a similar vein reflected the same misgivings many in the group felt about their own church lives. Timothy and Jaylene also heard unmistakable echoes of much that Stirling had addressed in his *Brief*. It was clear that God was stirring many individuals from diverse walks of life, and from around the world, in similar directions.

15

A JUDGE'S REFLECTIONS

2038

LINDA HUTCHINS Trent set down the newspaper and smiled to herself.

"It didn't take Jeff long to make a name for himself in Washington," she said to herself, not without sarcasm. "Cosponsoring a bill with the Senate majority leader to require the Gideons to place copies of the Koran in every motel, hotel, and hospital room where there is currently a Bible. If they did not comply, their organization would be shut down. He'll probably be on the short list of VP candidates by the next year. And then the brass ring."

Did she have regrets?

She had never asked herself that question quite so directly. She had been hurt, she wouldn't deny it. But did she really want to be married to Jefferson F. Rhodes?

She had a good life. She was a respected judge, and—

The ringing of her phone interrupted her thoughts. As Linda listened, her eyes widened.

Her husband walked into the room as the call concluded a few minutes later.

"What is it!" he asked. "You look like—I don't know what. Is it bad news—it's not your mom or your dad?"

"No, Cam, nothing like that," replied Linda softly. "I just got off the phone with a reporter in DC."

"What did they want?"

"She wanted to know my reaction to President Pérez's appointing me to western Washington's First US Circuit Court."

"Wow, honey—congratulations! You never mentioned it."

"That's because I knew nothing about it—this is the first I've heard."

Later that evening, playing the events of the day over in her mind—with the dozens of calls and interview requests—along with what was reported on the local newscasts, it all began to fit.

She and Jeff hadn't spoken in several years. But she could see his hand in this as clearly as if he had called her himself. *What is he up to?* she wondered. Jeff always had an angle. What would he want in return, and when would he expect payment?

Thoughts of Jeff again sent Linda's mind drifting in many nostalgic directions, some pleasant, others not so much. Jeff always prompted reactions inside her, most that she could never share with anyone, not even her husband.

That she had been in love with Jeff, of course, lay at the root of it. Those were the kinds of things a woman never forgets, especially being dumped by a man just when she thought he was going to propose. But her anger for the pain he had caused her could not entirely vanquish the memory of the youthful fascination she had felt, or the happy memories of being with him at Humboldt.

Had she really loved him or just been infatuated with the idea of being in love for the first time? She would probably go to her grave with that question unanswered.

No, she didn't have regrets. She loved Cameron. Whatever defined the feelings she had once had for Jeff might never be entirely clear. But she was glad she had been spared a life with him. Cam was, if not exactly her fairy-tale knight on a white horse, something resembling a more realistic version of it. Every day she was thankful for him. But that didn't stop the occasional fleeting thought of Jeff—nostalgia and anger intermingled in complex dissonance.

Now she had a new dynamic to add that she was sure would come calling in time—she owed him. She was, as the English novels put it, "under an obligation." But what was she going to do—turn the appointment down? That would be foolish. It was a dream come true. As for

Jeff's probable role in it, that was a can she would have to kick down the road for now.

Her thoughts could hardly help turning also to the younger of her two brothers. Her feelings were equally muddled as those toward Jeff, and her love for Ward equally complicated. How could she not love him, though she despised what he stood for? Whenever they saw one another, which could hardly be avoided, all they did was argue. Though Ward was traveling and speaking a good part of the year, few major events were scheduled during Thanksgiving and Christmas, which insured that he was usually home at such times. With their mother now living in a retirement community near Sea-Tac and thus all of them in the Seattle area, and both their parents, though divorced, expecting some level of family connection, holidays were awkward.

Their mother doted on Ward, relishing in the knowledge that her son had become an evangelical powerhouse. It was probably to be expected that the three children of the family would be divided, not in their parental loyalties exactly but in following the two very different outlooks of their father and mother. She and Sawyer had become Democrats like their father; Ward was a staunch conservative Republican like their mother. They represented the yin and yang of family life.

But Ward was so obstinately bull-headed. He would not listen to reason. Linda could forgive their mother for her backward views. She was from another generation. But Ward had no excuse. He should know better. These were different times. You couldn't talk like he did about certain kinds of people. The country had a gay president and Muslim vice president. Their reelection two years before was as historic as Obama's triumph in 2008. Men like Ward were cultural dinosaurs.

She wondered what Mark thought of Ward's outdated views. He had been the quiet one of the four college friends. Obviously he was a Christian—well, so was she—and now a well-known evangelical pastor. Ward would not have turned over the reins of Puget Sound Vine Ministries to Mark had they not mostly seen eye-to-eye.

Surely Mark was mature and objective enough to recognize the need of Christian churches to move with the times. The Episcopalian church she and Cam attended had a lesbian priest, and the church was thriving. People accepted transgenders and homosexuals now. It was no big deal. Mark had always been reasonable. If he hadn't been so conservative, she might well have fallen for him instead of Jeff.

But she hadn't seen Mark in years, not since college. For all she knew he had become as fanatical as Ward.

16

∧ Highland Blizzard

2039

THE SNOW that had been falling across the Scottish highlands for the past two hours would blanket the entire region under two feet of white before morning. Moira and Alexander Campbell knew they would be going nowhere tomorrow. They had already made arrangements for the shop with their assistant who lived in town.

Inside the thick stone walls of their home above Fort William, on most days they looked down on Loch Linnhe. Outside their windows today, however, nothing was visible but white—above, below, and everywhere in between. Inside, however, they were warm and cozy.

Given the storm and time of year, it would be dark by three o'clock. In truth, Alexander and Moira were looking forward to the time of enforced isolation. Two days before a parcel of books they had been eagerly awaiting had arrived from the United States. They had discovered an old dilapidated copy of the now-obscure American author's book on the commandments of the New Testament partially hidden behind a stack of other titles in their favorite used bookstore in Inverness. For some unaccountable reason, being struck by the title and buying the slender volume for fifty pence, a few days later they both realized that they had crossed a great frontier. Their outlook on their lives as Christians would never again be the same.

Immediately they began searching for whatever else the forgotten author of the past century had written. But all his books, they found, were no longer being published. And with Amazon's great purge of the late-2020s and cancellation of most titles their robots could discover with Christian content, spiritual books on the Christian faith were becoming harder and harder to find. Most of the other online sources, not wanting to be branded as "pro-Christian," soon followed Amazon's lead. Physical copies of Christian classics and personal favorites had thus become all the more precious and carefully guarded. Even Bibles were becoming more difficult and expensive to obtain.

Their discovery in Inverness led to a long and desperate search, until at last they located a treasure trove of eight titles—old and used, but who cared about that!—in an antiquarian bookstore in far off Seattle, Washington.

The box arrived two days ago. They had not yet had leisure to wade into its contents. They had waited, not patiently it must be confessed, until they could take their time and fully absorb what God had for them to learn from the man who had already become for them a literary spiritual mentor. The storm could not have come at a more propitious time.

With a long evening of delicious silence before them, as if they were opening a long-buried chest of hidden treasure—as the contents surely were to this man and this woman, sitting beside one another on their settee in their favorite room they called the Blue Lounge—Alexander and Moira slowly opened the cardboard box and gently, almost reverently, began to remove the carefully packed contents one title at a time. They handed now one, now another, back and forth between them, slowly opening one or another, scanning the contents, perhaps reading a few lines of the opening chapters, then perusing another. In addition to another copy of *Unspoken Commandments* were seven titles they had never seen—four novels and three non-fiction books, one bearing the peculiar title *Phantasms of Unfaith*. Half an hour later, both were seated in their favorite reading chairs—Alexander engrossed in a novel, Moira equally lost to the world in the lengthy introduction to what promised to be the most unusual New Testament commentary she had ever read.

"We should write to this man," said Alexander at length, as he set the book on his lap.

Moira glanced toward him. "These books are all so old, just like the first one we found," she said. "The address could be thirty or forty years old."

"Or more. The *Commandments* book was published in the 1980s, wasn't it?"

"The man might not even still be alive. Actually, that was over fifty years ago—it seems unlikely he could still be living."

"It's worth a try. We've got to get a list of his books."

"Wouldn't it be wonderful if we could find a group of people who thought this way about Christian living?"

Alexander thought a moment. "Do you think anyone would come if we invited a few people over to study the *Commandments* book?"

"Who are you thinking of?"

"I don't know—people who would understand, who would see how different this is from sleeping through church every Sunday while Steve tells his clever stories from the pulpit. The Grants, maybe—and the Jacksons—young Sylvia Fleming."

"I think the Hays might be interested, maybe the Mairs."

"You think they would come?" asked Alexander.

"I've sensed annoyance from Adela about the superficiality of services every Sunday. She can't stand Steve's stupid stories. That's her word not mine! She's hungry for more."

"You might be right. And Ted's a thinker. Pretty doctrinal, but I think he's open-minded enough to listen to the kinds of things Marshall explores."

"I like it!" said Moira enthusiastically. "I'll make some calls tomorrow. But we'll need more books."

"We don't need books. I'll make copies for us to discuss a page at a time."

"Then I will write to Stirling Marshall and see what he suggests about a discussion group using his book."

"Ask him how we can get more copies."

17

COURAGE IN LONDON

FURTHER SOUTH, the storm that was blanketing the Scottish highlands in snow was battering southern England with drenching rains. In their London flat high above the city, the sight of the swollen, brown, muddy Thames below in the distance was not a pleasant one.

Like their Scottish counterparts, Richard and Jessica Constable were looking forward to an evening "in." Richard was pastor of a small non-denominational church that had broken away from the Church of England thirty years earlier when the church began ordaining gay men and women into its clergy. He was now in the middle of a series of messages on the Sermon on the Mount and had been particularly intrigued by two books passed on to him by one of his members called *Does Truth Matter?* and *Unspoken Commandments*. The simplicity of the first title and the intrigue of the second arrested his attention. He had never heard of the author, but the topic of the latter, especially, dovetailed with his current study of Matthew's Gospel. After canceling the elders meeting at church because of the storm, he intended to take the opportunity to explore the book tonight. He was eager to see if it might provide material for next Sunday's sermon.

His was a small congregation and shrinking. Most of the original founding fifty or so members were either gone or aging, including Richard's parents, both now in their eighties. The fervor with which those in their church had been revolted by Anglicanism's acceptance of homosexuals in its pulpit, and later its endorsing same-sex marriage, had largely died out. Most religiously inclined men and woman in England had gradually followed the changing cultural norms and now accepted such things. The fiery stand that bound those first families together had waned. Most of their children accepted the new sexual order of the world and had left their congregation to join more "socially relevant" congregations.

Not that Richard preached on gender-related topics from the pulpit. He was no militant advocate for anything other than Christians trying to do what Jesus said. He did not wear his cultural or political perspectives on his sleeve.

Nevertheless, he had a reputation in London for speaking the truth boldly and plainly. It was not a reputation that brought in new members.

His more serious troubles began six years earlier, soon after outspoken lesbian Marcella Washburn became prime minister. The son of one of his parents' friends who had grown up in the church called to make an appointment with him with the request to be married in the church. Looking forward to meeting the young man and his fiancé, Richard was stunned when he walked in holding hands with another young man.

Assuming Richard enlightened and in step with the times, neither of the two suspected a thing. They sat and began to describe the specifics of the ceremony they had planned. Richard listened dumbfounded for twenty or thirty seconds, wondering if it was a dreadfully inappropriate joke.

Finally, he realized he had to interrupt.

"I am terribly sorry," he said quietly. "I had no idea of the nature of your—uh, your situation. I'm afraid I will not be able to perform the ceremony."

The two stared back, as surprised as he.

"Why not?" asked Richard's acquaintance, an edge in his tone.

"I'm afraid it is my policy not to officiate at same-sex marriages."

"I want to know why."

"It is simply a decision I feel conscience bound to adhere to."

"You refuse to give me a reason?"

"I don't refuse. It's simply my policy. I'm not asking you to agree or disagree, only respect that this is my decision."

"Well I don't respect it. You are obviously judging us."

"I hope I am not. If so, may God forgive me and open my heart."

"And there's no room for discussion?"

"I'm afraid not."

The young man's face grew red with suppressed anger. He jumped to his feet, his partner following him. Both stormed out, swearing violently and slamming the door of Richard's office behind him.

The following Sunday's service was solemn. Everyone had heard of the incident. Several prominent young people were missing. Included among the absentees were the boy's parents, who never missed a service and who, thirty years before, had been among the most staunchly opposed to allowing a hint of homosexuality through the church door.

Throughout the following week, a petition began quietly to circulate among the members calling for Richard's removal. The top signatures were the boy's mother and father. When the matter came up for a church vote, it was defeated forty-two to thirty-six, and Richard remained. Twenty-one of the defeated party were never seen in the church again.

The demonstrations began a month later, protesters in front of the church bearing Hypocrite! and Gay-hater! and Bigotry! placards. They rarely became violent, though there were occasional rocks through the church windows. But they did their best, often surrounding the church and shouting obscene taunts for an hour, to disrupt every Sunday's service. They were not so kind at the Constable home, eventually forcing Richard and Jessica to sell and move into a high rise where they would not be so accessible. After numerous threats, and fearing for their children's safety, Jessica quit her job and homeschooled their son and daughter through high school, then sent them to college in the Midlands where they had not been bothered. Eventually the weekly demonstrations stopped. With a congregation of less than thirty, they had accomplished their purpose.

Richard had scarcely finished reading the introduction of the book his friend had given him before he recognized it as a game-changer, a revolutionary new approach to Christianity. But not new at all—it had originated two thousand years ago with Jesus, in the very Sermon on the Mount Richard had been preaching on.

Continuing to read, his eyes aflame, Richard realized he was holding in his hand the Lord's answer to his discouragement. His congregation could shrink to twenty. It could shrink to ten!

What did numbers matter? If he was faithful to the message God had given him, faithful to the truth, God would see to the rest.

Jesus had begun with two then four. That four had grown to twelve, the twelve to seventy, the seventy to three thousand at Pentecost.

Why should he think he deserved to be listened to by more than two or four or twelve?

If his small church had begun as a protest against liberalism in the Church of England, perhaps it was time to redefine its commission. Times had changed. Perhaps that commission was no longer relevant to the people of England. Not that his convictions had changed or would change.

But perhaps it was time for a new defining manifesto of purpose.

Henceforth that purpose would be the commands of Jesus in a hostile and post-Christian world.

18

Spiritual Hunger on a Dairy Farm

SEVERAL HUNDRED miles east, dairy farmer Fynn Sievers had heard the weather reports and seen the ominous black clouds gathering far off over France and Holland all day. By afternoon the wind was whipping up. The storm would be upon them by morning. German radio and television were predicting flooding and power outages throughout the country.

He spent the afternoon getting the cows in from pasture, battening down all the doors and windows of the farmhouse and outbuildings, getting his two tractors safely nestled in their garages. Thankfully the last of his fields had been ploughed and laid to rest for the coming winter. There would be no more ploughing now. The fields would be muddy, if not covered in standing water, for weeks.

His wife, Monika, never minded such weather. She was such a bookworm that the confinement and rain on the roof signaled long evenings, and if she was lucky even daytime hours, curled up with a book. Her new favorite author, an American, had so absorbed her attention in recent weeks that every spare minute she returned to either of the two fiction series she had been reading. She had been badgering Fynn to read the author's book on the Reformation, which he was keenly interested in. The book had been translated into German, she said. He would love it. He might give it a try tonight.

Fynn wasn't much of a reader. Hands-on practicality was his most notable personality trait and greatest strength. He was a doer. He had a good head on his shoulders but was no philosopher.

After supper, Monika tucked away in the sitting room with her book, Fynn wandered outside into the dark. The wind had died to a whisper, and the temperature had risen several degrees. The eerie calm meant only one thing—the storm had come faster than he had anticipated. He was standing at its leading front—the eye, had it been circular like a hurricane—that would give way to a drop in temperature and sudden deluge of rain within half an hour.

He breathed in deeply of the warm air, fragrant with approaching moisture, then continued across the cobblestones to the main barn and inside. He turned on the light. He loved it here, so dry, so full of memories, now redolent with the rich aroma of straw and hay stacked high to the open rafters after the recent harvest.

He drew in a deep breath, exhaled slowly, and eased himself onto a stray bale of straw.

Maybe he should try to read the book on the Reformation, he thought. Last Sunday's service in town had been the final humiliation. He might as well have been sitting in an auditorium full of atheists.

The German church was dead. It had been dead for generations. So why did he keep going? There was no good reason. Yet he had continued to be faithful, week after week, year after year.

Why?

He received nothing from it. It was a vacuum of spiritual emptiness.

The once proud church of Luther, a church born out of the vibrancy of faith sought by Martin Luther, had lost its way. It was no more than an arm of the German government, as corrupt and political and devoid of life as the Catholic church Luther had fled from. Luther's church had itself become an institution of death in need of its own Reformation—a reformation out of Lutheranism and into life.

He wanted life, thought Fynn. He hungered for spiritual reality. Why he felt such yearning, he couldn't say. None of his friends did. No one in church did. Their pastor surely did not feel the same hunger.

But whenever he read the old copy of Kempis's *Imitation* his mother had given him, his heart soared. It was one of the few books he read. He wanted to be good. He wanted to be kind. He wanted to be humble. He wanted to live a Christlike life.

Where had such longing come from? Perhaps from the book. Perhaps from his mother's prayers.

Were there others, anywhere, who shared the passion to live a godly life?

There must be others. But where? How was it possible to feed his hunger in the spiritual vacuum that was present day Germany? The very air of the culture, the entire ethos of continental arrogance and independence, sapped the lifeblood of spirituality from his veins.

His thoughts drifted into incoherent unspoken questions that were prayers, though he did not think of them as such.

Several minutes later he heard the door of the barn open. Monika's soft footsteps came across the dirt floor. She sat on the bale beside him.

"It's chilly out," she said.

"Is it? I thought it felt warm."

"Are you feeling all right, Fynn? You look sad. Discouraged."

He smiled. "I think I am."

"About what?" she asked, placing a hand on his where it rested on his knee.

"I don't know exactly," he replied. "I was thinking about the church, how meaningless it is—that it needs a new Reformation. Maybe you put the idea in my head talking about the Reformation book you think I should read," he added, laughing lightly. "I want more from life. I don't mean that I am dissatisfied with our life together. I mean inside. I want to be more than I am. But the church isn't helping. If Herr Pastor Jonas heard me, he would probably laugh. He would have no idea what I was talking about if I mentioned Thomas Kempis or told him I pray to become like Christ. I feel that we're alone—spiritually I mean. In the middle of this vibrant, prosperous nation that gave birth to the Reformation but now is in such need of a new Reformation—you and I are alone." It fell silent.

"I had no idea you were thinking such things," said Monika after a minute. "I would have said it differently, but I was thinking much the same thing."

"Do you have any answers?"

"Only that God has something for us, something new, something that may even be frightening for us at first just because it is new and different. But it will be something that will lead only to good."

Even as she was speaking, a few random patters echoed down from the roof above them. Suddenly a great burst of light flashed, visible through the wood slats of the walls and the barn's two windows. Almost instantly a tremendous crash of thunder shook the ground, and the heavens opened above them.

They sat and listened, relishing the power of the onslaught. The cows had been restless before and now added their loud mooing to the thunder. But as the rain gradually steadied, so did the cows.

"If that's not a sign from God," laughed Fynn, "I don't know what else to call it. Whatever the something new he has for us is, it must be powerful!"

19

STELLA MASTERS

COURT MASTERS sat in his favorite reading chair holding the biography of the late Viktor Domokos. It was not a book he would have chosen to read for pleasure. He had waded into it from simple curiosity. The questions had plagued him for years. Why were some people seemingly almost genetically prone to embrace liberal ideas, even completely illogical ideas? Why did some people look at things, almost instinctively, from the wrong angle? Why would a man like Domokos, who had benefited from everything about Western culture and capitalism, make it his life's mission to tear down the very institutions that had given him so much? It made no sense. Although he supposed very little about people's reaction to right and wrong, truth and falsehood, made sense. Why were so many blind to clearly recognizable truth?

It was not exactly that he wanted to get to know his enemy. No man was his enemy. Yet he was desperately hungry to understand the liberal mind-set. What better way to get to the bottom of it than to read the life of the prototypical liberal of the past half century?

What made liberals tick? Why were they so incapable of seeing the obvious—that gender was physically, biologically, categorically binary, that socialism and communism were failed political systems, that capitalism worked, that unchecked immigration would ultimately ruin a nation's intrinsic fabric, and that in spite of its historic flaws the United States had been a nation that had brought good to the world?

Such truths, to him, in Thomas Jefferson's words, were self-evident.

Why were liberals blind to them? The mystery had baffled him for years.

The question was much closer than politics. Why had Stella become so mesmerized by Obama's charisma that she had completely changed her entire outlook? How could a seemingly Bible-loving Christian switch to the liberal side of the fence on everything? They still pretended to have a "Christian marriage." They still went to church together. But what faith meant to them was now worlds apart.

When he was honest with himself, he had no idea what her walk with God now meant to Stella. Embracing liberal ideas eradicated so much biblical truth and made a mockery of the character and purposes of God—how did liberal Christians rationalize the dichotomy?

He and Stella never talked about such things. He had tried for a few years after the sea-change in her perspectives. He quickly learned, however, to keep his mouth shut. Open-mindedness was not a key component of the liberal playbook. Liberals had all the answers. If you weren't a liberal, you were stupid. They had no interest in what those who didn't agree to the entire liberal playbook might have to say.

It was a terrible thing to know that his own wife looked down on him. He knew she loved him. But she looked down on him.

Thus the question remained—why?

How did their thought processes work in the face of such illogic? He didn't mind things like gun control. Even as a cop, that was a logical and legitimate point of view. But more than two genders! Did liberals really believe such lunacy?

He tried to resume his reading. Toward the end of the Domokos biography, he began to detect a subtle change in tone. Nothing he could put his finger on. But between the lines were whiffs of objectives that remained unidentified and hazy, hints of an agenda so sweeping it could not even be set down in print. He found himself reading more for what was not being said than for what was on the page.

The final quarter of the book was mostly taken up by ideas rather than events, long ramblings that Domokos's biographer had probably left mostly intact to convey the realism of his subject's gradually fading cognitive abilities. Yet the content of those tangents was of supreme interest. They revealed, though too vaguely to latch onto with certainty, the man's grandiose vision for world change. The word *manifesto* was only used once. But it jumped off the page as if printed in bright red.

Might there be such a document? Court wondered. But it was never mentioned again.

The gradually shifting tone of the book turned Court's interest toward the man Domokos had authorized to write his life story. The name Michael Bardolf meant nothing to him. The biographical information on the dust jacket revealed only that he had been Domokos's personal assistant for the final years of his life. That he was an excellent writer was obvious. What else might be involved in his association with Domokos? Might the changed tone indicate, more than a mere chronicler, that this Bardolf had gradually assumed the role of collaborator?

He turned over to the back cover and stared intently at Bardolf's photograph. He was certain he had seen the man somewhere. He'd noticed it the first time he picked up the book. The name too.

Faces and names filtered back into his brain from his Baltimore lists.

Of course! he thought as the light suddenly went on. How could he have been so blind?

Michael Bardolf had been at Patterson Park!

What was he doing there? What connection had put Viktor Domokos's assistant so close to the president? Nothing in the biographical information in the book indicated affiliation with the president or the Secret Service.

He'd been off the case for two years. Still, he had to know.

He picked up his phone from the stand beside him. He still knew the director's private number by heart.

"This is Parva," she answered.

"Erin, hello—Court Masters."

"Court," she said dispassionately.

"A quick question, I hope you don't mind. Do you know the name Michael Bardolf?"

There was a brief hesitation.

"Uh—the name sounds familiar."

"Yes, he wrote the Domokos biography."

"Ah yes, of course."

"Why I ask is that I have been reviewing my notes and hadn't noticed before that he was at Patterson Park. He was apparently among the Secret Service detail. I wondered what his connection was."

"I'll have to check my files and get back to you. But didn't I take you off the case?"

"Yes, just trying to close my files and tie up loose ends."

The call ended without further pleasantries. Parva's voice was stiff, thought Court, though she had never been the most personable of women.

His phone rang less than five minutes later.

"Court, you were right," came the director's voice again. "After checking my records, I remembered. I was requested to include Mr. Bardolf in the detail."

"By whom, if you don't mind my asking?"

"It came from the vice president."

"I see. Well, that clears it up."

"Why are you asking?"

"As I say, just tidying up loose ends."

"Let me remind you again, then, that you are off the investigation. Please make no more inquiries into the assassination. If there is anything to uncover, our own people will find it."

Again the call ended stiffly. Parva's voice did not carry the tone of a suggestion. She was giving him an order.

Court sat puzzling for several minutes over her strange reaction.

Footsteps interrupted his thoughts.

He glanced up to see Stella walking into the room. She sat on the couch opposite him. She wore a strange expression. Her face was flushed.

"What is it, honey?" Court asked. "Are you okay?"

She did not answer immediately but sat staring down. Court waited.

"Could I, uh . . . talk to you a minute?" she said softly.

"Of course. Is something wrong?'

Stella looked up, blinking hard. She forced a smile.

"Yes—actually, I think there is," she answered.

"Oh, honey—" began Court, rising and walking across the room. "What is it?" He sat on the couch beside her and took her hand.

Stella did not reply for a long minute or two. At length she drew in a deep breath.

"I think you met Wanda—you know, where I work?"

"I'm trying to place her—I think so."

"She's the company comptroller. She and I've worked together for years. She's probably the nicest person I've ever known—besides you, of course," she added, laughing lightly. "She so considerate, always trying to be helpful—kindness itself. She's been with the company since before she and I made the move to DC. In some ways she holds the whole thing together."

"Did something happen to her?"

"She was fired last week."

"Why?"

"It was out of the blue, no warning, no nothing. She's a widow without any other income. I don't know what she's going to do. She's fifty-six—how will she find another job?"

"There must have been a reason."

"She was reading in her New Testament at lunch time. Her office door was open. One of the young interns saw her and filed a complaint about religious influence in the workplace with the Bureau of Cultural Compliance. Mr. Gillette was served papers of noncompliance. He had no choice but to let her go or be shut down by the BCC."

Court shook his head in disbelief.

"Everyone knew she was a Christian, but no one minded," said Stella. "They know I go to church too. But once the complaint was filed, they had no choice."

"Does she ever talk about Christianity in the office?"

"Never. I don't know what it's like in your world, but in business and tech, she wouldn't have dared. On the poster about workplace rights and regulations they're required to post, Christianity is listed along with all the kinds of abuse and harassment and hate crimes that you can be fired for on the spot."

"What about Islam?"

"Not a word prohibiting Muslim dress, burkas, praying during work—that's all allowed."

"And you say Wanda was on her own time?"

Stella nodded. Silence fell again.

"It jolted me, Court," said Stella at length. "I don't know how to say it other than that suddenly my eyes were opened to many things you've seen all along. A light flashed into my brain. I don't know how I could have been so blind to it."

She paused and glanced away.

"The inconsistency of it all was suddenly so obvious," she went on. "Everybody's free to do and think what they like—unless they don't agree. Free speech applies—unless you disagree with what's acceptable. Pro-choice means you don't have the choice to be against abortion. The double standard of everything I had been pretending to believe exploded in my brain. How could I have been so blind to it? It's all a sham. There is no free speech, there is no freedom for Christians or conservatives. It's complete hypocrisy."

Again she stopped and looked away.

"Oh, Court . . . I'm . . . I'm so sorry I treated you badly. I'm sorry for not listening. You were right all along."

Stella burst into tears and covered her face with her hands.

Court gently reached his arm around her and drew her close. She wept quietly as they sat together for several minutes until the storm passed.

"You've been so patient with me," said Stella after some time. "There's nothing I can say except that I am sorry. It's like the man Jesus healed—I was blind and now I see. How they can be so intolerant, judgmental, and hypocritical, and all the while accuse Christians and conservatives of being those things—why couldn't I see it? You were the tolerant one. It was me who was intolerant."

"Don't worry about it," said Court softly. "All is forgotten. We'll move on from here."

"Thank you . . . but I am sorry."

"I know. I probably wasn't always as sensitive as I could have been."

A brief silence fell.

"Could we start reading that book together again?" said Stella after a minute. "You know the one on the commands. We haven't read it in a long time."

"I knew it made you feel awkward. That's why I put it away. I didn't want you to feel pressured."

"Always thinking of me," said Stella, turning toward him with a smile. "It did make me feel awkward. It challenged my blind spots. It made me angry sometimes. But I think I'm ready now. I'm ready to root out the blind spots. I want to see the world clearly again."

20

NEW GROUP LEADER

Dear Mr. Marshall,

I cannot thank you enough for your encouragement about the study group Alexander and I plan to host, and for arranging books to be sent for our group. We've contacted several couples we know in Fort William and they seem interested in joining us. I've told them about the Commandments book and they are intrigued. Alexander wants me to lead the group—at least at first. He says that my enthusiasm about your father's book is more important than anything he could say.

I'm a little frightened at the prospect. What am I thinking? I've never done anything like that in my life. But I feel it is important. The book has so revolutionized my daily walk that I feel it must be shared.

When reading the Commandments book, I underline and make notes as I read. I love that it is practical, not legalistic like the church I grew up in. I keep going back to the commands about being careful and watchful, and then the next ones—Take Heart, Take Courage and also Don't be Afraid. In the times we live we need to be alert. Even though everyone in the group knows we are not Bible teachers, I hope what your father has written will make them think.

I am so excited about being able to give everyone a copy. I am praying we will grow spiritually as we read and understand the commands.

Our first meeting will be in two weeks.

Sincerely,
Moira Campbell

Dear Moira,

I am excited for what God is going to do in your group. You will probably learn and grow from it more than anyone!

Let me share some thoughts of encouragement.

I love Deuteronomy. Continually Moses warns Israel to "be careful" or they will fall away. They have to be careful to obey the commands. It's exactly what you said. These commands about carefulness, attentiveness, and watchfulness are foundational. Look through at the number of times Moses commands exactly the same things Jesus does—Be careful and watchful. Maybe you can use some of this to tie in to your study.

I'd love to sit in on your Bible study! I agree with Alexander. You will do great. The others will feel your passion!

Timothy

21

ANGUISH OF THE OBEDIENT

Dear Mr. Marshall,

I have followed your father's life and writings for many years and have a number of his books. I was greatly saddened by his passing.

I managed to find your name and address, though it took some time—I did not see you online but wrote to your father's former university, and one of the men there gave me your address. I write to you as a discouraged and broken pastor who is feeling the onslaught of a tidal wave of the world's depraved practices sweeping over me with such force that sometimes I simply feel like giving up. It is not the world's worldliness so much. What is so debilitating is the church's worldliness, its acceptance of everything and anything the world forces upon it.

It doesn't even need to be forced—if the world says something is good and normal, the church jumps eagerly and follows blindly without even questioning it.

So much of what Christians universally would have called sin three or four generations ago—abortion, premarital sex, militant feminism, homosexuality, adultery, even the belief that Islam is a religion of truth and peace but that Christians and Americans should feel guilt for our history—all these most churches today not only condone and accept but in some cases actually encourage people to believe.

No wonder Christians are embracing so many untruths. The new Love Bible, being touted as the most accurate translation ever, the Bible that at last reveals God's love in its fulness, has ripped right and wrong from the pages of Scripture. I don't know if you have seen it. I was sent a free copy, as were all pastors and priests in Britain, with the offer that for every copy of an earlier translation turned in through Amazon's return depots, two copies of the Love Bible would be sent to our churches free of charge. The rumor is that the returned Bibles are being incinerated. How long will it take before reliable translations have all been destroyed?

The future of God's Word is in peril if its backers succeed in replacing the King James, RSV, NIV, NEB, NASB, NKJV, and the other true translations with this new atrocity against truth. I did some research to see if my natural skepticism was justified. Strong's Concordance has some 400 listings for sin and seventy for adultery and its forms. The Love Bible's concordance lists sixty-seven uses of sin, all in the Old Testament, and twenty-five of adultery, also only in the Old. Sexual sin has been almost entirely removed from the New Testament. Romans 1:26–27 has been removed. The text simply goes from verse 25 to verse 28. It was one of the first passages I looked up. I quickly began a more thorough search. Every reference to homosexuality, from Genesis to Revelation, is gone. The verses have simply been omitted—no mention of it in Leviticus—anywhere. And this Bible is being supplied to churches essentially for free. Of course hell, too, is gone completely. The word is not used once in the entire text.

A serious Christian who attempts to speak truth and stand up for God's creation as he intended it, and for the truth of the Bible, the true Bible, is ridiculed and mocked as backward, intolerant, judgmental, bigoted, even racist. Now liberals can turn to the "Bible" and counter anything a true believer in God's truth tries to say. I don't want to become a conspiracy theorist, but it may be time that Christians begin stockpiling Bibles—real Bibles. How much longer will they even be available?

*I am in a great quandary—how long can I remain in the
pastorate? Though I am trying to teach our people truth, am
I unwittingly still part of a dying institution, dying at its own
hand by daily absorbing the venom of worldly values and the
culture of progressivism, with no more awareness of its suicidal
drift than the frog in the frying pan?*

Perhaps I should back up and tell you a little of my story . . .

Timothy set down the letter ten minutes later and closed his eyes.
He drew in a deep breath and sighed. What to say to this hurting man
who had sacrificed so much for his convictions. He was a truth warrior
on the frontlines of the battle to preserve truth.

Lord, Lord—give me your wisdom, he prayed silently, then sat for
another five minutes. At last he set his fingers to his keyboard, and
began.

Dear Richard,

*Your letter arrived, and I'm delighted you were persistent
enough to find me. It is a privilege to dialogue on such pivotal,
important, though as you say, also heartbreaking matters.*

*I am shocked by what you say about the Love Bible. I have
heard of it, of course, but have had little interest in it. God's
people will certainly need to be more discerning than ever if the
world is now changing God's Word to subtly turn Christians
away from his truth.*

*There was a time when men were honored for standing
for their convictions. Sadly, no more. I can say, however, that
I share your grief at the drift of the church into the flow of the
world's current. My father used to call the church of man the
world's ally. As time goes on, I see more and more how prophetic
was his observation. I have recently sensed a time approaching
for me as well—a time of decision about how long my wife and
I can remain in our church as we observe the same trends you
do. I love our church and its people. But homosexuality and
progressive cultural views, same-sex marriage, have become so*

commonplace that no one thinks twice about what the Bible says.

These are difficult times for those of us who take God's truths seriously. I applaud your courage. I will pray that God will give you strength to stand and wisdom to discern his will for your small fellowship.

I don't know what your financial situation is or other responsibilities, but it would be wonderful if we could meet and pray and talk. These are pivotal times. I sense a kinship of brotherhood between us that I do not take lightly. Jaylene and I would love to put you and your wife up for a few days, a week, or whatever you could manage. We have a group that meets periodically, all of whose people are wrestling with their place in a world sliding toward the abyss. I think you would be encouraged to realize that you are not alone. God is invisibly raising up a new Church, which is an ancient Church, an eternal Church, Christ's Church, and you and I are part of it, my brother.

Consider this an official invitation to California!

Your fellow living stone of that Church,
Timothy Marshall

22

GOD'S LEBEN

2040

THE LETTER Timothy opened shortly after the opening of the new decade especially warmed his heart. The book referenced had always been one of his favorites of his father's. Coming as it did from the birthplace of the Reformation gave the letter all the more meaning.

Lieber Herr Marshall,

I hope you understand my broken English. I write to you from Germany. My husband and I own dairy farm. Being Germans we are Lutherans. Everyone in Germany is Lutheran. It is state church. In recent years we become dismayed that the church birthed by Luther now become bureaucratic and political institution no different than Luther day Catholic. The Lutheran Church in Germany is died. Yet no one knows it. It is chicken with head cut off—died yet still pretend to be alive. It grieve our hearts.

More faith than the church can give we desire. I remember of what Jesus say about shepherds with no life to give sheep. We feel alone. Spirituality to German people is church, nothing practical. Trying to talk about obedience or growing in Christ, is to brick building talking. They stare back as if you speak foreign language. They don't even know what words mean. The Leben of the gospel, its life, is nowhere in Germany.

Some time since I find your book The Reformation. It was old copy translated in German much years ago. My heart stirred as I read to pray for new Reformation in our beloved land, but also inside my own heart. Never story have I had move me so deeply. I am not the same since. Your words touch the hunger in my heart for more Leben—more of God's Leben!

My husband Fynn now read your book.

I know my English not so good. I hope you can read it and know what is in my heart.

Much thank you!
Monika Sievers

Timothy drew in a deep breath and slowly exhaled. He hoped she wouldn't be too disappointed to hear from him rather than his father.

PART 2

GESTATION

2016–2046

23

MINGLING WITH THE ELITE

2016

FIFTEEN-YEAR-OLD CHARLIE Reyburn had little idea when his mother signed him up for the exclusive summer conference for teens at Colorado's Gateway Canyons Resort that he would look back on it as the week he met two presidents. The draw, of course, which made the Gateway Conference one of the most difficult to get into, was the incumbent's highlight speech on Thursday evening. Its title alone, "The Bright Future of America's Advance," insured that every news outlet and hundreds of journalists would be haunting the teen conference all week looking for their own version of the inside scoop, and clues to the future leaders who would follow the transformational path on the world stage of the current administration.

When the evening arrived, the speech predictably brought the conference of eight hundred ambitious high schoolers from some of America's most high-placed and wealthiest families to their feet with fawning aplomb for the charismatic leader at the microphone, then riding high at the top of the world. With a good-looking powerful half-black, half-white man just like Charlie as its figurehead, the future of the progressive agenda had indeed never looked so bright.

The line to shake the speaker's hand following the speech was long, but no one was in a hurry. The aura of his presence would keep his youthful admirers energized all night. The mood was exuberant, electric, everyone talking excitedly. As he inched along, Charlie could not help being swept up in the energy of what was called in the speech "the moment to redefine America"—from its roots to the present and into the future. Predictably the greatest applause lines came from the speaker's swipes at the Republican nominee in the upcoming presidential election.

Not that Charlie had seriously considered a career in politics. But as had been said, the moment of destiny needed people in every sphere of endeavor—doctors, educators, authors, business leaders, entrepreneurs, teachers, laborers, nurses, shopkeepers, secretaries—all together to bring the new vision of a transformed America to the corners where they lived.

Charlie had no idea what he wanted for his future. But wherever life took him, he could be part of it—he could influence others and do his part.

As the line moved steadily forward, Charlie saw the speaker ahead, face aglow as he accepted the adulation of the adoring teens who moved past as quickly as his handlers could scurry them along. His face radiated pleasure at the praise heaped upon him, his broad smile mouthing bland platitudes as the blur of faces swept by.

Charlie stared ahead as the face of the powerful and admired man came closer. By degrees he was just able to make out his voice through the din, though the words remained indistinct. A momentary minor chord suddenly clashed in Charlie's brain with sour dissonance. For an instant the expression he saw changed in Charlie's mind's eye. The man was enjoying the adulation more than a man of humble character should. The praise fed something disguised as light but which, out of sight, was dark, sinister, hidden—invisible from public view.

Charlie shook himself back to the present. There was the speaker's beaming countenance in front of him.

The moment came.

He moved forward. Suddenly he was face to face with the legend and darling of third millennium liberalism—the very apex of everything the political elite of the Left had been trying to accomplish in American society for fifty years. Time slowed as if he were in a trance.

"Charlie Reyburn," he heard as the man glanced at his nametag. The very timbre of the resonant baritone made world leaders, media stars, even Hollywood celebrities swoon. "I am pleased to meet you."

Charlie stared deep into the light brown eyes surrounded by white, deep set into the handsome face. He reached up. As their hands met, an invisible current shot through his arm.

A faintly inaudible gasp sounded from Charlie's lips. Involuntarily he pulled his hand away.

The rest of the conference passed in a blur. He remembered almost nothing more until leaving for home on Saturday. But the moment when his hand met that of the week's honored guest remained with him, and forever changed him.

The train ride from Colorado back to Minneapolis gave young Charlie Reyburn ample opportunity to reflect on the week's events, and what had taken place in those stunning seconds.

He was only fifteen, but those moments aged him beyond his years. Though it would take decades for the reality to catch up with the promise, in a sense in that brief exchange he took several giant strides toward the manhood that was awaiting him.

☆ ☆ ☆

Charles Hart Reyburn was of that ambiguously styled "Generation Z," born in 2001, eldest son of Valerie Hart and Henry "Hank" Reyburn, Christian parents from Minneapolis where Charles and his two younger sisters were raised. They were a family of modest but comfortable means, Hank a self-employed contractor who built single family homes with a crew of three, Valerie a third-grade public school teacher. Valerie's brother was one of those Silicon Valley anomalies on whom fortune strikes. After Delwin's death in a private plane crash in 2004, Valerie was notified that his will named her as the sole beneficiary of his estate, then worth approximately thirty million dollars.

Hank and Valerie knew the money was not theirs. Nothing in their lives changed. They did not buy a new house or car. They took no lavish vacations. They both continued to work as usual, and very few of those who knew them had any idea of their wealth. They would keep it safe and continue to live as they always had. They did, however, set up a trust that left Delwin's fortune to their three children equally.

Hank's life changed little. In the educational system of an ultra-liberal state, however, Valerie could not prevent being drawn into the climate of the Obama years. She had voted for Obama not because she thought he was qualified to be president but to demonstrate her open-mindedness to help put a black man in the Oval Office. Having herself married a black man, no one would think of calling her prejudiced. But such were the complex movements of white guilt exploited by the Left that even the mother of three half-black children was not immune from them.

Gradually the indoctrination of political correctness in which she was immersed infiltrated Valerie's perspectives. Coming as it did so incrementally, she was hardly aware of the change. Like most teachers in the educational system, she had slowly absorbed the new cultural standards without holding them up to the mirror of truth. She accepted what she was supposed to think. When the curriculum she was mandated to teach her third graders began using subtle homosexual terminology and more explicit words like *choice* and *preference* for gender, she hardly batted an eye. She had been part of the educational morass for so long that she never considered what the effect would be on the young boys and girls placed under her charge.

Thus it was that she withdrew twenty thousand dollars from the trust account to donate, through circuitous means that were taken care of by Democrat operatives, to Hillary Clinton's 2016 campaign. Like many who adopted their perspectives simply by breathing the cultural air of the times, she hated Donald Trump with an irrational passion that clashed with the façade of her Christian faith. Her belief that, if elected, he would destroy America, prompted her to apply to the Future of America Conference for the summer of 2016 on behalf of her son. It was her duty to insure that he followed in the cause of men like Obama and courageous women like Hillary Clinton.

Once the name Valerie Reyburn was known because of her generous donation, and investigation revealed the substance of the family fortune, she quietly became a target for Democrat fundraisers. It went without saying that young Charlie Reyburn would of course be welcomed to the Gateway Conference along with eight hundred other young leaders of tomorrow.

Hank Reyburn was saddened by his wife's shift in outlook and her open acceptance of changes in the world that disgusted him. But the money had been her brother's, and Valerie had a right to it. Thus Hank did not squawk about her campaign contribution.

The campaign of 2016 produced more than a few arguments in the home. Eventually Hank realized that his logic accomplished little more than entrench Valerie more deeply into the defense of the anti-white socialist policies of Hillary's platform. It was a bitter pill to swallow to realize that his wife considered him, her black husband, an Uncle Tom and not a "true black."

Charlie was not oblivious to the rancor the 2016 election stirred up between his parents. He listened to everything, took it in, and after the conference weighed his own thoughts with deep solemnity. Valerie assumed from his bland but uncritical comments about the conference that his allegiance lay with her. On his part, Hank began to pray more specifically for his son, that God would protect him from imbibing the cancer that was endemic in the cultural air of the times.

He was unaware that his prayer was being answered even before he had been led by the Spirit to pray it.

24

CHARLIE
AND THE SCOTSMAN

2016

A FRIEND AT church first shared one of George MacDonald's books with Hank Reyburn—a book of lightly edited sermons published in California. Despite the dry sound of "sermons," Hank found deep food for his soul. A thinking man, though not an intellectual, Hank was well aware that his two years of junior college could not compete with his wife's two master's degrees in education. Yet he relished the theological stretching of the Scotsman's writings in his heart and mind. He found himself thinking in new ways, not merely outside the doctrinal boxes he was accustomed to but with the walls of those boxes blown to smithereens. Investigating his new favorite author, he was soon also reading MacDonald's novels.

One day Valerie picked up one of several MacDonald books lying about the house, saw that it was a fairy tale, began reading, and was enthralled by its similarity to the Chronicles of Narnia. Within a month she was reading *The Princess and the Goblin* to her class at school.

Thus it was, two months prior to leaving for the Colorado conference, that high school sophomore Charlie Reyburn also began reading the Scotsman, following his mother's example with the two Curdie books. The second of the two was admittedly strange. Valerie knew it would not be appropriate for her class and soon lost interest in the Scotsman.

Charlie, however, found himself especially taken with the more mature, if occasionally chilling, themes in Curdie's later adventures, perhaps because Curdie was near his own age. He found himself living inside the story as if every word was real.

Halfway through the book, he began feeling an unaccountable aversion to touching people, especially his mother. She wrote if off, along with his prolonged silences, to a teenage phase. It was just the opposite, however, with his father. Valerie never noticed the keen expression on Charlie's face as he stared deeply into his father's eyes whenever Hank shook his hand. Almost as if some unspoken rite of passage into manhood were taking place between them, Charlie often initiated the contact at the end of a day after his father's return from work, grasping Hank's hand, and always gazing intently into his father's face.

So caught up in Curdie's story, when Charlie came to the passage of the rose fire during his first read of the second book, he was overwhelmed, as if he were standing beside the fire with the terrifying imperative of plunging his own hands into its midst.

> *There Curdie saw another wonder: on a huge hearth a great fire was burning, and the fire was a huge heap of roses, and the heat of the flames of them glowed upon his face. He turned an inquiring look upon the lady.*
>
> *"Curdie," she said, "you have stood more than one trial already, and have stood them well: now I am going to put you to a harder. Do you think you are prepared for it?"*
>
> *"How can I tell, ma'am," he returned, "seeing I do not know what it is."*
>
> *"It needs only trust and obedience," answered the lady.*
>
> *"I dare not say anything, ma'am. If you think me fit, command me."*
>
> *"It will hurt you terribly, Curdie, but that will be all; no real hurt but much good will come to you from it."*
>
> *Curdie made no answer but stood gazing with parted lips in the lady's face.*

"Go and thrust both your hands into that fire," she said quickly, almost hurriedly.

Curdie dared not stop to think. It was much too terrible to think about. He rushed to the fire, and thrust both of his hands right into the middle of the heap of flaming roses, and his arms halfway up to the elbows. And it did hurt! But he did not draw them back. He held the pain as if it were a thing that would kill him if he let it go—as indeed it would have done. But when it had risen to the pitch that he thought he could bear it no longer, it began to fall again. At last it ceased altogether, and Curdie thought his hands must be burned to cinders, for he did not feel them at all. The princess told him to take them out and look at them. He did so, and found they were white and smooth like the princess's.

It was the ongoing result of the fictional rose fire that exercised the most profound impact upon young Charlie Reyburn. That impact would remain with him for the rest of his life. His eyes had been opened to deeper realms of seeing, and to the most profound lesson life has to teach humankind—the eternal truth of becoming.

25

WHERE IS THE LIFE?

2040

GRIGOR AND Anya Popov knew what it had been like trying to cling to faith in the former Soviet Union. Their grandparents never stopped telling them of the horrors of those days.

"You must never forget the price we Christians paid to keep faith alive," they told them over and over in a hundred ways. "Never forget— never forget."

If Russian Orthodoxy was a ritualistic empty spiritual shell before 1917, communism seemed to seal its fate once and for all. Though their daily lives as Christians were not as dangerous as they had been for their grandparents, Grigor and Anya wondered whether much had changed for the better after all. With the collapse of the USSR and the gradual resurgence of Russia's Orthodox church, its ritualistic underpinnings returned to fill the great onion-domed churches and cathedrals with robed and chanting priests leading a smattering of old black-clad men and women through lifeless liturgies as void of reality as the communist dictatorship it had outlived. The great relics of the past might as well have been mausoleums. The Russian church was a historic institution that gave some Russians pride, but it offered them no life.

The older Popovs, however, had discovered living, vibrant reality to their Christian faith under communism. Desperate to keep Christianity alive, they had passed it on to the two generations that followed. Having to live that faith in secret with a handful of others, knowing that its discovery could result in arrest, made faith and prayer and trust in God real.

They came under the influence of others in a thriving underground church, fed by the exploits—passed by word of mouth—of men like Brother Andrew and Sergei Kourdakov and Richard Wurmbrand, hiding Christian refugees, distributing Bibles when they could get their hands on them, walking through the dark of night to attend prayer meetings with three or four others, providing shelter to Christians hiding from the KGB, participating in the Rose network to get those in danger safely to the West, and revering Aleksandr Solzhenitsyn as a saint. It was at just such a secret prayer meeting that all four of Grigor's and Anya's own parents, children at the time, had met. All the while their grandparents longed for freedom and prayed for an end to the evils of the USSR.

Now their grandparents and the generations of Christians who had kept Christianity alive those years of terrible persecution were gone. Their prayers had been answered. Grigor and Anya now had the freedom to worship that their grandparents had prayed for. Yet they could not help occasionally gazing back wistfully at the underground church of their grandparents.

The Christians of those days did not know freedom, but they knew life.

Where was such spiritual life in Russia and Ukraine now?

Certainly not in its church. Most of those of their generation had no interest in church at all. There was said to be an evangelical fellowship in Kiev, but that was too far to travel. Were there others with whom they could share the deep things of God, whom they could pray with, who knew the life their grandparents had known with brothers and sisters of the underground?

All they had were their few treasured books. Grigor had taught himself English years before and was sufficiently fluent to be able to read most of what they were able to find from used bookstores in England or the US.

Their very old New Testament, however, he and Anya always read in their native Russian.

26

A Birthing Revelation

THE LETTER Timothy read one Sunday a month later was a surprise. He could not tell its origin from the envelope. Opening it, he saw that it had come all the way from Russia.

The moment he finished reading, he immediately began a reply.

Dear Grigor,

What a delight to receive a letter from so far away. Your English is very good—I hope I will be able to make myself understood as well as you did.

I am Stirling Marshall's son. My father and mother are now with our mutual Father, but I will respond to you as I hope my father might have.

To the extent I am able, I can say that I feel your frustration with the lifeless formality you see in your church. Finding the life of true discipleship is a challenge in such an environment. In a sense, that life is never found in a church at all but must be discovered and lived in daily life where we find ourselves.

If our involvement in a church contributes to that, it is a wonderful thing. But if it does not, we have to be willing to move beyond the church of man, even leave it behind, in order to live in God's true, higher, eternal Church. That high Church is built from hearts joined in the common bonds of discipleship.

Sometimes that is a lonely road to walk. It is possible to be an integral member of that great worldwide Church and yet still function in solitude. It is not a Church that meets on Sundays but that meets in the heart of God. It draws its members together in mysterious and unseen ways.

It may surprise you to know that the problem you are facing is widespread here as well. The liturgical forms of organized Christendom are all susceptible to the lifelessness of ritual from centuries of tradition.

Ritual cannot by its nature produce life, it only produces a continuation of ritual. It may for some be meaningful ritual. But it is still ritual. There are many forms of ritual in the Protestant and evangelical denominations as well.

Anything can become a ritual, as the churches of America reveal clearly. There exist many in our churches who feel the same isolation that you do. They too are struggling—whether or not to remain in churches where formula of doctrine and worship breed their own less obvious patterns of ritual. Some are leaving the churches of man, and their road can be a solitary one. Others choose to stay and pray for their brothers and sisters and for the revelation of the eternal Church.

Keep faith, brother. God is moving and you are part of it!

Wouldn't it be wonderful if somehow God could draw us all together? Oh, to be able to meet others of that Church he is fashioning among us. We are rough and uneven, broken and chipped. Yet we are the living stones of an eternal Church whose birth pangs, I believe, are underway.

Let's keep in touch, Grigor.

As that birthing revelation continues, I am,

Your brother in Christ,
Timothy Marshall

27

SPARRING BETWEEN HEAVYWEIGHTS

2041

THE STRATEGY hatched by the granddaughter of Viktor Domokos worked precisely as she had envisioned.

Throughout the two years leading up to the 2038 midterm, she increasingly thrust herself into the congressional limelight, making speeches and traveling the country. During that time she never once made an appearance, either for personal retreat or any of the cartel's scheduled meetings, at the Roswell estate in the hills of southern California.

The announcement in October of 2038 of her candidacy for the nation's highest office was greeted by the press exactly as she hoped it would be. She was instantly in the headlines and was virtually unopposed for the Democrat nomination twenty-one months later.

At forty-seven years of age, avowed Muslim Akilah Samara was elected in November of 2040 with 61 percent of the vote, sweeping into prominence her little-known running mate, forty-four-year-old Rhode Island governor Elizabeth Wickes Hardy. History had been made. The nation's two top offices were now occupied by women—the president a Muslim, the vice president a lesbian married to her gubernatorial chief of staff, Alexis Hix.

Midway through President Samara's first year in office, Mike Bardolf received an unexpected invitation to a private lunch from first-term senator Jefferson Rhodes.

"I am honored to meet you, Mike," said the senator as the two shook hands.

"And I you, Senator," replied Bardolf. "But why should you be honored to meet me? I hardly move in your circles," he added, his faithful Palladium vow to secrecy serving him well. If the truth were known, he moved in far higher circles than Jefferson Rhodes was even aware of. Oraculous did not have chapters in humble institutions like Cal Poly Humboldt. And though the junior Rhodes might have been recruited during his years at the University of Washington Law School, even his father's reputation had not marked him as a young man to watch. Those who thought so had obviously been wrong.

"Don't be so modest, Mike," laughed Rhodes. "You come with some lofty credentials—the Domokos biography is a masterpiece."

Bardolf laughed. "Well, thank you. But there have been no calls from the Pulitzer committee."

In truth, the head of that literary committee, a Palladium man, was one of Loring Bardolf's best friends. He had been dissuaded by Mike's father from nominating the biography, not wanting to call more attention to his author-son and the Bardolf name than the book had already caused. Mike's growing public reputation was an unforeseen development Palladium's elite, including Mike's father, were watching carefully.

"And your connections to the new president obviously places you in select company," Rhodes added.

Mike smiled. "We're not all that close."

"Even with your association with old Domokos?"

"We are both dedicated to his memory," rejoined Bardolf vaguely.

"I have noticed, however, that the new president has not been forthcoming in offering you a position in her administration."

"I would not take one if she did. Akilah knows it. I have no interest in a political position."

"Perhaps," rejoined the senator. "Still, it strikes me that the lack of an offer, even simply as a nod to your affiliation with her grandfather, is somewhat surprising."

Mike did not reply.

"Which brings me to the answer to your question, why you? To get straight to the point—I would like you to act as assistant campaign manager for my reelection next year."

Bardolf stared back with a blank expression.

"Again," he said after a moment, "why me? Especially after what I just said about not being a political man."

"Because I think you are the right man for the job," replied the senator. "I have done my homework. I know more about you than you are aware. Your biography of Domokos revealed as much about you as it did him. In you I see a man committed to the ideals we share and one willing to do whatever it takes to achieve those goals. You're the kind of man I want on my team."

Bardolf nodded thoughtfully.

A curious expression spread over the senator's face in the silence that followed.

"As I say, I have done my homework. You are not as divorced from the political arena as you like people to think," said Rhodes after a few seconds. "I know about your grandfather's association with the Gore campaign. I am asking nothing more than that you continue in your family's tradition. I also know about Four-Six," he added almost as an afterthought.

Bardolf's eyes narrowed imperceptibly. He did his best to divulge no reaction.

"Am I supposed to know what that means?" he said.

"You do know what it means," rejoined Rhodes with a sly smile. "But don't worry, your secret is safe with me. I am entirely supportive of your, shall we say, occasionally unconventional methods. That's why I want you on my team. I think you and I are two men who can work together to achieve our common objectives."

"Let's say for the sake of argument that I was interested," said Bardolf slowly, ignoring for the moment the question of what Rhodes really knew or whether he was fishing and how he knew whatever he thought he knew. "What's in it for me?"

"I would think that would be obvious. Power, opportunity. You know, change the world. Isn't that what we all want? After the election, you will be on my staff. You will have a friend in the Senate to keep you out of harm's way and insure that you are in the center of the action. Meanwhile, I will have a man at my disposal who isn't afraid to get his hands dirty for the cause. It might be different if President Samara intended to make use of your talents. As it is, I'm offering to put you in the game at the highest levels."

As he listened, Mike carefully scrutinized the senator's expression. He was a wily one, he'd give him that. He couldn't tell if Rhodes was toying with him, with innuendos that might mean more than he was saying, or if he was actually putting his cards on the table. It was a high-stakes poker game. For one of the first times in his life, he wasn't sure whether his opponent was bluffing.

"The highest levels?" he repeated, his own poker face revealing nothing.

"It doesn't get much higher than the Senate."

"There is one rung higher."

"True," smiled Rhodes.

"I will think about it," said Mike. "Don't construe my questions as indicating a lack of interest," he added, reverting to his best deferential tone, thinking it best for now to play along. "I am humbled by the offer and very appreciative. I just want to know which way the winds are blowing. If I were to take it on, what would I be doing? You must be aware that I have no experience in this sort of thing. And as I understand it, your reelection is a lock."

"Nothing in this town is a lock," rejoined Rhodes. "I would want you to be my inside man, one who, as you say, is comfortable out of the spotlight but who can get things done—sometimes private things."

"You're not talking about JFK kinds of arrangements?"

"Women—gosh no. Nothing like that. I'm a happily married man. I mean behind the scenes. As an example, there is one fly in the ointment I would want you to look into—stealthily of course."

"Which is?"

"An old friend of mine, Ward Hutchins?"

"The evangelist!" laughed Bardolf.

"The one and only."

"How close are you as friends?"

"Not close at all. We were friends. He would love nothing better than to take me down. He's a religious fanatic, but as squeaky clean as they come."

"And you would want me to do what?"

"As I said, you strike me as a man not afraid to get his hands dirty. I'd like to see what dirt you can dig up on him. I've tried, but nothing sticks. I need to take the sting out of his bite."

"Now that I think of it . . ." mused Bardolf weighing his words carefully—he couldn't say too much. Yet some well-chosen bait might lure the senator into revealing what he knew about Four-Six. "I believe Domokos may have had a dossier on him. I don't remember what was in it."

"Do you still have those files?" asked the senator, a little too eagerly.

"I may," answered Bardolf guardedly. "If I decide to take you up on your offer, I'll see what I can find."

"Be careful of his sister, Linda Trent," said Rhodes. "She was recently appointed to the Ninth Circuit Appellate Court and is a friend of mine. She and her brother parted ways years ago. I don't want her tarnished. She's on our side and has a future with—let me just say that she's one I want to protect."

"I will think about all you have said," said Mike.

"Here's my private number," said Rhodes as the two rose. "Call me any time. It goes without saying that we will keep this conversation between ourselves for now."

"Of course," nodded Mike.

28

THE TWO BARDOLFS

MIKE BARDOLF wasted no time after the interview getting his father on the phone. He recounted the conversation nearly word for word.

"Do you think he was on a fishing expedition with the Four-Six," asked the elder Bardolf. "He can't possibly know of the organization."

"I couldn't tell," replied Mike. "He wore an expression that said he knew more than he was saying. He must have picked it up somewhere other than from the periodic table. I doubt if he was a whiz at chemistry. But then all the talk about bringing me in on the action, into a position of power. He was either playing with me, perhaps baiting me into revealing something or he knows nothing."

"Ironic, though," chuckled Loring. "One of our puppets offering to put you in a position of power."

"Though it could be classic misdirection."

"True. The question remains, how much might he know? His father, Harrison, was pretty tight with a few of our number. Over the years, someone might have let something slip."

"That would mean someone broke the vow."

"All that vow stuff is mostly an Oraculous thing," rejoined his father. "We don't go in for it much at the higher levels. With things moving as they are and with your Domokos Foundation out in the light of day, it's not as if there is danger to the cause. If there is a leak, of course, it has to be plugged. I'll have our security committee investigate the fellow's known associates in the membership."

"What should I do about his offer?"

His father thought seriously. "It's almost too delicious to turn down. You, a man who could destroy his career with one word—with a word, that is, to the right people, namely me!—serving as his underling and hatchet man, from the sound of it. It might be hard to play second fiddle to him, but what an ironic juxtaposition—Rhodes thinking he's your boss, when you and I hold his fate in our hands."

"I'd like to accept his offer simply as a challenge!" laughed Mike.

"And it could prove useful to us in other ways. Let me convene a special meeting of the League. I'll talk to the other six. We'll decide the best way to handle it."

"Keeping close to him would give me the opportunity to find out if he knows more than he should."

"I'll get back to you. . . . Do you hear anything from your sister?"

"Are you kidding! Amy and I parted ways years ago?"

"She still involved with that church thing—Florida, wasn't it?"

"No idea. You've not talked to her either?"

"No. I had enough of her preaching at me."

"And Mom?"

"Your mother and I haven't spoken since the divorce was finalized."

"Dad, that was years ago."

"And not a moment too soon. You?"

"She and I had lunch together, three maybe four years ago. Silent and strained, you know the drill."

"Only too well. She was never one of us."

"By the way, Dad, I heard that old Spencer, chairman of the Fed, is on life support."

"Yeah—poor guy. Took a turn for the worst three days ago."

"Isn't it about time you put me up for the seventy-two?"

"Patience, Mike. Your day will come. We can't be nepotistic about it."

"That's never stopped Storm. He's going to have Anson on the seventy-two ahead of me. Anson's a fool."

"Storm's too eager. You leave your future to me."

Mike ended the call, waiting until his father was off the line to allow his irritation to vent. Sometimes it was all he could do to keep his cool. But his father still held the cards.

If he took this job with the senator, he would be playing second fiddle to two men—Rhodes and his father!

29

THE CULT OF ME-NESS

PADDY AND Charlene Ayscough had moved to New Zealand hoping to escape the fast-paced impersonal life running them ragged in Manchester. They intentionally settled in a relatively small town of several thousand, well away from Auckland and the other large population centers.

As they hoped, the pace of life was slower. They found a small church where they seemed to fit in. Once the church leadership learned that Paddy was a musician and singer, he was soon on the music team.

One of the things Paddy and Charlene hoped to escape was the obsession with technically perfect amplified, mixed, dubbed, and expertly produced music presentations with state-of-the-art electronic equipment and auditions for the music team. In the church they had left, only the most skilled musicians—and those who looked the part as well—were accepted. The fact that the congregation was singing Christian words to the accompaniment of electric guitars and amplifiers and drums and synthesized keyboards did not change the concert atmosphere. The sheer volume numbed their senses.

It was not music alone that had prompted a change. It was but one of many symptoms of a church, they felt, that had lost its way. Trying to be all things to all men, especially youth, their Manchester church had accomplished little more than turning Sunday morning worship into a rock concert. Therefore, when a job opportunity down under came along, they thought, *It's time for a change in life. Let's go for it.*

The music team in their new church was simpler—a real piano, though also an electronic keyboard, two guitars, a bass, and several vocalists. Though the guitars and bass were amplified, thankfully there were no drums. The congregational singing could actually be heard.

After he had been with the team for several weeks, however, practicing at the church every Thursday evening, Paddy came home one night, sat, and sighed in frustration.

"I'm not so sure it's any different here, Charlene," he said. "We practice and practice, trying to sound professional, getting everything just right, Bill at the controls of the amplifiers acting as if we're trying to put on a show. The girls at the microphones swaying to the rhythm—who are they trying to impress? It's not so loud as in Manchester. But it's still all about looking and sounding like we're putting on a concert. Before we broke up tonight, Ralph said he'd been approached by Jill who asked if she could join the team.

"She's a sweet girl," said Charlene.

"Yes, and a decent musician—a really nice voice. When she sings it's obvious she's in tune with the Spirit. You know how she is in the prayer group—sensitive and soft-spoken. A Christlike spirit."

"What did Ralph say?"

"He put it to the rest of the group for a vote. I was the only yea. Everyone else voted against letting her join. In their eyes, she didn't have a professional voice. No one would say it, but she's not as pretty as they want either. But Ralph, pounding on his guitar every week as loud as he can, but whose temper is legendary among the mechanics who work for him, is the example of what the music team is all about."

He sighed and shook his head.

"I don't know, Charlene. Something's wrong with this picture. The church and music team are small, and thankfully there's no leather jacket rock-star wannabe with nose rings and tattoos whacking his drums trying to pretend he's Ringo and completely obliterating the Spirit. But it's still the same informing spirit of the flesh animating the whole thing. It's the cult of me-ness—everybody look at me. I'm a rock star."

"Pretty cynical, Paddy."

"That's what it feels like. I nearly walked out of practice tonight and quit the whole thing."

"But you didn't."

"I didn't want to overreact. I knew I needed to pray that my own spirit was right before condemning the others. They're good people, mostly. They just don't know any better. The performance spotlight is fundamental to music. They've been part of it so long they are blind to it. We talk about ministering through music. But that's just a way of spiritualizing the self-centeredness of it. They've been in the me-environment of evangelical music all their lives. They are blind to its deeper currents of self and the flesh."

"What's the solution, then?"

"Get rid of music teams. Or at least get rid of amplifiers and drums and microphones and electronics, and sing unto the Lord rather than to the worship of our own talents. I've often thought that the real solution would be for the music leaders to be in separate rooms in the basement, unseen by the congregation or even by each other, with their music sent into the sanctuary speakers. The pastor would simply introduce every song, and the congregation and unseen singers would sing together. No one would know who was in the basement singing. No soloists trying to out-sing everybody—just quiet, worshipful singing. Anyone who wanted would be able to participate—everything done in anonymity. No one could ever know."

"But everyone would know," laughed Charlene.

"You're probably right. So the team could change every week. None of the participants would know who the others were."

"How would you keep it from sounding like a disorganized jumble?"

"I don't know. Maybe it's unworkable. I'm only saying that the solution to me-ness is anonymity. If no one was watching, if no one ever knew, that would go a long way to eliminate the concert atmosphere of people trying to show off. People would sing for love of the music, not love of the spotlight."

"No one would want to be on the music team if they weren't seen."

"If they are doing it to be seen, they shouldn't be on the team."

☆ ☆ ☆

At the following week's practice, Ralph asked Paddy to prepare a solo for the special music three weeks later.

Paddy thought a moment, then nodded.

"Any idea what you'd like to sing?" asked Ralph.

"I'll have to think about it."

"Well, let me know. The rest of us will need to practice with you."

"I'd rather have no accompaniment, Ralph."

He stared back in question. "Why not?"

"I just don't want one."

"But you'll at least want me on the bass, and Martha on the keyboard."

"No, Ralph—especially not your bass."

Ralph's eyes flashed.

"I want nothing electronic," added Paddy. "No amplifier, no microphone."

"What will you want for an accompaniment?" asked Ralph testily.

"Nothing, Ralph. Nothing at all."

No more was said. When the Sunday morning came, Paddy took his place well away from the bank of microphones where the music team sat.

"The old song I would like to share is taken from one of my favorite passages of Scripture," he began. "That's Psalm 139. It represents one of David's most personal psalm-prayers. It is a song you don't hear much anymore. It was written by Irish evangelist and historian J. Edwin Orr at an Easter revival service here in New Zealand in 1936. The regular Easter Sunday tent meeting was so crowded that a midnight service was scheduled. Afterward a spirit of revival began spreading into all of New Zealand. As Dr. Orr was preparing to leave the country a few days later, four Aborigine girls approached him and sang the beautiful Maori Song of Farewell: *Po atu. rau, I moe a i ho ne; E haere ana, Koe ki pa ma mao; Haere ra, Ma hara mai ano Ki-ite tau, I tangi atu nei.* He was so moved by the beauty of the Polynesian melody that he wrote new verses to the tune on the back of an envelope in the post office at the little town of Ngaruawahia. The words he wrote were based on the familiar words of Scripture found in Psalm 139:23–24."

Paddy smiled. "I'm sure I didn't pronounce the words I just quoted accurately," he said. "And this morning I will sing Dr. Orr's scriptural version. I hope you will close your eyes and pray with me, as we allow David's prayer to fill our hearts."

"You need to move over to the mic, Paddy!" called out the voice of Ralph's technical assistant from the rear of the church where he sat at the controls of the sound system.

"I won't be using the mic, Bill," said Paddy quietly. "Please turn it off."

He waited a few seconds, then in a low a cappella voice began to sing.

"Search me, O God, and know my heart today.

"Try me, O—"

"Can't hear you in back, Paddy!" called out a loud voice from one of the rear pews.

Paddy closed his eyes and drew in a deep breath. He waited, trying to enter a worshipful spirit.

"Search me, O God," he began again, "and know my heart today.

"Try me, O Savior, know my thoughts I pray.

"See if there be some wicked way in me.

"Cleanse me from every sin and set me free.

The church remained quiet. There were no more interruptions. He paused briefly then went on with the next verse.

"Lord, take my life, and make it wholly thine.

"Fill my poor heart with thy great love divine."

As he sang the words,

"Take all my will, my—"

Paddy's eyes suddenly came into focus on the faces seated in front of him. No one was looking down. No eyes were closed in prayer or quiet worship.

Behind him he heard Ralph shuffling in his chair getting ready for their next number.

This was just one more Sunday morning performance! Had David's precious prayer registered at all?

He struggled to go on.

"—my passion, self, and pride,

"I now . . . I now—"

His voice caught.

"I now surrender—"

With great effort he struggled to finish the line—

"Lord, in me abide"—then broke into tears.

Paddy turned and walked away. Already Charlene was on her feet. She hurried down the aisle to the front of the sanctuary and followed him through the side door behind the pulpit and outside.

30

THE HIGHER MUSIC OF GOD'S SYMPHONY

SPRING 2042

Dear Mr. Timothy Marshall,

Thank you so much for replying to my letter. I am sorry to hear that your parents are no longer living but equally honored that you would take the time to reply personally.

My previous letter was brief, as I was not sure it would reach you—your father actually. I would value your thoughts no less than I would your father's.

My problem is this—I am a musician and have long enjoyed music in church. Recently it has been revealed to me (I hope it is not presumptuous to use that word) that much of the music in our church is motivated by vainglory, not the Spirit of Christ. I don't know what to do, whether to speak up, quietly withdraw from our music team, or even leave our church. I am in great turmoil because I love music. I love nothing more than making music unto the Lord. But the Spirit of the flesh is so powerful in our church that I simply cannot watch it, much less participate in it, without being repulsed.

What are your thoughts? Can you give me any perspective? What do you think your father would say? What do you think God would say?

Sincerely,
Paddy Ayscough

Dear Paddy,

What difficult questions you raise! I cannot speak for my father, and I would not presume to speak for God. I can only speak for myself when I say that I identify completely with your quandary. We are part of a large church with a music team that I admit causes me to ask many of the same questions.

I think I can say with confidence that it is obvious that your heart is open to the voice of the Spirit as you pray for guidance. You can therefore rest in the sure knowledge that when God has a word to speak to you, you will hear it. I have every confidence you will be shown what you are to do.

Until then, live according to his commands, do nothing that makes you feel uncomfortable, yet neither be overly anxious to make significant changes. In all things, God moves slowly and steadily toward increasing his revelation and his wisdom. If you obey and move in accord with his revelation as it comes, more and greater steps will always follow.

You are where he wants you. You are asking the right questions. His guidance will come.

We will definitely be in prayer that God will speak his wisdom to you. Feel free to write anytime.

May God continue to write the higher music of his eternal symphony in your heart!

Timothy Marshall

31

SENATOR AND OPERATIVE

NOVEMBER 2042

THE DAY after Jefferson Rhodes's reelection in November of 2042, he called his assistant campaign manager into his office. A boy of fourteen or fifteen was just leaving as he entered the outer office.

"Ah, Mike," said the senator, "meet my son, Bradon. Bradon, I don't think you've actually met my recent assistant campaign manager, Mike Bardolf."

"Hello, Mr. Bardolf," said young Rhodes affably as the two shook hands.

"I am pleased to meet you, Bradon," said Mike. "Getting an early start, I see, in preparation to follow in your father's footsteps."

"I don't know about that," said the young teen. "I doubt if politics is my game."

"I'm sure your father will have something to say about that."

"And my grandfather!" laughed Bradon. "He's the family king-maker, right, Dad!"

"Indeed he is."

"I'll see you later, Dad," said Bradon, walking toward the door. "It was nice to meet you, Mr. Bardolf."

"And you, Bradon."

The two men walked into the inner office. Rhodes closed the door.

"Congratulations are in order," said Mike as they sat opposite one another, "and you have mine. Quite a victory yesterday—72 percent."

"Thank you. You did your part. You handled yourself very skillfully."

"Thank you."

"I've had a few calls, in fact, wondering if I was going to cut you loose after the election."

"Headhunters, eh?"

"That's about it—hoping you might be available."

Bardolf laughed. "Like your son, I'm not sure politics is my game."

"You may change your mind. Once they get a taste of it, most people can't stop. Now that the election is over, I want us to move to the next level. I said you could have a future with me. Having seen how you handled some of, shall we say, the delicate situations that arose, I am more confident than ever that I want you at my side. I think I . . ."

As he listened, Mike thought back to his conversation with his father anticipating this very contingency. They had decided to continue playing out "the Rhodes scenario," as they called it, to see where it might lead. Having a Palladium man—notwithstanding that he was still a non-voting member—so close to the center of power could prove advantageous in ways they hadn't anticipated. They still had not been able to determine how much Rhodes knew, however, or where the leak had come from. That was another reason to continue the relationship.

"I think I can trust you implicitly," the senator was saying.

Rhodes arched an eyebrow and gave Mike a knowing look that turned the statement into a question. The irony was not lost on him. It was whether they could trust the senator that concerned the two Bardolfs. Mike continued to play the role of subordinate.

"You can, sir," he said.

"Completely, utterly. I mean completely? Do you understand what I am saying?"

"Perhaps I don't," replied Mike, gently probing the ambiguous relational waters.

"Good answer. If you were too quick with a reply, I might not know where you really stood. People who agree to anything too quickly can't be trusted."

"I'll have to remember that," rejoined Mike without expression.

"That you are cautious tells me you won't make the commitment lightly."

The senator paused. Mike waited.

"Now that the election is over, I have no more need of my campaign staff. So what I've been beating around the bush about is—would you like to stay on?"

"I suppose that depends on what you have in mind."

"Again, a good answer. What I need is a man not only whom I can trust, but who can keep secrets. Might you be such a one?"

It was all Mike could do to keep from smiling. But he retained his poker face. The irony was so thick he might not be able to cut it with a knife. He had spent his whole life keeping secrets! The two major skeletons in his closet not a soul knew about—not even his father.

The question, however, was two-edged. What secrets might the senator have knowledge of, and how well could he keep them? It appeared the game of cat and mouse would continue.

"I would like to think so," replied Mike.

"And one who would do whatever I asked? One who believes in our cause enough to do whatever it requires?"

"I hope I have proven myself."

"You have. The future may require testing that loyalty to a higher degree. If you are interested, let me tell you what I have in mind. What I say now must remain between the two of us. No one can ever know of this conversation."

"I understand," nodded Mike, intrigued.

"If I so much as suspect a leak, let's just say the consequences will not be pleasant."

"Am I to take that as a threat, senator?" asked Mike. "Threats go both ways."

"Tut, tut, Mike," laughed the senator, momentarily jarred by the tone in the other's voice. "Forget I mentioned it. The first item of business is your termination from my staff. Then I want you to apply to the FBI for a position with the Secret Service. I will make sure you are accepted."

Hardly necessary, thought Mike. FBI Director Telford was of the Palladium seventy-two.

"Then learn the ropes," Rhodes went on. "Keep your head down. Obey orders. I will be watching your progress."

"I will not be working for you, I take it?"

"Not directly. However, I will want you to continue the work you were involved in with Domokos—Project Forty-Six I believe it was called," he added with a significant smile. "Very clever—who would ever guess what it means."

"I've never heard of a Project Forty-Six, Mr. Rhodes," said Mike, truthfully enough. How much the senator really knew, and how much was guesswork, remained the pressing question. In any case, Rhodes had just upped the ante.

"Have it your own way," smiled Rhodes. "Let me just say that you were not the only one who knew Viktor's secrets."

The revelation stunned Mike, but he kept his poker face intact.

"Meanwhile, develop your contacts within the FBI. Do your job and climb the ladder in the Service so that you will be ready when the time comes."

"The time?" repeated Mike. "When might that be?"

"When the time is right. That's all I can say. Six years is not really so long to work in anonymity."

"Ah, six years. I see," nodded Mike. "And then?"

"Then we will both be where we planned to be. You just go about your work and ignore me. From this day on, act like you do not even know me. When I need you, I will bring you back in. By then you must have a spotless FBI record. When an opening comes for presidential detail, apply for it."

"As I have alluded to, I am not President Samara's favorite. She still thinks I manipulated her grandfather to worm my way into his good graces."

"You leave her to me. And that is assuming she is reelected in two years."

"You don't think she will face a serious challenge?"

"Probably not. But one never knows. Assuming she wins, however, I'll make sure your path is clear."

They continued to talk for another twenty minutes. When Mike left the senator's office, though he had divulged nothing, he knew well enough why Rhodes emphasized secrecy. If a transcript of their conversation ever leaked out, they would both face a grand jury and be indicted on charges of treason. But it had been instructive in helping him learn much about the junior senator from the Evergreen State and the elder Rhodes. A suspicion had also grown within him as they talked where the senator's sketchy knowledge about Four-Six had originated. He was certain Rhodes knew no details. Still, if the hints he had picked up were accurate, the leak was serious and would have to be attended to. If he played the cards of what he had discovered shrewdly, they might be his ticket onto the seventy-two.

A long conversation with his father followed later that day. He did not, however, divulge everything he had learned. An ace or two kept even from his father would prove useful later.

32

THEATRICS AND GIMMICKS

2042

AN UNEXPECTED sight greeted Violet Langdon as she exited the Sunday morning worship services of ten-thousand-member South Park Christian Assembly in Albany, New York.

Outside the main doors as hundreds of worshippers filed out, on the pavement in front of them sat an eight-car, open-air tram. Each car could hold ten or twelve if they squeezed together. In front of the small electric-powered tram sat one of the church's five assistant pastors, decked in an old-fashioned engineer's uniform, with striped shirt and cap to match.

"What in the world is this?" exclaimed Violet. She had been daydreaming during Pastor Redmond's closing comments and hadn't heard the announcement.

"Didn't you hear what Arnold said before his final prayer?" rejoined her husband, Trevor.

"I must not have!" laughed Violet.

"He said the church had purchased a new tram in anticipation of the crowds expected for the Ward Hutchins meetings next month. He wants to try out the system. If everyone likes it, we can add as many cars to the tram as necessary to move crowds to and from the parking lots."

"As if we need to spend ten or twenty thousand dollars to keep people from having to walk to their cars," said Violet cynically.

"Fifty," corrected Trevor. "I'm on the Board of Trustees, remember. We had to approve the expenditure."

"All the more ridiculous! Fifty thousand dollars—you're really serious?"

"The church can afford it—a drop in the bucket."

"Why didn't you tell me?"

"We were sworn to secrecy. Arnold wanted to make a big splash—it had to be a surprise."

Their brief conversation was interrupted by a booming voice speaking through a vintage megaphone: "All aboard!" cried the pastor-engineer. "Next stop parking lot A, with stops also at B, C, and D. Don't be shy—jump in. All aboard!"

South Park Assembly was the most affluent church in New York's state capital—able to afford a fifty-thousand-dollar tram from half of one week's collection take. Most of its congregation was clad in thousand-dollar dresses and suits, appearing as if they had planned on a fashion show rather than a worship service. Yet the gleeful and excited scrambling that now took place—a hundred adults and children rushing, pushing, and shoving their way to nab the eighty or ninety available seats for the maiden voyage of the AA Express—gave the appearance of a mass of urchins who had never seen such a contraption in their lives. Matthew 19:30 was not so much in evidence as Darwin's law might have been paraphrased: the survival of the quickest.

A minute later Pastor Rick sounded the engine's bell then set off slowly until free of the enviously watching crowd that would have to wait for the next trip or walk to their cars.

"That was ugly!" said Violet as she and Trevor walked toward parking lot B.

"The children will enjoy it."

"But what example does it teach them? Rush ahead, squeeze everyone else out so you can get the best seat. What a spectacle. I suppose it will be balloons and jugglers next."

"Actually, you're not so far wrong," said Trevor. "We've arranged for six of those huge helium blimps to fly over the church for the week prior to the Hutchins meetings and two of those revolving spotlights for the night of the meetings—you know, like they used to have at car dealerships and theaters. I've seen them in old movies. We were lucky to find a company in Jersey to rent them from?

"At what cost?"

"Plenty. But to get the word out, how can you put a price tag on salvation?"

Violet stopped and turned toward her husband.

"Listen to you, Trevor," she said. "I can't believe what I'm hearing."

"What?"

"Do you really think blimps and spotlights will produce salvation? It's the Spirit of God that draws, not spotlights. People don't give their hearts to the Lord because of clever enticements."

"Sometimes people need a little encouragement."

"But spotlights and blimps! Jesus didn't announce the Sermon on the Mount with flyers and advertisements and spotlights. He sat then told people to live by God's commands. He didn't try to entice them to believe. He ended saying that those who didn't live by his words were houses built on sand."

"Come on, Violet—that's different."

"How it is different?"

"Well for one thing, there was no electricity back then."

"Trevor, that's ridiculous. You know that's not what I meant. Do you think that if Jesus were alive today he would use spotlights or trams or balloons?"

"I don't know—maybe."

"I don't believe this, Trevor. Of all people, you ought to know better. I expect it from Pastor Redmond. He lost the plot a long time ago, in my opinion. But you?"

"Arnold makes valid points. In this modern age, you have to make the gospel attractive so people will listen. Otherwise they will never darken a church door."

"I'll ask again—would Jesus try to make the Sermon on the Mount appealing and attractive? He said be perfect, put others first, sin no more, deny yourself. How do you make that appealing? No one scrambling to get on that tram was thinking about putting others first. Good heavens, Trevor—trying to make the gospel palatable is just another way of watering it down. If a church isn't teaching people to do what Jesus said, what's a church for?"

"It's different today, Violet. Different times require new methods."

"You don't think Jesus's methods are good enough for us? You don't think his methods will still work today?"

"That's not what I was saying—only that we have to change with the times."

"I'm not sure I agree, Trevor. It's changing with the times that has made the Christian church so lukewarm. There's no black and white anymore. Anything the world says, the church goes along with because we have to change with the times."

"That's not at all what I'm saying."

"That's exactly what you're saying. Because we must change with the times, you condone using the world's methods to spread the gospel—trams and blimps and spotlights. It's all gimmicks, Trevor— advertising gimmicks. It's the world's way. Pastor Redmond is turning the church into a circus. What's next, a big top in the parking lot?"

A sheepish expression came over Trevor's face. He was quiet a minute.

"Don't . . . not really. Don't tell me!" said Violet.

"Only for the week of the meetings."

"Lord, forgive our worldliness," sighed Violet softly. "Where?" she asked, turning toward her husband.

"One in front of the church for refreshments. Two others adjacent to the sanctuary for overflow crowds, each with two-hundred-inch monitors to broadcast the messages."

"Three tents! Unbelievable. Again, where is the example of Jesus? The Sermon on the Mount turned into a carnival. It reminds me of an old book I saw once at my grandmother's called *The Gospel Blimp*. A church bought a blimp to fly over the city to drop salvation tracts. It was satire but not so very different than the methods the church has been using throughout history—trying to spread the gospel any way except the one way Jesus said would actually work."

"And that way is?"

"Trevor, you know it as well as I do. I've heard you say it yourself. That's why I can't believe you're going along with these theatrics and gimmicks. Non-Christians coming to a meeting and watching people scramble to get on a tram—they will be turned away from the gospel. Watching Christians put others first—that's the ultimate salvation tract. It's just doing what Jesus told us to do. It's the Sermon on the Mount."

"You don't think the gospel sometimes needs a little help?"

"No, I don't. The only way to spread the gospel is by living the gospel, not dropping tracts on the city."

"I probably shouldn't tell you, but Arnold is looking into buying drones to fly over Albany to drop small cards announcing the meetings."

Violet could only shake her head in disbelief.

They reached their car and began the drive home in silence.

"On a lighter note," Trevor said when they were halfway home, "Pastor Rick asked me this morning if you and I would like to help chaperone the youth group trip to Haiti over Easter break. They're going to help rebuild an orphanage that was nearly destroyed in the hurricane."

"That might be nice. Putting young people to work doing some good. Who else would be going?"

"He wants to get six couples—us, the Jacksons, Wyatts, I think that's all he's got for now. Since we have no children that's why he asked us. I've got vacation time piling up at the hospital."

"You said we would?"

"Tentatively. I said I'd talk to you. Then he's got that gay man Spaulding and the lesbian lady Garnett to chaperone the trans and gay group. But there's only eight or ten of them."

"You have got to be kidding! They're going on the trip with our church kids?"

"They're church kids too. Some of them are from families in leadership. Jolie Redmond is contemplating a sex change I understand."

"That is disgusting. Her poor parents. The pastor's daughter—what an example for the church to set."

"They're backing her up."

Violet's mouth hung open a few seconds. "And all this is what you call changing with the times?"

"I suppose. Arnold is looking to bring a lesbian on staff as a new assistant pastor."

Again Violet shook her head and sighed.

"What has the Lord's church become to tolerate Jezebel in her midst," she said in a quiet voice. "The Lord's words have been turned upside down. It's no longer, 'neither do I condemn you, go and sin no more.' Now his words have become, 'no one here will condemn you, come join us, and continue in your sin as long as you like.'"

"So is that a no?"

"About the trip."

"Yes—the Haiti thing."

"It's absolutely a no. I will not be part of worldliness pretending it's for the sake of spreading the gospel."

"It would be a chance for us to visit Disney World. We've always talked about it."

"What?" said Violet.

"The group's going to spend three days in Florida at Disney World and Universal Studios before flying over to Haiti for two days."

Violet sat dumbfounded.

"It goes on and on," she said. "Three days having fun and two days at the orphanage. I wonder how much work will get done. How many of the teens would sign up, do you suppose, if there was no Disney visit— if it was going to be a whole week of hard work?"

"They won't have to decide. This way they can have the best of both."

"The best, Trevor. Best for whom? Do you think the orphanage directors consider two days better than a week? And then to cap it off, we would be transporting our American culture of gay and lesbian and trans teens to Haiti. I wonder how much the Haitians will appreciate that."

She sighed in angry frustration.

"It's like that book from many years ago—my dad told me about it," she said. "It was called *The Kingdom of God Is a Party*. I'm in shock by all this. Discipleship isn't a party. It's not trips to Disney World. That's presenting a false gospel to the world. There is no Disneyland gospel."

"But without Disney World, we'd probably only get eight or ten to sign up to go. As it is, sign-ups are approaching a hundred."

"I'd take the eight or ten in a heartbeat," said Violet. "Maybe I'd be able to talk to them about discipleship."

They rode the rest of the way home in silence.

Violet was thinking hard. She did not usually make snap decisions. Yet now that the day had come she realized that her subconscious had been thinking about it for a long time.

As Trevor opened the car door, she stopped him.

"Just a minute, Trevor," she said. "There's something I need to say. I've reached a decision."

"About the Easter trip—that's fine. I'll tell Rick no."

"It's bigger than that, Trevor. I've decided to leave South Park Assembly."

The words fell in the quiet car like a bombshell.

"I understand your loyalties," she went on. "This is my decision alone. I will love and support you no matter what you do. But I can no longer be part of it. I've attended my last service. I will not step inside that church again. I hope you can understand."

33

A Wife's Reflections

February 2043

IN THE huge ultra-modern sanctuary of Seattle's Puget Sound Vine Ministries, Grace Forster sat in their usual pew three rows from the front of the church between thirteen-year-old Craig and fifteen-year-old Ginger. Her husband Mark was preaching on the Beatitudes. He had just read the words, "Blessed are those who hunger and thirst for righteousness . . . ."

The words set off a chain reaction in Grace's brain. Gradually her surroundings faded. She was transported back through the years to the first time she had laid eyes on the young man who would become her husband.

She had been somewhat interested in a boy called Shaun Durant from the Baptist church where she had grown up on the coast of northern California. Being one of the top local runners in their high school, she had gone to watch Shaun run in a cross-country meet when both were Humboldt State sophomores. As the twenty-five or thirty young men lined up at the starting line, however, her eyes were unexpectedly drawn to one of Shaun's fellow Lumberjacks standing beside him.

The gun went off and they sprinted away, quickly disappearing into the redwoods. Grace waited with the handful of spectators until a few shouts in the distance signaled the return of the leaders twenty minutes later. As Shaun came racing toward the finish line in second place, she clapped and cheered. Yet instead of running over to congratulate him, she found herself waiting for the appearance of the other boy she had seen. He was about a minute behind Shaun, finishing in eleventh place. Her eyes followed him across the line.

There was no race scheduled the following weekend. At the Saturday Bible study hosted by the Christian group whose activities she had just started attending, there was the same boy again. Most of the girls of the group were talking about a good-looking boy named Jeff Rhodes, but she was unexpectedly taken by the boy whose name she didn't even know.

Then the president of the group stood up and introduced his friend who would lead the study that morning. It was him. His name was Mark Forster.

"I would like us to give serious thought this morning," Mark began, "to the Lord's fourth beatitude from Matthew 5:6: 'Blessed are those who hunger and thirst to be righteous, for they shall be satisfied.' I truly believe that in this simple statement Jesus has given us not only the key to the spiritual life but to everything in life. The desire to be good, the hunger to be righteous, as Jesus said, is . . . ."

Grace never forgot that day. Before they had ever spoken a word to each other, she knew what made Mark Forster tick. It was what had drawn her. He was hungry and thirsty to be like Christ, to live his life as the Lord's disciple. How could she not be drawn to him? Had she somehow seen it in his eyes, in his countenance, even standing at the starting line of a cross-country race?

By the end of that year, she and Mark were seeing each other almost daily. By the next, her junior year, Mark's senior, she knew that he was "the one." From the beginning, their love was bound up in their shared spiritual lives. There was no Mark and Grace apart from Mark and Grace the Christian college students whose desire was to serve the Lord.

Running was almost an equally strong passion for Mark, though he was totally unprepared for what he discovered to be her other passion.

"Have you ever run?" he asked one day after they had known one another a few months.

"What, me—no," Grace had replied. "I'm not very athletic."

"Anyone can run. And anyone can improve and do well at it if they stick with it and get in shape. I'm not that great an athlete either. I just love to run."

"I don't think I'd like it."

"What do you do, then? Everybody has to do something, you know, besides school and studying—a hobby, exercise?"

A sheepish look came over Grace's face.

"What?" laughed Mark.

"You'll laugh when I tell you."

"No I won't—what is it? You've got to tell me now!"

Grace looked down. It was quiet a few seconds.

"I want to fly," she said.

Mark began to laugh but quickly caught himself.

"Uh, well, sure. Who doesn't? I wanted to be Peter Pan when I was a kid. I dreamed of flying and wanted it so much I could taste it."

"That's not what I mean, Mark."

Mark finally realized from her voice that she was serious.

"I mean fly airplanes," Grace said after a moment. "I'm studying to get my pilot's license."

Mark stared back dumbfounded.

"Wow, that's pretty amazing. Not what I expected. You . . . I mean, can someone like you . . . can you really get a license?"

"I was in the NAHSAC all through high school."

"What's that?"

"The National Association of High School Aviation Clubs."

"What do they do?"

"We learned everything about flying. I got my student pilot license my senior year."

"You've actually flown an airplane!"

Grace laughed. "Just a small one. And with an instructor. But yes."

"That is a lot more adventurous than running! It would scare me to death."

"There's nothing like being up there," said Grace. "It's not just the view and the scenery. It's hard to describe—it's like a feeling of complete freedom."

Again it was quiet.

"What are your plans?" asked Mark. "Are you going to pursue it—I mean like a career or something? Or is it just for fun?"

"I want to get my private license first," replied Grace. "I'm old enough now. You can get a student license at sixteen, a private at seventeen, a commercial at eighteen. I'm almost nineteen. But the lessons are expensive, and I don't feel ready to take the test. Maybe next year."

"And your folks—they're okay with it?"

"Not my mom," laughed Grace. "She hates it. But my dad flew in the Air Force. That's probably where I got it. He thinks it's great. He takes me up with him a lot. I won't go for my private license until he thinks I'm ready."

"And then?"

"I've always wanted to do something with my life that mattered, to serve the Lord in some way. Ever since I got the flying bug, which was longer ago than I can remember, I've been fascinated by the work of Missionary Aviation Fellowship. I'm thinking about that."

"This is all blowing my mind," said Mark. "Who would know that about you?"

"That inside meek and mild Grace Thornton lurks a daredevil?"

Mark laughed. "Maybe something like that. Those are your words not mine. I've never seen you as all that meek and mild. When you have something to say, you say it. You've got, I don't know—pluck."

"That's what my dad says!" laughed Grace. "Maybe he's right. I tend to think of myself more as the meek and mild type."

"Not if you're flying airplanes! I'll now add bravery to the list of your character qualities!"

"If you say so!"

After finally qualifying for her private pilot's license a year later, she and Mark went to Murray Field with Grace's father. He saw them off for Grace's maiden voyage without father or instructor, Mark beside her in the two-seater Cessna.

Grace's father saw that Mark was nervous.

"You take care of your passenger here, Gracie," said Mr. Thornton. "His face is a little pale. If he starts to get sick, come back in."

"I will, Daddy."

"And you, Mark, my boy," he said turning to Mark, "I'm not going to tell you to take good care of my daughter because the shoe's not on that foot. It's she who's got to take care of you. You just relax and enjoy the ride. She knows what she's doing."

"I'll try, Mr. Thornton. But I've never been up in such a tiny thing."

"You'll be fine."

As they taxied out then turned around 180 degrees and sped down the runway, out of the corner of her eye Grace saw Mark's white knuckles gripping the armrests. She pulled back on the control wheel, and they soared into the air.

"You can open your eyes now!" she said laughing.

"My eyes weren't closed. Well, not the whole time!"

Mark drew in a deep breath and dared a peek. Soon they were banking gradually northward over Humboldt Bay then past the shoreline of the Pacific. Grace straightened out and flew along the coast until reaching Trinidad Head. Arcing steeply back in a semi-circle, their return route took them straight over McKinleyville, over the Humboldt campus, Bayside, and Jacoby Creek, until they descended and eased gently down onto the Murray Field runway. The entire flight lasted less than twenty minutes.

Mr. Thornton walked toward them as Grace taxied the Cessna to a stop in front of the hangers.

"That was amazing!" exclaimed Mark as they climbed out.

"You didn't lose your lunch?" laughed Grace's father.

"No—I couldn't believe it. Grace was amazing!"

"That's what I keep telling her mother—that she has nothing to worry about!"

"Well, you can tell her the same from me!"

It was the first of several flights together that year prior to Mark's graduation—including one up the coast to Crescent City and another inland over the Coast Range to Redding at the north expanse of the California valley.

Grace smiled at the memory. Their relationship wasn't only about her flying and Mark's running. Mark had been a spiritual mentor to her as well as a boyfriend.

As her thoughts drifted back to the present, Mark was still talking about the same passage that had sent her thoughts to the Bible study at Humboldt so long ago. Yet something was different today. His voice did not have the same passion, the same hunger. He almost sounded . . . what was it? As if he was reading from a commentary. She knew him well enough to sense that he was not speaking from his heart. Back at Humboldt his eyes glowed with the wonder of the Christlike life.

His eyes weren't glowing today. Mark seemed tired, bored, weary of preaching. He had lost the fire and enthusiasm for the Scriptures he loved so much.

It was almost painful to listen as he labored through the sermon. What did it mean? Was it possible that God had something different for them, something more than Mark preaching sermons he was bored with?

That same day, that very moment, Grace Forster began to pray in a new way for her husband. She prayed that Mark would either regain his enthusiasm for his ministerial calling, that God would supply what was missing, or that he would be led in whatever new directions God had for him.

What do you have for us, Lord, she prayed. *What are you saying—to Mark, to me? If you are getting us ready for a change, prepare my heart for it, too, as well as Mark's.*

She kept her reflections to herself. She didn't need to say anything. She didn't need to give advice or speak on God's behalf. If God had something to say to him, he would reveal it. Mark would hear what he was supposed to hear from God.

She trusted Mark. If something new was on his horizon, he would know God's voice when it came.

34

MINISTERIAL REEVALUATIONS

MARCH 2043

MARK FORSTER left the church, after the seemingly endless visiting following the service, more exhausted than usual from the handshaking and conversational superficialities.

Even as he stepped down from the pulpit after a sermon on the prodigal son, an undefined disquiet swept through him. He had noticed it during the sermon, a nagging feeling that he and the prodigal might have more in common than anyone listening would suspect.

When the misgivings had begun, he wasn't sure. A year ago, two years? When had he first sensed the hint of dissatisfaction?

To all appearances he was hugely successful, living a dream, now head pastor of a growing church, beloved by all, with wife and daughter and son considered one of Seattle's model families, chosen as one of the finalists last year as *Evangelical Times'* Man of the Year. That the magazine's award had eventually gone to Ward only showed how far the two friends had come. Ward was riding high and loving every minute of it.

Mark, not so much.

Reaching home, he was more subdued than usual during Sunday dinner. Grace noticed but knew he would speak his mind when he was ready.

After dinner, Mark disappeared into his study with the *Seattle Times*. Stories had been running ever since last November's election about Jeff's reelection to the Senate—Seattle's golden boy and the state's favorite son—interviews with his glowing parents, his patriarch father

---

Harrison Rhodes vicariously living his own dream. Today's Sunday issue devoted several pages to an in-depth biography of the forty-three-year-old senator.

Not that he had expected it, but there was no mention of himself or Ward and their college friendships. Those were associations it was best for liberals like Jefferson Rhodes to pretend had never existed, along with his own brief foray into the religious circles of Pinecroft and Humboldt's CCF group. Christian antecedents, however shallow, as Jeff's had been, did not look good on a Democrat's curriculum vitae. Mention was made of Linda, whom Jeff was quoted as calling "a dear friend of many years and a rising judicial star."

Mark could not help smiling a little sadly as he finished the article. Jeff's ambitions were being realized. He was in the national spotlight, as was Ward. His two friends were not really so different, both driven and ambitious and now stars in their respective fields—yet on completely opposites sides of life's spectrum. In spite of some of his theological differences with Ward, he loved him like the brother he was—and admired him as a man of conviction, integrity, and godly character. Poor Jeff, he thought on the other hand. What a bitter awakening awaited him one day.

And what of his own goals and aspirations, thought Mark as he set the paper aside. Was he envious of his two friends?

He didn't think so. Then what could account for the disquiet in his heart? Was it spiritual, professional, or somehow personal in a way he didn't yet understand?

The odd feeling remained the next day and the day after that—but still he could not identify its source.

A month or two later, he happened on a news item in one of the many evangelical news services he received that the longtime pastor of Foothills Gospel Ministries had announced his retirement.

He read it over a second time, unaccountably pensive at the implications. Though McAnarney's arrival at the Roseville church took place long after he was gone, he'd paid him several visits over the years when he and Grace and the children drove down to see his parents. Realizing that he was a minister of some repute in Seattle, with roots to the

Sacramento area, it had seemed appropriate to make contact with the pastor of one of the region's largest evangelical churches. McAnarney had invited him to take the Foothills pulpit for a guest appearance, but Mark had not accepted the invitation. During their visit two years earlier, he, Grace, Ginger, and Craig had been too busy moving his parents into a smaller home to visit the aging pastor.

Robert Forster always hoped his son would return to take over the Circle F. Though his mother was proud of him, Mark knew his father was disappointed with the career path he had chosen. Increasingly the ranch had become too much for him. Mark and his mother knew there had to be a change. For some time they'd relied on extra workers to make up for what Robert could no longer keep up with, but it was a temporary solution. Eventually they reached the decision—during a frank family discussion three Christmases earlier—for the two elder Forsters to retire from active ranching, sell off the livestock, rent the ranch house, and for them to move into a smaller house in Grass Valley. Robert was then sixty-seven. The change was both inevitable and necessary, though that fact did not prevent a good deal of grousing from Mark's father.

At the time Mark mentioned the possibility of leasing the ranch to one of their neighbors.

"David's ranching days are behind him, too," said his father. "He's two years older than I am. He sold most of his cattle stock years back. I suppose I could talk to D. S. Layne, but he's got his hands full with his own spread."

And so it had been done, and Mark's visit last year had been to the house in Grass Valley. A letter had come from his mother just a week ago. She still wrote real letters, Mark thought with a smile. Hers were the only such letters he received. Reading between the lines, he could tell she was concerned about his father.

His health was good, but the retired life did not suit him. He was a ranch man and would die a ranch man. His mother was worried about him.

Mark drew in a thoughtful sigh. Was it perhaps time to consider a change? His father might not have many years left.

As attentive as he had tried to be, there was only so much he could do from seven hundred fifty miles away. Did his father need him closer during these final years of his life?

His thoughts turned pensive as he recalled the happy days of his youth, riding everywhere on the ranch. His father was the very image of a robust, indestructible cowboy—Mark's own bigger-than-life John Wayne. Now he was gray and no longer sitting strong and tall atop one of his favorite stallions. He was on his way to becoming an old man.

Perhaps Robert Forster needed his son.

Mark read the notice about Foothills a third time. He would make a call to McAnarney later in the day to see what his plans were. First he wanted to chat with his father.

He reached for the phone.

35

CELL CHURCHES

FALL 2043

HEATHER MARSHALL was answering mail at the desk that would always be "Grandpa's desk" in the office she still reverently called "Grandpa's study." Though she had lived in her grandparents' house and had owned it with her parents for five years, in her mind it would always be Stirling and Larke Marshall's home.

She'd made the El Dorado home thoroughly her own, without changing the intrinsic ambiance so evocative of the man and woman she had loved. In the minds of many who came to visit, they had assumed almost saintlike stature. As much as she revered them, however, to Heather they would always be the grandma and grandpa who read to her and taught her to play the piano and played games with her, and made her feel like the most special girl in the world. The house would always be filled with the silent sound of her grandfather's laugh and the memory of her grandmother's smile.

Heather wanted people to feel Stirling and Larke Marshall's presence when they visited. Though her name was now on the title deed, she saw herself as caretaker to their legacy. The weekends hosting the GCG meetings four times a year were Heather's special delight. When people gradually began coming from farther distances to attend the gatherings, she was able to fulfill her passion for hospitality by inviting one or two of the couples to stay in her guest rooms, something they considered a great privilege.

A letter had just arrived that morning from New York. Heather had read it an hour ago, and her subconscious had been ruminating on the best way to reply. Ever since moving into her grandparents' former home, she had taken the correspondence far more personally and seriously. She realized what a solemn responsibility rested on her shoulders. When she replied to a letter, she was speaking on her grandfather's behalf.

Heather drew in a deep breath and looked down at the letter on the desk. At last she was ready.

> *Dear Mrs. Langdon, though I would rather call you Violet. Your letter was so personal, I feel that I know you as a friend.*
>
> *Oh, my—what a letter. You have really had a difficult struggle. What courage it must have taken to make the stand you did.*
>
> *I wanted to get that said first because it was on my heart. But now I need to tell you that I am Heather Marshall, granddaughter of Stirling and Larke Marshall. Their son, Timothy, is my father. Sadly, both of my grandparents died a little over ten years ago. Fortunately, their mail continues to reach us—sometimes by wonderfully strange pathways. My father and mother and I try to reply to every letter that comes.*
>
> *I hope you don't feel that you are getting the low woman on the totem pole. But I am really glad to have the chance to write you because I have felt many of the same misgivings in church— the theatrics, as you call it, the games and gimmicks. Sometimes I wish I had your courage just to stand up and say—This isn't what Jesus lived for or died for! But so far I have kept silent, except occasionally venting my frustrations when my parents and I are alone.*
>
> *We have been meeting semi-regularly with a group of people Dad calls a cell of the true Church. The reality is so much more fulfilling than the Sunday morning worship services of a mega-church. My father always distinguishes between the upper- and*

lowercase Church and church. He got that distinction from my grandfather.

It would be wonderful if you could find a few others to meet with periodically as well. You said your husband has continued attending services on Sundays but is reevaluating too. Has he felt any further leading about what to do?

Please write again. I am interested in how you and your husband navigate this in the coming months and years—especially as many of your concerns are ones so many others share. I know my mother will want to write to you as well.

Much love in the universal Spirit who binds us,
Heather Marshall

Two weeks later, a letter with a familiar address arrived at the Dorado Wood home, this time addressed to Heather.

Dear Miss Marshall . . . Heather,

Thank you so much for your kind reply. When I wrote I didn't know whether I would receive an answer at all, not knowing if the address in the book would reach you. I was so overjoyed, and honored to receive your letter that I immediately called my husband at work.

The group you mention sounds so wonderful. We could be a sister "cell" to yours! Actually, since my last letter, Trevor and I did invite some people over for an evening, mostly from our church, but a few from the hospital where we both work and where we have developed a few relationships. We didn't get into our "issues" with the church but just shared together. Then Trevor gave a little talk based on one of the passages from your grandfather's commandments book. Everyone seemed to want to get together again.

As for church, we are both at peace as things stand now. Trevor has decided, as I told you, to continue trying to maintain a presence at church until he is led differently. I am happy for him to go if he wants to. In the meantime, we will see where our little group goes.

Thank you so much for giving such thought and personal attention to my little world and its concerns. I already feel that God is opening new windows for me. I know I am not isolated in this new path I have chosen to walk outside the church—but not outside the Church at all. I know that I have found a friend, though you and I have never met. And that is the true Church after all, isn't it? I would love to hear from your mother!

With deep appreciation,
Violet Langdon

36

CURDIE HANDS

2016–2020S

THE MEMORY came back to Charlie Reyburn often.

Through his college years, then graduate school, and as his career in academia began, in one sense the Gateway Conference when he was fifteen continued to define his outlook on many things in life.

Especially that one defining moment.

He had finished the second installment of the Scotsman's Curdie's story two weeks prior to leaving for Colorado. He would never forget the day he first read the passage of the rose fire. He recalled how thoughtful he had been as he continued through the book. At one point he set the book down, too absorbed in his thoughts to continue.

He had not consciously prayed on that day. Yet perhaps something deep inside him had indeed begun calling out to God at that time— silently articulating what his conscious mind could not have formulated into words but which his heavenly Father knew expressed the deepest yearnings of his spirit:

May I have such eyes. May I have eyes to see truth. May I have Curdie eyes and hands to perceive truth. God, give me your eyes and hands.

He was only fifteen. But in that prayer, whether it was audible or merely the invisible groaning of a spiritually sensitive young man to the One who made him, his life's course was set. Without knowing it, Charlie Reyburn had given his life story to the Author to write.

It was only natural that he was still thinking of the fire and its result when he left for the conference two weeks later. He was still thinking of it on Thursday evening as he listened to the week's most publicized speech then later while standing in line to shake the speaker's hand.

As he pulled his hand away, the speaker had smiled.

"Don't worry if you are nervous, Charlie," he said. "I encounter it all the time. Meeting someone so well known is a momentous event."

Charlie hurried away, found his way through the adoring mob of young people, and out of the small amphitheater. Stunned by what he had seen as he gazed into the man's eyes and felt as their hands met, or thought he had felt, he walked fast. He had to be alone.

He had seen, and heard in his voice, something entirely different than the man meant to convey by his few words. In that moment, Charlie had seen into him. He beheld what lay deep beneath the smile.

What he saw was a void where the dignity of character should dwell. He was staring into the eyes of self-love.

As his hand pulled away, he had not felt the skin of a man's hand but the slippery scales of a reptile!

Obviously the book had filled his imagination with fancies. Surely he had imagined it!

Yet it had been so real! He had felt it!

He remembered nothing from the next day and a half. The world of politics had become disgusting to him.

About halfway home, as he sat in the train gazing absently out the window at the passing Nebraska countryside, the vision of the speaker's face returned with haunting vividness in his mind's eye.

Suddenly the words exploded in his brain:

It's all a lie!

He sat pondering what it could mean.

Slowly the truth dawned upon him—the speaker was not what he seemed. He presented an image to the world that was a façade. The public persona was a lie. Everything about the conference was a lie. The bright future of progressivism was a lie. It was leading the country into darkness!

After greeting his parents, the first thing Charlie did upon reaching home was close the door of his bedroom, take *The Princess and Curdie* from his bookshelf, and read the passage again. Suddenly it was fraught with more meaning than ever. He had to read again as the princess explained the reason for the rose fire and why she told Curdie to thrust his hand into its midst.

> *Have you ever heard what some philosophers say,* Charlie read, *that men were all animals once . . . It is of no consequence. But there is another thing that is of the greatest consequence— this: that all men, if they do not take care, go down the hill to the animals' country; that many men are actually, all their lives, going to be beasts . . .*
>
> *When you met your father on the hill tonight, you stood and spoke together on the same spot; and although one of you was going up and the other coming down, at a little distance no one could have told which was bound in the one direction and which in the other. Just so two people may be at the same spot in manners and behaviour, and yet one may be getting better and the other worse, which is just the greatest of all differences that could possibly exist between them.*

Charlie paused. The rose fire had endowed Curdie with unique and discerning hands that contained special power but also unique dangers. For the dozenth time Charlie asked himself if it was possible that he had indeed felt what he thought he felt the previous Thursday night.

Though he knew the passage nearly by heart, he continued reading.

> *Now, Curdie . . . listen. Since it is always what they do, whether in their minds or their bodies, that makes men go down to be less than men . . . the change always comes first in their hands—and first of all in the inside hands, to which the outside ones are but as the gloves. They do not know it of course; for a beast does not know that he is a beast, and the nearer a man gets to being a beast the less he knows it. Neither can their best*

friends, or their worst enemies indeed, see any difference in their hands, for they see only the living gloves of them. But there are not a few who feel a vague something repulsive in the hand of a man who is growing a beast. Now here is what the rose-fire has done for you: it has made your hands so knowing and wise, it has brought your real hands so near the outside of your flesh gloves, that you will henceforth be able to know at once the hand of a man who is growing into a beast; nay, more—you will at once feel the foot of the beast he is growing, just as if there were no glove made like a man's hand between you and it. Hence of course it follows that you will be able often . . . to tell what beast he is growing to.

37

New Pastorate

LATE 2044

NATURALLY CURIOUS about the man with whom he had been close for a time, one of Mark Forster's first inquiries after his arrival to assume the pastoral reigns of Foothills Gospel Ministries in Roseville, California, was about their neighbor and his father's best friend, David Gordon.

He was shocked to hear what was said about him among the church leadership—that he had drifted away from the Lord and was never seen in church. Specifics were scanty. No one seemed to know anything definite, only that David Gordon had changed and now held peculiar views about many things. Vague rumors associated him with a fringe group that some said had cultish leanings.

Mark could hardly believe the reports. Yet he had been away a long time and had not seen David for years. People changed, he supposed. He could hardly imagine David Gordon abandoning his faith. But one of the church's leading elders, Stoddard Holt, claimed to have it on good authority that the reports were true.

Mark glanced up from his desk as his sixteen-year-old daughter, Ginger, walked into his office.

"Hey, sweetie!"

"Hi, Dad—is it all right if I go out with some of the girls from church this evening?"

"Sure—who? I mean, somebody older will be driving?"

"Yes, Daddy," Ginger laughed. "Sally Jenkins's mom is taking Sally, Sylvia, and Tammy to the outdoor ice skating rink they just set up for Christmas."

"Sounds like fun. Of course, that will be fine."

His daughter turned to go.

"Ginger," said Mark behind her. She turned.

"I know this hasn't been an easy year for you so far—having to start a new school your junior year. I appreciate your positive attitude."

"It hasn't been so bad, really," she replied. "The girls my age at church have been super kind. Most of them are at Foothills Academy too. There's no weird stuff, you know, like questioning whether you're really a girl. I hate that! It's so stupid. There was too much of that in Seattle. Honestly, I'm glad for the change. I know I was a little grumpy when you first started talking about moving. I'm sorry. But once we got here, I felt a change right away—a good change. I like it here. And to get to see Grandpa and Grandma as often as I want—it's great."

"Thank you. That's very understanding of you. Sometimes a man has to make difficult career decisions that aren't always easy for his family."

"Well, Mom and Craig and I are part of your ministry too. I'm always so proud sitting in church to see you up in front."

Mark laughed. "What a nice thing to say. You are one in a million! What man is so fortunate as to have his teenage daughter say she is proud of him?"

"Well, I am. And if anyone doesn't like it, they can just . . . well, I don't know what they can do!"

Mark laughed again as she left his study. He only managed another ten minutes of sermon preparation before he was interrupted again, this time by his wife.

"Ah, Grace, my dear! I just had the most remarkable visit from our daughter," he said. "She said she was proud of me."

"Lucky you! What was the cause?"

"She came in to ask if she could go ice skating with Mrs. Jenkins and Sally and a few of the girls."

"She asked me too. I told her to talk to you."

"I said that I knew the move was hard for her. She said that you and she and Craig were part of my ministry, too, and that she was proud when she saw me in the pulpit."

"That is an extraordinary thing for a teen to recognize."

Mark nodded. Grace sat in the easy chair opposite his desk. The mood between them quieted.

"You remember David Gordon?" said Mark at length.

"Of course, though I haven't heard you mention him in a long time."

Mark nodded.

"Why?"

"It's just that I've heard some odd things since we returned. His parents were among those who started the church. Apparently David has dropped out. There are rumors he's connected with some questionable people. Stoddard Holt says there's a Christian cult that's sprung up in the area."

"I overheard Edith saying something about that too. I didn't think much of it—she's quite a talker. I guess a few of the women who have friends they haven't seen for a while think that's the cause—that this group is encouraging people to leave the church."

"Are these Foothills people you've heard about being led astray?"

"I think some of them may be, but I know nothing more than what Edith said."

"It's probably nothing to worry about. Edith Holt is not the most reliable purveyor of information."

"Could what they say about David be true?"

"It's hard to imagine. Now I feel bad that I allowed myself to drift away from him. If I had kept the lines of communication open, if he is involved in a cult, maybe I could have prevented it. He was my father's best friend. I should have tried harder."

"Are he and your father still close?"

"I haven't heard my dad mention him in a while. That may be because they moved into town."

"We should go see your folks again soon."

38

New Acquaintance at the Stables

FALL 2045

IT WAS the Forsters' monthly "family Saturday."

For longer than either Ginger or Craig could remember, the four Forsters devoted either the first or second Saturday of every month to whatever Craig and Ginger wanted to do. Usually the outings involved all four—a drive into the mountains, maybe camping Friday night and returning home on Saturday, hiking, sledding during the winter months, swimming—always one of Craig's suggestions—or sailing on Puget Sound.

Mark occasionally suggested a plane ride from one of the Seattle area's numerous private airports. As confident as she was, however, since Ginger's birth when they were in Oregon, Grace had not once taken Mark up with her. She steadfastly refused to fly with all four of them in a plane together.

"Things happen, Mark," she said. "Weather, engine trouble, a flock of birds. It can be anything. Flying's dangerous no matter how competent the man or woman at the controls may be. I'm just an amateur pilot. I will not put our family in a situation where there is even a 1 percent chance of trouble. I'll keep my license current in case it's something God might want to use one day. But as much as I would love for us to see Rainier or the Olympic peninsula from the air like when we flew out over the Pacific at Humboldt, I'm just not comfortable with it."

"What if we all wore parachutes?" asked Mark, more tongue in cheek than seriously.

"You and I are not going up together," rejoined Grace, who was entirely serious. "Nor all four of us. If something should ever happen to me, I want you safely on the ground to take care of Ginger and Craig."

As the two young people grew and approached their teen years, their interests diverged. Though moving to the Sacramento area eliminated sailing on the inlets of Puget Sound, at the same time it opened many new possibilities—sledding and snow sports in the Sierras rather than on the slopes of Mt. Rainier, hiking in California's foothills, or a day trip to Yosemite or the California coast.

One Saturday in September of 2045, Craig had chosen the Waves, a huge new water park in Rocklin. As he and Mark set out about 11:00 for a watery afternoon, Grace and Ginger headed in the direction of Auburn. Ginger had surprised them two evenings earlier with her request: "I want to go riding."

"Your grandfather and grandmother are no longer at the ranch," said Grace.

"I know, Mom," replied Ginger. "But I miss getting to ride like we did when we visited them. Isn't there someplace where I could ride?"

"What about the Wests' stables?" suggested Mark.

"Who are they?" asked Ginger.

"You know the Wests—from church."

"Do they have horses?"

"They own a horse ranch where people board their horses. I think they rent horses to ride. I'll call Dewitt."

So it was decided.

Pearl West greeted Grace and Ginger when they arrived, then walked with them to the stables to set about Ginger picking out a horse.

"Heather is getting several others ready to take out on the trail," said Pearl. "There will be six of you. Do you want to ride, too, Grace?"

"Not me. It's not my favorite thing."

"I thought you were the adventurer of the family."

"What do you mean?"

"Everybody knows the new pastor's wife is a pilot."

Grace laughed.

"Flying is one thing, riding a horse is another. I'll stay here. I brought a book."

As Ginger and Pearl brought the saddled horse out of the barn, Ginger noticed a girl with a decided limp leading a horse out into the nearby pasture, talking to it as they went. The horse's head was lowered as if listening, though the top of the girl's head barely reached its nose.

"Is she hurt?" asked Ginger. "Did she fall off a horse or something?"

"No," replied Pearl. "That's Heather. She had an accident when she was young. It left her with a limp. But she is the best horsewoman we have here. She'll be leading you on your ride today."

"What happened?"

"Let's just say that it was an unfortunate set of circumstances," replied Pearl. Not wanting Ginger to get cold feet, she said no more. "That horse you see with her had a hairline fracture in her leg. Everyone thought she'd have to be put down. But Heather wouldn't hear of it. She's nearly brought her back to full strength. Several months ago its limp was worse than Heather's. You can't even notice it now. She's worked miracles with more animals than I can tell you about. She understands them, and they seem to understand her. She's our resident horse whisperer."

Pearl handed Ginger the reins.

"Wait here," she said. "I'll be right back."

A few minutes later, Pearl returned with the short young woman at her side. From a distance she appeared no more than twelve or thirteen. Up close, however, her mature countenance revealed her to be in her late twenties or early thirties.

"Ginger, this is Heather Marshall," said Pearl. "She'll be your trail boss for the afternoon."

"Hello, Ginger," said Heather, offering her gloved hand, "—and hello, Mrs. Forster," she added as Grace walked up to join them.

"Oh . . . hello. But how do you—" began Grace.

"I grew up at Foothills," replied Heather. "I don't attend much since I moved to Dorado Wood. But everybody wants to hear the new pastor, right? So I've been a few times with my parents since you came. I've seen you all."

Grace laughed. "Are we that much an item of curiosity!"

"Don't worry," said Pearl. "Everyone loves our new Reverend Forster and his family."

"Shall we go, Ginger," said Heather, turning and leading Ginger to where the other riders were waiting.

Walking along beside her, Ginger wondered how a girl so short could even get on a horse, much less be in charge of the ride. She would soon learn that she could not be in more capable hands.

The small group of riders returned ninety minutes later. By then Ginger was chatting away with the others like they were the best of friends. With Heather giving instructions and helping as needed, they all unsaddled their horses and rubbed them down before turning them out into the pasture.

Ginger could talk about nothing but the ride all the way home. Grace knew it would not be their last visit to the Wests' ranch.

39

An Owned Man

2045

TODD STEWART felt qualms from the moment he met Mike Bardolf at the Oraculous banquet twelve years earlier at UCLA. Whether or not his major in journalism gave him unusual insight into people and situations, Bardolf definitely gave him the creeps, almost as much as the heavily scented young man next to him whose demeanor was as peculiar as the entire atmosphere of the memorable evening. Even in the incensed candlelit darkness, Bardolf's eyes had bored into him with an expression he could only describe as menacing.

All his instincts had been to decline the invitation two months later, presumably after a thorough vetting process, to join the highly selective Oraculous fraternity or society as they called themselves. The Society was the name by which the group was known to those on the outside. It was only after the prolonged, mysterious, and unsettling rites of initiation that the group's true name was revealed. Enough had leaked out over the years, everyone knew that to complete the solemn ritual and take the vow, not of mere silence but to uphold and further the principles upon which the so-called Society was founded, was tantamount to selling one's soul to the devil. No one in the group actually believed in God or the devil, which affirmation the new inductees had to make according to the rest of the solemn vow, followed by a swash of blood from their finger, self-produced by razor blade.

Disavowing belief in a supreme deity or a supreme evil, and their respective domains of heaven (with gold) and hell (with flames), was easy enough for one like Todd, who was completely unschooled in Christianity. He had only once set foot inside a church, at ten for the funeral of an uncle. His parents were as liberal and unreligious as any two millennials could be.

Disavowing belief was passive—that was the easy part. Affirming the commitment, sealed with blood, to do his best to bring about the demise and destruction of the God myth, as they called it, and all institutions that persisted in promoting it—that was different.

Even an acknowledged atheist, as he supposed he was, though he had never actually said it in so many words, could not help trembling inwardly as those in the darkened room began chanting, "Death to God. Death to God." As he began to mouth the dreadful words then say them aloud, quietly at first, then gradually raising his voice as the emotion of the moment took over, finally he chanted with the others, "Death to God!"

It was a fearsome thing. He shivered every time he remembered it.

Pascal's wager flitted through his brain every time the night returned unbidden to his memory—which it did more often than was comfortable, the great what-if of life.*

He didn't believe it.

But what if the old stories about cursing God held some mystical power?

He didn't believe in hell. But had he just sealed his fate with a one-way ticket purchased by his vow to kill God, to bring about death to God in whatever ways were presented to him?

Somehow, he made it through the initiation rites and probation period, during which he had been instructed to write a series of articles exposing the myriad fallacies of religion, with special emphasis on

---

* The famous wager with eternity at stake proposed by seventeenth-century mathematician Blaise Pascal in numbers 230–33 of his *Thoughts*: "It is incomprehensible that God should exist, and it is incomprehensible that He should not exist . . . . A game is being played at the extremity of this infinite distance where heads or tails will turn up. What will you wager? . . . You must wager. It is not optional. . . . Which will you choose then? . . . You have two things to lose, the true and the good; and two things to stake, your reason and your will, your knowledge and your happiness . . . . Let us weigh the gain and the loss in wagering that God is. . . . If you gain, you gain all; if you lose, you lose nothing."

Christianity. The Society could never be mentioned. The group's Latin name Oraculous nor its vow *Mors Deo*, Death to God—both revealed for the first time that night—could never be referred to under penalty, they said, of death, though no specifics of that consequence were ever given. Though the phrase was bandied about in the world every day, there were enough dark secrets to whatever, and whoever, existed behind Oraculous that no one wanted to test what happened if one broke the vow of silence.

Even though the whole experience gradually faded into the past, the hold of its voodoo-like vows and chants never left him. As time went on, their preternatural power continued to grip him, as if the chant Death to God, which often reverberated in his brain unbidden, kept the awful specter, the unknown Presence, at bay.

Whatever was out there in the Great Silence, in the black hole of metaphysical and existential uncertainty, shouting death to it—the great unseen It—acted like a juvenile talisman to keep it in its place.

Once deny the denial, once question the mantra, once disavow the vow, once open the door to the great emptiness, and the Presence would sweep in out of the void and bring death to those who blasphemed against it.

Or Him.

Curse God and die, the old saying was. Maybe there was indeed a chilling truth in the words.

No doubt the terrible dilemma, the ultimate dare of life in some measure explained the allure of Oraculous. The danger was the allure. Tempt fate. Play Russian roulette with your soul. Prove your bravado by cursing God!

What college student could resist such a life-or-death gamble?

Who had courage to appear a chicken in front of his peers? All the while the chant grew louder and louder. You had to go along.

And thus the hold of the secret vow deepened through the years. No matter how Todd tried to convince himself that it was pure hocus-pocus, in his deepest heart he yet trembled at what he had done. He knew his soul was no longer his own.

A thousand times he regretted going along with it, but he had done so for practical reasons. A month after the introductory dinner, he had been contacted by Mike Bardolf. He had personally delivered Todd's official invitation to participate in the initiation rites and thus become a member of the Society. The conversation was veiled, but gradually he realized why he had been invited though his family was not wealthy or prominent.

"We've had our eye on you, Todd," Bardolf had said. "We like what we see. You have a bright future in journalism, and we would like to help you achieve that future."

Todd's questions about the "we" were so vaguely answered it was not until much later that it became clear that the initiation chants were not the only way in which he had sold his soul to the devil. He had done so financially as well. And when you sell your soul, there is always a day of reckoning.

"We believe in you, Todd," Bardolf had said. "So much so that the $10,000 membership fee has been waived in your case. We would also like to help with the financing of your final two years. Consider it a scholarship, an investment in your future."

"That is very generous. Of course I am appreciative," replied Todd, hardly able to believe what he was hearing. "What will I have to do? Surely there are strings attached."

"Only write occasional articles for us, or perhaps help us research certain topics of interest. I assure you, we only want you to succeed."

Todd was not about to turn down such an opportunity.

"Who would I be working for?"

"Those who support the Society with their financial backing as well as some highly placed alumni of means. We are always on the lookout for future leaders whom we feel will make a positive mark on the country. For all practical purposes, you and I will remain in close contact, along with Mr. Roswell, whom you met at the banquet."

"How will I, as you say, be able to make a positive mark on the country?"

"By being the best journalist you can be. I will see that opportunities come your way. Occasionally you may be requested to look into certain things or pursue various stories. Mainly we are committed to seeing members of the Society advance in their respective fields to the highest level of their potential. Now it is your turn. We want to help you move up the ladder."

The inducements were intoxicating. If he wanted to complete his degree at UCLA, Todd knew he had few other alternatives. He hoped to pay his parents back too. If he could graduate debt free, that would surely help him do so.

So he agreed. He accepted the invitation, went through the initiation, took the money, and was now a lifetime member and alumnus in good standing of Oraculous.

Thus far the expectations had been minimal. He had little to complain of. His advancement had been rapid, almost meteoric. Even before his graduation in 2035, he had been contacted by Reuters and offered a mid-six-figure salary to join their Washington bureau. Three years later at only twenty-five he was in charge of his own division. He continued to be offered new job after new job, always more prestigious and at salaries he could hardly believe. Eventually NBC contacted him, adding him to their DC staff. Now at thirty-two, he was doing on-camera interviews as one of NBC's Presidential Manor reporters and was being touted as one of the Capital's up-and-coming media stars.

He hadn't seen Mike Bardolf or anyone from Oraculous for three years. He had almost begun to think the memories of that evening were nothing but a bad dream.

40

WAITING SILENCE AGAINST THE LIE

2020s–2030s

IT TOOK the maturity of years, and perceptions increasingly aware of the subtle cultural conditioning that dictated how people around him thought, before much he had sensed in those few days in Colorado fit together into a comprehensive perspective for Charles Reyburn. The process of seeing and waking paralleled and in a sense defined his education from that point forward and, it might be said, his entire professional career thereafter.

In time Charles came to realize that the series of moral and spiritual lies the country had been inoculated to believe went beyond public personalities and former presidents. The handshake that had begun his own waking exposed the Left's entire hypocrisy. It was all a façade, an upside-down pyramid where truth had been turned 180 degrees on its head. The two most worshipped naked emperors of progressivism who had once led what was called the Free World were not the architects of the Lie. They were merely pawns. As they passed from the scene, the Lie deepened. And still, decades later, it continued to spread its terminal cancer through the lifeblood of a nation that had no idea it was dying.

The entire country, the world, had been poisoned by the cancer. The small-minded egoists propped up onto the world's highest pedestal were mere lackeys in a much larger scheme. The Lie was against truth itself, God's Truth. Even those perpetrating the Lie at its deepest levels had no idea whose ends they were really serving.

As they spread the ancient venom of the Ancient Enemy's, *Did God really say?*, they remained oblivious that they were in truth killing themselves. They were laying waste to the fruitful garden of freedom, the very America they hated, where, in spite of its growing pains, the light of truth had flourished like no other nation before it.

Such perceptions were slow growing in the consciousness of the youth Charles Reyburn as he tried to understand what had transpired in Colorado. Had he told his mother about that night, she would have proceeded to lecture him about how wrong he was about the man she still adored. She was of the millions caught up in the hypocrisy of those early years of progressivism's triumph, thinking they were casting their votes against racism, when in truth they had only succeeded in exalting a man who had inflamed the racism of blacks against white America. Racism, too, had been turned upside down.

Charlie was therefore subdued when he reached home after the Colorado conference. He remained quiet for the rest of the summer. Hank and Valerie wondered if he had met a girl.

In fact, young as he was, their son had begun to ask profound questions about the meaning of life and the direction he wanted his own to go. To the prayer which gradually rose to the surface of his consciousness in coming years, *God, give me eyes to see truth*, he added its imperative corollary, *Show me what you want me to do.*

Answers to both prayers did not come all at once to young Charlie Reyburn. He was in his senior year of high school during the turbulent Trump years when critical race theory and wokeism emerged into national prominence. His civics teacher, a bitter Trump hater, embraced the new outlook with militant fervor. Daily he preached the new social normal. Nearly every one of Charlie's classmates could be found during lunch hour at the daily Impeach Trump rally waving placards and posters. To them, civics meant taking down the existing government so that a new social order could be built in its place.

By the end of the year, Charlie doubted that anyone in his class would know more about the Senate and Supreme Court than that they were elitist white men's clubs that had to be overthrown in order for equity in society to be achieved.

His own black skin fostered the assumption that Charlie went along in lockstep with the Woke agenda. He learned to keep his mouth shut. Even he could not help occasionally being seduced by the subtlety of the Lie. In his quiet moments alone in his room, having to write a paper which would not receive an automatic F on "Why Blacks Deserve Their Own 200 Years in Control of America," he thought back, as he often did, to his momentary encounter in Colorado. Surely the whole thing had the most logical explanation possible—that he was prejudiced.

More than once, he framed the shocking question in words: Am I a racist—am I a bigot? But a racist against what—a man half black and half white just like him? How could he be prejudiced against himself!

The question invariably brought another image to mind. Having seen her on television during her failed campaign just months after the Gateway Conference, he knew what he would sense looking close into the shocked candidate's eyes. The very thought made him shudder. He would be loath to shake her hand!

If people knew his father had voted for Trump, they would brand him an Uncle Tom. In the eyes of his mother's friends, men like his father were the worst—intelligent, thinking, open-minded, conservative black men. He knew better than anyone, possibly now even better than his mother, that his father treated every man or woman equally, and with more kindness and respect than any liberal Charlie had ever met. He had seen his father working alongside whites and Asians and blacks and Latinos for as long as he could remember. He had seen his father even give Latinos subtle advantages, cut them occasional slack that he might not have extended to one of his white or black workers for the simple reason that sometimes those who were struggling needed a helping hand. Nor could he forget the Mexican couple his father brought home to live in their spare bedroom for six months after being evicted from their apartment. The next day the man was working on his crew, though Charlie knew well enough that his father already had his quota of three full-time men.

And this was a man people would call an Uncle Tom because he voted for Trump.

Charlie Reyburn survived his civics class, in spite of his teacher's efforts to indoctrinate his students in socially correct dogma, and graduated from high school in 2019 just as the anti-Trump rhetoric was ramping up to the boiling point, in anticipation of the next presidential campaign. By then he was increasingly concerned for his mother's openly hostile rancor toward the president. Were Trump to have been assassinated, he was convinced his mother would have cheered. Though he hugged his mother affectionately, he never again touched her hand. He was afraid to.

Privately he and his father talked about the country, its future, and the issues that were likely to loom ever larger on the horizon if, in spite of the president's efforts, the direction of the nation was not averted. They never talked openly around Valerie or Charlie's sisters. Politics was not worth splitting a family apart.

Charlie enrolled in the University of Minnesota, lived at home for his first two years, then moved into a house with several other Christian young men. The bias saturating the university atmosphere was so blatant and visibly hypocritical that Charlie was in no danger of succumbing to its pressures. He wanted only to get as solid an education as was possible in such an intellectually tainted atmosphere, earn his degree, and move on.

In the first election in which he could vote, the acrimony of his mother toward Trump had reached such an irrational level that the entire political discourse disgusted him. A thoughtful college sophomore on the day of the election, he was by then questioning whether politics was the answer to the Lie.

The question was one he often asked himself: "Would Jesus vote?" It seemed clear that Jesus's agenda for world change existed in another sphere than the political realm.

Charlie was deeply interested in the public discourse. But he did not vote in 2020.

He dutifully gave himself to his studies, majoring in history and specializing in religious history, especially its influence on Western civilization and the founding of the United States. With his parents' blessing to continue funding his education with the investments his uncle made possible, he enrolled in Wheaton College's graduate school, eventually earning his masters—whose thesis followed the development of the major doctrines of the Christian faith—and finally his PhD in history, completed with a thesis exploring the gradual eroding of America's Christian foundations and the parallel rise of reverse racism, gender ambiguity, and wokeism.

After six years teaching high school history and civics, he was hired by Hillsgrove University in Lexington, Kentucky. After three years in Kentucky, he married Regina Stone. Four years after that, he attained full professorship in history and political science.

He continued to pray the two prayers that gradually coalesced into a defining life orientation: *Give me eyes to see truth. Show me what you want me to do.*

He read more of the works of the Scotsman, becoming intimately familiar with his most important works. Gradually he came to recognize that the many divergent manifestations of progressivism—however couched in the subtle and shifting nomenclatures of its interconnected agenda groups—were all tentacles of the Great Lie, which was the world itself.

If he was to change anything, Charles Reyburn realized, it would not be the world. Satan's world as it stood was beyond redemption.

People were not.

He wanted to turn people to the Truth. How best to do that was not through politics but through education—helping to train and teach and raise up future generations to think correctly, intelligently, objectively, implicationally, and wisely. And thus teach them to seek Truth.

Until God showed him otherwise, as he had learned from his father, he would remain silent about politics. He would not engage in the arena of the Lie. He would not combat the Lie by the world's methods.

He would try to teach Truth and let Truth combat the Lie.

41

UNFORMED SUSPICIONS

2040s

ANOTHER MAN who had been waiting for direction was Court Masters. Though he wasn't letting the waiting keep him idle. He was a man who kept busy.

He had been unsettled ever since Secret Service Director Parva had abruptly pulled him off the investigation of President Hunt's assassination. Like nearly everything surrounding the assassination and its aftermath, it smelled suspicious. Not that he suspected Parva of anything nefarious. But he was sure she knew more than she was telling.

She had that right, of course. She was the boss. That's why it was called the Secret Service—there were so many multiple layers of secrecy in the agency and its parent organization the FBI that no one person knew everything. He was an outsider, brought in for Parva's own secret reasons—whatever they were. He wasn't a member of the club. Fair enough. It's how the intelligence game was played.

But once he realized that she had only been using him to dig up dirt on conservatives, he began noticing other things. She was especially nettled after his call asking about the Bardolf fellow, reminding him in no uncertain terms that he was off the case, and should stay off it.

After that he'd had the feeling she had people watching him. He knew he had to be careful. Any further inquiries would have to be kept carefully concealed.

It was a year after that when suddenly he'd had a brainstorm—AI!

Stella had been talking about artificial intelligence for years in connection with her work for tech giant GIH, Global Initiatives for Humanity. She had become so adept using AI that she was put in charge of the Washington-based AI team. She was so skilled, in fact, that she could easily have dispensed with her entire team of six and used AI to do what the others did.

She never divulged this fact to her superiors. She believed in people more than machines, even so-called intelligent machines. For years Court had dismissed Stella's enthusiasm for artificial intelligence as one more "techie thing" he had no interest in. She kept telling him that AI was revolutionizing life as they knew it far beyond even what the internet had done. The years had proved her right. AI was everywhere, doing the unimaginable. It had influenced every aspect of life, business, communications, education, government. It had remade the internet into an entity unrecognizable from 2025. The internet of 2020 was as obsolete today as eight-track tapes and mechanical adding machines. There were those who now considered the internet, powered by its AI "brain," actually alive in some mysterious way not unlike actual human life. The unintended consequences through the years had been diverse and profound—devastating, said many, to humanity's sense of person-hood. Whether the cons outweighed the pros was still hotly debated by philosophers, theologians, and tech gurus.

Yet throughout the titanic changes of the 2020s and 2030s, he still wasn't interested. It wasn't real. The internet wasn't alive—who were they trying to kid?

One of the areas most profoundly changed by AI was the world of intelligence gathering. The spy game had not been the same since AI had stormed the gates of the FBI and CIA and every other intelligence network in the world.

Maybe it was time he joined the ranks and found ways to use AI as he would use any other tool. Might he even be able to use it to solve President Hunt's assassination?

He opened his file drawer and removed several thick manila folders containing his notes and research on the assassination—more than a thousand pages, all resulting in dead ends.

How might he use Stella's years of expertise in the Orwellian world of artificial intelligence to probe between the lines and ferret out clues he had been unable to find through traditional methods?

He began randomly looking through the folders again. Every one brought back reminders of months of work in a hundred directions but to no definite conclusions.

He had gone over the surveillance footage a dozen times, scrutinizing every face, from the president's people to the Secret Service and police contingents to those in the crowd he had been able to identify with face-recognition software.

He had conducted hundreds of interviews—with anyone and everyone imaginable, from Air Force One personnel to those along the route of the motorcade.

He had poured over the forensics of the water bottle a dozen times. Of course, there were no fingerprints or DNA other than Hunt's. But the traces of the poison led to a thorough investigation of homobatracho-toxin, its source and availability. Obviously the FBI had conducted its own massive investigation as well. But neither they nor he turned up anything solid. That the water bottle mysteriously went missing, and had never turned up, did not help.

Knowing his investigation was off the FBI's books, at Parva's orders he'd kept clear of the agents who'd been present that day. He now began to wonder if he had been looking at the FBI contingent all wrong.

Two days later, after a crash course with Stella about how to use the many AI websites to set up scenarios and possibilities, experimenting with the weird technology of interacting with a non-human but somehow "thinking" entity—almost like brainstorming with a living person about the case—Court was ready to get down to business.

He spread out the folders on his desk and looked over the written titles on each:

Motives

Forensics

Video footage—private from phones

Video footage—public cameras

Homobatrachotoxin

Witness statements
Air Force One
Motorcade—car, route, FBI personnel present
Presidential Manor staff and presidential detail
Foreign connections
Secret and underground organizations
Trump family
Personnel lists—official
Personnel lists—spectators
Theories

Taking each in turn, he began framing succinct questions that might prompt potential new avenues of inquiry to move him past previous roadblocks. Clearly AI was incapable of coming up with actual new information, but investigations all depended on asking the right questions. He hoped seeing what AI did with the questions he posed might get him looking in new directions.

By day's end he had twenty pages of printouts from his computerized "conversations" with various AI entities. The process had been fascinating beyond his wildest imaginings. He was under no illusions that he would instantly solve the case. Still, it had done exactly what he'd hoped—prompted questions he hadn't considered before.

Some of the AI suggestions were so obvious as to be pointless: Check footage from security cameras at the airport, the motorcade route, and the event site for all individuals in the vicinity of the president or the water bottle. Interview witnesses, such as the Secret Service agents and civilians who were at the event, to see if they saw or heard anything unusual. Investigate the source of the poison and how it might have been obtained, either legally or illegally.

And when one of the AI bots became technical, it was quickly over his head: Use data mining and machine learning algorithms to analyze large amounts of data related to political assassinations in general. For machine learning algorithms, techniques such as cluster analysis, association rule learning, and decision trees could be used to find correlations between the data. Cluster analysis would group similar data points, helping to identify common features between this and similar cases. Association rule learning would identify relationships between different pieces of data, such as locations, weapons used, and suspects. Decision trees could help make predictions about the potential outcome of the investigation based on the data gathered.

All gobbledegook to him!

Fascinating as the process was, however, his twenty pages of AI notes mostly pointed in directions he had already considered. A machine couldn't think like a detective. But he had to admit that the process of setting up the right queries helped him refocus and reexamine the case from several fresh angles.

As he did, his own memory of the day again grew vivid in his mind. It was one of those incidents that was frozen in time. After reading the Domokos biography and now recalling that its author, Michael Bardolf, was on his list of names, the image of him among the other Secret Service agents came back into his brain with forceful clarity.

He had assumed him to be one of the agents. Having no idea who he was at the time, his attention had been drawn by Bardolf's occasionally odd mannerisms, looking at his watch then back and forth at the president rather than the crowd, his fidgety behavior. Why he had been there, he still didn't know. And why had Parva declared him off limits?

Inserting Michael Bardolf's name into the inquiry, noting his disappearance after the president's collapse, the AI responses took on heightened interest. They now placed the mysterious Michael Bardolf at the center of focus:

Check surveillance footage for Bardolf's movements throughout the day and to see if he can be observed in the vicinity of the president—any opportunity for him to have given the president the water bottle—why was Bardolf there, under whose orders?—check phone records to see if Bardolf made or received calls or sent messages that could indicate involvement—investigate Bardolf's whereabouts leading up to and during event—look into Bardolf's political beliefs and affiliations—possibility of motivation or affiliation in the cause of another candidate—potential links to any secret organization—does Bardolf have hidden connection to the vice president, the obvious beneficiary of President Hunt's death?—check bank records to see if Bardolf made unusual recent financial transactions—any travel where he could have obtained or purchased the poison.

Court surreptitiously scrutinized Bardolf's background but learned nothing more than that he came from a prominent Denver family with shadowy connections that proved impossible to trace. There were hints that his family's connections to Viktor Domokos went all the way back to Bardolf's grandfather. The only thing he learned about Bardolf's movements was that he had traveled to LA shortly before the incident in Baltimore. The name Roy Aitken cropped up, but he'd been unable to learn anything about him or whether he even had a connection to Bardolf.

Sensing he was being watched, and realizing that AI could be used against him, he was severely limited. Just looking up the name "Michael Bardolf" could be easily traced to him. If he persisted against Parva's orders, he could find himself under investigation as a conspirator. He knew it was time to back off. It wouldn't do to run afoul of Parva and the FBI.

The Domokos biography had put Bardolf in the public spotlight, as did his affiliation with Senator Rhodes. If the man was indeed dangerous, it wouldn't do to have him as an enemy. Especially if he was in cahoots with Erin Parva.

42

THE CIRCLE F

APRIL 18, 2046

As THE spring of 2046 began to warm the earth and send out signs of new life, Mark Forster became increasingly nostalgic about the sights and sounds of his youth.

"I'd really like to see the ranch again, Dad," he said as he and his father walked outside their Grass Valley house after an early afternoon dinner. "Do you ever go up for a visit?"

"Not unless there's something they call about that needs attention," replied his father. "It makes me sad. I'd rather keep my distance."

"Is the place not—"

"Oh, no—it's fine," said Robert. "The family renting the house takes good care of it. They raise horses, and it's ideal for them. It's just that, you know, it's hard getting old."

"I know, Dad. I'm sorry the ranching life wasn't for me."

"Don't worry about it, Mark. You have your own life. You've done pretty well for yourself."

"I don't know about that!" laughed Mark. "But thank you. I would like to go with you next time you go out to the ranch. Do the people there have a horse they'd let me ride?"

"Probably even with your old saddle. I left everything behind when we moved here."

"That would be fun. You'll join me?"

"I don't know, Mark. I'm a little tentative about it now—falling is the biggest risk when you reach my age. I'm better off with two feet on the ground."

Three weeks later, with his father enjoying a glass of iced tea from the gracious hand of the present woman of the house, relaxing on the porch of the ranch house he still called "home," Mark Forster set out across the familiar fields on a borrowed roan mare that seemed not to mind a new rider on her back.

He sat straddling the saddle his father had given him on his fourteenth birthday. His heart was full as the pines gradually closed around him ten minutes later. The fragrance of their needles as they basked in the heat of an unseasonably hot day in early April filled his lungs with pleasurable nostalgia.

As if awakened by the aroma from the pines, his thoughts turned toward their neighbor, the man he had once so looked up to. Undefined feelings of regret swept over him for the long years of silence between them. He had become so caught up with the pursuit of his pastoral career that he rarely looked back.

After an hour's ride, he came to a fork in the trail. He stopped and smiled. How many times he had ridden this way in the past. That he had not taken it for many years seized his heart again with a pang. The memory of his father's friend and neighbor rose once more in his mind's eye.

David had a reputation for being a mystic. Soft-spoken, kind, gracious of manner, a gentleman in every way, he was also a tough, hard-riding, crack-shot cowboy of the old school who punched his cattle on horseback, not a 4 x 4, and who had been known in his youth as the best broncobuster for miles.

Almost without consciously deciding to do so, Mark gave the mare's flanks a gentle kick and turned her neck sharply to the left.

Thirty minutes later, he emerged from the trees. There was the familiar Gordon ranch spread out before him, the Bar JG sign, its gold and red paint weathered from the intervening years but otherwise just as he remembered it.

He reined in then sat for a moment taking in the scene.

What would he find? Had David changed, like everyone said?

After a few moments he urged the mare on.

PART 3

PREPARATION

2046–2048

43

STIRRING TO SPEAK

APRIL 18, 2046

CHARLES REYBURN, now Doctor and Professor Reyburn, was neither a visionary nor an ambitious man. He was content in an environment mostly free from the socialist drift of the country to teach the young people God sent him according to the values and perspectives he, and a shrinking minority of Americans, still cherished. He had learned from his father's example mostly to keep his mouth shut when politics became contentious. He kept his personal views to himself so thoroughly that most of his friends and students had no idea whether he was a Republican or a Democrat. His visible ethnicity led to the assumption, erroneous but useful in its own way, that his leanings were probably liberal.

But the years and the nation's slide were taking their toll, wearing away his commitment to silence. Hearing things his students said, and realizing how deceived even young people from Christian homes were from the subtle programming of the culture, it was increasingly difficult to keep quiet.

What good would it do to speak out? People like his mother could not be reasoned with. As for his students, the best he could do for them was teach them to think rationally, logically, and implicationally from a scriptural, absolutist, and accurate historical foundation. To attempt to sway them with his own opinions would be no different than the tactics of the Left. Changing the public discourse was not the job God had given him. Encouraging people to think with wisdom was.

Yet he was increasingly ill at ease. His silence weighed on him. Did his discomfort signal a change? Was God preparing him for a new season in which the demeanor of neutrality his silence conveyed would no longer be acceptable?

More and more these days he was given to prayerful introspection. When had the cancer infected the American bloodstream with the first cells of the disease? Where had it originated? Names like Karl Marx, John Lennon, Saul Alinsky, Jane Fonda, Angela Davis, Tommie Smith, Malcolm X, Timothy Leary all leapt to mind. But attaching individual names to the cancer was simplistic. The roots went deeper.

Who could identify the beginnings of an idea, especially an invisible and insidious one such as that by its intrinsic nature America's founding Christian ethic was evil?

For Charles Reyburn the question was deeply personal. It began on the day his eyes were opened. Suddenly he had seen all. Why could not everyone see?

Whenever the question arose in his mind, his thoughts went back to the rose fire. His entire outlook on life, relationships, and personhood had been altered. He had been burned by its flames—stunned, awed, overwhelmed by the power of the simple idea of truly seeing. Not merely seeing but seeing into people and situations and circumstances. Seeing with God's eyes.

Jesus's words had become explosively alive with truth—*Having eyes, they do not see.*

The greatest profundity of all, embedded within Jesus's words, was that it was possible to see God's truth.

Yet many intelligent, educated, seemingly good and well-meaning people, simply could not see.

Why?

If true seeing was possible, why did people not see?

What was the difference between see-ers and non-see-ers? He had not chosen on that pivotal day at fifteen to see.

He had simply *seen.*

His inner eyes had been opened. That was all he could say. He had seen truth. And life had changed.

As the new decade of the 2040s moved the country he loved closer and closer to the half-century mark, Charles sensed a shift. Much was stirring within him. His concern for the future of the country became palpable. The silence which the Lord had enjoined upon him for so many years became a weight upon his spirit.

A change was coming.

Sometime during the late afternoon of April 18, 2046, working at home during the week's spring break hiatus, Charles was reminded of the significance of the day. Thought of it was likely prompted by the novel he had been reading on the Reformation by the devotional writer Marshall.

He picked up the book from where it sat on his desk, flipped through the pages until he came to Martin Luther's famous speech at the Diet of Worms.

There was the date—April 18, 1521.

The novelist had reproduced the speech in its entirety. Charles knew it well. For good reason Luther's defense against the charge of heresy was considered one of history's most magnificent pieces of oratory, climaxing with Luther's triumphant declaration, "Here I stand. I cannot do otherwise. God help me."

Was a time coming when Christians in greater numbers would rise and follow Luther's example, saying with him:

Here I stand!

If so, where would it begin?

And with whom?

44

Reunion at the Bar JG

April 18, 2046

As MARK Forster rode toward the familiar ranch house, thoughts, memories, and an unaccountable nervousness came over him.

Mark dismounted, tied the mare to the rail in front of the house, walked up the two steps onto the wooden porch, lifted the heavy wrought-iron horseshoe knocker, and let it fall with a loud metallic clank. Even the sound sent a stab of nostalgic regret through him. He never used to knock at all. He had always just walked in, there to listen to the wise man and pour out his own heart, his questions, his uncertainties, his spiritual struggles. He would not be the man he was today without the gentle, loving, mentoring influence of David Gordon— guiding, goading, encouraging, leading him into maturity of faith.

At last he heard the latch turn inside. Slowly the door opened. The briefest expression of surprise was followed by a great smile exploding over the tanned, rugged seventy-five-year-old face.

"Mark!" David exclaimed. The next instant Mark found himself embraced in a bear hug that nearly deprived him of the ability to breathe. Despite his years, it was obvious that David Gordon had not lost his strength.

"Hello, David," said Mark, stepping back. The two men shook hands, warmly and vigorously. "You are looking well, and your grip is as strong as ever."

David was noticeably older and grayer, perhaps a little thinner and not quite so tall as before, face showing the lines of years in the sun yet with the same expression of subdued wisdom shining from his eyes.

"I doubt I can still wrestle you to the ground as I used to," laughed David. "But I still mend my own fences and set myself to break at least one horse a year. That alone forces me to keep fit."

"It is obviously working. It wouldn't surprise me if you could still pin me in less than a minute."

David laughed again. "I'd rather not try. Age takes its toll. Even if I could, I might not be able to get up again. But come in! The morning's second pot of coffee is still fresh. You cannot imagine how wonderful it is to see you!"

Mark glanced about the empty kitchen as they walked through.

"Is your mother . . . ?" he began.

"No, she passed away several years ago, the dear lady," replied David. "She was ninety-six."

"She was indeed a dear one—always with a cheerful smile. And this kitchen was always filled with tantalizing aromas."

David chuckled at the memory. "I do miss her cooking!" he said. "I manage, but she had a special knack. I'll pour you a cup of coffee. Half and half, no sugar, as I recall."

"Still my preferred recipe."

"I happen to have the necessary ingredients in the fridge."

A minute later the two men took seats in the expansive familiar living room, with cups in their hands.

"When I saw you standing there," said David, "for an instant I did a double take. I've been reading Stirling's book on the Reformation. I wanted to read the Luther speech again—today's the 525-year anniversary—five and a quarter centuries to the day."

"I'm sorry, I don't—"

"When Luther appeared on trial for heresy and delivered his famous defense and ended with the words, 'Here I stand, I can do no other. God help me.' A very timely speech for Christians of our time. I was just reading it when the clank came to the door. I was so caught up in the book, the sound jolted me out of a reverie. I almost expected to see Stirling Marshall standing there."

"I hope you weren't disappointed."

David roared with laughter. "Hardly! If there was one person in the world I would have asked God to bring to my door, it would be you. And here you are! I am so happy to see you."

"You knew we were back in the area?"

"Of course. I keep up on church news. How are your folks, Mark?" asked David.

"They're doing okay."

"And your father?"

"He misses the ranch. Mom says he's been depressed since the move into town. He always seems pretty much the same to me, though I'm sure he doesn't want to show it when I'm around. He puts on his boots and hat every day. But it hardly feels right living in town. He came to the ranch with me today, and I rode over. When I left him there, I could tell he felt like he was home."

"It can't have been easy for him. I miss him."

"He'd love to see you."

David nodded. A subtle expression of pain crossed his face.

"As I would him," he said.

"A visit would make Dad's day."

David smiled again. "To be honest, I've intentionally kept my distance."

"Goodness—why, David?"

"I've not been, shall we say, as active at church as some at Foothills think I ought to be. Especially after my mother's death. There are those who feel, as the last offspring of the church's original founders, that I ought to be a more visible presence. Your predecessor was rather strident in that regard. He paid me repeated visits and hammered me with all the scriptural proof texts why I should be in church every Sunday. After I respectfully declined to endorse his perspective of Christ's Church, I never heard from him again. Gradual whispers soon began to circulate through the congregational grapevine about me."

"What kind of whispers?" asked Mark.

"Oh, the usual—that my faith is slipping, that I am backsliding."

"Is there any truth to it?"

The snort of laughter that burst through David's lips contained both humor and annoyance.

"I will let you be the judge of that yourself. The most insidious form the rumors have taken is that I am involved in a cult that is wooing people away from the faith and encouraging them to leave the church. Some think I started the cult and am its leader."

An expression passed briefly over Mark's countenance that David was perceptive enough to recognize.

"You've been at Foothills over six months now," he said. "I can see you've heard all this."

Mark nodded. "You're right—I am sorry. I didn't want to bring it up. That's why I said nothing. But I don't see what this has to do with my folks. They don't even attend Foothills."

"I didn't want them tainted by the rumors about me. I thought it best they not be seen as too closely associated with a supposed cult leader."

"You must know that my father would put no stock in that. He would laugh it to scorn. He's never had much use for religious types, though he makes an exception in our two cases."

"I do know none of that would bother your father. It's more your mother I am concerned about. She's active in Grass Valley Baptist, and there is a good bit of mixing among the women. Everyone in Grass Valley knows the Gordons and Forsters. Our families go back to the gold rush. I didn't want to put her in an awkward position because of any gossip that might spill over."

Mark nodded. "That makes sense. It's exactly what I would expect of you, always thinking of others. Still, they would love to see you."

"Well, I will give the matter new prayer. Perhaps it is time."

A brief silence fell.

45

HOW MANY DOES IT TAKE
TO MAKE THE CHURCH?

"DO YOU mind, then, if I ask you a question?" said Mark.

"You know me well enough not to have to ask."

"I suppose you're right. But it's been a long time. We've both changed."

"I'm not sure I have, Mark—except physically of course. I'm still the same man you used to come to see. You, on the other hand, have become a man. Have you changed, Mark?"

The question took Mark by surprise. He did not have a ready answer. He had been assuming that whatever changes had taken place, on the basis of the rumors, were on David's side.

"I . . . I don't know," he replied a little hesitantly. "Everyone changes, don't they?"

"In some ways, of course. But in the bearing of their internal compass—if it is pointed toward God's North, that is one thing I hope never changes. But what was the question you wanted to ask me?"

"I guess I hinted at it already—sorry. But is there any truth to the rumor you've stopped being active in church?"

"If you consider a service every month or two, or perhaps three, not being active, then yes—that is true. I still maintain many close friendships and do still attend occasional services. Apparently that is not regular enough. But that is the extent of my involvement."

"Why do you not attend regularly?"

"Is this a pastoral call," smiled David, "or a visit between old friends?"

"Sorry again. Occupational hazard. Maybe both. Though I ask as a friend first."

"Fair enough. Then I will give you the twenty-five-word answer. I have increasingly arrived at the conviction that Christ's Church means more than as represented by the denominational churches of Christendom."

"I would agree. But do you think that fact invalidates the ministry of denominational churches?"

"A good question. You haven't lost your probing mind! To give you an honest answer—I don't know."

"You think it *might* invalidate the ministries of local churches?"

"Obviously not entirely. Where I have not yet seen what I consider truth, I will not speak my opinion. All I can say is that it may come to that eventually."

"In what way?"

"Only God knows. I think I've said enough. I don't want to debate the matter, Mark. You know how much I detest Christian debate. I respect and love you too much for that. I know you love the church. You have given your life to its service. I respect that. I honor you for it. You have no idea in what high regard I hold you for your dedication and service to God's people."

"Thank you, David. That is kind of you to say."

"To that I will only add that at present my personal conviction about what constitutes Christ's larger Church is not nurtured by being more involved than I think is appropriate from Sunday to Sunday."

"Perhaps that will now change, at least insofar as Foothills is concerned. I hope it will change if I am able to do anything about it."

"I would applaud such change. And I pray that the Spirit of God will enlighten me as he brings needful change to his Church."

"Might I hope to see you in church, then?"

"I will take you up on your good intentions," replied David. "Yes, you will see me next Sunday."

"Oh—well, thank you," rejoined Mark, surprised by David's easy consent. "If I can, uh, pick up on what you said about the church not nurturing you, how *are* God's people fed, then? Or how would you be fed?"

"Those are two different questions," replied David. "Let me clarify. It is not my being nurtured personally that I am so concerned about. God is well able to nurture me. What I tried to say is that I do not see what is called 'the church' nurturing the larger idea of God's eternal Church. Man's church is mostly concerned about nurturing itself and its small idea of the church, at which it succeeds very well. But it does not nurture the high truth of God's eternal Church."

"I'm afraid you lost me," said Mark.

"Then let me return to the other side of your question—how are God's people fed? They are fed by the gospel. They are fed by being taught to live by the gospel. They are fed as they are encouraged to be the Lord's disciples where they live twenty-four-seven. They are fed by being challenged to be sons and daughters of the Lord's Father by doing what he told his followers to do. It is a simple prescription for discipleship that is taught from very few pulpits but which is the lifeblood of God's eternal Church. They are fed by learning to be disciples."

"But it was Jesus who established the church."

"It was indeed."

"And we are told not to forsake it."

"Where are we told not to forsake the church?"

"In the Bible."

"I'm sorry, Mark, but I do not think you will find that anywhere in your Bible. You will certainly not find Jesus saying anything like it, though you will find similar wording from one of the other New Testament writers who did not see into God's purposes as clearly as Jesus did."

"Hmm, I think you're wrong. But perhaps I will look into it. But may I ask you another question?"

"Of course."

"Are you involved in a group that teaches people the church isn't important?"

"No."

"Do you consider the church important?"

"Not only important—imperative. Christ's Church will endure throughout all eternity and will defeat hell, which is something Jesus did say. Or implied, I should add."

"What is his church then?"

"The knitting together of the hearts of his disciples. Or to use the apostle Peter's wonderful imagery, the joining together of the living stones of God's men and women into a spiritual temple in which and in whom and among whom God dwells."

"I'm not sure I entirely follow you. But let me ask then, are you involved in a group that teaches everything you just said?"

"That is a little difficult to answer. I am involved informally with some people, yes. None of us teach what I just said, certainly not myself. Really, no one teaches anything. We are, however, attempting to live by the reality of the Church as I have briefly described it. But teach it as such, no."

"Do you meet together?"

"Occasionally."

"Weekly?"

"No."

"Monthly?"

"No."

"When then?"

"When we can."

"Are you the group's leader?"

"No."

"Who is?"

"There is no leader as such."

"What do you do?"

"We have no agenda."

"Do you consider a handful of people the church?"

"How many people does it take to make the Church?"

"I don't know, but it's more than just informal visiting. What is your program, your purpose? What are your objectives?"

"Being together."

"That's hardly the reason for the church."

"Isn't it?"

"And there's nothing more to it?"

"Mostly we talk informally. We are simply friends who get together occasionally."

"You are very mysterious, David."

"I'm sorry. I don't mean to be. There's nothing more to it than I have said."

"Are there others from the church involved—Foothills, I mean."

"I really would rather say no more."

"Why?"

"Because I do not want to add to gossip already circulating, probably most of which is unfounded hearsay. All you need to know, Mark, is that I am still the man you always knew. The only thing in my walk with God that has changed is that I hope it has grown deeper."

"All right. I will respect that, David."

"Thank you."

"I think I need to be going," said Mark. "I left my father back at the ranch. He'll probably think I got lost!"

"I doubt that. He knows you could never forget your way around the foothills."

Mark rose, and the two walked slowly through the kitchen and outside onto the porch.

"A fine-looking animal," said David as he watched Mark mount. "I think I recognize the saddle."

"The mare I borrowed from the people living at the ranch. And yes, the saddle is one that made this trek many times."

"I thought so!"

"Please give some thought to paying my dad a visit, David," said Mark.

"I will. I promise."

"And I will see you this Sunday?"

"You will!" laughed David.

"I speak only at eleven. The other two services are led by the assistant pastors."

"I shall be sitting inconspicuously in back. I don't want to start anything new in the rumor mill. But be assured—I will be there."

46

∧ CHALLENGE

∧S MARK rode pensively back to the Circle F, his thoughts were stirred in many uncomfortable directions. David always had an unusual way of expressing himself. His father jokingly called him a mystic.

The Christians Mark had associated with for the past fifteen or twenty years were predictable. They were, well, church people. They used the same jargon, expressed matters of faith in the same way, believed the same things, stayed within the boundaries of normal Christian thought.

David had never been one to keep inside the lines of other people's expectations. He had a way of unsettling comfort zones. He probed, made you think in unexpected ways.

Was that it—David made you think?

So much now returned to Mark's memory out of the past as he rode. Cryptic comments, especially about the church and its future, came to his mind. David always pushed and prodded. Discussions about the church, he now remembered, had arisen between them before. When he had been considering whether to take up pastoral training, he and David spent hours talking and praying. David had hinted at similar things he'd said today.

Somehow they had not penetrated back then. David's words today had gotten under his skin.

He remembered David's quiet exhortations to pay attention to the signs of the times, not to get swept up in what he mysteriously called the

Ally. Mark never had a clear picture of what he meant by the term. To his questions, David's only reply was that the truth would be revealed in its own time and in its own way. All Mark could discern was that it had something to do with David's unorthodox perspective of the end times. Back then he had been more concerned with his own future. He was viewing the church in a hopeful and positive light. David's subtle innuendos about the mysterious Ally fell on deaf ears.

One thing was certain, thought Mark as his reflections returned to the present, David was a man of his word. He had three days to prepare a sermon that he knew David would hear. He would preach on the church and speak entirely from the New Testament. There would be nothing David could argue with.

When Sunday came, Mark preached what everyone said was a powerful message on the importance of the church in the world and in the lives of Christians. He did not see David, nor was he among those shaking his hand at the conclusion of the eleven o'clock service. But he was there. He felt his presence. And so it continued for several more weeks. Only once, however, did he catch a glimpse of David's bushy gray mass of hair.

After a month and a half, as summer came to the foothills and after hearing from his parents that David had been three times to visit them, Mark decided it was time for another visit to the Bar JG. This time he drove.

He and David greeted one another with something of their former camaraderie. The conversation easily fell into the right channels.

"You have become an accomplished speaker, Mark," said David. "I have listened to you every Sunday since we last spoke. I am very impressed. I mean that in an entirely favorable way. You are soft-spoken in manner, personable, and speak from your heart. There is nothing of the cleric about you."

"Thank you. I take that as a great compliment coming from you."

"I mean it sincerely. You have a thought-provoking style. You challenged me many times."

"I suppose I learned more from you than I realized!"

David laughed. "I give the credit to you, Mark. You are a thinker. I could not have hoped for anything else. You are well on your way along the road."

"What road—to where?"

"To bold-thinking Christianity."

Mark took in the words with a puzzled expression. There was David again saying the oddest things! He refused to be boxed in with Christian jargon.

"So tell me," David went on, "have you resolved the matter we were talking about before—thinking that we have been commanded not to forsake the church?"

"Actually I hadn't given it much more thought," replied Mark, "other than what Hebrews 10:25 says."

"Do you think I am forsaking the church?"

"Not these last two months!" laughed Mark.

"Before that?"

"I don't know, David. The New Testament is clear about the danger of not gathering together. That seems to be what you have been doing?"

"Because I have not been participating regularly in a large gathering every Sunday—in a building that people call the church?"

"I don't know. Something like that."

"What about my gathering with the other Christians I mentioned?"

"That's not the church."

"Laying aside for a minute that Hebrews 10:25 says nothing about the church, why would you say my friends and I aren't the church?"

"You know what I mean—the organized church, a sanctioned church."

"Sanctioned by whom?"

"You're twisting my words, David. You know what I mean."

"Yes, I think I do know what you mean."

"You're just a group of independent people meeting occasionally. I don't see how you can call that a church."

"I did not call it that. I only say that we gather occasionally. You made the point that such was not the church, and I asked you why. But

I will say nothing further about whether Christians meeting together in a way not sanctioned by an organization calling itself a church is in fact an integral part of Christ's Church. That discussion will have to wait for another time."

A somewhat strained silence fell. David saw that Mark was uncomfortable. He realized he had pushed the discussion too far.

"Do you remember when you more or less challenged me," he said in a quieter tone, "or perhaps exhorted me, to come to church?"

Mark nodded.

"And I took you up on it."

"You did."

"Now I have a challenge for you."

Mark waited, not sure what was coming.

"I don't know if you remember when we used to get together, sometimes for very long talks about deep things, when I told you how I try to resolve any spiritual quandary in my life."

"Yes—I do remember," replied Mark. "You said you prayed for wisdom, then you went to the words of Jesus to see what he said. You always called them the red letters."

David cracked a smile.

"'See what the red letters say, Mark,' you said. 'Always what the red letters say.'"

David laughed. "You remember well. Those two things remain foundation stones in my life—praying for wisdom and the red letters. In praying for wisdom, I intentionally try to open my heart and mind to the Spirit's leading—laying aside my own opinions and preconceptions and wishes. Opinion is death to prayer. For God to speak, you need the self and its opinions to take a back seat and keep their mouths shut. I have to come to God with a clean heart-slate and ask him to write his wisdom on it. He cannot do that if the self is constantly interrupting. Then I go to the gospels and see what Jesus said. These factors working together nearly always bring light—the clean heart-slate, the wisdom prayer, and the red letters. It may take some time. But God nearly always gives guidance through the words of Jesus."

David paused to allow Mark to absorb his words.

"With that foundation," he went on, "I would like to challenge you to go to your New Testament as if you have never read it before. Then see what it has to say about the Church, about what the Church is and about what we are commanded to do about it. Find out what Jesus tells us to do. How are we to live in and function practically as part of His Church? If you find that you think I am wrong about anything I have said to you, I earnestly want to know it. I mean that. I am growing every day, Mark. I have much to learn. I do not throw out this challenge to try to prove a point one way or another. This has simply been the way I try to order my life—by asking what Jesus says and then what he tells us as his followers to do.

"How are we to live? See what the New Testament says about the essence of our discipleship and to what extent the church, and specifically church worship on Sunday morning, is intended to be the primary means to transmit and grow discipleship in our lives. See if my perspectives sound like they come from a man who is involved in a cult or if perhaps they come from the Gospels. Don't take my word for any of this. Find out what God's Word says. Find out how our discipleship is intended to be nurtured and grow. That is the pivotal question."

Mark took in his words thoughtfully.

He left the ranch a short time later in a quiet and pensive mood.

He could think of nothing else for the rest of the week. He realized he had to take David up on his challenge. His flesh shouted out all manner of objections. Who was David to counsel a minister with a reputation like his who had been to seminary and had formal training? David was presuming to lecture him on the church!

Even as such childish thoughts tumbled through his brain, he knew how idiotic they were. David had been his mentor, one of the humblest and most godly men he had ever known.

He would take David up on his challenge. He owed it to him.

He thought a moment. He also owed it to himself. If there was more truth to be discovered, he wanted to find it.

He not only owed it to David and himself. He owed it to God.

47

LIFE-CHANGING STUDY

EARLY JUNE 2046

MARK TOOK the second week of June off, drove into the Sierras, and isolated himself in a motel for as long as needed.

With him he had two Bibles, his laptop, plenty of paper, pens and pencils, his Strongs Concordance, and an ice chest and box filled with all the food Grace thought he might need for a week. His needs and habits were simple.

After checking in, his friend and colleague came to his mind as he walked to his room. He wondered what Ward was doing. He still wasn't quite sure what Ward thought about his decision to leave Seattle and move back to California.

He unlocked the door and walked into his temporary digs. It was not the sort of place he imagined Ward staying when he traveled. But with a café down the street and a grocery store in the next block, Mark had everything he needed. He settled into the small room with a sense of expectancy.

After a surprisingly refreshing night's sleep, he awoke to his first full morning eager to embark on his study. He had no plan other than to work his way through the New Testament with fresh eyes, as David suggested. He wanted to avoid simply reading it through. He couldn't lapse into familiarity-reading. He had to take off his minister's hat, put aside his seminary training and his years in the pulpit. David had exhorted him to read it as if he had never read it before. It would be difficult, but that would be his goal.

Setting his things on the small desk and making his workspace ready, he sat back and closed his eyes.

"Spirit of God, descend upon my heart," he whispered, the words of two of his favorite hymns mingling as he prayed. "I lay down my self with its opinions. Fill me, heavenly Father, with your thoughts, your wisdom. Guide my heart and mind in the channels you want me to pursue. Imbue me with your wisdom. Reveal to me the deep truths that the words of Jesus have for me. Guide my path, Holy Spirit. Search me and know my heart. Try me and know my thoughts. Take my life and make it wholly thine. Take all my will. My passion, self, and pride I now surrender, Lord, in me abide."

His heart stilled. He was ready.

He opened the favorite of his two Bibles to the New Testament and read Matthew 1:1 then stopped.

Over and over David's constant theme was not only the red letters but what Jesus told his followers to *do*. He could hear David's voice in his brain saying it in a dozen different ways: Doing what Jesus said. What does Jesus command us to do? How does Jesus tell his disciples to live—nothing matters but doing what Jesus told us. If we don't do what Jesus commands, how can we call ourselves his disciples?

The message from David Gordon was constant. The commands of Jesus were everything.

Suddenly a plan crystallized in Mark's brain.

Starting at Matthew 1, he would go through the New Testament all the way to the end of Revelation 22 and write down every command laid upon the Lord's followers.

It was the clearest prescription to find exactly how God wanted his people to live. Nothing else could give such a focused picture of what he, Mark Forster, was supposed to do.

What were Christians told to *do*?

How were they told to *think*?

How were they told to *behave*?

How were they told to *treat others*?

What were they told to *believe*?

Then there was the question that had prompted this study in the first place: What were Christians told to do and believe about the church?

David had said, find out what Jesus tells us. Mark would find out what Jesus said in all these areas. He would continue through the whole New Testament and find out what the apostles said as well.

He turned his attention again to the Bible open in front of him and read Matthew 1 and 2 then continued.

He completed three chapters without making a single entry. He began to wonder if this was such a good plan at all. He hadn't encountered a single do-command.

Then suddenly a single word from the verse 17 of chapter 4 hit him between the eyes: Repent.

He had found the first actual command of the New Testament! Excitedly he opened a file on his laptop and typed:

Matthew 4:17
Repent.

Two verses later came another: *Follow me.*

The next command didn't come until chapter 5: *Rejoice and be glad when you are reviled, persecuted, and spoken evil of falsely.*

His list now contained three entries.

As he completed the Beatitudes, Mark paused and read over Matthew 5:3–12 again. The Beatitudes were not phrased as direct commands. Yet surely Jesus intended his followers to live by their embodied truths. If such was his intent, might they not be considered *implied* commands?

Mark thought for another minute, then prayed, "I ask again for your wisdom, Lord. What is your intent here, your purpose for me, for your people? How do you want your disciples to live?"

He waited, trying to block out the rush of thoughts and pros and cons and suggestions that began swirling in his mind. He took several deep breaths and waited.

Two or three minutes later he began typing again, slightly rewording and indenting what he considered implied commands.

Forty minutes later, he had completed chapter 5. His list was beginning to take shape in front of him:

Matthew

> Direct Commands
>> Implied Commands

Repent (4:17)
Follow me (4:19)
> Recognize your spiritual need (5:3)
> Be humble (5:5)
> Hunger and thirst for righteousness (5:6)
> Be merciful (5:7)
> Be pure (5:8)
> Be a peacemaker (5:9)

Rejoice when you are insulted, reviled, persecuted, and spoken evil of (5:12)
> Be the world's salt (5:13)
> Be a light to the world (5:14)

Let your light shine before men (5:16)
> Do not relax even the least of God's commandments (5:19)
> Do not teach others to relax the commandments (5:19)
> Exceed the scribes and Pharisees in righteousness (5:20)
> Do not be angry with your brother (5:22)
> Call no one a fool (5:22)

Be reconciled with your brother before offering gifts to God (5:24)
Be reconciled with an accuser (5:25)
> Do not look at a woman with lust (5:28)

If your eye or hand causes you to sin, throw it from you (5:29–30)
> Do not divorce except for promiscuity (5:32)
> Do not marry a divorcee (5:32)

Swear no oaths (5:34–36)
Let your yes be yes and your no be no (5:37)
Do not resist an evil person (5:39)
If you are struck on one cheek, offer the other also (5:39)

If you are sued for your coat, give your cloak also (5:40)

If you are forced to go one mile, go two (5:41)

Give to him who begs from you (5:42)

Do not refuse one who wants to borrow from you (5:42)

Love your enemies (5:44)

Pray for those who persecute you (5:44)

    Be sons of your Father in heaven (5:45)

    Do not love and greet only those who love and greet you (5:46–47)

Be perfect as God is perfect (5:48)

He had completed only a little more than a single chapter. Even if he went no further, staring back from what he had typed was already a roadmap of obedient discipleship. The simplicity of it was breathtaking. How could it have seemed so complicated? The Lord's commands were simplicity itself!

David had said, "How are we to live? See what the New Testament says about the essence of our discipleship."

Here it was right in front of him! He had created a list of commands from a single chapter of the Bible, plus the first two verses, that exactly and precisely answered that question. And he had more than 220 chapters to go! The New Testament sitting in front of him suddenly appeared to him as a potential gold mine he had only begun to explore.

What treasures might he unearth in the following days!

All day he sat at the small desk. By day's end he was only halfway through the gospel of Mark. But the profound import of what he had begun deepened within him all day.

A roadmap to discipleship was taking shape. Never had the red letters been so alive with purpose.

He almost had to laugh. The whole point of the exercise, for him at least—though he suspected David knew it would take on much greater significance if he undertook it with an open and prayerful heart—was to discover what the church truly is and how God's people are to live in the church. Yet thus far he had found only a single verse about the church—Jesus's words to Peter in Matthew 16:18. But no command was attached to it at all, not even an implied command—nothing to give enlightenment about what Jesus meant by the church that would be built on Peter.

The list of other commands, however, was so overwhelming in its importance, even in its simplicity, that his interest in the church began to fade alongside the obvious daily practicality of the rest of the red letters.

48

FRACAS AT A GRADUATION

MID-JUNE 2046

"THIS IS Todd Stewart, NBC News. I am standing outside the main auditorium of Hillsgrove College where commencement ceremonies will begin in about thirty minutes."

Lights, vans, cameras, and several film crews had begun arriving an hour before. They had turned the normally sedate town and campus into a hubbub of confusion and expectation. No one knew why the network would cover the small institution's graduation exercises of a mere five hundred plus scholars. The only thing noteworthy about the event was the high-profile guest commencement speaker whom Hillsgrove's president had been publicly thrilled to secure for the occasion. The buildup to his arrival had been all over the local news for a week.

Yet Hillsgrove had never been on the national radar. Why the national media was here, led by their rising new "golden boy" and Presidential Manor correspondent, no one knew. But handsome, articulate, blue-eyed, blond—and compelling at six feet three—Todd Stewart drew eyes wherever he went. He made sure his private life was off limits. But considered one of the capital's most eligible bachelors, there was no shortage of speculation on that score.

"In recent days," Stewart continued, "after months of investigation, facts have come to light that have the potential to rock the world of evangelical Christianity and undermine the career of Rev. Ward Hutchins—the man more than any other who represents the public face of Protestantism in our time. Whether Reverend Hutchins will indeed mount the podium in the building behind me to deliver the Hillsgrove College commencement address after the bombshell about to be made public, or whether at this eleventh hour he will be withdrawn from the program, we must wait to see. As you watch events unfold live, you will know everything as soon as we learn of it."

As Stewart's words, not immediately heard above the din, gradually circulated through the crowd, a hubbub of expectation mounted and spread. Those filing inside the auditorium were abuzz with speculation, which gradually reached the ranks of the robed graduates standing some fifty yards away, waiting to begin their processional.

The auspicious moment of Stewart's telecast had been carefully chosen and scripted for maximum impact. He and NBC's executives had known the supposedly "unearthed" details for over a month. They had managed to keep them under wraps until this day, choosing to go on air live at the most propitious time after Ward Hutchins and Hillsgrove's faculty were already inside. Stewart would make the announcement at the very moment the strains of "Pomp and Circumstance" began. Their intent was not only to smear Ward Hutchins but to discredit all of Hillsgrove College, whose conservative and traditional reputation was anathema to the academic establishment that had ruled the nation's educational system for decades. To take down Ward Hutchins and give Hillsgrove a black eye in one fell swoop would be the ultimate two-birds-with-one-stone scenario.

Thus Todd Stewart had been flown from DC down to Louisville with the full might of NBC's production crew on hand to make an event of it.

Stewart continued with bland and unremarkable background filler on Ward Hutchins and Hillsgrove's growing reputation as one of the last remaining bastions of conservative educational tradition, one of the only accredited universities where evolution was presented as "theory" not fact. Everything proceeding from Todd Stewart's mouth was colored with the bias his scriptwriters at NBC had perfected years before, and which his short tenure in front of the camera had made him shrewdly skilled at presenting as unassailable. Preserving a façade of respectful objectivity—the persona his handlers wanted to create—the actual content of his remarks left no doubt that Hillsgrove's faculty was comprised of dimwitted fools, and that its mission statement was rooted in nineteenth century white supremacist Christian bigotry.

He continued until the opening strains of Elgar's classic processional filtered through the open doors and the graduates began to file behind him, two by two, into the auditorium. The cameramen had been prepared for the moment and now zeroed in for a tight close-up of Stewart's face.

"After exhaustive investigation and hours of interviews," he went on, "combing through documents and bank records and three personal interviews with the women involved, whose names remain confidential at this hour, the story has broken just today, uncovering massive financial improprieties in Hutchins's organization including millions of dollars apparently diverted to offshore accounts in the Cayman Islands, which I have documentation to reveal are controlled by Reverend Hutchins. Furthermore, three women have come forward to reveal multiple instances of sexual misconduct, including two affairs of more than six months with Hutchins. These trysts occasionally took place at a private love nest in the Caymans and at locations throughout the US. Reports are sketchy at this hour, but Mrs. Hutchins has reportedly filed for divorce and is quoted as saying that life with Ward Hutchins was, and I quote, 'a living hell—like living with the most arrogant and egocentric man on the planet.'"

Stewart paused briefly then turned.

"As you can see, Hillsgrove's graduates are making their way into the auditorium where even now Rev. Ward Hutchins sits on the dais with faculty and other dignitaries planning to address them. Let me just see if I can . . ."

Microphone in hand, he walked toward the processional. Lights and cameras followed.

"Excuse me," he said, muscling through the crowd and into the processional and interrupting its orderly march. "What do you think of the report of Reverend Hutchins's multiple affairs—"

He shoved his microphone toward one of the graduates.

"—wondering if you have heard the allegations."

The robed students continued, though several had to swerve aside to do so.

"Have you heard the report that Ward Hutchins embezzled from the donations to his ministry?" he continued, squeezing forward and stepping in front of two graduates, again breaking the flow of the chain. "What will you think listening to him give you advice as you graduate—"

He shoved the microphone into the face of the young man in front of him. But he pushed Stewart aside, and he and the girl with him continued in line.

"—should he be dropped from the program? What does it say about Hillsgrove that a man like Ward Hutchins . . ."

Doing their best to ignore him and shove past, the graduates continued. Finally the end of the line filed inside, and the doors closed behind them.

"As you can see," said Stewart, turning again to the cameras, "no one is talking. Whether the students were instructed not to talk to the press or whether the news took them by surprise, one thing is clear, as has been the case through its history—transparency will not be forthcoming at Hillsgrove. As the doors close behind me, this mausoleum of conservativism in America's educational system, a relic of times long put to rest in our nation, continues its tradition of secrecy, closing ranks to protect one of its own. For its professed love of truth and intellectual honesty, you have just seen one more example of the two faces of Hillsgrove College and of those who cling to the dying ethic of conservatism and its Christian foundation, and its refusal to look at the truth of its own hypocrisy.

"I will bring you more on these breaking revelations about Rev. Ward Hutchins as they become available. This is Todd Stewart, NBC News, reporting from Hillsgrove College, Kentucky."

49

ENOUGH!

DR. CHARLES Reyburn sat watching the NBC broadcast in rising indignation. Why he had tuned in it was hard to say. He never watched the major news channels without a specific reason to do so. NBC was the worst, nothing but a propaganda machine—the modern Democrat party's Pravda. Meaning "truth," ironically the underlying objective of the Russian newspaper was to control news in order to hide truth, exactly as was apparently NBC's current raison d'être.

Hearing through the grapevine, however, that young Todd Stewart would be making an appearance in town, and not attending the ceremony because of a bout with the flu, Reyburn decided to watch. He had been following the young man almost since he broke onto the national scene fresh out of UCLA with a report for Reuters on the new face of the LGBTQ agenda in America as the first century of the third millennium approached its halfway point. Something about the young man, even seen on television—something in his eyes, his expression, his demeanor—caught Reyburn's attention.

What it was he couldn't say. Young Stewart drew him. He had followed his rapid rise through the media ranks ever since, dismayed at his obvious bias—no doubt a result of a thorough brainwashing from UCLA's journalism school—yet still intrigued. The young man had talent, it was clear. He was articulate, perceptive in some ways, yet clearly mired in progressivist ideology.

For inexplicable reasons, he began praying that young Stewart's eyes would be opened, praying that arrows of truth would pierce his heart and brain. He had been doing so ever since.

Tonight's telecast had nearly destroyed whatever dedication remained to continue what seemed like a hopeless prayer, along with the goodwill he felt for the up-and-coming journalist. The entire broadcast was scripted. He had seen and heard such reports hundreds of times in the past twenty years. He could always recognize them as biased hit pieces. He had seen it so many times—they put out the allegations with great fanfare, presenting them as undisputed fact. Once the damage was done, lives ruined, the public thoroughly believing what the media knew to be lies, their objective had been gained. The later revelation discrediting the report was never made widely known.

He was certain tonight's Hutchins story was complete fiction. He was no great fan of celebrity Christianity. But he had enough trust in Ward Hutchins's character to sense that this whole spectacle was a hatchet job.

He turned off the television, praying now not for Todd Stewart but for Ward Hutchins and his poor wife.

Reyburn was ill at ease the rest of the evening and slept but fitfully.

He awoke sometime after four in the morning, still agitated, with a phrase reverberating in his brain that struck a familiar though dissonant chord from long ago:

It was all lies!

He was fully awake in an instant. More sleep was out of the question. Careful not to disturb his wife, he crept from the room. The flu seemed miraculously to have left him.

From the moment his eyes shot open in the darkness, he knew that the constraint of silence had been lifted. It was time to come out of the closet, or, as he preferred to think of it, out of the Narnian wardrobe. The lies had gone too long unrefuted. He could remain silent no longer. It was time to speak. Someone had to stand for truth.

Even if he was only one man, no matter what persecutions he might endure, it was time Christians stood against the Lie.

Even if it was just one Christian who did so, he was willing to be that man.

Charles Reyburn's Martin Luther moment had come.

With almost feverish anticipation, he hurried through a shower as his coffee was brewing. Seated at his desk fifteen minutes later, he hurriedly opened a new file on his computer. Within seconds his fingers were flying across the keyboard.

"I am writing this as an open letter," Reyburn began, "to my mother and father, my wife and family, my friends, my colleagues, my students, and my nation. Those who know me well are aware that I have taken a somewhat unusual spiritual journey over the past thirty years, one that might be described in Robert Frost's immortal words, as the road less traveled . . ."

His fingers scarcely slowed for three hours. Finally, he paused and glanced over what he had written.

"All my life I have been what is loosely called traditional in my general outlook and perspective. I am an unapologetic Christian and an unapologetic American who believes in America's Christian and absolutist foundations. During these times of change, especially as I am an academic and educator, I have found it necessary over the years to rethink many particulars of my Christian belief as well as the particulars of my perspectives of what the underlying idea of America is and should be. These reflections have led to an exploration of the larger implications of my entire outlook as a historian, an American, a Christian, and a man.

"What follows is not an autobiography by any means of my particular journey in these areas. It is rather an attempt to place my sojourn into a wider context. I have felt the necessity to explore Christian thought and America's political, cultural, and religious foundations beyond the boundaries of what might be considered the views and perspectives held by most in our nation today.

"I recently turned forty-five. It seems a good time to pause and reflect where I have come from, where we as a nation have come, and where we are going."

All trace of illness was gone. For four days Charles Reyburn hardly ate, with but six hours of sleep between those days. His wife had never seen such a look in his eyes. The resulting ninety pages was like nothing he had planned or could have envisioned. It was a statement of faith, a manifesto of belief, a warning of concern, and a prophetic challenge.

But before it was completed, he knew the time was still not yet. But that time was approaching. He had been given the freedom to write or begin writing what he saw but not yet to make it public.

Keeping what he had written to himself, it could not be helped that occasional remarks and themes found their way into his lectures that attracted attention. Questions began to circulate whether Dr. Reyburn had had an epiphany or perhaps had terminal cancer. He was speaking with new confidence. His voice sounded different. He walked with a jaunty stride of purpose.

But no one knew the cause.

50

Stunning Conclusion: What Is the Church?

June 2046

AFTER EIGHT days, Mark reached the end of Revelation 22.

With an enormous sense of satisfaction, he took his file to a local computer center to print it out then returned to the motel with thirty-five single spaced pages of what he had identified as the direct and implied commands of the New Testament.

They were almost infinitely diverse, every one uttered or written with different wording, the context adding distinct nuances.

He realized he had only begun to explore the complexities of Scripture's commands. As a youth he had been so taken with Stirling Marshall's *Unspoken Commandments*. How was it that he had never perceived the more comprehensive scriptural backdrop upon which that study had been based?

After further thought, he concluded that the first thing to be done was to group the list of some 1,500 individual entries into headings of related commands. Then it would be helpful to order the commands in the approximate sequence of their frequency of use—listing such commands as *love* and *pray* at the top, and more individual one-time commands such as *turn the other cheek* and *have salt in yourselves* at the bottom of the list.

These categorizations and groupings, however, did not turn out to be as easy as he had assumed. Did *forgive your enemies* and *forgive seventy times seven* times both fall under the general command to forgive, or did important distinctions exist that needed to be identified, one pointing toward treatment of others and the other pointing toward long-suffering, endurance, and never ceasing to do good? Every entry had its own distinctive shade of meaning and context.

Before he had progressed much further, he saw what an ambitious undertaking it was. Listing the commands was only the beginning. Fitting them into a sequence and order of categorization—he was facing a mountain of work.

It could take him months!

It was time to bring the first phase of his study to an end. He would continue at home.

On the evening of his eighth day, Mark glanced back over his typed list. He smiled as he looked again at the first page and what had been his first three entries.

Repent.

Follow me.

Rejoice when you are insulted, reviled, persecuted, and spoken evil of falsely.

He had been out of communication with the world for a week. He had not turned on the television or listened to a word of news. Wanting to keep his focus absolutely single-minded, he had not even spoken to Grace. He was completely unaware of events in far off Kentucky that were sweeping his friend, Ward, into a new round of controversy or how deeply Ward would be called upon by God to obey this final beatitude of Matthew 5:11–12.

The next morning, with a full and thankful heart, Mark packed up his things and headed out of the mountains back toward the valley. The week had changed him. He did not yet fully realize how much.

All the way home, the most startling revelation of the week deepened within him. David had been entirely right. There wasn't a single word in the New Testament commanding attendance or regularity or membership or any kind of involvement in what would be termed an institutional or denominational church. Not a word remotely suggesting it had been spoken from Jesus's mouth.

There was only the familiar yet vague verse in Hebrews 10:25 about not forsaking assembling together, with no definition whether that had any bearing on meetings and groups and worship services and everything else that had come to define "church."

The commands were full of instructions about how to treat one another and how to think and behave toward the brethren. But formal weekly meetings or services—not a word. And Jesus's words in Matthew 18:20 were positively pregnant with significance in answering David's question about how many it takes to make a church.

These revelations shook him. The modern denominational image of what he had assumed was the church was nowhere to be found in the red letters. Whatever Jesus meant by his words to Peter, denominational Christendom could hardly be it.

51

REFLECTIONS
ON THE RED-EYE

THE RED-EYE from Louisville back to DC hadn't been Todd Stewart's preference. But he wasn't about to miss tomorrow morning's briefing in the Presidential Manor's press room. His elder NBC teammate was in New Hampshire for an event laden with implications for the next election where second term Vice President Hardy would be speaking. Todd's colleague always made a point of attending the first official event of every presidential cycle. Though this appearance was coming months earlier than Hardy had anticipated, everyone knew this represented her campaign kickoff for the '48 election.

So Todd would be the lead NBC presence in the press room. The higher-ups had been told that President Samara liked him and had been waiting for an opportunity to call on him. Hoping to build on his five minutes of fame the night before at Hillsgrove, Todd had his question on Ward Hutchins prepared.

He leaned back in his first-class seat and reflected on the day and evening. He had certainly stolen the spotlight from Hutchins, though reports were that the popular author and speaker had not mentioned the fracas outside, nor the charges, and that his commencement speech had been well received in spite of it all. Hutchins would probably call a press conference tomorrow, though none of the national news crews would be there to cover it. The suits at NBC were already preparing a response to what would be Hutchins's obvious denials.

Todd drew in a deep breath and closed his eyes.

An indescribable sense of disquiet had been gnawing at him ever since the telecast. It was not just that the stories about Hutchins were fabrications. He had put out false stories before. It was part of the game. They were in a battle. The battleground was the world of ideas. There were no rules, no etiquette, no ethics. You won battles by framing ideas to your advantage and to the disadvantage of your opponent. Fiction was one of the weapons of engagement.

Yet he'd had misgivings about the hit piece on Hutchins from the beginning. Whatever his beliefs, the man was a man, a brother human being. He had a wife and children. They would all suffer because of what he had said tonight. Who could tell what pain he had inflicted?

And he, Todd Stewart, had done it. No one else. How many lives might be ruined by what he had done tonight?

He had been just following orders. If he wanted to keep his job and continue climbing the ladder, he had to be a good soldier. Yet wasn't that the Nazi justification—we were just following orders?

If he suddenly found himself alone with Mrs. Hutchins, what would he say?

"Yes, Mrs. Hutchins, I knew that they were all lies. But it wasn't my fault. I was just following orders."

What kind of coward makes such excuses?

Whose fault is anything? Who was to blame for the suffering that would fall on the Hutchins family? If he had refused to run the story, they would have given the microphone and scripted story to someone else. Nothing he did could have prevented the story or the pain to the individuals involved. So how could it be his fault?

Another oft-used Nazi excuse—if I don't do it, someone else will.

Where did the justifications stop? If individuals don't make a difference, who will? Where were the Martin Luthers in the media, who had courage to say their rules of engagement were wrong, who had courage to stand against the lies?

He thought back to his encounter with Mike Bardolf seven months ago. He had not heard from him in so long that he had almost begun to hope he had seen the last of him.

But he wasn't destined to be so lucky.

"Todd, Mike Bardolf," he'd heard on the phone. "We need to talk. Meet me at Giralto's tomorrow at 1:00. There's a private room. You will be expected."

He hadn't asked if the time was convenient. It was clear Todd had no option but to be there.

"I have an assignment for you," Bardolf began when they were seated in the luxurious back room of the swanky watering hole for Washington's elite. He took a long swallow of the brandy in his hand. "You've heard of Ward Hutchins, the religious kook?"

"Yes."

"I need you to get some dirt on him. The dirtier and juicier the better—sex and finances preferable. See where it takes you. Here are some names that will get you started."

He handed a folded sheet of paper across the table.

"You mean . . . are there allegations?"

Bardolf stared back expressionless. "There are allegations if we say there are allegations."

"What does that mean? What is the basis for looking into him?"

"That we need dirt on him. We need to take him down."

"Without basis?"

"Everyone has skeletons. No one's clean, especially religious types. There are no Boy Scouts. That's the basis for it. I don't care if we know it yet, that's your job—to find it. If you don't find anything, write up the story anyway you like. But who knows, maybe you will find something. If not, it doesn't matter. You just have to make people believe you."

Todd took his words in thoughtfully.

"I'm not sure I am comfortable with that," he said.

"I didn't say you had to be comfortable with it."

"I mean, if there is no basis for it, what are you saying—make it up out of thin air?"

Bardolf's eyes narrowed. Even in the dim light, the intimidation in his expression was enough to silence Todd's objections.

"Surely I don't have to remind you," he said with an evil glint in his eyes. "You took vows that are lifelong. This man is a menace who must be stopped. By any means possible."

Todd had always known a day of reckoning would come when he would have to pay the devil to whom he had sold his soul.

That day had apparently arrived.

He didn't know what would happen if he flatly refused. He doubted it would come to his body being found floating in the Potomac, though he wasn't sure even that was out of the question with a man like Bardolf. But he did know he could find himself descending the professional ladder as quickly as he had ascended it.

The president of NBC was an alumnus of Oraculous. Todd knew he hadn't become a member of the Presidential Manor press corps at thirty-two because of talent. He was decent in front of a camera, but so were a thousand other guys.

It was a double-edged sword. He had joined their weird and secretive society, taken their money, and had risen high and fast. Now the debt came calling.

He wasn't quite ready to find out what would be the consequences of refusal. He would deal with his conscience later.

Now here he was seven months after that conversation, his hit piece on Ward Hutchins in the books, the damage done, the pain on his family and reputation inflicted, while his own star continued to rise.

But he couldn't let himself reflect too closely about the lives his complicity with Mike Bardolf might ruin. Thinking about such things only raised the specter of guilt.

At this stage of his career, he couldn't afford that.

52

OBEDIENCE IS
THE OPENER OF EYES

AUTUMN 2046

WHETHER THE timing was unfortunate or ordained would depend on one's perspective. But the reality was that within a year of returning to California as head pastor of Foothills Gospel Ministries, Mark Forster's spiritual frame of reference had shifted on its axis.

His week's listing of the New Testament's commands turned his world upside down. As time passed, he realized that it had in fact not really changed much at all. He had heard the same thing from David Gordon many years before. Somehow he had forgotten. Or at least the perspectives of those years had slipped into the background of his subconscious. Suddenly now they clamored to be taken seriously.

He was twenty years older. He was ready to hear more than he had been capable of when fresh out of college. The intervening years, though perhaps sending him down a few tangential byways, had also matured him in preparation for this season.

He was at last ready to dig deeper.

Whether the elders and congregation of Foothills would greet the changes with rejoicing or skepticism remained to be seen. For now they little suspected the upheaval taking place within the heart and mind of the man they had called as their pastor, mostly because of his reputation as a Bible teacher and associate of Ward Hutchins. One of the fringe benefits of that calling, which they still hoped would materialize, was one day to see their pastor's famous friend in the Foothills pulpit.

By the end of the summer, a few were noticing a subtle change of tone in the pastor's sermons. His altar calls, too, became less frequent. Reverend Forster seemed to be speaking more to Christians about discipleship, whatever he meant by that, than to new people in hopes of involving them in their many ministries.

But ministers always followed subjects of interest, some said. Mark's repeated sermons from Matthew 5–7, could easily be explained on that basis. At least, so the elders hoped.

Had they been privy to Mark's discussions through the summer and autumn of 2046 with David Gordon—whom everyone could not help noticing in church regularly now, a fact they attributed, as was true, to their new pastor—they would have seen how transformational Mark's study of the commands had been to his spiritual outlook.

As he was driving up to David's ranch one Monday afternoon, which he did on most Mondays, usually with Grace, Mark's thoughts returned to his visit with Stirling Marshall before deciding to enter seminary. The exhortation Marshall gave him about the decision came back into his mind with extraordinary vividness. He could still hear the older man's voice—soft, peaceful, and powerful.

"Be very prayerful and sober minded, Mark," he had said, in words very much like those that now filled Mark's mind, "as you count the cost of a lifetime in the ministry. Many well-meaning men find themselves falling into the spiritual black hole of organizational Christendom, without realizing it until it is too late. The ministry is a high but also a perilous calling. It is difficult to keep life at the center as your focus in the organized church. You must recognize that most within that church will not share your focus. Your most determined efforts will be powerless to change that fact. If you preach the commands and obedience to the commands, there will be repercussions, and not always pleasant ones. The challenge to obedience always brings opposition."

The words were almost bitter to recall. How quickly he had forgotten. He *hadn't* focused on life at the center. He *hadn't* preached the commands. Was that perhaps the reason he had enjoyed what would be called success in the pastorate—he hadn't followed Jesus's example?

If the challenge to obedience always brings opposition, what did that imply about the fact that nearly everyone in the Seattle congregation had loved him?

The church and its myriad organizational demands had drawn him into its maelstrom. He had been swept into the vortex just as Marshall had warned, caught up in the life and activities of the church, not the life of the commands.

Suddenly twenty years had gone by. It had taken his old friend David Gordon to challenge him, to open his eyes, and bring him back to the center.

53

A Tribulation Church

Two hours later Mark and David were riding slowly on horseback through the pine woodland of David's ranch. Their racing days were over, when a challenge from one or the other might lead to a madcap gallop to the summit of Rustler's Butte by different routes. But though the rides were more sedate, their conversations were much as in former days. Now, however, they probed increasingly deeper regions of discipleship.

"Why do Christians focus on everything except the commands?" Mark had just asked. "They are so central to everything Jesus taught. Yet they are rarely mentioned. I suppose I should be able to answer that—I was guilty of the same thing for years myself. Why did I focus on everything except the commands!"

"It is always easier to dwell on externals," replied David.

"How do you mean?"

"Keeping character, growth, and personal accountability at arm's length. The commands require two things—constant self-evaluation and obedience. Neither is pleasant. It's easy to play games with the outsides of truth. That's why some churches are full. Probing the heart of God's intent, that's hard."

"I am beginning to learn that!"

"Men who preach life at the center don't attract large congregations. Depend on it—the larger the church, the more the emphasis you are likely to find on external superficialities of Christianity."

Mark thought seriously a minute.

"What does that say about me, then?" he asked. "Here I am pastor of a huge church. Most of my congregation isn't attuned to life at the center either."

"It says that you are a growing man. Perhaps you have been sent to lead them toward it."

"I would like to think so," sighed Mark in a melancholy tone. "But how can I not regret how clueless I have been?"

"We all grow into God's depths by a different timetable, Mark. Yours may still have some painful trials ahead."

"Such as?"

"Sooner or later, you may have to face the difficult fact that the church of man is not the best vehicle for the transmission of the centered life."

"Is there such a vehicle?"

"The will, of course, is where the centered life originates. We must choose it."

"You said the transmission of the centered life. I assume you meant how it is passed on to others. How is that done?"

"Through example, certainly, and then through the Church."

"I thought you just said the church wasn't the best means?"

"I meant the Church, not the church."

"I don't understand you."

"There is a Church of God and a church of man. We've talked about that many times. They are not the same. It is unfortunate that the same word is used for both because they could not be more different. That is not to say there is no overlap. But in the fundamental direction they are going, in their underlying objectives, methods, and purposes, in many ways they are diametric opposites. You've heard me make the distinction a dozen times."

"Of course," nodded Mark.

"If I recall, when you and Stirling Marshall had that long conversation, he said it too. The distinction between the two was one of his signature tunes."

David broke off what he was saying as the two horses separated to wind around opposite sides of a row of trees.

"I believe a time is coming," he went on when again they came side by side, "and you may be part of it, when the Church of God will be revealed as a much different thing than the organizational church of man. Most ministers and pastors and priests will be blind to the distinction. The revelation may go on without them. At the same time, the church of man will become increasingly joined with the world. This unholy marriage between the church of man and the world has always been going on. But in recent times the linkage has become inseparably linked to the world's outlook. That objective is nothing more nor less than to write God and his principles and his truths out of the lives of modern men and women. In other words, to make God's truths irrelevant to modern Christendom. The word *God* will remain. But the adopting of cultural progressivism will have effectively turned the members of most churches into practical daily-life atheists."

"That is a frightening assessment," said Mark. "Do you really think it is as serious as that?"

"I do," replied David. "That is what is so different about our time. The church and the world have always been filled with evil and hypocrisy. But never has there been a time other than Stalin's Russia when the civilized cultures of man have set out with a concerted plan to wipe God out of the human equation. But that is exactly what the political and cultural radicals of our time are bent on doing. That is what makes the present cultural battle unlike any other. It is what makes the present marriage between the world and the church so much more lethal."

"I assumed that the godlessness we see in the world was not so different than the godlessness of all eras."

"I believe it is very different. The churches of Christendom are unknowingly embracing this death-to-God agenda. They would be aghast to hear me say that. They have no idea how their compliance with the world's outlook is spreading the world's cancer throughout their churches. They have been seduced into thinking it their duty to be open and tolerant and accepting toward the shifts modernism is imposing on the culture.

"It is a fool's game. It's the same as Chamberlain's attempt to be pals with Hitler over a hundred years ago. Churchill understood what many Christians today don't. Allying itself with the world's tolerance of sin is a cancer that will destroy man's church. You can't befriend the devil without becoming one of his pawns. In the end, those who remain in it—the clergy and laity alike—will be left behind."

"You don't mean . . . not left behind by the rapture?"

"No," laughed David. "Nothing like that. You won't find me using that 1990s jargon. No, I mean left behind by the revelation and expanding life of God's Church, the true Church, the eternal Church."

"Surely you're not saying that every Christian, or every pastor, who is involved in a denominational church is deceived?"

"Of course not. It is a very fluid mix of people and motives and life directions. We know there were honorable and righteous Pharisees in the first century too. Yet a change was coming. The old was in the process of being swept away, even though in that transition, there were good and obedient and righteous people in the old system for a time. But eventually it was swept away."

"You believe that we are in such a time now, that the church will ultimately be swept away?'

David was thoughtful for a long time.

"God's Church will never be swept away. But the church of man, the structural and organizational institution that goes by the name church is increasingly becoming the ally of the world—yes, it will be swept away. It will not happen all at once. It will doubtless not happen in my lifetime, perhaps not even in yours, though it may.

"A time of tribulation for the church of man is coming. Whether it is the great end-times tribulation of Revelation, I would not hazard a guess. That tribulation may not be marked by wars and rumors of wars but with prosperity and ease and self-satisfaction.

"Prosperity may be the Achilles heel of the church of the tribulation. It may be that prosperity will blind Christians to deeper spiritual realities. We may be in that tribulation even now. The church of man, the world's ally, may actually be the antichrist, not some many-horned evil world figure."

"You honestly think that could be!" exclaimed Mark.

David paused and sighed.

"I see but through a glass darkly, Mark," he said. "One thing I know is that the church of man, the ally, and perhaps even the antichrist of a far different tribulation than evangelicals anticipate, will be swept away. God's true men and women, his disciples of Christlikeness and obedience, must come out before that time comes. They must come out so that they can be part of the remnant awakening that will raise God's eternal Church from among them."

54

Birth of a Remnant

"But to return to your questions," David went on after a moment, "yes, for now good and honorable people remain in man's church, bringing light and salt where they find themselves, some even teaching the commands as you have been doing, leavening the body of Christ in preparation for the great shaking. At present you are one of them. You are serving where you felt called, and I believe you were called."

"When will this shaking come, this transition, this coming out as you call it?"

"It will come in phases, not all at once. You and millions like you remain in man's church at present. The remnant will gradually arise, recognize the ally for what it is, and gradually come out from among their self-satisfied brethren and be separate. The institution itself, which goes by the name of church in the world, will ultimately die from within. Don't get me wrong. It may not cease to exist. It may continue prosperous and self-righteous to the end. But whatever life it once contained will slowly evaporate until there is nothing left but the shell of many country clubs that still call themselves churches."

"That is very sobering. Even frightening."

David nodded. "That's why it will be a time of great tribulation for many Christians. They will not understand what is happening or why it is happening. Yet they won't try to understand. They won't want to understand. They will be too complacent to care. Many good souls will one day weep bitter tears when their eyes are opened to the reality that much of what they took for granted as having come from God actually originated in the sinful heart of man."

"A hard thing to say, David."

"Perhaps, but would you prefer I pretend it is not as serious as it is? You have been in the institutional church long enough to know it is true. You must have seen it."

Mark nodded. "I suppose you're right. But much of what you say I don't want to believe."

"Neither do I want to believe it. But the reality is impossible not to see. Most Christians would more readily embrace suffering and persecution and even bloodshed than they will be able to accept the grievously painful truth that the church of man may actually be the antichrist and that they have been part of his great lie."

"You don't mince words, David."

"I will always be straight with you. These are eternal issues, Mark. Those playing games with Christianity are nothing but modern-day Pharisees. Malachi's fire awaits them. There's no way to sugarcoat it. Those left in man's church will eventually be pawns on the enemy chessboard, which is the world. When the remnant has come out of the church of man, then indeed will God's Church begin to flourish, though the world may not see it. From the lifeless church of man, the remnant will burst out like a tiny yellow crocus through winter's snow, reaching into God's eternal sun out of a lost and frozen world."

"Are you saying it will be an underground remnant?"

"Not in the cold war sense, meeting in dark basements, hiding out, fearful of talking to one another openly. It may come to that, I don't know. But I meant the term differently. I mean that the remnant Church of the end times will be invisible to the world and probably invisible to those poor souls left in the church of man, who are either too fearful or too self-satisfied to leave it. God's Church will be in plain sight all the time, yet as unseen as that winter crocus springing to life in the world's out-of-the-way places, full of God's life yet unseen as a lost world hurries by. The remnant Church will boast no buildings or signboards, pass out no tracts, put no bumper stickers on its cars. Its invisible strength will be built from the interlacing bonds of unity that exist between its members, functioning in the world of men but of a different world altogether."

Mark shook his head and sighed.

"As I say," David went on, "the time for that revelation is not yet. For a while longer the church and the Church will comingle, the true discipleship Church seeding what life and light it can into the hearts of the sincere and growing men and women of man's church.

"Gradually those with eyes to see, in ones and twos then fives and tens then hundreds and thousands, will recognize what spirit animates the church of man. They will know that they can no longer be part of it and that they are called, like the Israelites of old, to come out and be separate. Then indeed will tribulation be upon them, for the battle lines will be drawn. But only those of the remnant birthed during the era of birth pangs will recognize where and how the tribulation battle will be waged. It will not be in the Middle East."

Mark did not reply. It was almost too much to take in.

55

A Memorable Weekend

NOVEMBER 2046

As THE chill of late fall came to the California foothills, those of its trees destined to lose their leaves, scattered amid the evergreen pines, exploded into red, gold, and orange.

Though the Forsters and Marshalls were casually acquainted from church, especially as Timothy was a former elder, the two families had not established a deeper level of intimacy since the Forsters' arrival. One Sunday afternoon in November, Timothy and Jaylene invited Mark and Grace and their family for dinner along with their daughter Heather and David Gordon. Receiving Jaylene's call, David suggested that they get together at the Bar JG on a Saturday instead. The atmosphere would be more relaxed without the pastor and his family having to sandwich it between morning and evening Sunday services.

"If you still want to be the hostess," laughed David on the phone, "you can provide the main dish."

Mark and Grace were happy with the change. They loved the ranch, and Mark had now resumed regular and frequent visits to David's lifetime home. Thus it was arranged for the two families to meet at David's at noon on Saturday for an early afternoon dinner.

In their conversations of recent months, Mark had not again asked David about the mysterious group he had heard about. Vague reports had also reached him associating the Marshalls with whatever kind of group it was, no doubt prompted by Timothy's resignation

from the board of elders and the gradual lessening of their involvement. Mark hoped the dinner invitation might prove an opportunity
to learn more.

It was a thorough mix of age groups that arrived at the ranch about
noon, from David at seventy-five to Timothy and Jaylene at sixty-six
and sixty-three, their daughter Heather, thirty-two, Mark and Grace at
forty-six and forty-five, and their daughter and son, Ginger and Craig,
eighteen and sixteen.

"Hello again, Heather," said Grace as the two made their way
toward the house, each holding a "potluck" dish from their respective
two cars. "I haven't seen you for a while."

"When I am at church, I go to the ten o'clock service," replied
Heather, walking beside Grace with her characteristic limp.

"That's the trouble with multiple services," rejoined Grace. "You
don't see everyone."

"To be honest, Mrs. Forster," said Heather, "I usually attend a small
church in Dorado Wood where I live. I like the small church atmosphere better. And it's a long drive to Roseville."

"You're still working at the assisted living facility?" asked Grace.

"I'm the resident nurse and activity director."

"What a wonderful ministry."

"I love the work. Your Ginger and Craig have sure grown since the
last time I saw them, which was probably soon after you arrived from
Seattle."

"Ginger will soon be in college!" laughed Grace. "I can hardly
believe it."

"What are her plans?"

"She's thinking about some of the state universities—and Jessup.
That pleases Mark and me, of course."

"She could take classes from my mom and dad!"

"We thought of that."

"She graduated last year and is taking this year off helping at the
church."

They reached the house just as Craig came bounding out, David,
Mark, and Timothy on his heels.

"Mom, Mr. Gordon's going to let me ride one of his horses after dinner!" said Craig excitedly.

"Strap him in tight, David!" laughed Heather.

"I'll let you supervise when the time comes," said David.

"Jaylene and Ginger are waiting for you ladies in the kitchen," said Timothy. "We're going to do the man thing and stand around the corral looking at horses."

"If there's any riding to be done, Dad, don't leave without me!" said Heather.

"I wouldn't think of it!" replied Timothy.

"Craig is still a boy at heart!" laughed Grace as she watched them go. "He's a high-school junior on the outside and still ten on the inside!"

Two hours later, as the eight stood from the table, a lull descended.

"I don't know about anyone else," said David, "but I think I'm ready for that ride. What about it, Craig?"

"Yeah!" exclaimed Craig. "Can I, Dad?"

"You bet," replied Mark. "I'll join you."

"The air is crisp, hint of snow in the air," said David. "There might not be too many more chances. Who else wants to come along?"

"Me!" chimed in Heather and Ginger almost at once.

Everyone left the house for the stables to help with the saddling and preparations. Thirty minutes later the three horsemen and two horsewomen set out across the pasture toward the woods, David in the lead with Craig talking excitedly beside him, one of David's cowboy hats two sizes too big down over his ears.

"Run inside, Timothy," said Jaylene, "and grab the phone. We have to get a picture!"

As they disappeared into the trees and the three turned back for the house, Timothy glanced toward the northwest.

"Those are some nasty looking clouds off there," he said. "They were calling for rain tomorrow. I have a feeling it'll be here by tonight. We should head back down to the valley before dark."

Half an hour later as Timothy and the two women were finishing up in the kitchen, Jaylene and Grace talking like old friends, a sudden blast of wind turned all three toward the window.

"You may be right about that rain, Tim," said Jaylene. "The wind seems to be kicking up."

Timothy opened the door and walked out onto the porch. A gust nearly blew him off his feet. He hurried back inside.

"The temperature's dropping too," he said.

Another hour went by. The three were still seated in David's great room reading and dozing. The howling wind outside prevented them hearing the return of the horses until suddenly Craig burst through the door.

"Mom," he yelled running through the kitchen. "It's snowing. David made us gallop all the way back!"

Timothy shook off his drowsiness and rose from his chair and walked to the window. The entire landscape was white, covered with an inch of snow. Huge flakes were falling so thick he could not even see the barn.

He turned toward the door. "I'll see if they need help with the horses," he said, hurrying outside without a coat. Wanting to miss nothing, Craig dashed after him.

Ten minutes later everyone was inside, the riders and Timothy chilled to the bone. They had left on the ride in a pleasant sixty-five degrees. The thermometer on David's porch now read thirty-seven.

"We should get going," said Mark. "I think the remainder of our afternoon together has been canceled."

"Why don't you call your folks, Mark?" said Grace. "See what it's doing in town. We've got to go that way."

"Good idea," said Mark, taking out his phone.

"Hey, Dad, it's Mark—yeah, we're over at David's. This sudden storm caught us by surprise. What's happening there?"

The others waited as Mark listened.

"Yeah . . . when was that . . . oh, boy—wow . . . hmm . . . okay, yeah, I'll keep you posted, Dad."

He turned toward Jaylene and shrugged. "Started there two or three hours ago. Four inches already and coming down like a blizzard. No one predicted it. The road crews weren't even on duty. By the time the plows get out, it'll be a mess."

He looked around the room. David was outside on his porch gazing into the whiteness. He walked back inside and closed the door behind him. "Temperature's down to thirty-four," he said. "There's already three inches out there. Even if you left immediately, by the time you reached Grass Valley, you'd be looking at six. I hate to tell you, Mark, but I think you'll be spending the night here. You Marshalls too."

"Yay!" cried Craig excitedly.

"We've plenty of leftovers for supper," said Grace.

"Probably no chance of getting out early tomorrow?" asked Mark.

"You grew up here," said David. "The plows will hit town first, then 49 into Auburn. But they won't have the local roads around the ranches plowed till late tomorrow or even Monday morning."

Mark thought a minute.

"I'd better make some calls to Stoddard and a few of the others," said Mark. "They'll need to cover tomorrow's eleven o'clock for me."

"David," said Jaylene, "if you show us what to do, Grace and Heather and I will get started making up the rooms."

"You've stayed here enough times over the years, you know where everything is."

"Just tell us where you want everyone."

When evening came, the accumulation had grown to nine inches. Never could any of the eight remember a more pleasurable evening, snow outside, everyone cozy inside with a warm fire crackling in David's huge stone fireplace. When Grace went to the piano and unexpectedly began playing Christmas carols, rousing singing spontaneously filled the house. Popcorn and apples followed.

"I don't like stores rushing the Christmas season," said Grace after finishing "Joy to the World." "But with the snow and all of us here like this, it just put me in a Christmas mood. It feels like Christmas eve."

Again her fingers began flying over the keys to "Ding Dong Merrily on High."

The snow and unexpected isolation, with more Christmas carols, added to the festive atmosphere, with hot vanilla drinks and leftover pie about 8:00. Conversation continued lively. By the end of the evening, the Marshalls and Forsters were on their way to becoming lifelong friends. Though thirteen years separated them, Grace hit it off with Heather no less than had her daughter.

56

SURPRISE GUESTS

MORNING CAME with bright sunlight and a cloudless blue sky, with the Bar JG buried in a foot of snow. Craig was out in it before most of the household was awake, returning with jeans and shoes soaked and his fingers frozen. Half a snowman sat in front of the house.

The men declared themselves in charge of breakfast and insisted on waiting on the women. Coffee and tea were served. For the next hour the sounds in the kitchen kept the women in stitches. The aromas that began to fill the house were reminiscent of Isabel Gordon's kitchen. At last breakfast was served—eggs, bacon, sausage, hash browns, and a sumptuous coffee cake—one of his mother's favorite recipes David had practiced enough times to perfect.

As the morning progressed, it was obvious to everyone, especially David and Grace who knew him so well, that Mark grew quiet as 8:00 then 9:30 and finally the eleven o'clock hour arrived. No one said anything, but David had some idea what he was thinking—perhaps akin to surprise that lightning did not fall because they were not "in church" at the appointed time. In a subtle way, however, the absence from Roseville—and a surprisingly happy and pleasant absence—subtly confirmed the undercurrents of change taking place within Foothills Pastor Mark Forster.

When the echoes of eleven chimes from David's large pendulum clock slowly died away, the room was left in momentarily silence. Thankfully, no one suggested an impromptu church service. Grace made no move to the piano to start playing hymns. As if to prevent anything artificial beginning, David stood.

"Hey, Craig, how about you and me seeing what we can do with that snowman!"

Craig leapt to his feet and ran for the door.

"Not so fast, partner!" said David. "Let me get you some gloves first and a jacket."

"Wait for me!" said Ginger, hurrying to join them.

"Make that two pairs of gloves!"

The ice thus broken, conversation in the great room resumed. No one mentioned church or what might be going on at that moment in Roseville.

About 1:00, suddenly the kitchen door opened and two men and two women walked in. David rose to meet them.

"Ora . . . D. S.!" he exclaimed. "What in the . . . oh my goodness—" he added as another couple walked in behind them. "Dewitt, Pearl! This is unbelievable! How did you all get here?"

"In the four-by-four," replied the man called DS, a fellow rancher from the other side of the valley. "We were going to come over today anyway. Ora wanted to ask you about that *Phantasms* book. Then Dewitt called. He'd heard through the grapevine that the Forsters were stranded up here, so we drove down, picked them up, and came to check on you. Had to put chains on when we started up your road, though—too thick even for my Jeep."

"Well this is fantastic—but no one's stranded," said David. "We're having a great time—come in, we've got left over coffee cake. Hey everybody, look who's here—it's the Wests and Laynes!"

David led the newcomers through the kitchen into the great room. Hearing the exuberant greetings, the others were by now out of their chairs, curious to see what the commotion was about.

"Timothy and Jaylene," said David, "you know everyone—Mark, Grace, let me introduce—"

"Hello, Dewitt—Pearl," said Mark in obvious surprise. The two men shook hands. Grace stepped forward and embraced Mrs. West.

"Of course, you would know each other from church," said David. "What was I thinking?"

"We heard from Stoddard that you were here," said Dewitt, one of Stoddard Holt's fellow elders at Foothills.

"Were you at the service?" asked Mark.

"No. D. S. called when we were getting ready. We decided to come up with them instead."

The three Marshalls greeted the Wests and Laynes warmly.

"I don't believe the two of you know Mark and Grace Forster," now said Timothy. "Mark and Grace Forster, meet Ora and D. S. Layne from across the valley."

Grace and Mrs. Layne smiled and shook hands.

The rancher offered Mark his hands, eyeing him carefully. "You're Bob Forster's boy?" he said after a few seconds.

"I am indeed!" laughed Mark.

"I knew it the minute I saw you—the spitting image, as they say!"

"I recognize your name too," said Mark. "But I don't think we've met, have we?"

"I saw you a time or two when you were a kid and I was an over-grown teenager punching cattle with my dad. We came over to the Circle F to borrow a couple horses from your dad. Now we're both grown up, and you're a big-time pastor, I hear."

"Let's just say I am a pastor," said Mark, glancing with a hint of embarrassment toward David. "And this is our daughter, Ginger, and our son, Craig."

More greetings followed all the way around.

"How is your dad?" asked Layne. "I heard he moved into town."

"They're doing okay," replied Mark. "He misses the ranch."

"They leased it out, didn't they?"

Mark nodded. "A nice family's living in the house."

"What are their plans for the place, or maybe I should say your plans?"

"We haven't really talked much about it, to be honest. We've only been back in the area two years. My two sisters are scattered across the country, so it will eventually fall to me and my folks to decide what to do. It's hard on my dad to talk about the future, much less selling."

"I get that. Well, if that time ever comes, talk to me. I'd take some of your dad's land off his hands if that's what you and he and your mom decide. But a man and his land—that's sacred. You're right not to rush him."

"Thank you—I appreciate that. It's good to know there are people around who care about my folks."

"Your dad's a legend around here, just like David," Layne added. "They're the last of their generation left of the Grass Valley ranching community."

Within ten minutes, the four wives and Heather were bustling about the kitchen making fresh coffee and setting out cups and plates and what remained of the three pies from the day before.

An hour later the twelve were seated in the great room chatting informally.

"You had something you wanted to ask, Ora, about Stirling's *Phantasms* book?" asked David.

"Yes. I know some of you love it, but I am having a hard time understanding it."

"Well," replied David, "we have Stirling's own son right here. Why don't you ask Timothy?"

"I had planned to," said Mrs. Layne, "the next time we . . . I mean, if I happened to see you sometime," she added nervously. She turned toward Timothy. "There's nothing much more to it than that. I just find it hard to understand."

Timothy thought a minute.

"Many people write to Jaylene and me who feel the same way," he said at length. "They love *Unspoken Commandments* and the novels, but they struggle with *Phantasms*."

"That's me exactly. I love the characters in his novels—the women, the men, the children. It's what sets your father's writing apart—real people living their faith. But some of his other work is too mystical for me."

"Dad's writing was diverse, that's for sure. He appeals to such a broad cross-section of people, probably no one reads all books in the same way. Everyone has their favorites, though I would say that *Unspoken Commandments* is probably the foundation for all the rest."

"And *Phantasms*?" said Dewitt's wife, Pearl.

"In a way I think the title says it all," replied Timothy. "Some of my father's titles are really clever. He used his titles and subtitles to convey hidden meanings that probably escape some but which illuminate the deeper purposes he intended. *Unspoken Commandments* is a perfect example. We are all familiar with the two great commandments that Jesus spoke, and the many other spoken commandments—*do unto others, turn the other cheek, love your enemies,* and so on. These are vital, of course. But by digging into the Gospels more deeply and uncovering more subtle aspects of behavior and thought to be gleaned from Jesus's teaching, though he may not have commanded them directly, my father opened a far more expansive, and I believe a far truer, way to read and understand the gospel message. In a way, too, I think that the somewhat perplexing title forces people to dig to discover what he meant. The title itself aided my father's purpose."

As he listened, Mark's eyes widened. He had read Stirling Marshall's book several times. He had not realized until that moment how it might have subtly been influencing him during his week alone with the New Testament and his investigation of its indirect commands.

"In a similar way," Timothy continued, "I think his title *Phantasms of Unfaith* is also a brilliant title. By couching his message in a somewhat mystical and allegorical way as the book does, hinted at by the unfamiliar word of the title, it is true that some aspects of it tend to be obscure. In *Phantasms* he was trying to expose those aspects of religiosity that masquerade as faith but which reveal the self strutting about trying to disguise itself as more spiritual than it is. Thinking itself walking in faith, the self is living a dream, a fantasy, a mirage. It is living in a phantasm of unfaith."

"I think I understand," nodded Ora.

"But his novels and *Unspoken Commandments* represent the meat of my father's message. If you don't care for *Phantasms*, don't bother with it."

A brief silence fell. Mark had been listening intently.

"So would I be overstepping, David," he said, glancing around the room as he spoke, "by asking if this is something like the mysterious group you are part of?"

David burst into laughter.

"Very clever, Mark!" he said. "Trying to bait one of us into divulging more than I have told you."

"Honestly, I just—" began Mark.

"All in good fun!" said David. "I'm only teasing. But yes, this is exactly like it. There's no big secret. This is what we do—get together informally. We might even call this a meeting of the group. What do you think, Timothy?"

"Sounds good to me. The meeting is hereby called to order. What's next on the agenda."

"I would say to see how much of Jaylene's chess pie is left!" said David.

The others laughed.

"You see, Mark," David went on. "There is no agenda. We just enjoy one another in the Lord's name."

"In other words, as a Church where two or three are gathered together?" said Mark.

"A Church indeed! You have been paying attention."

"And you seem to have lured one of my elders into it," said Mark, with the hint of a smile on his own face, glancing toward Dewitt.

"Just coming along with a neighbor to see if David was okay from the storm," replied West.

"If you say so, Dewitt!" rejoined Mark.

"No comment."

"Though it might be best if you didn't mention to Stoddard that Dewitt and I were here," added Pearl. "There would be no end of the mischief Edith could stir up."

After the weekend of the snowstorm, the discussion when the threefold cord met two weeks later was inevitable.

"It seems more than clear to me," said Timothy, "that it's time to officially invite Mark and Grace into the GCG group. But you have known Mark far longer than we have, David. What do you think?"

"It's absolutely time," replied David. "They're ready. Had you not suggested it, I would have. Not to put too fine a point on it, but after the Wests and Laynes walked into my kitchen, the jig was up. I couldn't help smiling to myself—the Lord sometimes has such a wonderful sense of humor!"

"Mark knew and everyone knew he knew, and he knew we knew he knew!" laughed Jaylene. "That was such a funny exchange you and he had. I completely agree—Mark and Grace are one with us."

Having made the decision to talk to Mark and Grace, there was no inclination to delay. The Marshalls and Forsters, with Heather and David, met at the Marshall home in Roseville the next Monday afternoon Mark was available.

Neither Mark nor Grace were surprised. They took in everything the others shared seriously, recognizing the potential pitfalls of becoming more involved. Yet they were excited and eager to learn more.

57

A Senator Makes News

August 2047

MIKE BARDOLF put down his phone, drew in a breath, poured himself another glass of Scotch, sat back, then picked up the remote and turned on his television. It was nearly time. After six or eight minutes of preliminaries, the program's highly publicized guest was finally introduced.

". . . so please welcome," the host said, "the senator from the great state of Washington, Jefferson Rhodes!"

Applause from the live audience followed as the senator walked on stage looking trim, handsome, and supremely confident. At forty-seven, his abundant crop of brown hair was just showing the right tinge of gray around the ears to give him the distinguished air of a national leader. His trademark had always been his winning and subtly mischievous smile. It had aged well. It was still a smile that made women swoon and drew fellow politicians into his confidence. Even Republicans couldn't help liking him. With an ambitious father, his age, looks, and mannerisms invited JFK comparisons, which he always deflected with the roguish smile that confirmed them all the more, though saying nothing to dissuade the idea.

"Hello, Senator," said the host, "very good to have you with us. Welcome to the Big Apple."

"Thank you, Phil," replied Rhodes, sitting down adjacent to the king of late-night television, Phil Simons. "My pleasure of course."

"You will be coming up for reelection next year."

"I will be indeed."

"You've become one of the best-known young senators on Capitol Hill. Many are calling you one of the Senate's future powerhouses."

Rhodes laughed. "Don't believe everything you hear, Phil. You should know as well as anyone that there is always talk in Washington. Actually," he added with his trademark grin, "you probably know that far better than most. You make your living exploiting the rumors that circulate down there."

"Touché!" laughed Simons. "How else would I attract guests and keep my audience but by the help of the capital's political machinations?"

"Speaking for myself and my esteemed colleagues, we are glad to be of service to your profession, dubious as may be some of the tactics you use against us."

Again came the grin. By now Jefferson Rhodes had both the live and huge television audience in the palm of his hand.

As he watched, Mike Bardolf could not help smiling. The man was a master, he had to admit.

"In keeping with your kindness, then," Simons went on, "and hoping that you will continue to provide me newsworthy tidbits that pay my salary—"

"Which is more than mine," I might add, interrupted the senator, much to the delight of his listeners. "Probably many times over!"

"No comment!" laughed Simons. "As I was saying, there is talk that after your reelection, which I think we may take as a fait accompli, in spite of the fact that you are at present only in your second term, that you may be put forward as senate majority leader, or if not that as chairman of one of the important committees. I've also heard your name mentioned in connection with the Supreme Court. Would you care to comment, Senator?"

"Only to say that I am honored to serve the people of Washington and hope to continue doing so and representing their interests in the nation's capital."

"Spoken like a true politician. However, would you care to comment about, shall we say, any higher professional ambitions?"

"No, Phil. As I say, I am honored to serve my constituents and my country in any capacity whatever. If my colleagues should think me suitable for a role in leadership, I would be humbled and honored."

"And the Supreme Court?"

"I think such speculation is fruitless at this point. As you know, justices are usually chosen after many years of judicial experience in the lower courts, which I do not have. My law degree might technically qualify me, but I reiterate that I am happy where I am. I will leave the Supreme Court to my old friend, Linda Trent, appointed last year by President Samara."

"It has been said that your influence was a significant factor in her appointment to the bench. She was, after all, relatively young and still an unknown on the Ninth Circuit."

"Perhaps. But Linda possesses a gifted legal mind. She is imminently qualified and has proven herself so since her appointment."

"Did you help persuade President Samara to appoint her?"

"I am on the Senate Judiciary Committee. We made a number of recommendations. And yes, Linda was among them."

"But you did not put your finger on the scale?"

"I made no secret of the fact that I knew Linda personally. But my vote on the committee weighed no more than anyone's."

"You and she were engaged at one point, were you not?"

The hint of a flash burst from the senator's eyes, seen only by Simons and not caught on camera. He shifted slightly in his seat, and Simons knew he had scored a major point on the fight card. But Rhodes quickly masked his annoyance.

"We dated in college and during our first year of law school. But no, we were never engaged."

"And you see no conflict of interest in recommending her to sit on the bench given your history?"

Again came a brief flash from the eyes. But there was no uneasy shifting of position, and Simon's blow glanced off. Jefferson Rhodes was not a man who allowed himself to be sucker punched twice.

"Not at all. That was a long time ago. Linda and I have remained friends. We are both happily married and have pursued very different careers. I did not show her anymore favoritism than I did the other worthy candidates the president had to consider. In the end, it was the president's choice. I think Linda's track record as a modern thinker this past year and a half has proved the president's decision an excellent one."

"And her brother Ward?"

"Ah," laughed Rhodes, glad to move the conversation away from Linda, "now you've opened the proverbial can of worms!"

"How so?"

"It is no secret that Ward and I are poles apart in outlook. He has nothing but disdain for what his sister and I stand for in moving this country into the future."

"Do you share that disdain?"

"Toward Ward?"

Simons nodded.

"Oh, gosh no! Ward and I are old college friends—roommates for a time. I may disagree with his religious convictions, but he was always more inclined toward such things than I was."

Rhodes chuckled. "We were living in an apartment together during the Trump-Biden campaign of 2020. Oh boy! You should have heard some of our arguments! But I respect Ward's passion for his beliefs."

"He has spoken out publicly against your views and campaigned for your opponent ever since you first ran for Congress."

"Yes!" laughed Rhodes. "Ward has been a thorn in my side—I will admit that. But everyone is entitled to their opinion."

"They say that he has insinuated that you were behind the allegations that circulated last year about his marital troubles and financial misconduct."

"Ridiculous. I would never stoop to such tactics. As I say, Ward is an old friend and I wish him well. Besides, his efforts on behalf of my opponents have made no difference. I've not lost an election yet."

"Actually, that brings me around to another rumor that I've heard. Just pretend that it's you and me in private having a beer together."

"Right! No one else is listening, is that it, Phil?"

"Exactly."

"If you say so," rejoined Rhodes, flashing the camera a grin.

"All right, I asked you before about higher ambitions. I've heard that you might not seek reelection."

"An interesting rumor. But why would I not?"

"I would think it would be obvious."

"I can't imagine where you heard such a thing."

"Just one of those little tidbits one picks up around the water cooler."

"Again, why would I not seek reelection?" rejoined the senator, arching a quizzical eyebrow.

"Because of, shall we say, higher ambitions."

The entire auditorium where the popular talk show was filmed went deathly silent.

A playful smile parted Jefferson Rhodes's lips. The mantle of the Kennedy mystique had indeed fallen on the northwest's favorite son. He needed to say nothing. The impish expression said all there was to say. The words that followed were meaningless. Everyone knew they were meaningless.

"I told you earlier, Phil," he said slowly, "that I am honored and content where I am. I will continue to serve my constituents in the Senate for as long as they want me as their senator."

"No loftier ambitions?"

"I have no ambition other than to serve the people of America and do my part to advance what our great statesman, Barack Obama, at the conference where I first met him years ago, called the bright future of America. Such is my only ambition—to help take America forward into the second half of the twenty-first century."

58

HIDDEN PAIN

MIKE BARDOLF was not the only one of Jefferson Rhodes's colleagues and friends among the four million viewers watching the interview with Phil Simons.

The youngest justice appointed to the Supreme Court since Clarence Thomas in 1991, Linda Trent, watched with conflicted and ambiguous feelings. She had smiled at the reminder of their bitter political debates back then—she and Jeff taking on Ward and Mark with all the acrimony of their youthful hatred of Trump, often, she had to admit, imputing to her brother and Mark the most unkind and untrue of motives. That was one benefit, she supposed, of the single-party system that American politics had essentially become. Since the Trump era and its aftermath had passed from the scene and the Democrat party essentially owned the presidency, election campaigns had been far less strident. Not gentlemanly, by any means, but not so vitriolic.

It was Simons's questions about her appointment, however, that unsettled her. She had not wanted to admit that Jeff had anything to do with her rise from state circuit to appellate, and thence to the Supreme Court in a mere six years. But after watching Jeff's denials, she knew it was true.

She knew him too well. But whatever gratitude she might feel was mingled with annoyance, even the silent elephant in the deepest room of her being—the pain of rejection.

She might be a Supreme Court justice and one of the most respected women of a new generation of glass-ceiling-shattering women. But she was still a woman with her own private demons. She and Jeff had parted ways. Now they were at the top of the political world—though Jeff wasn't quite there yet. Both regularly graced magazine covers and Sunday supplements in the *Seattle Times*.

Yet the "what ifs" sometimes crept unbidden into her mind.

She hated them. She didn't want to think about Jeff. But sometimes she couldn't help it.

59

PRAYER FOR A ROOMMATE

LINDA'S BROTHER Ward Hutchins turned off his television with thoughts curiously similar, yet entirely dissimilar, to those of his sister. He, too, found himself reflecting on the old college days. It was hard to imagine Jeff as a former roommate. Then they had been a world apart. Now they were a universe apart.

How did it happen, he wondered. Why did people perceive reality from such different perspectives? To all appearances, Jeff was a Christian back then. Whether he had been a true Christian, Ward would never know. That was for God to know not him.

How did the liberal cancer get so deep inside him?

Exactly as Simons suggested, he suspected Jeff as having orchestrated the smear campaign against him. He had not breathed a word of his suspicion. Simons had obviously floated the trial balloon trying to get Jeff to take the bait. Even if Jeff was behind it, he did not hold it against him. Jeff was so immersed in the great deception of the times that he could hardly be blamed.

And he had spoken forcefully against Jeff's politics. Jeff had imbibed the dangerous ideas of the times—what could he do but speak against them? But he would never attack Jeff personally. In some way, he still liked Jeff. At the same time, lies must be countered for truth's sake.

He often thought about trying to arrange a meeting with Jeff, just the two of them. Might a flicker of the old friendship still be alive?

Now that they were both in the national spotlight and with the media losing no opportunity to fan the flames of acrimony, he supposed such a meeting was unlikely. Jeff was too much a politician—he would never agree.

Still, maybe he ought to try.

Lord Jesus, he prayed, *give me wisdom. Give me an opportunity to meet with Jeff. Open the doors for healing in his heart toward me. Give me love for him, and perhaps give him love for me as well. Open his eyes, Lord. Reveal truth to him. Awaken him to see the lies in which he is immersed, and that they are lies against you. If he once knew you, even faintly, bring a glow back to those embers of Spirit life. Oh, Lord—open his eyes!*

60

UNLIKELY SENATOR

FIFTY-SIX-YEAR-OLD WYOMING Senator Harvey Jansen had also seen the interview and knew exactly what it portended. Jefferson Rhodes was going to run for president.

Sometimes he hated this city. There was nothing real about it. The entire culture of the capital reeked of ambition, money, deception, greed, the cult of personality, and the raw lust for power. He had only been here eight months, and he hated everything about it.

Why he had allowed himself to be roped into this he would never know. Had the fleeting desire for importance made him vulnerable to a decision he now regretted? God forgive him, he probably had a dose of ambition in his bones. But no longer. It would be over in fifteen months. Then he and Harriet could go home.

He'd never met Rhodes. People like Jefferson Rhodes did not mix with the likes of a temp congressman from the Union's least populated, and to most in this town, least important state, a mere schoolteacher who had never even been to Washington, DC, before his swearing in. But he could tell simply from watching the interview what manner of man the senator was.

Who would his party put up to run against Rhodes, he wondered. Poor old Jedediah Waters had tried for the Republican nomination four times—the twenty-first century's Harold Stassen—had been successful twice, and had been trounced both times in the general by Akilah

Samara. Finding a Republican willing to undergo the humiliation of it had become more like finding a sacrificial lamb than nominating a credible alternative to the Democrat juggernaut. But willing though he would likely be, the party's powerful leaders would doubtless quash another attempt by seventy-six-year-old Jedediah before it got off the ground. Whoever it was, thought Jansen, he didn't envy anyone going up against Rhodes. Even from the television screen, he could see the mean streak in the man's eye.

The combination of circumstances that had landed him here was as improbable as the pilot of *Designated Survivor* whose reruns now had a cult following. He had been perfectly happy as an eighth-grade science teacher at Laramie Christian Academy. Not only happy—he loved his job, looked forward to school every day, lunch with Harriet, school librarian, and whichever students felt like joining them, weather permitting, on the lawn outside. For the two childless educators, it was a dream job, pouring their lives into a new generation of Christian young people. They would never have been allowed such freedom in the forty-five states where private Christian schools were banned. Thus far Wyoming had managed to keep them legal, though for how much longer was anyone's guess. They even still had their supply of pre-2030 Bibles, though in that case, too, there was the constant threat of confiscation by the Federal Education Oversight Unit, or FEOU.

The state's Republican governor and legislature had been unable to prevent environmental legislation over the past decades from being rammed through by successive Democrat presidents. The popular bumper sticker around the mountain states, "Wolves Love Democrats," essentially said it all. The burgeoning wolf, grizzly, and mountain lion populations were threatening every ranch between the Canadian border and the Great Basin, and sightings in towns and cities were worrisome. The danger was real, not only to livestock but increasingly to humans.

As a precaution, every school in Laramie had been issued a rifle, held in a locked safe in the office, whose combination was known to only two individuals—the principal and one other faculty member of his or her choosing. In the case of Laramie Christian, that faculty member happened to be Harvey Jansen. Having grown up on his father's cattle ranch, Harvey knew his way around guns. But he had gone through the required training with the rest of Laramie's two-man, or woman, safety teams and thought little more about it. Though the campus was situated on the outskirts of town just beyond the Sioux subdivision, he never expected to see a wolf or mountain lion anywhere near the school.

For eleven years the safe in the office was never opened. It was nearly forgotten. There had not been a single incident in all of Laramie.

Until three years ago.

Eighteen-year-old high school dropout Brad Childress, whose father had recently divorced Brad's Christian mother for reasons of "spiritual fanaticism," walked onto the Laramie Christian Academy campus during the lunch hour carrying a Colt .45 from his father's collection. Having listened in court to the liberal judge deliver a stinging harangue against his mother for attempting to indoctrinate her children into a dangerous and subversive cult—by which he meant Laramie Christian Academy—Brad had taken it upon himself to exact vengeance for the breakup of the marriage. He planned to do so at the school where his mother taught.

From the other side of the school, Harvey heard the first two shots, leapt from the grass to his feet shouting to Harriet and the others nearby, "Get inside, all of you," and sprinted for the office.

In the emotion of the moment, it took him three fumbling tries to get the safe combination right. As he opened it and grabbed the pre-loaded rifle, two more shots echoed from outside.

Emerging from the front door of the main building, holding the rifle at his side and looking about for the source of the gunfire, he appeared more confident than he felt.

The screaming and pandemonium that had erupted with the first shot gradually quieted. From across the grass in front of the school, Brad saw him coming and squared around to face him. The terrified students slowly backed away, then when they thought it safe, ran for cover. By now no fewer than fifty hand-held phones were recording the event.

Brad Childress, clutching the Colt .45 but not pointing it at anyone, and Harvey Jansen, with the school's Winchester still at his side, walked slowly toward each other as if enacting the climax of *High Noon*.

Seeing the Winchester, and the look in the man's eye staring straight at him, suddenly Brad found himself more intimidated than he had expected. He always thought the school was run by women and wimps. This guy meant business. He hadn't bargained on a suicide mission.

About twenty yards from each other, both stopped. Young Childress was shocked by the first words he heard.

"Nice looking gun, Brad," said Harvey, still without raising the rifle.

"How do you know my name?"

"I've seen you with your mom. She told me. Colt 1909, isn't it—your dad's?"

"Yeah, it's his. What do you know about it?"

"I know guns, Brad."

"So what—so you know guns!"

"I'm a pretty good shot too. That Colt's got six rounds."

"Yeah."

"You've already fired four. What do you think your chances are against my Winchester?"

"Pretty good, if I get one through your heart!"

"Maybe. But I doubt you're that good a shot. By the time I hit the deck and you're trying to aim, I will have put one between your eyes. Is that what you want, Brad? Did you come here to get killed?"

In the momentary silence, sirens could be heard screaming toward the school.

Keeping his eyes locked on Brad's, Harvey shouted in a loud voice, "Anyone hurt! Are there any injuries!"

"No, Mr. Jansen," came several voices at once. "He just shot in the air!"

"Good for you, Brad," he said. "That was smart."

Slowly he began to walk forward again, eyes piercing into Brad's, though with the rifle still at his side.

"You can hear the police coming, Brad," said Harvey. "They're coming for you. You've been smart so far. No one's hurt. But it's going to be a little intense when they get here. They're going to arrest you. You're going to need a friend. I'll be that friend, but you've got to trust me."

He stopped five feet in front of Brad.

"Hand me the gun, Brad," he said then gradually stooped and laid the Winchester on the ground. "I'll make sure it gets back to your dad." Slowly he took two more steps toward Brad.

Almost as if mesmerized by Harvey Jansen's calm voice and demeanor, Brad slowly handed him the pistol. Harvey laid it on the ground beside the rifle then led Brad a few feet away.

Instantly Harriet Jansen ran through the door and outside with Brad's mother, weeping though doing her best not to completely fall apart.

"Harriet, you go meet the police when they get here," said Harvey as the two women ran toward them. "Tell them to calm down. Tell them everything's fine and not to draw their weapons."

He glanced over at his wife so that she could see he had it under control. She nodded.

"We don't need them turning this into a circus. Sylvia," he said, turning to Brad's mother, "you stay right here with the two guns on the ground until the police come. Keep the other kids away. Don't let anyone near them. Brad and I will be in the office. Don't tell them where we are until you're sure they're going to handle it calmly. We don't need them charging in with a SWAT team. Tell them to send in one officer and calmly. This is no time for macho police heroics."

Harvey turned and walked toward the building, his arm around Brad's shoulder as they went.

Film of the event exploded throughout Wyoming for the rest of the day, making several of the national news programs that evening. Newspapers throughout the mountain states led with a variety of headlines the next day to accompany photos of the brief incident in front of the school, which coincidentally took place only a few minutes after noon:

"Clint Eastwood of Wyoming," "Gary Cooper Rides Again," and "The Man from Laramie." Harvey Jansen was hailed as a hero for his calm handling of what might have been a far more serious incident.

Brad Childress was arrested. Harvey went to visit him every day in jail and spoke on his behalf at his trial. Brad pled guilty. Largely on the basis of Harvey's testimony that he was convinced he had meant to harm no one, Brad was leniently sentenced to a year in jail followed by probation. During the year, he was visited by Harvey Jansen every weekend. Under Harvey's tutelage, and arranging to bring teachers from the high school, Brad resumed his studies, and earned his high school diploma the same month his sentence was over.

When his year was up, Brad was met by his father and Harvey Jansen together.

That might have been the end of it had Wyoming senator Whit Yancy not died in January of 2047, two-thirds of the way through his third term.

Two days later, the Jansen landline rang shortly after seven in the evening.

"Hello, Harvey," said the voice on the line. "It's Governor Foxe."

"This is an honor, Governor."

"The honor is all mine, Harvey. I haven't had the chance yet to thank you for the way you diffused the situation at that school in Laramie. It was heroic, Harvey."

"All in a day's work, Governor," laughed Jansen.

"Hardly that. Not everyone would have been able to maintain their cool like you did. You're just about the most famous person in Wyoming."

"I doubt that!"

"You could run against me and probably win."

"I have no political ambitions, Governor—believe me."

"I'm hoping I might persuade you to change your mind, Harvey."

"How so?"

"You heard about Whit Yancy?"

"I did."

"I am appointing you to fill his seat until the next election."

The line went silent.

"Harvey, are you still there?"

"Still here, Governor. Why me?"

"Because like it or not you are now a national figure. You would be a great asset to Congress, and you could be a voice for Wyoming. Your approach to that school incident has you respected by Democrats too. You're the perfect choice. Jimmy Stewart was the man from Laramie. Now you can follow him in another role—Mr. Jansen goes to Washington."

"But it would only be for the remainder of his term?"

"True. By then, you might want to run for reelection."

"I doubt that."

Again it was quiet.

"I am honored you would think of me, Governor," said Harvey after a moment. "All I can say is that I will give the matter serious thought and prayer. My wife will have an equal vote."

"Of course. I understand completely. That's all I can ask."

61

A Friend's Thoughts

MARK FORSTER'S reaction to the Simons interview was more personal and poignant. He sat for several minutes in silence as the ticking clock in the living room approached 11:30.

"It's hard to imagine you and he as roommates, Daddy," said Ginger.

Mark smiled sadly. "Not only roommates. BFs. That's what we called ourselves. He's been to the ranch. We rode all around together. We were inseparable. Pike and Pine, that was us."

"What happened?"

"Life, I guess you'd say. Life, ambition, liberalism—who knows? When as a Christian I couldn't go along with the directions he was moving and the new values he was adopting, that was the end of it. I think he despised me as backward and judgmental. He looked down on anyone with conservative viewpoints. In his tolerance for everything new and modern, he became completely intolerant of anyone who didn't agree with him."

"Now he's one of the most important men in the country," said Grace. "Any regrets, Mark, about your own career path?"

"Good heavens, no. Ward and I followed our spiritual leadings. Jeff and Linda got drawn into the world's current. My regrets are for what they allowed themselves to become part of. I still pray for them. I know Ward does too. We've talked about them. Of course, Linda's Ward's sister and he loves her. That doesn't change the fact that she's lost in a world going more wrong every day."

"Do you think you'll ever see Mr. Rhodes again, Daddy?" asked Ginger.

"I don't know, Ginger. I doubt it. I'm sure he's forgotten his old pal Pine." Mark turned to his wife. "Are you still planning to get together with Heather?" he asked.

"I forgot to tell you. I called her today. We're having lunch tomorrow."

62

ONLY ONE HOPE

OF THOSE who had seen the Rhodes interview, most were in bed within the hour. In a window of a Hillsgrove, Kentucky, home, however, a single lamp still burned at 2:30 a.m.

Prof. Charles Reyburn had been writing feverishly for nearly three hours. He was not thinking of tomorrow's schedule, which fortunately had no early lectures. Neither was he specifically thinking of Jefferson Rhodes or the Simons interview.

But seeing Rhodes in the light of what he was certain the interview portended sent his brain off at lightning speed. He had been writing sporadically ever since the fateful night of the Hillsgrove graduation ceremony fourteen months earlier—taking notes, researching various historical trends apropos to his central idea, gradually adding to the initial rush of writing prompted by the Stewart interview.

For whatever reason, as he watched tonight's interview, the random months of thought and prayer suddenly came into focus as if coalescing into a blinding arrow of light.

Nothing less than a rebirth of America's true heritage could save the country from joining all the world's failed experiments in governance. The US would follow the USSR into oblivion as surely as night followed day unless the present godless downward spiral was halted.

America's only hope was a spiritual rebirth.

Instantly he saw the completed book that had been an unformed chrysalis until that moment. He saw it clearly and saw it whole.

He had not stopped writing since.

63

HEATHER AND GRACE

AUGUST 2047

"PEARL TOLD me briefly about the incident with the snake," said Grace Forster. "I hope you don't mind."

She and Heather Marshall sat opposite one another at the coffee shop where they had agreed to meet halfway between Auburn and Granite Bay. It was Heather's scheduled day to work at the West stables. She left Dorado Wood an hour earlier. The coffee shop was on her way.

"Not at all," replied Heather. "It's no secret. Everyone knows. But we don't broadcast it when beginners are heading out for a ride. They would refuse to go another step for fear of rattlesnakes!" she added.

"But there are snakes?"

"This is definitely snake country. You have to be careful."

"Where I grew up on the coast there were no poisonous snakes. It was too cold."

"Where was that?"

"In northern California, a town called Eureka."

"I know where it is. In all honesty though, what happened to me was a fluke. I was nine, now I'm thirty-three. In all that time I've never seen another rattler when out riding."

"What did happen, if you don't mind my asking?"

Heather recounted the day to the extent she was able to remember it.

"That's awful," said Grace. "You must have been terrified."

"It happened so fast I hardly knew what was happening. I barely felt it when the snake struck because I hurt from the fall off my horse. As Dewitt galloped back to the ranch hanging on to me, I was barely conscious. It's all a blur in my memory. I faintly remember sirens when I was in the car with my father. Then the next thing I remember is waking up in the hospital. They said I had been unconscious for three days. My father and mother never left the hospital."

"It must have been agony for them. I can't even imagine."

"When I started to come to, I felt empty, lifeless, and so tired I could hardly open my eyes. But when I did, the first thing I saw was my mother's face. She was crying a river of tears!" laughed Heather.

"I'm not surprised!"

"The first thought to enter my mind, with the confused images of laying in the back seat of the car and the sirens, was that we had been in a car accident. I felt like I'd been run over by a steamroller. But as I came to myself, there was my dad behind my mother looking fine. Anyway, slowly life returned, thanks to Dewitt and my dad and the policeman. They saved my life."

"A remarkable story."

"To show how confused I was by what had happened, when I went back to school I told everyone that the policeman and my father had driven five hundred and one miles an hour to get me to the hospital. I think my dad told me he had hit a hundred and five briefly, and I mixed up the numbers."

They both laughed.

"At first everyone was nice and made over me. But it didn't take long for it to be obvious that I was different. Even at a Christian school, children can be terribly cruel. My limp was noticeable. It wasn't until the next year, and the year after that, when it became apparent that my left leg was going to be shorter than the other, and that my body wasn't growing as fast as the other girls. When I reached high school, which is a dreadful time for anyone who is the slightest bit different, I was probably the shortest person in the whole school with a limp in my left leg. Luckily eventually I crept up to five feet one. What a milestone it was to pass five feet! All I can say is that high school was a miserable time. I couldn't run or play volleyball or hit a baseball. I couldn't do anything the least bit athletic. I was so clumsy. The other girls laughed when I fell in PE. The boys called me a freak. Many days I went home and cried. My poor mom and dad—they suffered with me. In their own way, they probably felt the pain deeper than I did."

"At least as much."

"No boy ever looked twice at me," said Heather, "unless it was with a look of pity or to laugh at me. I never went to a school dance. I don't know the first thing about how to dance. Even in college I never had a date. I've never had a date in my life. That was just a part of life I knew I wasn't going to experience. So I accepted that I would be single.

"But there was a part of me that was determined to make something of my life. I was a Marshall after all. I was proud of my name. I knew my grandfather had been a great man. He died when I was eighteen. I remember him and my grandmother, Larke, well. I treasure the times I spent with them. I also revered my father and mother. They were the most loving parents imaginable through the pains of my teen years. By the time I reached college, I decided that I would carry on the Marshall name with pride and dignity in spite of my physical limitations. I would find work I loved, and I hoped I could help people less fortunate than me. I would seek people who didn't fit in, people on the edges of life—people who were like I had been in high school. I would try to make life a good thing for them."

"What an admirable ambition for a young person to have. So many become bitter and blame their parents for everything. What you did is such an example."

"I hope so. But I don't feel so noble about it. As I said, I am a Marshall. My family taught me respect, and I hope a little selflessness along with it. I have a legacy to live up to."

"What you say reminds me of something I read in a little devotional I've been reading. Actually, I have it in my purse. It's a small book from over a century ago. I'll read it."

Grace pulled out the tiny volume, flipped through its pages, found the passage, then began reading.

"'There is a wondrous charm in a gentle spirit. The gentle girl in the home may not be beautiful, but wherever she moves she leaves a benediction. Close beside every young girl stands One who holds in His hands all gifts and graces. He looks into her face and asks what new adornment He shall give. Let her pray for the spirit of gentleness, for no other gift will make her such a benediction to others.'"*

She closed the book. It was quiet a moment.

"That describes you," said Grace. "You wear the benediction and grace of a gentle spirit. It is obvious that the Marshall legacy lives on."

"That is gracious of you to say," smiled Heather. "As you read I thought of my grandmother. I would like to think that in some small way her spirit has been passed to me."

"How did you get involved in nursing?"

"I didn't know what I really wanted to do," Heather replied. "I majored in English at Jessup, mainly because I loved to read. Books were my solace after the snakebite when I was in the hospital and then at home recovering. In high school, books became for me probably what dating and sports are for other high schoolers. The English major was natural, though what can you do with a college degree in English but teach? I didn't think I would make a good teacher. I suspected that my handicap would make it difficult for me to gain the respect a teacher needs. I thought about special education and working with handicapped children. But the school environment had been so painful for me that I didn't pursue it."

She paused and laughed lightly.

"That's a long way around to explain how I finally decided to enter Jessup's nursing program. After receiving my MSN-RN degree, I went to work at Alpine Meadows Care Facility. I have been there ever since."

"You are still involved at the Wests' ranch?"

"That's my other life!" laughed Heather. "I work four ten-hour days at Alpine and spend two days a week—or sometimes three!—at the Wests'."

"How do you have time for it all?"

---

* J. R. Miller, *Help for the Day* (London: Andrew Melrose, 1904), 139.

"I don't!" Heather laughed again. "But I love my people at the facility, and I love animals. I could never choose between them. They are my family."

"You lead a busy life."

"I am so blessed with the opportunities God has given me."

"And your gift," said Grace. "Ginger is positively taken by what you do with horses."

Heather smiled. "I am very thankful," she said. "I don't know if it really is a gift. People ask me that all the time. All I know is that immediately after I recovered from the snakebite and started going to the stables again, horses seemed to sense that I was different. Some of them already knew me, but I think they knew that something had changed. Maybe it was my limp. Whether it was, as time went on, for whatever reason, as I limped toward them, even when other people were around, horses came to me. It might have been nothing more than animal curiosity. Maybe they sensed that a limp meant pain. Maybe they had empathy for me. Maybe it's that horses with something wrong seem to sense that I share something in common with them. In a mysterious way, I think I understand them too. I don't know why or how. Maybe God did give me a gift, I don't know."

"You obviously still enjoy riding."

"I love to ride!" said Heather. "I'm too short for a big horse. But sitting in a saddle is one place where I don't have to think about this leg of mine. Not that I do think about it anymore. I've been lame since I was nine. I feel like it is from God to remind me how precious life is. But on horseback, my legs don't matter so much. By the time I was fourteen, besides having two horses of my own stabled with Pearl and Dewitt, they often called me to help with troubled animals."

"In what way? What do you do?"

"At first I just spend time with them, let them get used to me. Usually that gives me some insight how to help them through their own issues. Sometimes nothing comes to me. But at other times I sense what might be helpful. Everybody talks to horses. But I think they like the sound of my voice, and maybe that contributes to why they are drawn to me."

"Well it sounds amazing."

"I think my handicap—which isn't a handicap at all, but you know what I mean—is one of the reasons the old people at Alpine Meadows respond to me as they do. It isn't that they feel sorry for me, but that it brings us together. We're both dealing with life's hard things—they are aging, I am going through life with a limp. It puts us on the same level, in a way. And the women sort of want to mother me. It's so sweet. They'll do things for me that they don't do for the other workers."

"I think I understand."

"Best of all is how everything that has happened affirms Romans 8:28. It is the most wonderful truth—that I might not have the camaraderie I do with horses, or with people, if I was normal, so to speak. God truly gave me the desire of my heart, which was a love for horses and being able to spend my life with them. He wanted to deepen that connection. His way of giving me more of what I wanted was through pain. Surprising as it is to say, that rattlesnake was God's way to bring fulfillment into my life. To look into a horse's eye and know that in some way I might know a little of what he is thinking, and maybe that in some way he senses my love for him, it's like nothing in the world. Then to be able to share those same connections with people—with men and women going through their own personal struggles—and to be able to give them something of myself, it adds all the more to the blessing of what God has given me. And I owe it all to a rattlesnake."

"An amazing story. Thank you for sharing, Heather. I will never forget your example."

64

SCIONS IN THE CAUSE

SEPTEMBER 2047

"MIKE, ANSON Roswell," Bardolf heard on his phone. He hastily rummaged through his memory to place where he had last seen Talon Roswell's grandson. "Hey, Anson, good to hear from you. It's been what—" He paused.

"Three years—that fund raiser for President Samara's reelection back in forty-four—not that she needed it!"

"Right," rejoined Bardolf without missing a beat. "The last thing she needed was our help! You were in California interviewing for that internship your dad set up for you with the governor. Did my letter help?"

"Did it ever! I think he'd heard of you. He glanced over the letter and nodded. 'Well, you certainly come highly recommended, Mr. Roswell,' he said. 'And from a highly placed Secret Service agent—most impressive.' Our fathers may be on the League, but nobody knows it. The Secret Service, that's different. At least you get to operate out in the open. Thank you again."

"Anything for an Oraculous man."

"I'm still uncertain why my dad didn't just tell the governor what he wanted, though as far as I can tell, he's not one of us, if you know what I mean."

"We don't have everybody on the team yet," laughed Bardolf. "Though we're getting there!"

"Well, no matter. He hired me on the spot. Now I'm on his staff in Sacramento, second in command in charge of communications. I've got an office down the hall from the governor's."

"That's where we want our people—controlling the narrative. That explains how you were able to track down my private number."

"You FBI guys aren't the only ones with resources at your disposal." Mike laughed.

"And with our two names, even if we're not at the top levels yet, we can find out anything we need. Actually, I'm surprised you're not a voting member yet."

"My father's got some peculiar notions about my advancement," said Mike with thinly disguised scorn.

"Maybe we can help each other out," rejoined Anson. "We third generation scions of the legacy have to stick together. That's why I'm calling—at least I hope I can return the favor. I saw that hit piece you arranged on Ward Hutchins. I assume you were behind it. Using my fellow alum Stewart—though I realize he is only at the Oraculous level—that was the perfect stroke. Listening to him, I almost believed it myself!" Anson added laughing. "But Hutchins is drawing bigger crowds than ever. Once he refuted the thing, with his wife vouching for him so convincingly, the allegations lost their sting. It was no Hillary Clinton standing by her man through clenched teeth. Mrs. Hutchins was so believable, even I believed her."

"Regrettably, so did I," said Mike.

"I don't like to say it, old man, but the end result was a flop. As good as your strategy was, you didn't think through the implications."

Mike Bardolf's blood surged to be upbraided by an underling, no matter what his name was!

"Get on with it, Anson," he said, now through his own clenched teeth. "What did you call about?"

"Something's come up here. I was thinking that if we put our heads together we might take another crack at Hutchins that would be more successful. Like I said, returning the favor you did me."

"I'm listening."

"There's a guy on my staff—energetic and a whiz with technical computer stuff. His only flaw is that he's a gung-ho Christian. Dad's a developer in the area, got him the job on the governor's staff, and he was assigned to me. I think he's made me his personal project—bringing me tracts and articles—witnessing they call it. I had a friend at UCLA who was just the same—really obnoxious. Anyway, this guy on my staff has been inviting me to a big do at his church. It's twenty miles from the city. He's convinced I'll get swept up in the excitement and get saved. Anyway, you'll never guess who is the guest speaker for the extravaganza his church is putting on—Ward Hutchins."

"I see. The plot thickens."

"It occurred to me that, with some planning, you might be able to use the event to your advantage. This guy is so talkative, if I play along and feign interest, there's no telling what I might learn."

"Does he know Hutchins?"

"No, but he's a wealth of info about the church. His dad's one of the big wigs. Inside information is always good. Maybe there is something that might stick. What if the reports Stewart floated before are true, and we could get proof from the inside?"

"Why is Hutchins going there?"

"He's an old friend of the pastor—college buddies, I think. They pastored together in Seattle before Hutchins hit the big time."

"Anything we can use on the other guy?"

"Don't know a thing about him."

"See what you can find out. That would be a coup—take down two high-profile evangelicals at once. Any chance there's a gay connection? Church people are still squeamish about that."

"I doubt it."

"Doesn't matter. We didn't make the affair angle work on Hutchins. Maybe we could smear the other fellow. What's his name?"

"Forster."

"If we could dig up something on him and make the dirt stick to Hutchins—I like it! It doesn't take much. Everyone knows those guys are all hypocrites pilfering from the collection plate. We've just got to hit on the right angle to give the rumor traction."

"If kids are involved, so much the better. Our two grandfathers nearly destroyed the Vatican and its lackeys with that one. Church people are squeamish about pedophilia too."

"You're right, if we could get one kid to come forward, we could bring down the entire Hutchins organization. I'll look into some possibilities on my end. I have a guy whose specialty is planting rumors—actually, you may know him, another Oraculous guy, Nolan Halstead—came up through the Penn State chapter. In the meantime, see what you can dig up about the church and Hutchins's friend."

65

DEEP THROAT REDUX

OCTOBER 2047

BY MID-AUTUMN of 2047, most of the following year's presidential hopefuls had declared their intentions and their schedules began to fill. New Hampshire and Iowa and the other early primary states once again took their four-year place in the sun.

It was true that with the outcome a foregone conclusion, presidential campaigns had lost much of the excitement of former times. Only the Supreme Court retained a pretext of neutrality, though the six-three liberal majority insured that no major roadblocks were erected to slow the cultural agenda.

The fact was, presidential politics contained no drama. The primaries were all that mattered these days. That fact held consequence on the Democrat side. But for the Republicans, it was mostly an exercise in futility. Their squabble for the nomination held the passing interest of a wildcard skirmish whose victor might enjoy a brief bump in ratings but would get killed in the Super Bowl on November 3, 2048.

Meanwhile, the Democrat lock on both houses of Congress also seemed permanent.

Next year's election in this particular case seemed equally boring on the Democrat side. Notwithstanding the smiles Phil Simons had managed to elicit from Washington's junior senator, no serious candidate had stepped forward to challenge the inevitable nomination of Vice President Elizabeth Wickes Hardy and her eventual election. With the good graces and support of outgoing President Akilah Samara and hailed as the great triumph of the LGBTQ and like-gender marriage movements, the election of Wickes Hardy was an assumed fact. Hardy's appearances in New Hampshire and swings through other primary states—with her wife, Alexis, at her side—were duly noted but raised few eyebrows except in the few remaining enclaves where fundamentalist Christianity remained a factor.

Two days after the director of the FBI's Secret Service had reassigned Mike Bardolf from the presidential unit, where he had been for three years, to head up the detail protecting the VP in light of her likely election, Bardolf received a call on the private phone whose number only one other person on the planet knew. That man had given him the phone several years ago as a means to keep open a line of discreet communication.

"Mike—it's time."

"I thought I might be hearing from you," said Bardolf.

"The VP's in town for a few days?"

"Yeah."

"We need to meet face to face. Usual place—Thursday night. I'll be there at 11:30. Take the usual precautions."

"I won't be seen."

The "usual place" was a mostly deserted parking garage in a seedy part of the capital, which Bardolf had selected when their relationship had gone underground. A bit more cloak and dagger, as if his accomplice were trying to channel Deep Throat, than the senator liked. But it had worked so far. And Bardolf was now a skilled operative who always carried a gun. The senator was never worried about his safety.

Rhodes wheeled his son's vintage Mustang into the deserted garage. He always used Bradon's old rattletrap Ford on such occasions. If it were spotted, his son's reputation provided a ready excuse for why the car was out so late.

Slowly he made his way up to the open-air top level then drove to the far corner. Not another car was to be seen.

Bardolf, without benefit of a car, was waiting.

Rhodes turned off the engine and got out.

"Senator," said Bardolf as the two colleagues—to call them friends would be stretching credibility—shook hands.

"Mike," said Rhodes. "Bit chilly for October. How long have you been waiting?"

"Not long."

"You walk up?"

"Always. Won't do to have my car seen anywhere around here. So you said it was time."

"I've been weighing many factors," said Rhodes. "I had originally planned to wait until '52. But that would put me up against an incumbent. And '56 is too far away. So I've decided to jump in and take on the VP."

"I thought you might. A bold move. She is the president's darling. They are already touting two successive double-digit terms with women in the Oval Office. They want to set a trend of permanent female leadership."

"I can handle Hardy."

"They have the demographics to make such a thing possible. You're white, Senator—a huge hurdle to overcome. Do you really want to take on President Samara, not to mention the LGBTQ lobby? Hardy is their poster girl."

"Akilah is a fool," rejoined Rhodes. "She would never have become president had she not been a woman and Viktor's granddaughter. She was the female Obama, just as out of her league as he was. Her conversion to Islam gave her a lock on it. As for Hardy, I'll take her on and whip her fat—"

He paused.

"Let me answer your question by saying, no, I am not afraid to take on the president and vice president together."

"I thought you might be thinking of a run when I saw you on the Simons interview. I'm not sure anyone will be surprised."

"Did I give away too much?"

"Probably. But you kept your cool. Your low profile since has prevented speculation. But I know you well enough to read between the lines."

"So are you with me?"

"Of course, Senator. I told you that six years ago. Nothing has changed."

"I had originally planned to bring you back onboard my staff like before."

"I'm ready."

"I'm now thinking that your appointment to Hardy's detail may be the best thing that could have happened. As long as you're with me—"

"Have no concerns about divided loyalties, Senator. Elizabeth is an airhead. How she got so far up the food chain in this town is beyond me. She is unqualified to be president as was Kamala Harris."

"When has that prevented imbeciles from getting elected?"

"True. That list would be a long one. But she is a pretty face whose 10 percent black blood allows her to play the race card along with her gender preferences. She ticks all the boxes. But yes, you can count on me."

"Then stay where you are. If there are things you learn that might help me sling some dirt—"

"That goes without saying."

"We won't use any really juicy stuff unless she begins to rack up primary wins. For now, I want to take the high ground. I'll be magnanimous, respectful, the perfect gentleman as I take her down. It will be tricky going after a lesbian. So you just have the goods on her ready to break if my position becomes precarious. My hands have to be clean."

"Of course."

"I'm more concerned about what Ward could do to me," said Rhodes.

"Hutchins? Honestly, what could he do? I know you hate the man. And actually I do have some irons in the fire hoping to take another crack at him. But the evangelical vote is so miniscule at this point, his ability to influence a national election wouldn't amount to three or four percentage points. Why bother? The Christian electorate is split—they don't care about cultural issues anymore. We've won that battle. Christians have been swallowed into the rest of the country."

"You might be right," rejoined Rhodes. "But that three or four points could be six or seven in the old Bible Belt. That could be the difference between myself and the esteemed Ms. Hardy in the primaries. If Ward was able to sow doubts about me in the South, he could swing the nomination to her. Unwittingly, Ward could be the kingmaker."

"Or queenmaker," added Bardolf dryly. "I see your point. But the Bible Belt would never support a lesbian. More likely is that Hutchins would come out against you both."

"Nevertheless, I want to take no chances. We have to take him down. If I am elected, he could be a permanent thorn in my flesh throughout my presidency. I do not want to have to deal with Ward for the rest of my life. That is your most important assignment," said Rhodes emphatically. "Deal with Ward Hutchins."

66

SOWING SEEDS OF DOUBT

LATE 2047

WHATEVER GOSSIP may have been circulating in the rumor mills of Foothills Gospel Ministries about the mysterious group that some said Pastor Forster had become involved in, along with the shifting tone apparent in his sermons, all that was forgotten in the excitement leading up to Ward Hutchins's visit to the church in early December of 2047. The highly anticipated event, at which Hutchins promised to make a major announcement, given all the more festive atmosphere by the Christmas season, had begun to attract national attention. The church would not hold nearly the crowd that was anticipated, but Hutchins was adamant that he would speak in his friend's church, not an impersonal stadium at Sac State or the Sacramento Arena or anywhere else.

Anson Roswell's friend had passed on little more than details of the event and the biographical facts of the two college friends. Mike Bardolf made sure all the former rumors resurfaced in the media build-up to the event but was hoping for more.

"Keep digging," he told Anson. "None of these guys are clean. Find me something."

A week before Thanksgiving, Anson telephoned his Palladium colleague.

"I may have something," he said. "I told Lionel I would attend the meeting if he could get me a seat. He's sure I'll fall under Hutchins's spell. He happened to drop in passing a tidbit about the church's pastor."

"Yeah—Forster, the college friend. I've got a full dossier on him."

"My guy said his mother is in a lady's group in the church and is tight with Forster's wife. He said the pastor and his wife belong to some group no one knows anything about—like a secret club or something. My friend's mother asked the pastor's wife about it, and she became evasive. He says some people in the church suspect the pastor and his wife of being involved in some offbeat goings-on?"

"Like what—right-wing militia stuff, hoarding guns, what?"

"No idea. But there's talk. This guy Forster has secrets."

"Interesting. Secrets are always good—skeletons in the closet. Keep on it. I'll have plenty of my own people on hand too."

"There won't be seats."

"How are they deciding who gets in? Your guy ought to know that."

"I'll ask him."

"Pews for sale to the highest bidder," said Bardolf. "That would make an interesting angle—Salvation for Sale—Tickets to Heaven Only $50. But I'm not talking about getting people inside. We'll have cameras and microphones blanketing the place. Like the Hillsgrove strategy. I'll get Stewart there again. That will insure publicity. The mystery group angle is good—what is your pastor hiding sort of thing."

"You are devious!" said Anson.

"It's how the game is played. I don't suppose you've heard anything about the announcement Hutchins says he's going to make?"

"In my circles the scuttlebutt is that he's planning to announce a run for the Republican nomination."

"That would be big news. A little late to get into the primaries though."

"They say he might mount a write-in campaign."

"That never works. But Hutchins is popular, and old Waters is about as dull as a candidate could be. Hutchins might pull it off at that. But my primary political contact—"

"The VP?" queried Roswell.

"Someone even more reliable. He says Hutchins will never run for office."

With the primary season gathering momentum and the Iowa and New Hampshire contests looming, Thanksgiving came and went, and Ward Hutchins's California appearance approached. As it descended on Sacramento, the media predictably rehashed all the former stories of sexual indiscretions and financial improprieties.

Mike Bardolf had also been successful in leaking innuendos about Foothills pastor Mark Forster, an unknown to the national media but whose shadowy past with Hutchins in college—as the Bardolf/Roswell team managed to spin the narrative—was shrouded in mystery.

Hints were spread of a secret organization to which both belonged, whose activities were so dark that not even their closest friends knew what really went on. No one actually accused the two evangelical pastors of satanic rituals and seances. But it could not be denied that there were many unanswered questions. The origins of such innuendos were themselves cloaked by so many layers that no one in the media imagined their source to be none other than Vice President Hardy's personal Secret Service agent, then crisscrossing New Hampshire on the opposite side of the country in two feet of snow and fed through the media pipeline by the Palladium network.

Bardolf had done his work with devilish ingenuity. Intrusive journalists shoved microphones in the faces of the hundreds pouring into the 8,000-seat capacity Foothills sanctuary for a two-hour pre-arrival concert by the popular rock band Heaven's Glory. The questions were forceful, persistent, and disturbing.

"What is your pastor hiding?"

"Is Ward Hutchins a sexual predator?"

"What is the secret society your pastor and Ward Hutchins belong to?"

"How much will Ward Hutchins take home from tonight's collection plate?"

"Does your church conduct seances?"

"Was your pastor involved in satanic rituals in college?"

"Is your pastor involved in an affair."

These and a dozen more disgustingly suggestive questions were hurled rudely at those moving toward the church. They were not intended to be answered, only to sow doubts.

Where he watched from the East Coast, Todd Stewart cringed at the questions thrown at the unsuspecting crowd. He knew there was nothing to the allegations and was glad Senator Rhodes had specifically requested him for an event in the capital. Otherwise Bardolf would have had him there in person to sully the reputation of what were probably two honorable men.

He was beginning to hate this business.

67

EXTRAVAGANT ARRIVAL

DECEMBER 6, 2047

LATE ON the afternoon of December 6, the highly anticipated moment arrived. Comparisons with Billy Graham notwithstanding, Ward Hutchins was a man of the new millennium in which image was everything. He was not one to let an opportunity pass. If it meant thrusting himself into the limelight for the gospel's sake, he would do it. He had become the face of Christianity in not merely a post-Christian world but a hostile and anti-Christian world. He needed to put himself out on the front lines, showing the world that Christianity was not dead, that Christians had courage to stand against the world's tide, and that they were not opposed to a little good old-fashioned showmanship.

Landing by private jet at the Sacramento airport, his brief helicopter flight to Roseville north of the city was filmed by hundreds of cameras, while spotlights brought in for the occasion zeroed in on the chopper coming through the dusk toward the gigantic parking lot of Foothills Gospel Ministries.

Settling slowly to earth, ablaze in light, Ward's arrival held all the spectacle if not of the Second Coming, given the season, certainly the arrival of Santa Claus at nearby Galleria Mall. The suggestion of a joint appearance of Santa welcoming Ward as his helicopter touched down had been floated by some of the more visionary elders of Foothills.

Pastor Forster flatly refused. Having already conceded in the matter of the preliminary concert, Mark was in no mood for compromise. They could have Ward or Santa. Not both. He was willing to call

Ward and cancel his appearance on the spot in the middle of the meeting, which would be followed by his resignation. With two or three elders in a huff, the Santa suggestion was withdrawn.

Inwardly regretting he had invited Ward in the first place, Mark and Grace Forster, with Ginger and Craig at their side, stood in front of the roped-off crowd of at least 6,000—half made up of the exiting concertgoers following the conclusion of the entertainment thirty minutes before—as the helicopter came to a windy set-down. The blades whirred to a gradual stop as the door opened and the man of the hour stepped out.

Ward waved, smiling and ebullient, to the cheering throng. Mark slipped under the rope and ran out to meet him. The two old friends embraced warmly.

"Hello, Ward," said Mark as they stepped back. "Quite the entrance!"

Ward laughed. "Who'd have thought it, huh—back at Humboldt—us, here in the spotlight. None of our Saturday breakfast Bible studies were like this!"

"Can we walk for a minute?" said Mark, slipping his arm through Ward's, then turning and leading him away from the crowd across the pavement.

"What's on your mind?" asked Ward.

"Nothing," replied Mark. "I just wanted a few quiet seconds alone with you—haven't seen you in a while. I wanted to explain personally why I left Puget Sound. I know the church meant a lot to you. My folks—"

"No need, Mark. You explained yourself in the letter you sent. I'm happy for you."

"Thank you, Ward. But I've felt unsettled about it. I know the Seattle church was your baby. You left it in my hands, and—"

"Hey, my friend. Your parents are your primary responsibility at this stage of life. You had an opportunity, just like I did. I am truly happy for your success here, as well as the chance to be near your mom and dad. Who can put a price tag on that? You did the right thing. You have my blessing!"

"Thank you, Ward. That means a lot coming from you. You've been my pastoral mentor—your opinion matters to me. What about you—any regrets?"

"Are you kidding! I'm the luckiest guy in the world as the man said. God is using me to reach people—at least I pray he is. We have both been blessed to accomplish some things for him."

"I'm glad you feel that way. I appreciate your coming."

"Anything for an old friend."

"My people here can't believe we used to be roommates. They think you're a saint."

"And you're telling them just the opposite, right!"

"I'm not in the bubble-bursting business!" laughed Mark.

"All I will say is that God has been good to me."

"And your surprise announcement?"

"Ah, you may be one of my best friends. But you have to wait along with everyone else."

Mark laughed again. "Then we had better get back and not keep your fans waiting."

They turned and returned, still arm in arm, then separated as Ward greeted Grace, Ginger, and Craig.

"Hello, Grace," said Ward with an affectionate embrace. "Great to see you again."

"And you, Ward."

"I thought maybe you would be piloting my helicopter."

Grace laughed. "If you'd wanted a Cessna, maybe," she said. "But a helicopter is above my pay grade!"

Their security detail led them under the rope and through the throng toward the church.

In his hotel room in Peterborough, New Hampshire, Mike Bardolf grinned proudly at the photographs that had just been transmitted to him from Ward Hutchins's arrival, as well as the transcripts from some of the interviews that would be aired on local California television stations for that night's ten o'clock news.

He took a long swallow of whiskey. "We can use this!" he said to himself. "This should take him down for sure—the proverbial smoking gun!"

It wasn't often that Mike Bardolf allowed himself to celebrate victory prematurely. But this was one of those times.

They had him nailed to the cross!

68

Two Announcements

THE MAN who thought of himself—erroneously, though he did not know it—as Mike Bardolf's boss wasn't feeling so optimistic. He too had seen the telecast and had read the morning's news stories. Not a word about the rumors and allegations. Only Ward's triumphant arrival and his rousing Christmas sermon, which many were hailing as one of his landmark speeches that had the Christian world abuzz. He was more popular than ever.

What did they have to do? thought Senator Jefferson Rhodes. Did nothing stick to his old nemesis!

Then there was his press conference this morning at which Ward had promised to make his supposed "great announcement" before flying from Sacramento to Mexico City for a huge Christmas celebration lasting several days. He would be speaking before crowds estimated to be enormous.

Christianity was supposed to have died out years ago. What was going on!

He had planned his own announcement for noon on the same day to coincide with Vice President Hardy's campaign rally in Peterborough. He had hoped to steal the spotlight from her.

Now it appeared Ward might steal it from him!

He had initially skipped both New Hampshire and Iowa, hoping to make a bigger splash by coming in as a late entry. It would all be for naught if they couldn't muzzle Ward.

At noon eastern, Senator Jefferson Rhodes took his place on the steps of the US Capitol building, the white rotunda gleaming in the light of a cold December sun as backdrop, a bank of microphones in front of him. Several hundred members of the press corps were spread out behind them.

"Ladies, gentlemen, and others," he began, "thank you for coming. I have a few remarks—"

Three thousand miles away, on the tarmac of Sacramento International Airport, with a private jet waiting in readiness, Rev. Ward Hutchins stood before a considerably smaller crowd, but one which likewise contained reporters from two dozen local television stations and all the major networks.

The timing coincidence of 9:00 a.m. and 12:00 with the Rhodes press briefing at the capital on the opposite side of the country was just that—a coincidence. Neither man had known the other's plans. Yet the perfect concurrence of fate—or destiny if one was so inclined to interpret it—contained such exquisite irony that it almost seemed foreordained.

Though having no idea what was coming, Mark Forster had reluctantly agreed to introduce Ward and stand beside him for the press conference.

"As you know," Senator Rhodes was saying, "during my years in the senate, it has been my privilege to work for the people of America. That commitment will continue as . . ."

In Sacramento, Ward Hutchins had finished thanking his friend, Mark, for his introduction—a little too brief by Ward's estimation. "I thank the good people of the Sacramento area and all California for their warm welcome," Ward went on. "Though my time here has been all too short, I have felt your love and will always consider myself part Californian. Before I leave you, I want to make two brief announcements that I think will be of interest to you and . . ."

"As I say," continued Senator Rhodes on the Capitol steps, "my commitment to this country has never been stronger, which is why today . . ."

"In my hand here," said Ward, pulling an envelope from inside his coat pocket and holding it up, "I have a brief letter addressed to my longtime friend, Mark Forster, your own Californian favorite son, inviting him to join my team as full-time Bible teacher, evangelist, and coordinator for the Ward Hutchins Evangelistic Crusade team."

He glanced to Mark at his side and threw an expansive arm around his shoulders. In obvious shock, Mark stood dumbfounded.

"As you can see, he is speechless!" laughed Ward. "I'm sure he will make a public announcement himself, after he has the chance to speak with his lovely wife, Grace, and make plans with the leaders of his church for a replacement."

★ ★ ★

". . . I am announcing my candidacy for the Democrat nomination for the presidency of the United States."

The crowd of DC reporters burst into raucous shouts. Whether his voice could be heard above the others was doubtful. But Senator Rhodes knew that one young man's popularity, not to mention that his crop of blond hair stood two to three inches higher than most of the men around him, would insure his being seen on tonight's news.

"Yes, Todd," he said.

"It hardly seems coincidental," began Todd, "that Vice President Hardy is at this moment speaking in Peterborough, New Hampshire. Did you schedule this press conference at this particular time to upstage her?"

The senator laughed. "You should know better than that, Todd," he said. "The timing for my announcement was set some time ago after I decided to throw my hat in the ring. To be honest, this is the first I've heard of Elizabeth's event—she's in Peterborough, you say?"

"As everyone in Washington knows, Senator," laughed Stewart. "But taking on a sitting vice president from your own party seems a bold move. Is there bad blood between you and the present administration?"

"Not at all. I have the greatest respect and admiration for President Samara and Vice President Hardy. Decisions such as these, Todd, are deeply personal, often having little or nothing to do with the personalities involved. It is simply that I consider it time for fresh blood in the Presidential Manor."

"In the meantime, my second announcement is this," continued Ward. "In the coming months leading up to next year's presidential election, I will be writing a series of articles that will be released through the national media and will be free for all to read. These will outline the basic tenets of biblical prophecy as it relates to the second coming of Jesus Christ and what the Bible calls the great tribulation."

Ward paused briefly to allow his words to have their intended impact.

"The articles will not be copyrighted," he added, "nor will I receive a penny from them. As the Spirit of God gives me wisdom, discernment, and insight into the Word of God and our times, it is my hope, prayer, and intent that these articles will culminate on or around the time of the election."

"Have you kept abreast," shouted out Rachel Maxwell from CNN, "of what your friend Ward Hutchins has been saying?"

A shot of adrenalin surged through Jeff Rhodes's frame. An expletive of fury nearly burst from his mouth. Controlling himself, he forced a laugh.

"I don't spend my time following Ward's antics these days," he replied. "He was once my friend but is now a buffoon and fanatic. I am sorry to have to say it, but to hold such outdated and disproven views—there is simply no excuse for it. The national discourse left people like Ward Hutchins behind decades ago."

The senator spun and walked up the steps of the Capitol building, reporters running after him shouting more questions. He did not stop until safely inside the Senate lounge, incensed that in the moment the eyes of the whole country should have been on him, whose name should come up but Ward's!

He was trembling with rage as he quickly downed a stiff belt and sat trying to calm himself.

Meanwhile in Sacramento, the man at the center of the new candidate's wrath was about to make a headline even more incredible than that of his politician friend.

"If the Lord leads and gives me the insight into events and the Scriptures I am praying for," Ward went on after a brief pause, "I am hopeful and expectant that my articles will culminate approximately a year from now with my being able—with the Lord's help—to name the potential identity of the antichrist, who is even now, I believe, in our midst as a figure of rising reputation on the international stage."

69

REACTION

REACTION TO Ward Hutchins's startling announcement was swift. The national media lampooned him as a clown. Mike Bardolf laughed every time the video clip of the moment replayed itself in his mind. No other factor mattered now. The fool had completely destroyed his credibility.

The evangelical world, however, ever eager to embrace some new prophetic scenario, was instantly injected with new life. Ward's television and weekly radio program ratings went through the roof. If he had been a star before, he was a mega-star now. Even the liberal news outlets began vying for rights to be the first to make his series of prophetic articles public, offering him nosebleed sums of money.

Had he incorporated his articles into a book, he could have named his price and publishers would have lined up at his door to pay it. But he stuck to his guns. He would not profit a penny from his revelations. He would publish them on his own blog. After that they were free for the taking.

As to the identity of the mystery antichrist—about which even the liberal media had to run a few stories to educate the public on Christian second-coming terminology—speculation ran rampant. Journalists from around the world clamored for an interview.

Did he have a list of potential candidates?

Was it a long list or a short list?

Was the antichrist an American?

Was he a politician or religious figure?

To these and a hundred other questions, Ward would divulge nothing.

"I honestly know no more than I have said," he repeated over and over. "There is no list. I am not speculating. I await God's revelation. I have no agenda but to open my heart and mind to the leading of the Holy Spirit. If I sense no leading from God, I will say nothing. If he has no revelation for me to make, then I will make none. Above all I must emphasize that I said the *potential* antichrist. I will be no more definite than that."

The news outlets were as stymied by what was meant by "the leading of the Holy Spirit" as they were by the meaning of the strange term *antichrist*, eventually his apparent sincerity won the day, and most Christians believed him. The rest of the country, however, considered him a kook. An honest one, perhaps, but a kook nonetheless. They awaited events with interest, and Ward continued to appear on news programs from the major outlets. Mostly, however, for the comedic value.

Within a week Las Vegas oddsmakers had begun compiling a list, posting opening odds. Betting was brisk. The list of names grew exponentially as bookies saw a chance to cash in.

NBC began running a weekly "Antichrist Watch" sixty-second segment every Friday, which gave the current odds of the top twenty contenders and other betting details. CBS countered with a Thursday evening spot called the "Hutchins Circus," which was usually highlighted by more laughter from the reporters hosting it than fresh news.

☆ ☆ ☆

"What are you going to do about Mr. Hutchins's offer, Dad?" asked Craig one morning at breakfast.

"Yes, dear," added Grace. "You've been uncommonly quiet for the past two weeks. No one at church is talking about anything else."

"Do the two of you really need to ask," replied Mark sardonically.

"I don't suppose we do," rejoined Grace. "Maybe I just want to hear you say it."

"Fair enough," nodded Mark. "All right, then—obviously no, I'm not going to join Ward's team. If it was a serious possibility, I would have talked to you three, and we would have discussed it as a family. Still, Ward is one of my best friends, and I felt he deserved my respect enough for me to at least pray about it—for a week or two. But God would have had to move mountains for me to accept. However, I am happy to report that the mountains remained firmly in place. I wrote Ward last night turning down his offer. I will send the letter today—by snail mail. I want him to see it in my own handwriting."

"And the other thing?" asked Craig.

"What other thing? asked Mark.

"The antichrist announcement."

Mark sighed. "I hardly know what to make of it. It is so outlandish, so contrary to Scripture, I still cannot believe Ward's presumption. It's as brazen as LaHarr's prediction that the Lord would return before 2025. I hate to say it, but as much as I love Ward, on this one I think he's gone off the rails. This puts him up there with all the prophetic writers of the last century. I'm still stunned by it."

"People at church are excited," said Ginger.

"The kids in the youth group are talking about it," added Craig.

"I'm asked every day if I know when Ward's first article is coming out," said Grace. "I have had at least a dozen calls asking, you and Ward being friends, if I know who the antichrist is!"

Mark shook his head in annoyance and frustration.

"If I announced a new sermon series on Revelation, after Ward's visit, the church would be filled to overflowing. As it is, I try to speak earnestly and personally about the commands of the Bible, and they fall asleep in the pews. Sometimes I wonder how long I can continue."

He paused and chuckled lightly. "Come to think of it, that is actually an interesting idea. Maybe I should do a series on prophecy," he said. "That would knock their socks off—though it would be like no prophecy they've ever heard."

"You should, Daddy!" exclaimed Ginger.

"Do you want to see your father unemployed?"

"What do you mean?"

"The moment I began preaching some of my own perspectives about the Church in prophecy, I think the elders would request my resignation forthwith."

70

CHRISTMAS

DECEMBER 25, 2047

TIMOTHY AND Jaylene invited Timothy's four siblings for Thanksgiving and Christmas every year when they were planning no trips to visit Jaylene's relatives. To their amazement, as the year 2047 wound to an end, all four accepted their invitation for Christmas. It would be the first full family reunion for years. David Gordon spent most holidays either with them or with Robert and Laura Forster. As the Forsters would be out of town with Mark and Grace and their family, reluctant as he was to intrude on the family gathering, David nevertheless consented to Timothy and Jaylene's entreaties to spend Christmas day with the five Marshalls and their families.

Woody and his wife, Cheryl, drove up from San Luis Obispo and stayed with Timothy and Jaylene. Jane and Wade Durant flew in from Houston on the twenty-third and spent four nights with Cateline and her husband, Clancy, in Marysville. Graham and his wife, Lynn, drove up early Christmas morning from Sunnyvale and stayed over, also with Timothy and Jaylene.

Six of Stirling and Larke's eight grandchildren by then had families of their own. Only Heather and her best friend and cousin Robyn, Cateline's unmarried daughter, were present from their generation of Marshalls.

The few days together at Timothy and Jaylene's in Roseville rekindled the five-way relationships of Stirling and Larke's children such as they had not experienced since their junior high and high school years. There was much laughter, fond recollections, favorite card games, a few practical jokes, and several opportunities for Jane and Timothy getting good-naturedly back at Woody and Cateline for some of the older brother and sister pranks they had perpetrated on the two youngest of the family.

The excitement around the Christmas tree on Christmas morning after Graham and Lynn arrived about 10:00, adding their carload of wrapped packages to the mix, could not have been more exuberant had they all still been ten-year-olds.

They did not draw names for gifts. All five seemed eager to make up for the years by going all out for each other. The result was a veritable cornucopia of gift giving between the thirteen. Along with gag presents, there were some exquisite gifts where money had obviously been no object.

The next two hours were filled with more fun, laughter, and tender moments of gratitude than they would have imagined possible.

Timothy's eyes filled when he opened a framed eight-by-ten photograph of himself, in full laughter at eight or nine on his father's shoulders hanging on for dear life as his father ran across the lawn of their Santa Barbara home.

"Thank you, Jane," he said in a husky voice. "I don't remember ever seeing this before."

"I don't know why it was with my keepsakes," replied his sister. "I only stumbled across it a year ago. I knew how much it would mean to you."

"I will treasure it. I can't thank you enough."

By 1:00 the turkey in the oven was filling the house with the aroma of Christmas. The five wives were busy in the kitchen and dining room, gabbing away, while the brothers, brothers-in-law, and David were sitting in front of the television shouting encouragement to the Packers in respect of Wade's antipathy for the Cowboys.

Around the dinner table at 5:00, Timothy took the opportunity to explain in more detail about the ongoing correspondence in which they continued to be engaged with readers who wrote in response to their father's writings.

He mentioned again their quarterly meetings with those who had benefited from their father's books, adding that they would all be welcome and his hope that they might want to join them.

The two photographs taken by Heather of the five brothers and sisters, beaming and with arms around one another, and of the ten with husbands and wives all together—which she later framed and sent to her aunts and uncles and presented to her parents—turned out to be the most treasured memory-gift of all.

Surely Stirling and Larke were watching with eyes full of whatever tears of joy were possible in heaven.

Mark, Grace, Ginger, and Craig Forster spent Christmas with Grace's parents in Eureka on California's north coast. To their delight, Mark's parents, Robert and Laura, accompanied them on the drive up through the redwoods to Grace's hometown. They spent four days with the Thorntons, delighting in taking Ginger and Craig around to the places of their college years, showing them where they had both lived as students, as well as to all the special haunts of the north coast they knew so well—from Patrick's Point to Eureka's Old Town and Garberville and the Avenue of the Giants.

Christmas eve was festive and lively. Grace and her mother took turns on the piano for an evening of carols, with spicy apple cider, hot vanilla, and an assortment of Christmas cookies Grace's mother had been baking for a week. Even usually taciturn old Robert Forster let his hair down for the evening with a dramatized reading of *The Night Before Christmas* that held everyone spellbound.

"I haven't heard you do that since Janet and Gayle and I were kids, Dad," said Mark. "That was a treat! You need to do that for their families sometime too."

Christmas day at the Thornton home was all about Ginger and Craig. Never had they had such a haul, as Craig so indelicately put it. With two parents and four grandparents doing their best to spoil them, it was indeed a Christmas for the two teens to remember as the bonanza of all Christmases.

By the end of the day, the hearts of the three mothers were full to overflowing to see the love spreading out in so many directions within their two families. Midway through the afternoon, as the two grand-fathers left the house and walked slowly along the sidewalk talking between themselves, the three women stood at the kitchen window watching in contented silence.

Though it was too cold for much beach activity, the sky was blue, and the predicted storm heading their way from the Gulf of Alaska held off. On the day after Christmas, the Forster and Thornton parents went to lunch together in Eureka's Old Town then walked along the harbor and browsed through several antique shops. Mark and Grace drove north with Ginger and Craig to Trinidad.

"We used to attend Easter sunrise services up there when we were in college," said Grace, pointing to the top of the huge outcropping from the town called Trinidad Head.

"You should see it from the air," Mark said. "The first time your mom took me up, we flew from Eureka up the coast to here. I was terrified."

"You should have seen him!" laughed Grace. "He held on so tight and kept his eyes closed when we took off."

"Really, Dad?" said Craig. "You were afraid?"

"I'd never been up in such a tiny plane. When we banked to turn around over Trinidad Head there, I thought I was going to fall out! But I got used to it. After that, I couldn't wait for your mom to take me flying."

They left Trinidad and drove by the old coastal road then down to Moonstone Beach.

"I used to run races along here," said Mark. "Your mom came to watch occasionally. But she mostly came to see one of my teammates she had a crush on."

"Mark! I did not!" laughed Grace.

"You told me you liked Shaun."

"Sort of. But only until I met you."

"Shaun who, Mom?" said Ginger excitedly. "I want to hear about it!"

"It's nothing, Ginger," said Grace, still laughing. "Now look what you've done, Mark. Honestly!"

She turned again to Ginger. "Your father swept me off my feet the moment I saw him. End of story."

"Is that true, Dad?" said Craig.

"What can I say!" grinned Mark.

Linda and Cameron Trent, with Sawyer and his wife, Inga, celebrated the holiday with Eloise Hutchins in Seattle. Surprising everyone, their father Truman accepted his former wife's invitation to Christmas dinner. The two were not only cordial to each other but laughed and reminisced happily, leaving Linda and Sawyer looking at each other wondering if some of the old spark still lingered.

They had arranged a video call with Ward in Mexico City. The result was like a Hutchins family reunion. After the call, however, Linda and Sawyer could not help getting the giggles about Ward's plan to name the antichrist. Only too late did they realize that making sport of their brother raised tears in their mother's eyes.

"I'm sorry, Mom," said Linda. "I didn't mean anything by it. I love Ward, you know that. I apologize."

"Thank you, dear. I understand. Ward's outspoken ideas aren't for everyone. I don't even know if I agree with all his prophecy talk. But I respect him for standing up for Jesus."

"I understand."

"I'm sorry, too, Mom," said Sawyer.

The six crammed into Sawyer's car just after dark and went for a drive north into the city and to Westlake Center. They walked to the brightly lit Christmas tree, which Sawyer and Linda remembered from their younger years, then returned to the car and loaded up again, this time for a drive up Queen Anne Hill. They stopped at Kerry Park, climbed out, and set out walking in the cold night air. The storm was expected the next day, possibly bringing snow. For now, they were able to enjoy the festively lit city skyline under a clear starlit sky. Linda and Sawyer and their spouses wandered away, not by intent, until they realized they had left their mother and father behind.

They turned back to rejoin them. Linda touched Sawyer's arm to stop him. They stood for several moments silently watching. Eloise and Truman were standing with their backs to the others, gazing toward the city hand in hand.

Linda leaned her head against Sawyer's side. He put his arm around her shoulder. It was a sight neither of them ever expected to see.

They returned to the house for eggnog and a quiet peaceful evening together.

As he was leaving, Mr. Hutchins paused at the open door and turned.

"Thank you for inviting me, Eloise," he said. "This has been one of the happiest days I've had in a long time. And you haven't lost your touch with the dressing and mince pie! How it took me back!"

"Thank you. The way to a man's heart, you know."

"There must be something to it. You snagged me all those years ago!"

He paused and a wistful look came into Truman Hutchins's eyes.

"Would you, uh . . . would you like to get together again sometime—maybe for lunch or a walk in Discovery Park?"

"I would like that, Truman."

"I'll call you, then."

She closed the door behind him, wiping at her eyes before turning back inside to rejoin the others.

Three or four miles away across the water, at the Rhodes estate on Bainbridge Island, looking across Puget Sound at the Space Needle, father and son stood together on the deck that stretched out on the Seattle side of the house, drinks in hand, waiting for Sandra and Marcia to announce that final dinner preparations were complete.

"A year from now, Jeff my boy," said Harrison Rhodes, "you will be president-elect. "What say we rent the Space Needle for the victory party?"

"Only you could think of something so grandiose, Dad!" laughed Jeff.

"I mean it. This will be our crowning moment."

He turned to his son then lifted his glass.

"A toast," he said, "to my son, the next president of the United States."

71

NEFARIOUS INNUENDO

EARLY 2048

THE ELECTION year of 2048 opened with Vice President Elizabeth Wickes Hardy leading in delegate count and popular vote by a wide margin, having run unopposed in the first three contests. But the polls among registered Democrats showed her trailing newcomer Senator Rhodes by a point, which widened through January and February. By March, the delegate count was a tossup, with the senator leading the VP in most polls by six to seven percentage points.

Ward Hutchins, however, continued to be a fly in the senator's ointment, speaking out against the policies of both candidates. His continued high profile ensured that he was central to the political discussion, with the potential to decide the primary of the party he vehemently opposed. His ties to Jefferson Rhodes were impossible for the media to ignore. The candidate was regularly asked about Reverend Hutchins's prophetic articles and if he held any store in them. Rhodes laughed off the questions, yet inwardly fumed that eventually his association with Ward could well prove his fatal undoing.

Rhodes was also asked about his and VP Hardy's relative standings in what was now called the Antichrist Sweepstakes—which had opened in January with Rhodes in 27th place at 11,000 to 1, and the vice president in 35th at 13,500 to 1. In the months since, both had risen in the rankings, the VP now in 13th with the senator trailing at 21st.

Asked if the rumors that outgoing President Samara had encouraged her vice president to convert to Islam in order to enhance her chances of being named the antichrist, Rhodes wisely offered no comment. The entire Hutchins factor was difficult to know how to handle. Being high on the antichrist list would probably help with cynical secularists, if for no other reason than to elect the candidate most reviled by Christians. On the other hand, in the Bible Belt, the anti-antichrist vote could turn it the other way.

What the effect would be in the age of non-gender, no one could predict. But at last, judging the time right to inflict a mortal blow on Ward Hutchins and put the senator's angst about his old friend to rest once and for all, Mike Bardolf arranged to leak a blockbuster story to all the news outlets, giving it first to the *New York Times* a day in advance, with the ironclad agreement that they agree to run it on the front page of their print edition, and with photos. It would hit the newsstands at the precise moment Bardolf emailed the full files to all the networks.

The headline in the *Times* read:

Gay connection between Hutchins and college roommate.

Photos of their Sacramento embrace and walking away from the camera arm in arm took half the space above the fold of the *Times*.

Of course with a same-gender-married lesbian running for president, the secular world could have cared less. The most conservative pockets of the evangelical world, however, were rocked. Ward Hutchins's reputation took a major pounding, with the readership of his next article less than half the preceding three. A telephone call with Mark convinced him to meet the onslaught of negative press differently than he had all the accusations hurled at him up to that point.

"Ward," said Mark seriously, "say nothing. Not a word. Do not deny it."

"Are you kidding? We have to deny it."

"No, we don't, Ward. The Lord is our advocate. The stronger the denial, the more people believe it."

"You are not going to make a public rebuttal."

"I will not say a word. I urge you to do the same. Believe me, Ward, silence is the best defense. Remember Jesus at his trial."

Ward thought a minute.

"It goes against the grain, Mark."

"It does. It is one of the hardest things a man can be called upon to do—meet false accusations without defending oneself. But it is the only way. I'm asking you to try it my way. Silence is the best defense."

Ward reluctantly agreed. Neither man nor their wives nor anyone associated with them issued a response or made any comment whatever. Gradually Ward's readership recovered.

Few at Foothills believed a word of it. Not a whisper about the allegations was spoken, but Mark's friends and wife and son and daughter ached for him. As Mike Bardolf knew, the suggestion is enough to tarnish a man's reputation for life. Mark would always carry the invisible pain of wondering if even a single person might have believed it and their faith stumbled as a result.

A serious talk with David followed.

"You can expect more of the same, my friend," said David seriously. "Those who set themselves to stand against the world's depravity, whether publicly like your friend, Mr. Hutchins, or privately and seemingly invisibly, will increasingly be targets in the days ahead. You may face worse than this. A season of trial is coming. The remnant will be in the crosshairs."

Mark continued subdued. Much remained on his mind as a result of his lengthy talks with David about the Church and the end times. His own future in a church whose priorities and outlook he no longer shared occupied a predominant role in his prayers.

72

∧ Birthing Grows

FEBRUARY 2048

When Timothy Marshall arrived home from the university one day in February when Jaylene had had no classes, her enthusiasm was not hard to notice.

"You look like you've had a good day away from school!" laughed Timothy.

"You know how we occasionally mention the GCG meetings to the people who write?"

Timothy nodded.

"And invite them to visit if they ever happen to be in California?"

"But they rarely do!" laughed Timothy, "—except for Matthew and Sarah from Idaho."

"Well that may be about to change," rejoined Jaylene.

"How so?"

"I received several letters just today asking when the next gathering was planned."

"Really!"

"One was actually from Sarah. And Violet Langdon telephoned from New York. We had such a nice visit. As we were saying goodbye, I happened to mention it. She perked up and said maybe they could come too."

"That would be great!"

"It can't be a coincidence. It's a sign, Timothy. I think God is preparing to expand your father's vision. It crossed my mind as I was thinking about it that the time might even be approaching to share your father's *Brief* with a few select people. Matthew and Sarah were the first people I thought of, and Pearl and DeWitt. And of course there is Mark and Grace to think of."

Timothy took in her words thoughtfully.

"Not to the whole group—I don't mean that," Jaylene added. "We would have to pray very hard about such a step. Maybe it would be only one or two or three couples—I don't know. But the thought crossed my mind."

"You're right. Something is stirring. It's obvious that as God births his remnant, it will happen organically in many places simultaneously, arising in diverse ways. What we are part of is only a tiny part of a whole. We will never see but portions of it. Many of the people we've written to have started their own groups. I have the feeling there are thousands of small fellowships springing up for similar reasons—coming out from among them to be vibrantly and separately alive in fellowship with the brethren. Maybe a new season is dawning for our little segment of that birthing too. We need to talk to David and Heather."

It fell silent a moment. Jaylene's expression became serious.

"I had another thought today," she said at length. "I've also been thinking about your brothers and sisters. I know we see them periodically, and I realize they know generally what we are doing. But should we make a stronger effort to bring them more fully into it? They're part of your father's legacy. Our Heather shouldn't be the only one of the next generation to know what that legacy represents."

"I don't think my brothers and sisters want to be involved."

"That may be true. If so, that's their choice."

"I do want them involved, don't get me wrong," said Timothy. "You heard what I shared at Christmas."

"The unity between you all was heartwarming."

"I loved it. But none of the four have asked more about what I shared since. I've broached the subject with all of them through the years. Thus far they haven't seemed interested. Dad's spiritual vision hasn't meant the same to them as it has to you and me and Heather. I don't understand it."

"You're different, Timothy."

"I shouldn't be. Everyone ought to revere their parents. What Dad said about sharing his *Brief* with them only when the time is right is a burden on me, his realization that they hadn't made his life's vision their own. I'm sure that was sad for him."

"Maybe it's time to reassess that. We're all getting older, Tim. I think maybe you need to leave what they do about it in their hands. You don't want them saying to you some day, 'Why didn't you tell us? We had a right to know.'"

Timothy nodded. "That's a hard question—did they have a right to know, in a sense, against what Dad himself wanted? We have honored Dad's words for fifteen years. He left the decision in our hands. Maybe now it's time to leave that decision in their hands."

"Why don't we specifically invite them to come to the next gathering in April. We'll tell them that we really want them to come."

"I like it!" said Timothy enthusiastically. "I will write and begin badgering them immediately."

"For your brothers and sisters to participate and see what God is doing through their father's writings would be wonderful."

"That's my father's vision of the Church."

"If it turns out that today's mail and the call from Violet aren't just flukes, there may be too many to meet at Heather's."

"I'm sure David would love to host the next GCG at his ranch."

"That would be fun, especially if the weather is nice. People from church will be bound to hear about it. Somehow rumors continue to circulate."

"We'll have to be careful to do nothing to hurt Mark's ministry. He's walking a delicate tightrope between the group and his ministry. Along with David, we need to talk to Mark and Grace before deciding anything."

"And the *Brief*?" asked Jaylene.

"That's another big question," said Timothy thoughtfully. "Dad would be the first to say—he did say—that we must be cautious. I don't think the passage of time has changed that underlying injunction."

"Nor do I."

"It is not my dad's message, but God's. He has to make the next step known. Yet I see the possibility that God may want to use this gradual heightening of interest to reveal the next step. It may indeed be time that more are intended to read it. I'm sure God is raising up many men and women like my father. There may be other so-called *Benedict Briefs* being written around the world even now. My father is but one whose writings are intended for the Church of the future."

73

PERSONAL ASSESSMENT

MARCH 2048

FOLLOWING PRESIDENT Samara's final State of the Union address, the annual Presidential Manor's Correspondent's Dinner in March of 2048 promised to be even more a superficial praise-fest than the usual syrupy fawning over the Democrat commander-in-chief.

It was becoming obvious by now, however, that the president's VP and her personal choice for a successor had a stiffer battle on her hands than either had anticipated. President Samara's partisan speech in support of her VP was an obvious snub toward Senator Rhodes. The press, generally favorable toward Hardy, was nevertheless not opposed to a good old political brawl, knowing that at the end of the day another Democrat would sit in the Oval Office. Every journalist had his or her favorites, but they didn't much care which Democrat came out on top in the end. VP Hardy had been around a long time and did not light everyone's fire. Though no self-respecting progressive would come within a mile of actually saying that her marriage to Alexis Hix and their flamboyant public displays of affection bordered on the kinky. They would admit no more than that new blood in politics always made things more interesting.

Todd Stewart sat listening to speaker after speaker drone on. It was the same partisan palaver he had heard so many times before.

He was getting tired of it. Did such a thing as objective journalism exist anymore?

Where was the objectivity in this world he was part of, the balance, holding Democrats accountable, not just praising everything they did while bashing everything the Republicans did?

He knew this was supposed to be an evening for fun. But these speeches were absurd. The daily press briefings were no different—the Democrats could do no wrong, the Republicans could do no right.

Who was he to talk? He was a cog in the same giant machine. He parroted the company line night after night on the news and lobbed the same meaningless softballs to the president or her press secretary. It had been out of his mouth at Hillsgrove that the accusations against Ward Hutchins had been broadcast to the country. He knew they were lies. Yet he had dished them out to the country on a silver platter.

Was it possible, as conservatives had been saying for years, that the media was nothing more than a propaganda arm for the Democrat party? Had Bernie Goldberg been right?

Had Trump been right all those years ago to call it fake news?

He had grown up immersed in a culture that hated the former president, routinely placing him at the top of the worst presidents list. Even after a quarter century, Trump hatred still fueled left-wing passion.

All the way back in his university days, he had read Tom Woodstein's final book before his death: *Donald Trump: An Accounting, An Assessment*. From being a lifetime liberal and Nixon and Trump hater, Woodstein had shocked the nation by recounting the personal story underlying his writing of the book on Trump.

The result was a complete reversal and change of perspective, not only about Trump—whom he concluded was one of the three most effective presidents since Lincoln, along with FDR and Ronald Reagan—but of the framework that had informed his political outlook for his entire journalistic career.

In his afterword, the famous journalist had candidly admitted his lifelong bias. The words jolted Todd with such force that they had been rattling around in his subconscious for more than a dozen years.

"All my life," Woodstein wrote, "I have been a partisan Democrat, a fact which colored my writing and was foundational to the presuppositions undergirding all my books. I was not, until very recently, capable of recognizing that intense partisanship is poison to journalistic integrity. I flattered myself that I could be partisan and objective. It has taken me a lifetime to recognize the fallacy of that assumption.

"Watergate was the personal watershed of my career. It planted an endemic suspicion, even hatred, of the conservative right and of Republicans in general as the enemies of truth, justice, progress, freedom, and every other virtue one could think of. Conservatives did not merely hold different opinions—they were the enemy. Their views were not just wrong—they were evil.

"I was unable to see what a myopic vision of the world this gave me. Forever after I was tainted, not with Richard Nixon's presidency but with my own violations against objectivity, even against truth. My crime was more personal—it was a bias so deeply ingrained that it kept me from being an objective truth seeker.

"Such I remained until very recently. I did not love the truth. I was in love with a political and cultural agenda. As difficult as it is to admit, I was in love with my own intellect, with my own objectivity. I was in love with a lie. I was not the least bit objective. That blindness and its bias poisoned my work for half a century. I regret it more than I can say."

Woodstein's book had shocked him. He had gone along with the media of the 2030s in repudiating and denouncing its one-time hero as a senile has-been. His own excoriating review in the *Daily Bruin* was one of the reasons he had come to Mike Bardolf's attention. It might have been the reason he had been invited to the Oraculous banquet in the first place.

But what if Woodstein was right, thought Todd. What if Trump was right, and he, Todd Stewart, was part of an institution committed to lies and fake news rather than to the truth? Was Woodstein in fact a man of courage for finally admitting his lifelong bias?

The questions were almost too staggering to look squarely in the face.

Todd's unsettled thoughts sent his mind back to the plane flight returning from Hillsgrove College, when the ethics of what he was sometimes forced to do had troubled him. It wasn't Mike Bardolf this time. It was the entire atmosphere around him at this moment in the grand ballroom of the Washington, DC, Marriott. This was nothing more than a mutual admiration society between the Democrat Party and the media.

He glanced over at the FNN table—stuck at the back, none of its correspondents ever asked to speak, just as the president never called on them at press conferences.

And he, NBC's golden boy, dutifully went along. Not only because Mike Bardolf's hooks were deep into him, but because the mainstream press always went along.

What if he refused to do Mike Bardolf's bidding? What was the worst the man could do—get him fired? The man wasn't going to kill him. He wasn't a murderer. Maybe getting fired wouldn't be so bad. At least he would be his own man again.

His future as NBC's new star, whom more than one of the corporate suits were touting as their eventual anchorman, no longer looked so glamorous.

Was fame worth selling his soul to a culture where truth and objectivity mattered so little?

74

UNEXPECTED CALLER

FRIDAY, APRIL 17, 2048

THE IMPULSION continued to grow on Timothy and Jaylene throughout the spring months that the time was approaching to selectively share Stirling's *Benedict Brief* with a few others. At the same time, they felt strongly that it was to remain private. Stirling's warning of the principle of Matthew 7:6 remained at the forefront of their prayers. More and more Timothy saw the wisdom of David's words from years earlier, that the higher the truth, the more Satan is able to use it to deceive, that even truth in the enemy's hands can be a powerful tool to promote falsehood, breed evil, and work division in the hearts and minds of those willing to be deceived.

Stirling's sweeping vision of a Church of the future knit together by unity rather than organizational structure was one of God's highest truths. It was therefore also one easily susceptible to the subtle machinations of the enemy to destroy it. They must do their part to keep that truth in the hands of the Spirit to work God's will, and only his will.

More and more of the questions raised by the people writing to them, and the quandaries Christians were facing worldwide, were almost directly answered by Stirling's *Brief*. Over and over they saw issues Christians were grappling with, about the church and the culture, echoed with uncanny precision by what Stirling had written fifteen years earlier.

Heather was on their minds too. Now in her thirties, they were in awe of the spiritual maturity evident in her character. It was obvious that their daughter understood the depths of her grandfather's heart far more than any of his own children had at the same age. Her occupying their home had taken on a spiritual significance that extended far beyond it simply being a place to live. As deeply as he wanted to be faithful in doing his part, an image occasionally came to Timothy's mind of his parents' spiritual legacy overleaping the generation of their own children and coming to rest even more powerfully in this one of their granddaughters. Hopefully she would not be the only one. But for now, the anguish he and Jaylene had felt to see their little girl suffer in her teen years was bearing fruit in God's garden in the flourishing of nothing less than a radiant countenance of Christlikeness. Though the youngest by more than a decade, she had become one of the foundational pillars of their GCG group.

It seemed clear that the Lord had been preparing their own Heather to carry Stirling Marshall's writings and vision, and perhaps his *Brief*, into the generations of the future.

As the day for the next GCG meeting drew near, they were delighted that all four of Timothy's siblings had responded to their invitations and planned to attend. It was also their intention, at long last, to share Stirling's *Brief* with them, along with a few others.

The doorbell of the Marshall home rang at 2:15 Friday afternoon on the day before the meeting planned for the following day at David's ranch. Timothy had come home from school early to check over his notes one final time for the talk he planned to give on his father's obscure book *Phantasms of Unfaith*. By now the acknowledged leader of the group, even though the GCG get-togethers were informal, he always had something planned if it seemed appropriate. If the sharing between everyone else was spontaneous and vigorous, he was happy to sit back and say nothing.

Timothy rose from his desk, left his office, and walked to the front door. He opened it to see an imposing figure standing in front of him. The man was several years younger, probably late fifties, powerful of appearance, broad-shouldered and easily six feet two.

The man smiled somewhat awkwardly.

"Hello," he said, obvious nervousness belying his arresting physical presence, "are you, uh . . . Mr. Marshall?"

"Yes, I am Timothy Marshall," nodded Timothy.

"I'm sorry to call on you at home. I was hoping I could talk to you for a few minutes. My name is Court Masters."

"I am pleased to meet you, Mr. Masters," said Timothy, extending his hand. "Won't you come in?"

"Thank you. I appreciate it. I realize this is an imposition."

"Not at all. My afternoon is free. I'm a professor at a local Christian university, and I have no classes on Friday afternoon."

He led his visitor inside.

"I actually know quite a bit about you," said Masters as they sat in the living room. "I know about Jessup. I looked up your class schedule. That's why I came on Friday, hoping to catch you."

"You seem to know all about me!"

"I hope you don't mind. I've also read several of your books."

"I see."

"And many of your father's. That's why I'm here. I know your father is gone, but I had to tell you what an impact his book on the commandments has had on me, and my wife as well. As much as any other single factor, that book helped save our marriage. That's not to say that your books have not been equally meaningful—"

"Have no fear," laughed Timothy. "My father was something special. He saw into the heart of God like no one I've ever known, and no writer I've read other than Kempis and MacDonald."

"Yes," nodded his guest, for the first time cracking a smile, "I am familiar with both men—thanks to you and your father. For that, too, I am enormously grateful."

"So—do you live in the Sacramento area?" asked Timothy.

"Hardly!" chuckled Masters. "Washington, DC."

"Goodness!" exclaimed Timothy. "You're a long way from home. How did you manage to find me?"

"It wasn't so hard, especially for me. I should explain—I'm a detective. DC Metro."

"Ah, so finding my schedule and address would have been child's play."

"In a way I suppose you're right," smiled Masters. "I'll be sixty in a year. I've scaled back some. I'll probably retire in a year or two. But finding people is part of the job description."

"I hope I'm not under investigation!" laughed Timothy.

"My wanting to see you is strictly personal," chuckled Court.

"Are you on business out here?"

"Not really. Two errands brought me to the West Coast. Seeing you was definitely one of them. I could have written or telephoned. But I wanted to see you face to face, shake your hand, and tell you that the books of both Marshalls, yours and your father's have been life changing."

"Thank you," said Timothy seriously. "I appreciate that. We rejoice in the ongoing impact the books continue to have."

Court went on to share in more depth about his and Stella's reading of *Unspoken Commandments* together. Conversation between the two men flowed easily and spontaneously until they were sharing deeply, laughing together, then growing serious again, as if they had known each other for years. Timothy put on a pot of coffee, and two hours sped by. Long before that, Timothy realized that a lasting friendship had begun, that another living stone had been placed beside him in the growing temple of God's Church. He scarcely hesitated with what he said as Court prepared to go.

"I don't know how long you're planning to be in the area—" Timothy began.

"For several days. My wife and I are staying at Larkspur Landing in Roseville."

"I know the place. You should have brought your wife with you."

"We didn't want to presume."

"No fear of that!" said Timothy. "The timing of your trip to California couldn't be better."

"How so?"

"We get together periodically with some people who have also benefited from my father's books. It so happens that our next gathering is tomorrow. We would love for you and your wife to come."

Court hesitated. "That is very gracious of you. But really . . . I didn't come expecting—"

"We are just ordinary Christians who get together away from a church environment to enjoy one another's company and talk about what God is doing in the world and in our own lives. You know me well enough by now to know that we would love to have you. If my wife were here, she would insist."

"Thank you. I'll talk to Stella," replied Court, nodding with a sincere expression of gratitude. "I know she will be as appreciative of your hospitality as I am."

"That reminds me," said Timothy, "you never mentioned the other matter that brought you so far from home. Unless it's confidential—"

"Not at all," rejoined Court. "There is another man I also wanted to make contact with—a pastor. I was fortunate that you both lived near Sacramento."

"What's his name?" asked Timothy.

"Mark Forster."

"No kidding! That's wonderful—another of the Lord's divine coincidences!"

"Why do you say that?"

"He's one of my closest friends. He and his family will be there tomorrow. A perfect chance for you to meet."

"Unbelievable! God has been directing our steps since the moment we left DC. I suppose that seals it. I know Stella will be delighted."

"Why don't we swing by Larkspur around eleven tomorrow. You can drive up with us. We'll be meeting at the ranch of one of my father's closest friends in the foothills."

75

WIDENING CONCENTRIC CIRCLES

SATURDAY–SUNDAY, APRIL 18–19, 2048

THOSE PLANNING to attend the April meeting of the Gold Country Gathering had indeed swelled beyond its usual number. They thus enjoyed an outside meeting in the foothills at the Bar JG ranch, treated to a balmy and fragrant seventy-two-degree spring afternoon, complete with a lavish potluck, spirited fellowship, much laughter, and profound discussions on many things.

The larger group ensured that many new friendships formed, the regulars from the Sacramento area making ten or twelve newcomers from around the country feel welcome—including Violet and Trevor Langdon from Albany, New York, the Stevens from Kansas, as well as Sarah and Matthew Gardner from Idaho whom several already knew from a previous visit to California.

The highlight of the day proved to be Court and Stella Masters, who, being almost accidental attendees and trying to hang back unobtrusively, found themselves instead the center of attention. Court's sheer appearance was enough to turn eyes. If he wasn't a former NFL linebacker, he could have been a movie star. The reality was hardly diminished that he was neither. A detective, a policeman in the nation's capital, who had known Trump and been present at the assassination of President Hunt, was enough to keep the younger people following him about all day and the others brimming over with questions. His stature was heightened in David's eyes by his quiet demeanor, his desire to listen more than talk, and that whenever he did share, his comments focused on a favorite quote from Kempis or a question to Timothy about something his father had written.

Curious as many were to learn more about the world of Washington, which was home to Court and Stella Masters, hardly a word touching on politics was heard all afternoon. Certain matters pertaining to that world were indeed privately raised when Court and Mark were seen walking alone together midway through the afternoon. They arranged to meet again on Tuesday, after the Masters' planned visit to Yosemite on Sunday and Monday. Court and Stella would return late Monday afternoon in time for supper at the Marshalls', to which Mark, Grace, and Heather had also been invited.

Midway through Saturday afternoon, during a lull when everyone was walking about stretching their legs and Court and Mark had wandered across the pasture toward the woods, Woody took Timothy aside. His expression was serious.

"Thank you for including me, Tim," he said. "This has meant the world to me. I just didn't realize—" He shook his head, hardly knowing what to say. "Please, keep me posted on everything you do from now on," he added. "I'm sorry I didn't listen to you before. I know you wanted to include me. I just . . . I don't know—I guess I wasn't ready."

"It's all about the right time," smiled Timothy. "I had to go through the same thing."

"That may be," rejoined Woody. "But you wised up sooner than I did."

The two brothers embraced. As they stepped back, a sheepish expression came over Woody's face.

"I have a favor to ask," he said. "It's embarrassing, but would you send me a list of Dad's books. It's time I had them all. I want to read everything."

After the Saturday afternoon at David's ranch, a much smaller group gathered for breakfast on Sunday at the Marshall home in Dorado Wood, Heather Marshall's home now. Present were Timothy's four siblings and a select handful of others with whom, after much prayer, the threesome of Timothy, Jaylene, and David had decided to share Stirling's final communication to posterity, the *Benedict Brief*. Out of respect for Mark's position, wanting to cause him no awkwardness rather than because they felt him less prepared for its reception than the others, Mark and Grace were not present.

They had prepared copies ahead of time. Timothy shared about its history, read aloud Stirling's injunction to care, discretion, and privacy, urged upon them the same exhortation with the request, if they did not feel they could abide by it, that they excuse themselves, adding that no one would feel the least ill will toward anyone making that decision.

No one moved.

Timothy then handed out twelve copies of his father's *Brief*, telling those gathered, after reading them, that the copies must remain behind. He hoped they would understand that they must allow no printed copies circulated or the *Brief* mentioned or shared after they all went their separate ways, and he equally encouraged them to live by it as much as they could. Still, it was to remain a private document.

Then everyone went out for a walk in the neighborhood or sought a private place in the house or back yard. The weekend continuing to be warm, most chose the out of doors.

They gathered three hours later, each returning his or her copy to either Timothy or Jaylene.

"I do not feel discussion or further talk is necessary at this point," said Timothy. "We must each prayerfully decide how God would have us use the word he gave through my father—our father," he added, glancing toward his brothers and sisters. "Let us be in prayer for one another, that we will be faithful to my father's cautions and counsel, and that we will be wise stewards of what he has passed on to us."

What God would do next remained to be revealed.

76

WHAT IS THE SPIRIT SAYING TO THE CHURCH?

JUNE 2048

GINGER FORSTER found her father in his study, two Bibles and several books spread out on his desk.

Mark heard her steps and turned.

"Could I talk to you, Dad?" said Ginger.

"Sure, sweetie," replied Mark. "You're a welcome interruption."

"Working on your sermon?" she asked, sitting in one of the easy chairs.

"Not really. Maybe a future one. For now I'm just trying to get a handle on some thorny scriptural questions."

"I thought you understood everything in the Bible."

Mark broke out in laughter. "Ah, the innocence of youth! No, my dear, I am but a neophyte in God's high mysteries. I am learning a few things that I have been slow to apprehend and should have understood sooner."

"What is it you are trying to understand now?"

"Only that most perplexing book in the whole Bible—Revelation."

"Ugh—I don't like it."

Mark laughed again. "Well, I am hoping to find more in it than is commonly taught. I'm trying to get new perspective on the whole prophetic scenario, I suppose you'd say."

"The rapture and tribulation and all that stuff?"

"Yep—all that stuff. However, you didn't want to talk to me about that."

"No," replied Ginger. "The mail came an hour ago—"

She hesitated.

"And?"

"There was a letter from Jessup. I've been accepted."

"That's great, honey—congratulations!" said Mark enthusiastically. "Have you decided, then?"

"I've still got my applications in at Sac State and Davis. And I'm still thinking about Humboldt since you and Mom went there."

"For purely selfish reasons, I hope one of the others is your final choice. What are your thoughts about living at home?"

"I'd like to stay with you and Mom—if you're not sick of me."

"Never! We would love to have you here for as long as you want to live with us. It's a parent's dream. Financially, too, that would certainly make it easier. We'll be able to help with your college expenses, of course. But you know that pastors don't get rich. Have you thought about Hillsgrove's California campus?"

"I would love that too. I have their catalog but haven't applied yet."

"Are you leaning toward one of the Christian colleges?"

"I think so. I'm not afraid of the secular colleges exactly. But I don't want to be surrounded by all the ungodliness and gender nonsense, with every professor pushing socialism and diversity racism."

"You are wise to be cautious. Most colleges aren't educational systems anymore but greenhouses for bias, intolerance, and religious prejudice."

"The catalogs are full of all that," rejoined Ginger. "Though everything is couched in progressive-speak to sound like sweetness and light. It's so deceptive. Why would I want to be taught by Marxist teachers and sit in class with transgenders who think I'm abnormal? I'm not worried about the lies rubbing off on me. But it's obvious how sick our culture is. Why would I want to be around those influences? I want to be influenced by goodness. I want to associate with decent and honorable people."

"Well, I honor you for that. Several of Jessup's and Hillsgrove's faculty are church members. The Marshalls of course. Any more thoughts on a major since the last time we talked?"

"Taking this year off has been good for me," replied Ginger. "I'm glad for the experience of helping with the church's school. It has confirmed that I think I want to teach."

"That's great, sweetie. You'll be a terrific teacher. You have a gift with children. You ought to go out one day and have a look around the campuses."

"I'd like that. Would you go with me, Dad?"

"Love to."

Mark watched Ginger leave his study a few minutes later with a feeling of pride and gratitude. His little girl was nineteen and nearly grown, he thought with a smile.

The realization was a melancholy one. No parent is eager to see a son or daughter leave the nest. He was thankful that the time was not quite yet and that Ginger had chosen to stay close to him and Grace through her teen years. He believed that teen independence and rebellion as a natural and genetic inevitability was nothing more than a myth. He had often said to Grace that young people choose either independence and rebellion, or respect and obedience. Life's directions flow out of the foundation of those teen choices. He was grateful to God that Ginger's life choices had begun early to follow the principles of Proverbs 2 and 3.

Mark returned his thoughts to the books and papers spread out before him. There were many things on his mind other than Ginger's future. Foremost among them at this moment was how to respond to the prophecy fever that Ward's articles were stirring up. He felt Ward's perspectives were leading people into unscriptural perspectives about the end times.

He returned his attention to the pages of notes and the book in front of him. One of his Bibles was open to the first three chapters of Revelation, another to the troublesome rapture passage of 1 Thessalonians 4:16–17, and a third to Matthew 24.

How could he make sense of so many futuristic passages pointing to apparently conflicting conclusions?

His eyes strayed to the printout he had made of Ward's latest public post from three days earlier on the seals, trumpets, angels, bowls, and other signs and visions of Revelation.

"Ward, Ward, my friend—you've entirely missed the point," he sighed inaudibly. "You've skipped over the most significant part of the book, the first three chapters. The messages to the churches build the foundation for all that follows. You can't interpret Revelation without that foundation. Any attempt to understand Revelation that has not been built on the first three chapters will be laced with falsehoods."

He closed his eyes and silently prayed again for his friend. Millions were lapping up Ward's every word. His explanations and so-called revelations were shallow and incomplete. Like so many authors through the years, Ward was building on faulty foundations because he, like they, did not understand the first three chapters of Revelation.

Mark's prayers drifted into inarticulate groanings for his friend and how he should respond.

Several minutes later, he reached for a fresh sheet of paper, picked up a pen, and began to write.

Ward, my dear friend,

I have read all your prophetic articles. I must hand it to you—they have certainly stirred up the evangelical world. The people in my church are talking of nothing else. They eagerly await every new installment.

If you do not mind a few words of caution, however, from a friend and your pastoral protégé, I would only say—

Mark stopped, set down his pen, thought a moment, then crumpled up the sheet and tossed it into the can beside his desk. God had answered his prayer sooner than he had anticipated.

It was not time. God bless him, Ward was a dear and honorable man. Yet he was so mired in the doctrinal traditions of the elders that the light of deeper truth could not yet penetrate the thick crust of that theology.

At least for now. He knew Ward well enough, however, to know that at its root his was a truth-loving heart. Seeds of deeper truth would sprout in time, as they do in the hearts of all lovers of truth. Though doctrinal traditions retard that sprouting, the eyes of true hearts always come open. He only hoped Ward's season was at hand.

He had been such a one himself. It had only been recently that the seeds had sprouted and begun bearing fruit in his own heart—thanks to David's persistent prayers and patient prodding. Perhaps he was such a persistent, patient, prodding pray-er in Ward's life.

Lord God, my Father, Mark prayed, *keep me from judging those who perceive truth differently than I do. Deepen my hunger for an increase of truth. Reveal your heart to me. Show me where I need to delve deeper. Reveal to me the truth of your purposes in the days ahead, especially for your people in the Church. Reveal the mysteries of your Word, that I might be your faithful voice to speak truth as you give me opportunity. Show me, as your servant John exhorted, what your Spirit is saying to the churches.*

Mark had again turned his attention to the study spread out on his desk and was trying to refocus his thoughts when Grace walked through the open door.

"I'm afraid I may have some unwelcome news," she said. "Edith Holt is here. She wants to talk to us. She's not smiling."

Mark sighed. "Let's have her," he said. "Might as well face the music."

77

THE ELDER'S WIFE

JUNE 2048

THE WIFE of influential elder and probably the wealthiest member of Foothills Gospel Ministries, Stoddard Holt, was of that class of church activist that is the special blessing and challenge of most pastors. She was involved in everything, served on three boards and most ad hoc committees, and felt entitled to know every secret and to demand to be consulted on every decision.

Grace led Edith into the study. Mark rose and offered his hand.

"Hello, Edith," he said as she shook his hand limply. "Please have a seat. What can we do for you?"

"I have been talking to some of the other ladies," she began stiffly, "and to Stoddard, who also knew nothing about it. I want to know why Stoddard and I were not invited to the gathering you had three weeks ago at, er . . . David Gordon's ranch."

She spoke David's name hesitantly, as if whatever it was about him that was held in such suspicion might taint her by speaking his name.

"There has been far too much favoritism toward certain people in the congregation," she went on, "while others are ignored. We are not at all happy about it."

"We? You mean—"

"Myself and some of the other elders' wives."

"And Stoddard?"

"Stoddard too."

"I wish he would have come to me about it," said Mark. "We could have cleared it up easily. Are you here on his behalf? Does he know you've come to see us?"

"I thought it best I handle it myself," replied Edith. "Sometimes Stoddard has difficulty expressing himself forcefully enough."

Whatever his wife might think Stoddard Holt capable of, the man had been a disgruntled elder and thorn in Mark's side almost from the day of his arrival. For years the two Holts had been pulling most of the strings at Foothills. Under Mark's leadership they felt demoted to the level of everyone else. They did not like Mark's way of treating everyone equally.

"I see. Well, let me just say, Edith, that I am very sorry you or Stoddard or anyone else felt slighted. But it was not a church function, nor did Grace and I have anything to do with its planning."

"Why were you there, then, and the Marshalls?"

"They've known David Gordon for decades. As have I. I grew up as his neighbor. We're old friends. There's nothing so mysterious about it."

"Other people from the church were included."

"A few, I think."

"Why weren't we?"

"I can assure you that you and Stoddard were not singled out. Most of the people who were there had no connection to Foothills—some were from other states. The gathering had nothing to do with Foothills. As I say, we have been friends with David for years. The others were friends with whom there have developed spiritual connections on the basis of our reading of Stirling Marshall's books—Timothy's father."

"I've heard of him. What does he have to do with it?"

"Most of our discussions were based on the ideas in his books. I'm sure you've heard me refer to him from the pulpit. It's sort of like a book club. Have you read any of Stirling Marshall's books?"

Ignoring Mark's question, Edith went on with her second grievance.

"Betty Macratchen told me she heard from Hazel Hubert that Faith Silva has been attending a secret group that no one in the church is supposed to know about."

"Ah, I see—you know of this third hand—not always the most reliable way to get truthful information, Edith."

"Never mind how I came by my information. I came by it—that's the important thing. Hazel says the two of you are involved," Edith added, glancing toward Grace.

"And you know this because Hazel told Betty who told you?"

"That's what I said."

"But it concerns none of the three of you?"

"That has nothing to do with it. I simply want to know why this has been kept from the church and why others have not been invited to participate. Even the elders know nothing of it."

She sat up erect in her chair as an angel of truth on behalf of the aggrieved, crossed her arms, and waited.

"Well, Edith," began Mark, "you seem to feel there has been some sort of favoritism at work here, and I can assure you such is not the case. Yes, Grace and I meet with a group of people who get together occasionally every few months. But it has nothing to do with the church. Like the get-together at the Gordon ranch, we are not part of the group's leadership."

"It's held at the Marshalls."

"Sometimes. At their daughter Heather's home."

"They're members of Foothills."

"Heather is not. Sometimes the group meets at homes of people from other churches. As far as the Marshalls are concerned, you're right, it's usually held at Heather's, which is natural enough as it mostly concerns her grandfather's writings."

"Why is it so secret?"

"It's simply that the kinds of things discussed would not be of interest to everyone. If there was a group meeting to talk about boat building, for instance, I personally would not go. Maybe you wouldn't either. A quilting group, Grace might want to be part of, but I wouldn't."

"Don't be ridiculous, pastor. I'm not talking about boats or quilts. What kinds of things are discussed at your group?"

"Just what I said before—the ideas in Stirling Marshall's books. Call it a book discussion group if you like. No one is intentionally excluded—not you or Hazel or Betty or anyone. It is simply that Timothy and Jaylene and Heather have invited people with whom they have discussed the writings of Timothy's father. It mostly began from correspondence with people outside the area altogether long before we were at Foothills. We didn't become involved until very recently after we, too, took an interest in Stirling Marshall's writings through the influence of David Gordon."

"Him again!"

"Yes, a very godly man, Edith. A true example of Christlikeness."

"Humpf!"

"As I say, the only purpose is to discuss ideas that are of interest to those who come. I think for the next meeting Timothy said we would be discussing one book in particular. If you and Stoddard are interested, I will tell Timothy and perhaps you and Stoddard would like to read some of Stirling's work. Timothy wants people to come who have read the book or books that will be discussed. The discussions are sometimes very serious. As I said—much like a book club. Have you read anything of Mr. Marshall's?"

"No."

"If you would like to, I have a copy of one here about becoming more Christlike that I would be happy to—"

"I'm not interested."

"Do you want me to ask Timothy to talk to you and Stoddard about it?"

"It doesn't sound like anything we would be interested in," said Edith, rising.

Grace led her from the study. Mark heard the front door open and close, then Grace walked back in.

"I'm not sure I handled that as deftly as I might have," he said.

"I thought you handled it perfectly. It is exactly a book club. You were up front and truthful. With people who are determined to take offense, there's not much you can do but apologize and muddle through. They're going to get offended whatever you say."

☆ ☆ ☆

When told the gist of their conversation with Edith Holt, Faith Silva was remorsefully apologetic.

"I had no idea our daughter was still awake and listening when Brad and I were talking about the meeting at David's. She mentioned something about it in passing a day or two later, and I thought nothing of it. I told her not to mention where Brad and I had been. But she and Mary Hubert are best friends. That must be how Edith got wind of it. I am sorry."

"Nothing to worry about, Faith," said Jaylene. "The Lord is the leader of this thing. We're not trying to be secretive, just prudent."

"We'll see what comes of it," Mark replied. "I have the feeling the road we're trying to walk will increasingly be misunderstood. But no sense in worrying about it yet."

"If that happens," added Grace, "we'll shower the disgruntled with kindness."

78

"You Must be Ready"

JUNE 2048

IT IS not often in life that answers to prayer come either so quickly or with such specificity. In the present case, David Gordon was so suspicious of getting his heaven-to-earth signals crossed that he waited two months for confirmation before setting about to obey what he thought he had heard.

Who can say how thoughts, ideas, and prayers coalesce and intermingle. Probably the roots of it began long ago with his earliest association with Stirling Marshall.

Changes in the world . . . the discussions with friends in the group . . . the radical Left's increasing militancy against Christianity . . . the growing parallels with Hitler's attempt to eradicate Judaism from Germany, and Stalin's horrifying cruelty against Christians, with progressivism's war on Christianity . . . his conviction that dark days were ahead for Christians . . . that persecutions would drive many fellowships of believers into hiding . . . that God had some role for him to play in the unfolding of the days ahead . . . perhaps even a prophetic role, a shepherding role . . . all these and many more stirrings had swirled vague and unformed in the groanings of his inarticulate prayers probably for years.

It was a year ago when his eyes fell on a small group of books that were among his mother's favorites sitting together on one of his bookshelves.

He rose, walked to the shelf, and pulled out *God's Smuggler* by Brother Andrew and leafed through the pages, abundantly filled with his mother's penciled notes. He had read it as a young man. His mother had said to him often, "These times will come again, David. You have to be ready. Most in the church will not see them coming. But you will see. The Lord's hand is on you. God's people will need you."

He finished his mother's old worn copy two days later, mesmerized, his mother's words with him every moment. He followed with *The Book Thief, The Diary of Anne Frank, Escape to Freedom,* Corrie ten Boom's *The Hiding Place,* then several titles by Richard Wurmbrand and Aleksandr Solzhenitsyn, and finally a biography of Dietrich Bonhoeffer. As he read, the conviction grew upon him, overspread by his mother's quiet voice, that he was not reading about the past—but of the future.

The radical notion suddenly blossoming on the tree from these diverse roots came to him early on the Monday morning after the most recent GCG meeting at his ranch. Walking out of the house, still feeling the glow of the weekend just past, about halfway to the barn, as his eyes fell on his backhoe sitting behind his barn, suddenly he stopped dead in his tracks. His eyes opened wide, and he looked down at the dusty dry ground beneath his feet.

Surely, Lord—you don't really want me to . . .

Almost immediately he heard again his mother's voice: "You will see. You must be ready."

He could hardly even formulate a prayer. It was the craziest idea he had ever had!

Almost every moment for the next two months, the hazy, crazy, far-fetched idea haunted him. It grew more vivid as the weeks went by. Finally, it ceased to be a mere fantasy. It became palpably real, a voice like that of Revelation, speaking of the days to come:

> *"As I was lifting my thoughts to the Lord came a vision*
> *of a nation—a once great nation—as a flourishing garden of*
> *former times now lying abandoned, unkempt, windblown and*
> *overgrown, like the desolation of Israel overrun and taken into*

*exile. Behind the desolation, stretching into the distance beyond,
I saw a long line of men, women, and children, exiles and
refugees from a time of great trial, seemingly waiting to enter
that garden, desolate as it appeared.*

*"That Church will soon also be a Church in exile from the
nations of a world plunging into darkness. To be of its remnant
will mean joining an exiled community of people even as
God's people Israel have lived for two thousand years. True
Christianity will be a faith of exile, persecuted and ostracized
for refusing to embrace the manifold lies of the age. An exile is
coming to God's true Church. But he who endures to the end will
be saved."*

Finally, the vision could not be ignored.

In early summer, David informed both sets of Forsters and Marshalls that he would be out of touch for two, maybe three weeks. He had something he needed to attend to, he said, though would give no details. They assumed he was going away, but where and for what purpose he did not divulge. He requested that they ask him no questions, either now or later. Though curious, they willingly complied.

The next morning he was up with the sun, closed and locked the gate at the end of his long driveway to prevent visitors then spent most of the morning working on his ancient rusting backhoe. After draining the tank and adding fresh diesel and oil, cleaning the plugs and carburetor, and checking the belts and hoses and tires, the decrepit old thing somehow sputtered into life. A good deal of expected exhaust followed for several minutes as it coughed and choked and blew its lungs clean from years of inactivity. Meanwhile, David gingerly experimented with the levers that controlled the boom, stick, bucket, and loader.

By early afternoon he was at work, first digging the twenty-five-by-forty-foot perimeter trench he had laid out earlier between his house and the barn, loading the dirt on the back of his flatbed to be hauled into the woods and spread about, and also to fill in various low spots about the ranch where he would plant pasture grass to keep the change from being noticed. By evening he was well underway, the thousand-square-foot rectangle completely excavated to a depth of three feet and the dirt nowhere in sight.

It was a good beginning. David went to bed that night weary but with a sense of satisfaction. It was an enormous undertaking for a seventy-seven-year-old man. He told himself years ago that he would undertake no more huge projects on the ranch. But this project had grown imperative.

In the following two weeks, with planks, timber, two-by-sixes and -eights, and four-by-twelves, rebar, piping, and two dozen new fenceposts with rails to match—all of which he had judiciously purchased during the past month from different suppliers so as to raise no questions—now stored in the barn, the clandestine project slowly took shape. With the initial phase of the most backbreaking work in place, the final week of his isolation was spent making multiple trips back and forth into Grass Valley and Auburn and down into the valley to haul back more than a dozen trailer loads of U-haul concrete behind his pickup.

After three weeks, he was thoroughly spent. What a month before had been a crazy idea on the drawing board of his mind, was well underway, and the new corral for his horses between the house and the barn mostly completed. The fence posts surrounding the thirty-five-by-fifty-foot enclosure were in, solidly encased in concrete.

He would ask Mark and Timothy to help set and bolt the corral's horizontal rails. That kind of work would be easier with three men.

> *"Unless a grain of wheat falls into the earth and dies, it remains alone; but if it dies, it bears much fruit."*
> — JOHN 12:24

PART 4

BIRTH

2048

79

Tumult in Denver

June–July 2048

ONCE HIS momentum began to build, Jefferson Rhodes won most of the remaining primaries between March and June with eight- and ten-point victories over Vice President Hardy. She was close enough, however, with delegates spread between the candidates proportionally, that she kept the race interesting. Her early uncontested victories from New Hampshire and Iowa actually preserved her delegate lead into April.

But Rhodes intended to leave nothing to chance. On the basis of several clandestine late-night meetings on the top floor of the Fourth Avenue parking garage, the senator was made privy to certain confidential facts relating to the vice president's personal habits even more kinky than her so-called marriage. When shrewdly leaked to the press from "unnamed sources," these resulted in a marked decline in her ratings even among the LGBTQ community. The remaining primaries easily put Rhodes over the top. Never suspecting the faithful and trusted Secret Service agent who was at her side every minute, Ms. Hardy yet had no doubt, however he had learned of it, that Jefferson Rhodes was behind the leaks. He had a reputation for playing dirty. But she had not expected such a level of backstabbing even from him.

After being selected as VP four years earlier, she had assumed the Oval Office was as good as hers after her predecessor stepped down. It was her turn, not some upstart junior senator from the northwest. She stewed for days after his public announcement of his intention to offer her the second spot on the ticket. Fortunately, she had two months to consider a response to the humiliating offer—whether to rebuff it out of spite or swallow her pride in LBJ fashion and accept. Maybe she would get lucky and Rhodes would be assassinated.

The Democrat convention in July was a coronation of Jefferson Rhodes, not as the party's nominee but as the next president. President Samara was as furious at the senator as was her VP. She had already decided she would not campaign for him. She consented, however, to give a lackluster speech on behalf of the nominee, spending most of the time extolling her VP Elizabeth Hardy, who gritted her teeth and accepted Rhodes's offer to continue in her current job.

The only political drama of the summer came where no one expected it—from the Republican convention in Denver. Most of the news outlets barely gave it two hours a night, not like the eighteen-hour-a-day coverage of the Rhodes coronation.

As the week progressed, however, and no Republican stepped up to challenge aging perennial hopeful Jedediah Waters, rumors began to circulate on the convention floor that a coalition of party heavyweights was pressuring Waters to withdraw. Waters, who had run essentially unopposed in all the primaries, had secured far more delegates than needed. If he went ahead with a third run, however, he might suffer the ignominy of suffering the greatest loss in American history.

The party bigwigs put the question to him bluntly: Was that how he wanted to be remembered? If he withdrew, allowing the nomination to be thrown open to the delegates, they promised to make it worth his while, adding suitable blandishments that promised to cast him as one of the leading Republican statesmen of his era and a man of enduring stature.

Sensing a brewing story, news teams began rolling into Denver on Thursday of convention week. Once the rumor of a possible withdrawal was confirmed, the networks jumped on the story.

On Friday morning a hurried press conference was called. "Republican stalwart Jedediah Waters," began the party spokesperson, "has decided to withdraw his name as the Republican presidential nominee for health reasons. He will, however, address the convention on prime-time Saturday evening in support of the eventual nominee. He has also agreed to act as chairman of the Republican National Committee for the following year."

The convention exploded into a tumult of conjecture about Waters's replacement. Reporters from the networks and western regional stations prowled the floor for any tidbits that might lead to a breaking story.

Suddenly the first brokered convention by either party in decades scooped the news cycle. Would they select a well-known Republican senator, one of four Republican governors, or a new face that might inject fresh life into the dying party and make a legitimate race of the election?

Or might nominations come from the floor in a free-for-all with every state's favorite son?

For the first time since Trump, the Republicans were in the news!

At noon on Friday, fully two dozen names were being floated. All the Trump children were mentioned, which sent the liberal media into a frenzy. By late afternoon the prevailing opinion, however, held that party dealmakers were looking for a fresh face, an outsider.

Midway through the evening, with speeches droning on from the podium, the convention floor suddenly ignited with the rumor that the leading contender was the nation's most visible Republican that year—a true outsider who made news wherever he went.

The name that would be placed in nomination the next day, by the contingent from Senator Rhodes's own home state of Washington, was that of none other than the Democrat candidate's former college roommate Ward Hutchins.

Reached at his home for comment by a sudden flurry of telephone calls, Hutchins repeatedly disavowed the slightest interest in political office. But as every reporter covering the story knew well enough, and expressed on air, politicians always denied their ambitions.

Until standing on the podium, that is, basking in applause, when they uttered the words that had been inevitable all along, "It is with great humility that I hereby accept . . ."

So it would be with Ward Hutchins.

That he left his home hurriedly that same night for the airport and was on his way from Seattle to Denver within two hours all but confirmed that, come Saturday's floor vote, the Hutchins nomination would be unanimous.

80

SURPRISE IN LARAMIE

NOT ALL Republican senators and congressmen attended the nominating convention. In spite of its geographic proximity on this occasion, one particular westerner who declined considered it a pointless waste of energy. He had done his duty to state and country. He had no intention of subjecting himself to a week of funny hats and balloons.

He followed the news as the week progressed, more out of loyalty than interest. He knew he would be asked about it and should at least be abreast of developments. As far as Ward Hutchins's denials went, as a Christian he wondered if he might possess more inside information than the journalists who made light of Hutchins's denials. He reflected that Matthew 5:37 might have more bearing on the outcome of the convention than any of them realized, and that Ward Hutchins might actually mean what he said.

Harvey Jansen was right.

It turned out that he would be asked about the convention much sooner than he had anticipated.

Returning from a late afternoon summer ride with his wife along the Laramie River south of town, as they neared their home on its ten acres at the end of Chimney Lamp Road, neither the accidental senator nor his wife took much notice of what seemed an unusual level of activity at the Laramie Regional Airport two miles north of them—four or five small planes landing in quick succession within minutes of each other.

They were just reaching their stables when two helicopters swooped down, seemingly coming from out of nowhere, circled, and set to the ground in their own pasture on the opposite side of the house. Before they had a chance to dismount, several vans and a black limousine turned from the highway three quarters of a mile away into their dirt driveway. The assortment of vehicles came roaring toward them, the vans spraying dust and pebbles, and thoroughly spooking their horses.

"What in the world is going on?" exclaimed Harriet Jansen doing her best to calm her mount. "If one of our parents has died, I don't think we would be notified with quite this much urgency."

"All I can imagine," said her husband as he dismounted, "is that there is a crisis in Washington. The Senate must have been called into emergency session."

"There's been nothing on the news," rejoined Harriet. "It's been non-stop convention coverage."

"What else could it be?"

"I don't know, Harvey," she said. "But here they come, and they're certainly not here for me—you'd better go face your public. I'll take care of the horses."

Harvey dismounted and walked toward the house. A dozen men and women were now running toward him. Most carried microphones or were lugging video equipment. Within seconds he was surrounded by reporters all shouting questions at once.

He held up his hands until it quieted enough that he thought he might make himself heard.

"I have no idea what any of you are saying!" he said loudly. "Quiet down, please—one at a time!"

"What do you think, Senator?" he heard a voice call out above the rest.

"About what?"

"The convention. The vote."

"I know nothing about it."

"You haven't been watching the news?"

"Not since noon. My wife and I drove into town then went for a long ride."

"You don't know, Senator?"

"I tell you, I have no idea what you're talking about."

"Senator, the convention nominated you. You're the Republican nominee for the presidency!"

81

HERE WE STAND
FOR LIGHT AND TRUTH

AN HOUR later, two men and a woman were seated in the living room of the Jansen home in earnest conversation. Outside were now camped no fewer than fifty journalists and a dozen news teams that had been arriving by plane from Denver and Salt Lake City and from throughout Wyoming for the past hour.

The curtains of every window in the house were drawn. The entire country was watching, waiting for the front door to open.

"I know how much you detest the limelight, Harvey," Harriet Jansen was saying. "But I think Governor Foxe is right. You didn't choose this. But maybe history has chosen you."

"I have done my duty to the party," said Harvey softly.

"I appreciate what you have done, Harvey," said the governor, who had also declined to attend the convention. He had arrived by limousine from the state capital in Cheyenne fifty miles away at the behest of the party leaders. He had been on the road soon after their call, his arrival coinciding with the fleet of private planes arriving from Denver 130 miles south.

"I asked you to accept the appointment to the Senate as a favor to me," Foxe continued. "You did. You have done your duty, as you say. You may consider that obligation fulfilled. But I believe your wife is right. History has chosen you."

The room was silent.

"Harvey," said Mrs. Jansen at length, "the last thing I want to do is campaign for the presidency. I realize we would embark on it knowing we will lose. But what if, in the midst of our country's decline, you and I could bring some spark of light and truth to the national debate? Speaking for myself, that would be worth it. I will support you whatever you decide. But know that I am willing to stand at your side and be a light for Christ even in a losing cause."

Jansen knew that his wife hated politics. She would not have said what she did unless she felt deeply that something important was here for them.

"The Lord said, 'Let your light so shine before men,'" she went on. "Maybe we are being called to do that, Harvey. We may not want to. But what if, for some reason we do not understand, we are being called to say, we are God's man and woman. Here we stand—for light, for truth—for America."

Though only the two men heard them, her words reverberated with the powerful reminder of the crossroads of history in which Martin Luther had taken his stand more than 400 years before.

"We may not be a bright light," Harriet continued. "However, if every Christian stood and shone for truth where they live, insignificant as they may think they are, all those lights may not stop the world's slide into darkness, but they are still God's lights. I believe they will shine bright when the full story is told in eternity. The world may mock us, Harvey. Alongside Senator Rhodes, they may make fun of you. They will laugh when they think of me as first lady. I don't care. I want to let the light of my faith shine, Harvey."

Harvey could only sit in silence absorbing such an outpouring from his wife. Governor Foxe, too, had been mesmerized.

"I once heard you say, Harvey, that the Republican nominee is nothing but a sacrificial lamb. Maybe they nominated you to be exactly that. Maybe they chose you because you were the least significant national Republican they could think of, so that none of them would be tarnished with defeat. But we have the opportunity to willingly choose to be sacrificial lambs. There's no greater privilege than to walk in the footsteps of our Lord's example. He was God's Lamb, and we can be his baby lambs."

After the three inside rose from their knees twenty minutes later, the front door of the house opened. Fifty cameras instantly began rolling.

They walked outside together. Shouts erupted. The three approached the small crowd but remained silent. They stood side by side patiently waiting. It took fully two minutes for the assembled journalists to realize that none of their questions would be answered until they were completely silent.

At last Wyoming Governor Foxe took a step forward. The cameras zoomed close on his face.

"Ladies and gentlemen of America," he said, "let me be the first to congratulate, and to present to you the Republican nominee for the presidency of the United States and his wife, Senator Harvey and Mrs. Harriet Jansen."

82

WARD HUTCHINS
GOES PRIME TIME

JULY 2048

SENATOR RHODES was relieved that his old friend and nemesis Ward Hutchins had been true to his word and declined to be nominated. He had flown to Denver to appear personally to prevent happening to him what had happened to unsuspecting Harvey Jansen—being drafted by the convention knowing nothing about it.

Had Ward agreed to the nomination, he might have put up a credible fight. As it was, however, in the week following Jansen's nomination, in spite of the sentimental appeal of a hopeless underdog, the Las Vegas odds gave Rhodes a twenty-five-point advantage. Jansen wouldn't carry a single state.

Savoring the glow of his victory and his place atop the party, Jefferson Rhodes still worried about Ward's popularity with the far right. Small though the religious faction was, Ward remained capable of inflicting damage.

A week after the convention, Mike Bardolf was named to head the Democrat nominee's Secret Service detail.

Ward wasted no time weighing in on the election. He had kept in the background throughout the primary season, concentrating on his prophecy articles. He continued to tease his readers with the promise that the series would culminate toward year's end—if the Lord gave him the insight he expected—with the revelation of the identity of a potential antichrist. As much as his readers ignored that all important word, he continued to emphasize it. "No one can know such things for certain," he said, "until the tribulation is well underway. I can only reveal what I believe the Lord is showing me about possibilities. Nothing more."

Had his articles been purely religious, they would have attracted little attention in the wider world. But Ward's association with Jefferson Rhodes, and the obvious political undercurrent to his name recognition after the brief convention buzz, kept the general public intrigued. When he gave a speech, even the liberal press now covered it in hopes of catching something outlandish.

Why Jefferson Rhodes let him get under his skin was curious. No one cared what a right-wing religious fanatic said about the Second Coming.

Yet Ward haunted him.

A force he could not resist almost compelled him to tune into Ward's highly publicized telecast on prime time in the last week in July. Rhodes poured himself a full glass of Scotch and sat to watch alone, both trembling with trepidation and in rising anger that Ward could exercise such a hold on him—angry at himself for allowing him to do so.

As intrigued as they were by his antics, none of the liberal networks agreed to Ward's terms. FNN, however, gave him three uninterrupted minutes of airtime at 8:56 p.m. eastern, the slot reserved for five minutes of ads between the two hourly news programs. It was billed as "A Vital Address to the Nation." In spite of being snubbed by the liberal media, FNN had so widely publicized the event that its viewing audience surpassed all the other networks, cable and broadcast, combined.

"Good evening, my fellow Americans," Ward began. "I come to you tonight to speak about the future of our nation. As you know, I have never been a political man. The ministry God has privileged me with is a ministry for the hearts and souls of men, not to sway their political allegiance. However, we are at a critical time in our history when the destructive ideas that have become commonplace over the past four decades are threatening the foundations upon which our country was built as a nation 'under God.'

"Sadly, we are no longer a nation under God, but under man and under woman and under gays and lesbians and atheists, under people from other countries who have swelled our numbers, a country under judges who do not uphold our laws and who legislate to further their progressive agenda, a country under doctors who slaughter the unborn, a nation under politicians who continue to find ways to circumvent both man's law and God's law to legalize the murder of innocents. I repeat, because it is so important—we are no longer a nation under God.

"These people and groups have as much a right to be Americans as I do. Please do not call this hate speech. I hate no one. I only say that truth is truth, and we must live by it. My point is that the rights and agendas of such groups and the abandonment of our founding laws and principles have replaced God's truth as the foundation of our country. This is the message I would leave you with.

"If you remember nothing else from my words this evening, I pray you will remember this: if this divergence from our founding principles continues, America will cease being a light on the hill to the people of the world."

He paused, seemingly well aware that his controversial words would inflame the country.

"I say what I have just said to judge no one but to call us to repentance and to a return to our core values. Though many in our country no longer believe in right and wrong, I stand before you tonight and declare that there *is* a right, and there *is* a wrong, just as there *is* truth, and there *is* falsehood. Of course, in many aspects of life, individual choice determines right and wrong. But on a higher plane some things are *always* right and other things are *always* wrong.

"Abortion, for example, is always wrong. It is simply wrong. Our nation's system of laws now says that abortion is legal. But it is still wrong. This is but one example in which the politicians of our nation have legalized what is wrong. Same-sex marriage is also legal, but it, too, is wrong. It is a slap in the face of the Creator who made us man and woman and who created traditional families as the primary institution of humanity.

"My message this evening is simple. I ask this one question: Do we want our nation to continue down the road of legalizing and encouraging what is wrong and condemning those like myself who call it wrong? Or do we want to stem this tide and turn our nation back toward virtue and truth?

"We stand at a crossroads in our history. It is not too late to reverse this downward trend. We must reverse it, or we will join the many other failed nations who now lie on the dust heap of history. The utopia preached by progressivism is a mirage. Beneath its happy talk of equality, justice, tolerance, and unlimited personal freedom lies a foundation built not on truth and right but on untruth and wrong. If we do not awaken to that fact, those falsehoods will destroy us."

Again he paused.

"I am not here to endorse any candidate in the upcoming election. I do not know Harvey Jansen personally. I cannot speak knowledgeably about his ethics or character, though he is a Christian man. I do, however, know Jefferson Rhodes. Jeff is a friend, as is well documented. I like Jeff. We have enjoyed some good times together. I love him as a brother.

"So it would clearly be inappropriate for me to encourage you to vote for or against either of these men. This election is not about these two men. It is about our future as a country. I therefore encourage you to examine the platforms of the two parties. What do they stand for? In November, this nation will not merely decide on the presidency. You will also be voting for congressmen and senators, for mayors and governors and state legislators.

"In November this nation will decide the direction of its future. I ask you to examine the principles undergirding the platforms that all candidates endorse, at every level. Examine the values represented. Do not be deceived by radical and utopian promises from those who have abandoned right and truth and sold the soul of this once great nation to—"

Jefferson Rhodes leapt from his chair. With a mighty heave he threw his half-full glass of Scotch across the room. It shattered into a hundred pieces, spewing what was left of its contents against the wall.

"D— you, Ward!" he cried aloud. "I'll see you rot in hell before I'll let you destroy me. You're finished, Ward! I will destroy you!"

83

Λ DVICE FROM WIFE AND FRIEND

JULY 2048

PROBABLY LIKE most unpublished authors, and a good many published ones, even having completed a book, Charles Reyburn had no idea what he had.

Had he spoken truth? How might people respond? Should he try to get it published? Would any publisher even look at it?

Following the beginning he had made two years earlier, he had written the complete manuscript almost in a single gush of inspiration during the past summer, never pausing to ask such questions until it was done. He had written it because he had to write it. He had been compelled.

But what came next?

With no clear answer to that question, he put it aside. Without more direction, waiting was always best.

His wife knew he had been consumed by it, but he had divulged nothing to her. When he finally gave her the manuscript to read, almost a year had passed. She had no idea what to expect. Staying up half the night until finally falling asleep, several loose pages falling on the floor beside her chair, she finished the 225-page manuscript the next afternoon.

She found her husband in his study. He turned and saw a look on her face he had never seen before.

"Charles," she said, "this is the most remarkable . . . I don't even know what to call it. You have to publish this!"

"Would anybody read it?"

"Charles, the country needs it. This could change everything."

"I wouldn't even know how to find a publisher."

"Talk to Dr. Harrison. He's published several books."

"Good idea. He might be able to point me in the right direction."

On the following Monday, Charles Reyburn sat in Dr. Nicholas Harrison's office as his colleague looked over his manuscript. He was not nervous, neither was he looking for praise, flattery, or criticism. He was simply seeking honest information from a knowledgeable author who knew the world of publishing better than he did, and spiritual counsel from one of his closest friends whose wisdom he trusted.

He waited patiently. His friend read the entire introduction, half the first chapter, then began skipping ahead, reading in succession the first half page of every chapter that followed.

After about twenty-five minutes, during which time neither man said a word, he set the pages down on his desk and exhaled a long sigh.

"Do you know what you have here, Charles?" he asked.

"I don't suppose I do," replied Reyburn. "That's why I came to you."

"Then I will tell you what you have—you have a prophetic document."

Reyburn stared back with blank expression.

"I mean that in the full scriptural sense of the word. This is no cartoon like *Left Behind*. This is what the Church has been waiting decades for. I believe it is a word from God. It has to be published."

Reyburn still sat listening though unbelieving.

"You're not, I don't know, Nicholas—exaggerating a bit?" he said at length.

"I mean every word."

"But will anyone publish it? It's obviously not a message that will resonate with the public at large."

"You may be surprised. I doubt you wrote it for the public at large anyway. You wrote it for the true Church. I have the sense that there may be more in this country besides conservative evangelicals who are tired of what's going on. I believe this may hit an unseen chord with millions who see America disappearing before their eyes."

"I hardly know what to think," said Reyburn. "What do you suggest?"

"With your permission, I would like to show it to my publisher. They are a small evangelical house. You wouldn't want a secular publisher handling it."

"Of course not."

Reyburn thought a minute.

"Would it be best not to use my name?" he said.

"Why? Are you concerned about the repercussions?"

"I wasn't thinking of that. I am just aware that I am an unknown. I have never written a book. It seems the message might be more powerful if no one could question my motives or lack of credentials. Might anonymity be a benefit?"

"I will be honest—if you pursue this, your life will change. You will be ridiculed and praised. You will be hailed as a prophet and despised as a fanatic and Uncle Tom. Even with your black skin, you will be called a racist, even anti-black. Logic will be gone. You will be excoriated. You and your wife must be prepared. You could even be in danger. The Left hates courageous Christians more than anything. It is becoming increasingly dangerous to be a Christian. They will mobilize their full arsenal to discredit you. Your family will suffer. That is certainly a reason to publish it anonymously."

Reyburn took his words in seriously.

"On the other hand, doing so will give the book's critics ammunition to call the author a coward, afraid to show himself, and to undercut your credibility. Your story about shaking the hand of their most revered icon and its impact on you—unbelievable. I've not read the whole thing, but that may be the most powerful image in the book. It's all lies! Charles, my friend, that is a singular moment that will be quoted and re-quoted. For that moment to have the power it does, you have to come out from behind the curtain and show yourself as the unpretentious, soft-spoken professor from Hillsgrove College. You have to take your place with history's men whom God called to stand tall at the crossroads and say, 'Here I stand.'"

84

∧ Sevenfold Cord

August 2048

David GORDON and Mark Forster had been meeting together for two years, revisiting many of the themes they had discussed during Mark's collegiate and post-university years. Now that he and Grace were involved in the GCG, Mark was fully drinking from the fountainhead of David's wisdom. David's years of prayer for his neighbor and son of the best friend of his own young manhood had born hundredfold fruit.

Mark's regular visits to his parents in Grass Valley contributed their share to the deepening sense of his own sonship as well as of the divine Fatherhood. As he learned the imperative lesson that God's Fatherhood was reflected in all human fathers, not only seemingly spiritual ones, his love for his own father deepened, as did his gratitude for his father's friend who was truly a spiritual father.

Many of the principles in Stirling Marshall's writings that had been a mystery to him before now opened windows in his heart into an entire new world of spiritual consciousness. What he had considered his role in the ministry paled alongside the high and eternal purpose of God, which David called "God's High Logos."

David also continued to meet regularly with Timothy and Jaylene, as they had been for years. He was enjoying supper with them in late August. They had been discussing Charles Reyburn's new book—rushed into print with new publishing technology literally within weeks of landing on the publisher's doorstep—along with their sense that Stirling's writings were about to expand to a wider audience.

"I believe it is time to share your father's *Brief* with Mark and Grace," said David. "We always said we would not share it without unanimity between us. We've now opened the door with a few others. So I am putting before you whether Mark and Grace are next."

Timothy and Jaylene glanced at one another but said nothing for several seconds.

At length Timothy smiled. "Short answer—I concur. I have been feeling exactly the same thing. I said nothing to make sure we left it in God's hands. If he was indeed speaking, then I knew I could wait until he spoke the same thing to one of you."

He turned toward his wife.

"I hope what I am about to suggest isn't the partisanship of a parent," Jaylene added. "But I have been thinking the same about Heather—that she is ready as well. I felt strange back in April sharing it with the others and not Mark and Grace and Heather, especially asking to use Heather's home without her present. I understood our reasons, but I definitely feel they should be next."

"Heather indeed may be next in line," nodded David. "That she is a Marshall who seems thoroughly one with her grandfather's spiritual vision and is attempting to live her life according to its principles places her in a unique category all her own. I think both your parents, Timothy, would absolutely want her included."

A week later, the three Marshalls, two Forsters, with David and Heather met at Heather's. They gathered on Saturday afternoon. Heather provided snacks and coffee and tea but this was not a social visit.

When they were seated, Timothy launched into the reason why they were there.

"After my mother died," he began, "my father was given what he felt was a final message from God to the Church, or perhaps to a remnant of it that would be revealed at some future time. Essentially it was a call to the true Church to recognize itself as called out, not merely out of the world but out of the institution of man that goes by the name 'church.' He called the document the *Benedict Brief*.

"At his death, my father entrusted his *Brief* to the three of us with cautions about how and when to share it, including certain stipulations how it was to be handled to protect the message and keep it from falling into the hands of those who would misunderstand and misuse his message in ways that were the opposite of God's intent."

Timothy went on to share how his father had kept it even from them at first, how the *Brief* had changed their perspective on many things, how they had had to grow into their own understanding of his father's vision, how the GCG group had emerged slowly, that they had gradually sensed a time coming when his father's document was to expand and that they were to share it with selective others.

"In short," he concluded, glanced around at his daughter and Mark and Grace, "it is time for you three to read the *Brief.*"

"Naturally we are honored," said Mark with sober expression.

"You must understand that reading it comes with a great responsibility—such as we have been carrying all these years. You will be taking on with us the responsibility to pray for direction for how and when the *Brief* is to be used. We have been especially hesitant," Timothy added, glancing toward Mark, "given your position in the church. The last thing we want is to add further complications to the balance you have to walk between the group and church. Yet we feel you are one with us in this. It is not a responsibility to be undertaken lightly. So at this point, the choice whether or not to take this next step has to be yours."

Mark and Grace looked at one another.

"We understand," said Grace. "It is a great honor, all the more so that it comes with such a heavy responsibility.

"I would caution you, too," added David, "that your lives may change. Your ministry at the church may change. The times ahead, as Timothy's father foresaw, may be perilous for the remnant of the Church."

The house fell silent for several long seconds.

"I have been sensing changes coming to my role in the church," said Mark slowly. "I don't yet see what those changes are. But being involved with you and others in the group, David, I am not the same man I was when we moved to Roseville. If this is the next step God has for us, how can we not embrace it?"

Again the room was silent.

Jaylene glanced toward their daughter.

"And you, Heather?" she said.

Heather was looking down, obviously deep in thought. She drew in a deep breath.

"I don't know what to say, Mom," she said. "All I can think of at this moment is Grandma and Grandpa, and how much I want to know everything that was in their hearts, all the wisdom God gave them over the years. I want to know them. I am so honored by this, there are no words."

She turned away as her eyes filled with tears.

"Lord, give us wisdom," prayed David.

It was enough, for it was everything.

85

CONTROVERSIAL INTERVIEW

SEPTEMBER 2048

NICHOLAS HARRISON was not mistaken. His editor at Sonrise Path Publications had a contract drawn up within a week of Harrison's visit, committing the full weight of the small publishing house behind a major marketing campaign. Still in awe over the rapid developments, Reyburn designated that all proceeds from the book be donated to the Bold Thinking Christianity Reading Room at Hillsgrove College.

The book progressed at lightning speed through the editorial and production stages, fast-tracked to coincide with the election season. Word of mouth was instantaneous. Within two weeks sales had topped 50,000 and the secular publishing world began to take notice. By the end of August, it had crept onto the *New York Times* non-fiction best-seller list despite the paper's most diligent efforts to disregard it.

Requests were immediate for interviews and regional radio programs. The networks were watching developments. Talk-show requests began pouring in.

Nor did it escape the media that Jefferson Rhodes's lead over Harvey Jansen, once unassailable and virtually unaffected by the Hutchins appearance on FNN, had shrunk by ten points since the release of Reyburn's book.

Something unexpected had been kindled. No one quite knew what.

In the first week of September, reluctant but willing to agree for the cause, Charles Reyburn found himself waiting in the wings listening to Phil Simons introduce him.

"Good evening, gentlepeople," Simons began. "I have with me this evening as my special guest Dr. Charles Reyburn, professor emeritus at Hillsgrove College, whose book *Roots: America Reclaims Its Heritage* has ignited something in this country. In just four weeks since its release, it now tops the *New York Times* bestseller list, an unheard of accomplishment in our time for a so-called religious book. The response has been so enormous that it appears to have had an impact on the presidential election. Democrat Senator Jefferson Rhodes has dropped several points in the polls since the book's release. Has a swing in this nation's outlook on religion, and Christianity in particular, begun? Has a return swing of the pendulum set in toward traditional spiritual values?"

Simons paused as the live band now brought his guest onstage. The two men shook hands then sat in their respective seats.

"Welcome, Dr. Reyburn," said Simons. "I will put that exact question to you—are we witnessing a return of America, as the title of your book has it, to its roots, its heritage?"

"Honestly, Phil," replied Reyburn, trying to remain calm in spite of being awestruck by his surroundings, "I don't know. I am probably more surprised by the response than anyone. All I can say is that reading a book does not change a culture. For people to change themselves, for a country to change itself—that's harder. Most people don't want to change. Institutions by their nature are resistant to change."

"That sounds pessimistic, as if in spite of its sales, you think your book may not have much impact in the long run."

"That may indeed be the case. Change is hard work. It takes a recognition that in some respects we have been going down a wrong road. That's what change implies. People don't want to admit that. At its most basic, change means admitting something is wrong."

"I had never thought of that."

"It is gratifying that people are reading my book. But three years from now, will anything be different? Will people have changed? Will the country have changed? If history is any judge, probably not. People don't learn from history. They don't learn from their mistakes. They don't want to admit that things are wrong, that *they* have been wrong, as G. K. Chesterton once pithily said. So they don't change."

"That's a bleak outlook!" laughed Simons.

"Or a realistic one," rejoined Reyburn. "I'm a historian. Most cultures don't heed the warnings of those who see danger ahead."

"And you believe that the trends of our times are dangerous and will lead us to our demise?"

"I do."

"You're in a tiny minority."

"I realize that."

"What is so dangerous about trying to better people's lives, which, as I understand it, is the foundation of liberalism?"

"Nothing, if that were all there was to it. Bettering people's lives is what the gospel of Jesus Christ is all about. But liberalism's soft underbelly is the same fallacy of all socialist experiments. Their utopian dreams are based on so many untruths and inconsistencies that they always fail in the end. I say that not as a political partisan but as a historian. They fail because they are not based on truth, on right and wrong."

"Perhaps you could give an example of what you mean."

"The most lethal example is also the most obvious. Progressivism is supposedly based on tolerance, freedom for all, inclusion, justice, equality. Would you agree?"

"That's what they say."

"So where is tolerance, inclusion, equality, and free speech for Christians who express belief in traditional Christian ideas? Why are Christians excluded—singled out and subjected to intolerance and their ideas not given equal respect in the public discourse?"

"You make an interesting point."

"Another example from all the way back in the 2020s. It became completely commonplace for men to compete in women's sports. If he said he wanted to be a woman, if he identified as a woman, progressivism said that was his right. The absurdity of it was obvious to common sense, but few liberals back then lifted an eyebrow. Few complained about the injustice toward the women athletes who were displaced in the early years of this movement. Those women were treated unfairly, to prop up the progressive fiction that gender is a choice. Now, of course, there are four categories of high school, collegiate, and international sports competitions, and four sets of records, rather than the former two. But are the Olympics really better off lasting two months, with a full slate of events for men pretending to be women and another for women pretending to be men?"

"You believe that gender neutrality is a pretense, a fiction?"

"Of course. You believe it, too, though you probably won't say it. Everybody knows it's fiction. It is a biological impossibility. But people go along with it because they know they will be condemned by the Left if they speak up."

Simons did not reply.

"Take another example," said Reyburn. "If I speak candidly about what I believe as a Christian, I will be bullied, ridiculed, and accused of hate speech. You know what will be said about me tomorrow after this interview. The media will applaud a man for wanting to be his true self by competing in women's sports. The two trans categories in the Olympics get as much coverage as the men's and women's events. The participants are hailed as cultural pioneers and heroes. Yet my belief in right and wrong is universally condemned by progressives as judgmental toward such individual freedoms. Why am I not free to express my beliefs without condemnation? Can you explain the logic of that to me?"

"No, I can't," replied Simons.

☆ ☆ ☆

Amazing, thought Mark Forster, at what he was witnessing on nationwide television.

He had never heard of Charles Reyburn before reading his book. He knew little about him. This was the first time he had actually seen him. The man was bold and courageous without being pushy or arrogant. His calm demeanor, his quiet confidence in who he was in God, gave such powerful dignity to his articulation of truth that even an experienced interviewer like Phil Simons could not rile him.

Mark was reminded of Jesus at his trial before the high priests. Though not remaining silent as had the Lord, Reyburn was relying on truth, not argumentation or the forcefulness of personality, to be his advocate. He was a visible example of how God's people could effectively be salt and light to the world by Christlikeness of character speaking the truth in love and humility.

As the interview continued, Mark's thoughts strayed to his own position as the pastor of Foothills. Compared with what Reyburn was doing, his audience was miniscule. And his was a friendly audience of Christians, not the hostile audience of an anti-Christian culture. Yet even in his tiny world, did he have the mettle to stand with the level of courage that was being demonstrated in front of him? Especially in light of the fact that a lesbian and transgender sat on his own board of elders. He had been uncomfortable about it ever since coming from Seattle but had no idea what to do.

Mark was but one of thousands who, as they watched, took the interview very personally. Reyburn was giving them a practical example how to meet the culture with the imperatively twin virtues of boldness and humility working in harmony, each strengthening the other.

86

THE GREAT LIE

"LET ME make the example more pointed," Reyburn continued. "I believe in sin. I believe sin exists. There is real right and real wrong. Sin is not an imaginary, outdated concept. I believe it is real. It is sin to do wrong. Yet I'm certain you are aware that there are some countries, and many in our own who would support it, where I could be arrested and jailed for what I just said. In those countries, the term *sin* is considered hate speech."

"I have heard that," nodded Simons.

"So where is tolerance, freedom, inclusion, and equality toward those who believe in right and wrong and sin? Is progressivism tolerant of me? What are progressives saying about my book? Are they hailing it as a triumph of free speech? Or are they quoting selections in their reviews and calling it hate speech? What will progressives say to the hate speech directed against me tomorrow? When I am condemned, will the ACLU come to my defense? You know the answer as well as I do. You asked for an example of the fundamental fallacy of progressivism. It is in front of us every day—intolerance, injustice, and hate speech toward those who do not go along with its ideas. This is pure hypocrisy."

"I see your point. But that is a strong accusation. You consider progressivism's ideals hypocritical?"

"No. Its ideals are noble. But its practice is hypocritical. There is no tolerance unless you agree. Disagree with progressivism and you will be attacked with the full force of its intolerance. You will be attacked by hate speech. When it comes from the Left, however, hate speech is called enlightened thinking. When those on the Right express their personal beliefs, it is called hate speech. That is hypocrisy. Progressivism is laced with the cancer of all totalitarian systems—the attempted eradication of all who oppose them. That is the very opposite of freedom."

"You do not mince words."

"I see no point in sugarcoating it. The slide of our culture into what Rod Dreher years ago called soft-totalitarianism has been lethal since the Obama years and has thoroughly infected politics, educational systems, Hollywood, and the media with its cancer of elitism, intolerance, anti-white racism, and anti-Christian bigotry."

"You as a black man are speaking of anti-white racism?"

"Why should I not? My fellow blacks have become the nation's racists."

"You will be condemned for saying such a thing."

"Of course. Those speaking uncomfortable truths are often condemned. Shopenhauer said two centuries ago, 'What the herd hates the most is the one who thinks differently; it is not so much the opinion itself, it is the audacity of wanting to think for themselves, something they do not know how to do. All truth passes through three stages. First, it is ridiculed. Second, it is violently opposed. Third, it is accepted as being self-evident.' Because of untruths being universally accepted by the youth who have allowed themselves to be brainwashed, for years I have had little hope that our nation can survive, or at least the nation that was once the United States of America. I have tried to teach my students faithfully according to the principles upon which our country was founded. Yet I have been but one of a tiny minority trying to bail the waters of liberalism out of our sinking ship of state with my little thimble. The fundamental values of our nation are simply gone."

"Don't you think that's overstating it?"

"Freedom of speech, freedom of religion, equality to all including people who believe as I do, tolerance toward people who believe differently than the culture tells them they should—our values don't get much more fundamental than that. As I said, you know what will be said of me after this interview. Do you think my freedom of speech and my freedom of religion will be respected or lauded? Where do you find silencing Christians and curtailing their right to free speech in the Constitution?"

"There are those who say the Constitution is outdated and should be changed."

"Are they saying that because they want to give Christians more freedom of speech and more freedom to believe as they do without recrimination?"

Simons thought a moment.

"It sounds like you are a man on a mission," he said, laughing lightly.

"That would be a grave mischaracterization, Phil. I am just an ordinary man who finally realized I had had enough of the hypocrisy and the media's complicity in it. I wrote what I wrote because it welled up inside me and I had to write it. I had no thought of publishing a book. It was my wife who said I should have a friend look at it."

Simons laughed. "Perhaps we should have her on the show!"

"That would be a hard sell!"

"But you must have sensed that the country was ready for an awakening, or you would not have written it."

"Honestly, no. I did not anticipate anyone reading it but my wife. I always say she is paid to read what I write, so I take her occasional praise with a grain of salt. I say that tongue in cheek, of course—she is very gracious but will also nail me when I say something I shouldn't. She was the only person I expected to read it. I certainly never imagined this kind of response."

"And she was enthusiastic?"

"Yes, and suggested I show it to my colleague at Hillsgrove, Nicholas Harrison. He asked if he could show it to his editor at Sonrise Path. That's how it happened."

"A remarkable story. You honestly did not intend to publish it?"

"I was simply compelled to write. I had no plans. I worked on it sporadically for two years. Then a day came when the Great Lie overpowered me."

"What great lie?"

"The Great Lie of progressivism. I was filled with what you might call a righteous indignation that the Left has gotten away with foisting its hypocrisy, bigotry, elitism, intolerance, and, yes, blatant racism on a gullible public for too long. Something arose within me and shouted *Enough!* I didn't think about what I was doing, I just wrote. I hardly thought of anything for weeks but my attempt to combine history and spirituality with what I might call the foundational ethos of the United States of America. When I came up for air, I had over two hundred pages on my desk."

"Remarkable," repeated Simons.

87

A Detective
and His Wife

WHERE THEY sat watching the unprecedented interview, Court and Stella Masters could hardly believe what they were hearing. Never in their lives had they heard the agenda of modernism repudiated so forcefully and intelligently.

As a longtime liberal, until her inner eyes had been opened, Stella was especially intrigued.

Court found himself reflecting on the circuitous paths that had brought him to this moment. In the fourteen years since Secret Service Director Erin Parva had enlisted his clandestine help to investigate the assassination of President Adriana Hunt, much had changed for Court Masters.

The biggest change was that he and Stella were now on a firm marital and spiritual footing. Stella had left her tech job at GIH after the firing of the company's comptroller, no longer able to tolerate what she suddenly saw as an atmosphere of liberal elitism. She had been doing temp work ever since, specializing in training people to understand and use artificial intelligence tools. Even so many years after the murky world of AI had gone mainstream, there was still enough confusion to keep her appointment calendar booked for weeks. People called her the AI Guru. They were now talking about retirement and refining their mutual bucket list. Without children, they had enough put aside to do whatever they wanted.

For some time, too, the realization had grown upon them that church no longer fed their spiritual hunger. They had been praying to be drawn to people with whom they could share what was sometimes a solitary spiritual journey. After their visit to California in April, Court knew that prayer had been answered. He and Stella were eagerly antic-ipating the next meeting of Timothy and Jaylene Marshall's group two weeks from now.

They had also begun writing a book together. It was turning out much differently than the book Court had vaguely considered about his life as a policeman. They hoped to share—candidly and honestly—their personal journey as husband and wife, the difficult years when they had drifted apart because of different perspectives on the culture, coming together again, changing, growing, learning many new things. They hoped their different perspective—Court's as a career policeman, Stella's as one who had been surrounded for years by a cocoon of liber-alism—would give readers two vantage points from which to view the changes taking place around them.

What would not come into the book was Court's now back-burnered investigation into the assassination. Whether it went into the book or not, Court's perplexing, and he now admitted worrisome rela-tionship with Erin Parva, now FBI director after Greg Telford's retire-ment, wove as a sub-theme through the past fifteen years of his life.

It hadn't been long after Parva had enlisted him to investigate the assassination when he began to sense hidden motives behind her request, the suspicion that her true intent was to use him to infiltrate underground enclaves of conservatism that might be considered sub-versive to the objectives of the administration.

Whether she really believed Trump supporters were behind the assassination, he soon began to doubt. It was an excuse to cast a wider net, using Court as her lackey.

Was she aware of his spiritual and political leanings? Had she known all along? Is that why she had chosen him, to act as a mole to penetrate pockets of so-called sedition she would never gain access to through normal FBI channels?

He tried faithfully to learn more about the assassination. He followed dozens of leads, easier to work on unnoticed after his promotion to detective, some of them intriguing but with no hint of a conspiracy or Trump connections.

All the while his suspicions about Parva grew. Her subtle questions deepened his conviction that more was on her mind than the assassination. Their conversations became like interrogations, her tone probing, wary, guarded.

Stella's help with AI had given his investigation a shot in the arm yet also increased the danger the more he pursued it. The dots leading to Mark Forster, prompting his visit to California, were admittedly thin. First there was the sinister figure of Viktor Domokos lurking like a giant shadow behind the American political scene, to his biographer Michael Bardolf who had been at Patterson Park that fateful day in the fall of 2033 and was thus linked to Parva through the Secret Service, possibly also to then Vice President Perez. He then followed Bardolf's movements to his affiliation with Sen. Jefferson Rhodes. From there the trail led from Rhodes to evangelist Hutchins, where at last the far-right wing of evangelical conservatism came into the picture, just as Parva had insisted all along. He had painstakingly investigated Hutchins but without a shred of evidence that he was a Trumpite or connected with anything nefarious. The accusations by the press led Court to the connection with the senator's other friend, pastor Mark Forster. Hence had followed his trip to California where he also hoped to meet the son of the author of *Unspoken Commandments*.

The rest, as he might have said, was history. His visit with the Marshalls and Mark Forster convinced him beyond doubt that they were among the most honorable people he had ever met.

The Marshall group was exactly the kind Parva had wanted him to uncover. No doubt she knew all about his trip to California. That she did not grill him about it after his return convinced him of it all the more.

There was nothing among his new friends to arouse suspicion. They were simply people of deep spiritual conviction trying to live by the commands of the Bible. But if she were to learn of the group, that purpose would not be one Erin Parva could understand. Court was not about to let that happen.

The sequence of thoughts flashed through Court's brain in a few swift seconds. Just as quickly his attention returned to the interview in progress.

Charles Reyburn, he realized, was cut from the same cloth as those he had met in California. He was a man whose being was anchored in God's truth. With Reyburn's every response, Court wanted to shout, "Amen!"

It was time for Christians to stand up and be counted.

It was time for *him* to stand up and be counted!

88

WHO WILL CONTINUE
THE LEGACY?

"WHEN YOU say you were compelled," asked Simons after a brief pause, "—by whom, by what?"

"I wouldn't want to over-spiritualize or dramatize it," replied Reyburn, "but I hope God had a hand in it. I am a Christian. I view my life through a supernatural lens. I realize not everyone does. On the other hand, therefore, I would just as truthfully say that my love for America compelled me. Or my love for truth, my hatred of falsehood and hypocrisy. Or my heartache and concern for the younger generations of America who are being raised on the falsehoods of the Left."

"You have children of your own?"

"I do."

"And you are concerned for their generation?"

"I am heartbroken for them. Can you fathom the damage done to the self-image and self-perception of an entire generation of people—adults now—who were taught in school from the time they could read that there is no such thing as male and female, that their gender is a matter of choice not biology? The idiocy of it is indescribable. Yet the Left has foisted this lie upon the public, and an entire generation has no idea what to think when they look in the mirror. Not to mention the new racism being taught from kindergarten up. CRT is just a new form of racism, promoting division and hatred no less than old forms of racism."

"Those on the Left would call that narrow minded and judgmental."

"I hope you will not react so simplistically as that."

"But honestly, Dr. Reyburn, many Christians live in a bubble. They don't recognize the real world for what it is. When you tell a young person they need to change, that their lifestyle choices are wrong—some Christians would go so far as to call them sinners—you don't think that is judgmental?"

"When progressives tell people to embrace homosexuality and abortion and that those who oppose them are bigoted, is that any less judgmental? But to your question, I never call anyone a sinner."

"But you think pursuing gender options other than birth-biology is a sin."

"Have you heard me say that?"

"I assume that to be your view from your remarks. Do you think it's a sin?"

"That's a gotcha question, which I will not answer. If I say no, you will ask why I think they should change. If I say yes, you will call me judgmental. It's a dishonest question, Phil."

"So you don't try to confront young people with their sin?"

"I do not. That approach may appeal to some but not to me."

"What do you do instead?"

"I try to accept people where they are—with kindness and I hope with understanding."

"What do you say to them, then?"

"I talk to them about the character of God, about how he created his universe, about the happiness and fulfillment he desires for his sons and daughters that can only be found by falling in with the created order of the world. The foundation of everything is the recognition of who God is as a good and loving Father. That is the basis for living by his created order. There are confused and unhappy young people in the world, Phil, who realize they have been betrayed by progressivism. They have questions. They want to be given a path to clarity."

Reyburn paused briefly.

"My position is really not so difficult to understand," he went on. "I try to help everyone toward personal wholeness, guided by kindness. It is the same quest I am on myself—toward wholeness and maturity of personhood, toward becoming the man God created me to be. The psychological damage to untold millions by modernism's sexual and gender delusions is incalculable. People are confused and suffering because of modernism's lies. Getting back to your question why I wrote the book—all these factors rose up within me and over-whelmed me. I had to write what I saw happening to our nation and its young people."

In speaking of the next generation, Heather Marshall realized that Dr. Reyburn was talking about her. She was of Generation Alpha. She was even too young to be called a "Millennial."

She took Reyburn's words, and his warnings, far more personally than most of her age, whether Millennials or Generation Z or Alphas like her. More important than all that, she was a Marshall. She felt the imperative of her grandfather's spiritual vision—as well as that of her parents—resting on her shoulders. She was the generation who must take the spiritual truths they had implanted into her forward into the future.

But Reyburn was right. The times were perilous. What would become of her generation? What would become of Christianity and America under her Generation Alpha and Beta and whatever the young people of the future would be called? Would the Alphas be the generation that allowed Christianity in America at last to die a slow and ignoble death?

No! she wanted to shout. We mustn't let it die, my brothers and sisters of the third millennium! We must fight to preserve the heritage that has been passed to us! We must be strong and of good courage! We must follow the examples of my grandfather Stirling Marshall, the examples of my mother who stood against secularism in education, the example of Dr. Reyburn who is proclaiming truth to America! It is up to us—the Millennials and Alphas who love truth and love America, we who represent the posterity of our forebears—it is up to us to pre-serve the legacy!

She thought back to her grandfather's *Benedict Brief* which she had just read a month before. He had issued the same challenge—for Christians to stand up for their convictions.

The *Brief* put so much into focus. She had heard her parents and David talk about the same principles in the gatherings. Reading the *Brief* also explained why she often felt uncomfortable at church.

But what can I do, Heather thought. *How can one like me help preserve America's legacy?*

She was a crippled young woman of no consequence. No one took notice of her. She was not the kind of person anyone paid attention to. By all reason, she should be dead. She had nothing to give, nothing to say. She wasn't even married. It wouldn't be many more years before she would be considered a spinster, an old maid.

And yet—I am still a Marshall—a Christian—an American!

She would be faithful to her grandparents' and her parents' legacy and spiritual vision. She would promote their vision and their writings however she could. If she could not change the world, she would try to change her place in it and the people God sent across her path.

Dear Father, she prayed, *I don't have much to give. All I can do is offer you myself as I am. All I can say is that I am willing to do what you want me to. Let me be a faithful steward of my generation to preserve the heritage that has been passed down to me by my family, by my country, and by my Lord. Thus, heavenly Father, may I be an instrument in my small corner of the world for the ultimate salvation of mankind.*

89

DECLARATION OF WAR

PHIL SIMONS'S next question to Dr. Reyburn contained the subtle bait to lure him into an admission that would undercut his entire message in the eyes of many listeners.

"If God inspired or compelled you," he said, "would you call your book a message from God to America? Did God *tell* you to write it?"

"I would never go that far. I am just a man, a historian, a husband, a father. I am a man who loves his country. I am no prophetic oracle."

"The mere fact that you mentioned God in connection with the book will bring attacks from the country's progressive element."

"I would expect nothing less. I am already being ridiculed by the media. Democrats are outraged. They assumed that the world was theirs forever, that they would be free to continue brainwashing the public with ever more absurd ideas. They never dreamed that a backlash might one day arise and ask if the emperors of progressivism are wearing any clothes. Naturally they are incensed. They have had it their way for decades. Such are the tactics—falsely condemn those who disagree. Saul Alinsky preached it, and they have been using his playbook ever since. I have no doubt that I will continue to be characterized as a dangerous homophobe, racist against my own kind, an Uncle Tom, and a religious fool. I would not be surprised that I might even be called a terrorist for using such terms as *sin*."

"Are you prepared for that?"

"No. Is anyone prepared to be lied about. But I recognize it as inevitable. It goes with being a Christian who stands for truth. Liberalism by its nature hates true Christianity. They don't mind Christianity-and-water, C. S. Lewis's famous term for pretend Christianity. The progressive army is full of professing so-called Christians who do not take the words of Jesus and Paul seriously enough to make the difficult attempt to live by them. And they despise Christians who *do* try to order their lives by the Bible's truths."

"Why do you think that is?"

"I have been puzzling about that for years. They love Muslims who take their faith seriously. Why do they hate serious Christians? I honestly cannot figure it out. It may be because Christianity professes to possess a truth that is absolute, not relative, a truth that exposes the lies of the times."

"Islam might be said to do the same."

"You are exactly right. So why the tolerance of Islam and the hatred of Christianity and Judaism? It is a great mystery. Yet Christianity is the world's great absolute, and thus the archenemy of that fundamental deception of modernism. Once admit that there is *true* Truth, an *absolute* Truth to which all men and women are accountable, once admit that to deviate from that ultimate Truth is not a matter of personal choice but is wrong, once admit these truths, and the entire progressive agenda is dead. Therefore, Christianity *must* be destroyed."

"You obviously see the cultural war in almost apocalyptic terms—the great battle between good and evil."

"Good and evil, yes. Apocalyptic, no. I see it in *historical* terms. The story of the Soviet Union was not apocalyptic, but it was a story of good vs. evil. The communist dictatorship was an evil system. To sustain itself, Christianity had to be destroyed. Our nation is engaged in that same battle. I am not an apocalyptic thinker. However, I do see the battle for the future of our nation as one of truth vs. falsehood. I would not call those who disagree with me evil. I don't think in those terms either, though many on the Left do. They will call *me* evil. But I do not call them evil. I think in terms of truth and falsehood.

"The Christian foundations of our nation will either be reclaimed and strengthened anew, or the underpinnings of our history and culture will wither and fragment and eventually decay. It is those foundations that gave America its strength. Their loss will ultimately doom our future. The mainstay tenets of the liberal agenda for seventy years have been symptoms of a culture that has abandoned truth in favor of unlimited and bizarre levels of personal freedom, which is nothing more than narcissistic hedonism. Systems based on such falsehoods cannot endure."

"You're saying individual and personal freedom are lies?"

"That is too simplistic. Understood in a larger context, they are intrinsic to the gospel. But as ends unto themselves, as gods to be worshipped as the Left worships them—yes, they are lies. There is no such thing as *complete* individuality or unlimited freedom. Seen in perspective, and with a foundation of truth, right, wrong, and personal accountability, then of course individual freedom within such a framework is a worthy objective, which every society should work toward. They are intrinsic to Christianity, intrinsic to our national ethos. But the Christian gospel places individual and personal freedom into the larger context of absolute truth, not relative truth."

Timothy Marshall listened with a mounting sense of prophetic import. Charles Reyburn was delivering no mere "book interview." The world, and Satan working in the world, would take Reyburn's bold proclamations as a call to arms. He was stripping the façade off the progressive agenda, laying its illogic and hypocrisy bare, and doing so on national television!

America had long been on the brink of an ideological civil war. The first tremors of the conflict had been felt in the 1960s. Ever since, the black clouds and ominous rumblings of its approach had loomed on the horizon. As it drew closer, alliances, causes, unwritten pacts, political and societal factions, and back-room diplomacies remained in flux. All the while the sides in the approaching clash of values maneuvered to stake out their positions. When this multitude of complex group-ings, partnerships, bonds, and cultural forces at last came into clear focus, every American would be drawn into the conflict.

And now, from the most unassuming and unlikely quarter, war had suddenly been declared!

The cultural earthquake would be felt across the nation. To the Progressive World Order, assuming its transformation of America and the world a fait accompli, the Simons interview was nothing short of the first offensive salvo.

And Prof. Charles Reyburn had placed himself in the crosshairs!

A chill swept through Timothy's frame. The realization suddenly overpowered him that from this night on, this bold, courageous, humble man of God was in danger.

Liberals would view Hillsgrove's unassuming professor as a wolf in sheep's clothing, as the standard bearer of their mortal enemy. Their lies, their venom, would now be unleashed against Charles Reyburn—just as they had been against Donald Trump, just as they had been against Ward Hutchins.

Oh God, Timothy prayed, *cover this man with your grace, your care. I lift him to you along with his wife and family. Proverbs says that you are a shield to those who walk in integrity, as this man surely does. Be a shield to him against the onslaughts that are sure to come. If there is anything I can do as a support and encouragement and even somehow a protection to Dr. Reyburn, make it clear to me, Lord. Keep him in your hands.*

Even as the interview continued, Timothy pulled out his Bible, turned to Psalm 91, and read it over slowly as a prayer for Dr. Reyburn's protection.

90

I Stand Too!

"WHAT DO you say to those who argue that America's foundations were laced with systemic racism?" Simons now asked, giving the black descendant of slaves a rope to hang himself with. Again, however, Reyburn deftly refused the bait.

"I would say they are right," he replied.

"Doesn't that invalidate your premise that we should get back to our roots?" Simons persisted.

"Of course not. That again is a simplistic response. All nations and people grow and mature. Am I going to forever condemn you because of something you did as a boy or you me? We grow and mature and change. Forgiveness and tolerance enter the equation. I forgive you your shortcomings as you mature out of them. You forgive my immaturities, even for ways I may have hurt or injured you. Then we go forward arm and arm, flawed and imperfect, but growing, forgiving, brothers in our common humanity. Nations have to do the same, their racial groups learning to move forward in the brotherhood of a common humanity. That cannot happen unless at some point the grievances of the past are put behind us. Forgiveness is essential to national growth and national health. Progressives, however, seem intent on keeping hatred against whites and Christians alive forever."

"That message, I take it, is intrinsic to the theme of your book."

"That is the theme. Certainly America has darkness in its past— child labor, slavery, slaughtering buffalo, eminent domain, forcing

Native Americans onto reservations. All nations and cultures have had similar issues. But Mexico isn't ravaged with terrible national guilt over Montezuma's butchery toward other native groups. We do not condemn our native Indian tribes for their atrocities toward one another. Curiously, it is only white oppressors that are condemned, with a hatred that is preventing us moving out of the racism of the past. This lets the cat out of the bag that it isn't oppression or racism that progressives hate, it is *white* racism. Other forms of racism and bigotry get a free pass. But white racism will never be forgiven.

"Will I refuse to be kind to you because my many-times great-grandparents were slaves? That is ridiculous. You have nothing to do with it. The entire premise of systemic white racism and critical race theory such as gained traction in the 2020s is based on an absurd presupposition, injecting young white children with guilt for being white. Far from curing racism in America, critical race theory accomplished nothing more than providing an illogical excuse upon which to base a whole new form of racism. It set the country back decades, inflaming racism against whites. Then came the backlash, with a resurgence of white racism in the 2030s against the so-called browning of America. All caused by critical race theory. Again, I emphasize that without forgiveness, there will never be wholeness.

"The liberals of America are unique in expecting our nation—the whites of our nation only—to feel permanent guilt over the past, and for those aspects of our past to be ongoing never-healed scars on our national psyche. But we have grown. It's the founding principles I am talking about. We were a nation whose founding principles were unlike those of any other nation in history. If Washington and Jefferson owned slaves, that only means they were men of their times, just as you and I are."

"And you feel that excuses them?"

"No. It explains them. It gives historical context to the times. We ought to be mature enough to understand the nature of history. People and nations grow. We have put slavery behind us. It was a travesty, yet that was over two hundred years ago. Because my ancestors were slaves gives me no special rights, especially the right to hate whites."

"So we should forget it?"

"Of course not. But we need to understand it as history—accurately not anachronistically."

"Perhaps you could explain what you mean by that word to our audience."

"Judging the past by the standards of the present. We cannot judge slavery or past racism by the standards of today. We have been the greatest nation in history because of our Christian roots. That foundational ethos of exceptionalism—notwithstanding our myriad blind spots and the men and women who did not live up to the nation's ideals, and who were cruel and did terrible things—is in danger of being lost. What I have written is not a religious tract. I am not an evangelist. I am a historian. As a honest historian I must look at America's flaws. That does not mean I invalidate the strengths that are the lifeblood and fabric of what I have called our foundational ethos.

"We have primarily been a good people, yet often an immature people who, in spite of our goodness, have done some terrible things. We need to make sure we do fewer bad things in the future and give dignity to all those of our national family who are trying to live by goodness and truth, not just satisfy their own desires. Like all of humanity, we are a flawed nation, we are a good nation. There are no Hitlers, no Stalins, in our national history."

It was silent for several long seconds.

"Do you see hope for America's future?" asked Simons seriously.

"I want to. But I am pessimistic. Most people are too lazy to change. So they drift along with the status quo. That's why progressivism has been so successful in deluding the public with its lies. People go along without recognizing that the emperor is naked. If we do not as a nation recapture the foundational ethos that recognizes our history for what it is, our exceptionalism for what it is—an exceptionalism based on right and wrong, based on truth that is not individually determined and that is different than falsehood—then we are in grave danger.

"We stand at a precipice toward which we have been inexorably moving since Obama brought the radicalism of the sixties into the Oval Office. In making the government itself complicit in that radicalism, he launched a systematic agenda to undermine our Christian heritage. It may not have been what he intended. The damage of the consequences of his tenure continues to ripple through the years. We are in mortal peril unless we somehow rediscover our roots—not by electing a single conservative president but with a wholesale repudiation of modernism's radical agenda."

At last he could sit still no longer. Court Masters leapt from his chair with an exuberant, "Amen! I am with you, brother. I stand too!"

Beside him, Stella broke out in laughter.

"What do you mean by that?" she asked.

"I don't know," replied Court. "Martin Luther, you know—here I stand. People who love this country and its roots and values can't stand on the sidelines forever. The Left has had it their way too long. Its lies have to be unmasked. I don't know what I will do. But if this man can demonstrate such courage, can I do less? I have no idea what will come of it. I only know that it is time for me to take a stand with him!"

91

Cost-Counting Time

SEPTEMBER 2048

AS CHARLES Reyburn made the rounds of more talk shows following his appearance on Phil Simons Live, he became a national figure. As he had predicted, he was portrayed as a hatemonger. There were calls for his arrest for hate crimes and cultural terrorism. They were taken seriously enough that the FBI opened a case file on him.

Reyburn's book was so historically logical and well researched that it was generally accepted across the spectrum except by the extreme Left. He had touched a chord in the public consciousness that had been waiting to be set in motion. His book did not exactly cause the sudden groundswell of nostalgia for America's roots that dominated the narrative. It was apparent that an undercurrent of unrest with the trends of recent decades had been smoldering in the cultural subconscious for some time. It had been waiting for someone to stand and say, as Reyburn had said to himself, "Enough!"

Soft spoken, apolitical, unpretentious family man Charles Reyburn, as unlikely a man as could be imagined, proved a catalyst for protest against the excesses of what was being dubbed "the progressive era." Even ultra-liberal *Time* magazine ran a cover feature article, with Reyburn's picture on the cover, titled, "Is the Progressive Era Over?"

Suddenly a rising wave of commonsense Americans began calling for that era to end. It was totally unprecedented for the networks to give such a platform to an evangelical Christian. But the unexpected success of Reyburn's book took the country by storm. Reyburn's name became a household word—millions of the books flew off bookshelves and from Amazon's warehouses almost faster than they could be printed and were downloaded into every imaginable kind of electronic device as fast as the orders could be processed. Progressively radicalized Amazon, which had effectively banned 90 percent of Christian books and only carried one version of the Bible, the Love Bible, in this case put profit ahead of its dedication to the Left's agenda. If they didn't carry Reyburn's book, other outlets would. One of them might develop a niche market that could threaten their monopoly on book sales.

By the third week of September, Reyburn had been on every talk show of the networks. Asked whether he was associated with any group or movement or church, he insisted that the response to the book was an organic movement. It had no leader. People were invisibly bound by the common belief in the standards and traditions and values upon which America was founded.

Threats from the Left were predictable and malicious. He was branded as an ignorant Uncle Tom and homophobe. Yet when the network's rating gurus sat him down alongside their favorites for on-air debates, assuming their progressive darlings would make mincemeat of him, Reyburn's calm, gracious, considerate, historically sound, and logical responses made his adversaries appear the ranting fanatics. He was so well spoken, knowledgeable, and straight-talking with a likable and quiet demeanor, that their attacks had no more effect than water off a duck's back. It rapidly became clear that the traditional conservative Christian, a black college professor, was actually the tolerant, rational, and historically astute thinker, while the liberals pitted against him were revealed as judgmental, shallow, knee-jerk thinkers.

It happened that the next meeting of what they still called the GCG group was scheduled two weeks after Charles Reyburn's appearance on several of the Sunday talk shows.

Now numbering between fifty and sixty, the group could talk about nothing else. Court and Stella Masters were among them.

"Dr. Reyburn's book is obviously a wake-up call to America," David was saying, "though how many will heed the call, as Reyburn said, is probably doubtful. Most would rather sleep through their alarms than rouse themselves to the wakefulness necessary to make changes in their outlook. It may be a wake-up call to us as well."

"How so?" asked Dewitt West.

"The far Left will not be content merely to refute and discredit men like Reyburn. They will seek to destroy them. The same danger may eventually face us. Reyburn has unwittingly drawn a line in the sand. Thousands like us may be called to take a stand on one side or the other. I fear the organized church may not have the courage to stand for truth. It will be up to the remnant—those who have heard the call to come out from among them and be separate—to stand where man's church is too weak to do so."

Court Masters, a policeman and detective, listened intently to David's words about potential danger. Thoughts began to revolve in his mind.

"Those like Reyburn," David continued, "who stand and say, 'Enough!' will find themselves facing persecution the likes of which they may not be prepared for. They will be persecuted by their churches and their friends, those who have gone along with the world for so long their alarm clocks have run down. Such may call themselves Christians, but they are asleep. Those who are awake to the signs of the times must count the cost too. Tribulation is coming. It may look very different than what many expect.

"As this group has been, a time is coming when all groups like this will be called cults. Not only by the world but also by the rest of Christendom. Meeting like this may very soon actually be against the law. I can envision a time, and not far off, when to meet like this we will be required to have a government official present to monitor what is said. Dr. Reyburn has sounded the battle cry. Progressivism will fight back. We have not yet seen the true face of its evil. But it is coming."

Everyone sat spellbound. They knew David was no conspiracy alarmist. If he said such things were coming, the danger was very real.

"Much may be about to change. We applaud Reyburn's courage. But he may have stirred up the hornet's nest in the same way Trump did. Things will get worse for Christians rather than better."

David paused and grew serious.

"I am going to go so far as to suggest," he went on, "that we do not meet again until after the first of the year. Not because I am afraid, but so that we can each take time to earnestly pray about our own role in a future that may require great courage. Each one of us needs to count that cost. I would submit this idea to our mutual prayer."

The room was silent.

At length Grace Forster opened the copy of Reyburn's book she was holding.

"I just read a passage this morning," she said, "that resonates exactly with what David has said. It may indeed be time for us to count the cost of our own courage to withstand the onslaught that the Great Lie will amass against God's people."

She began to read:

"'The Lie will not be exposed by marching through the world with blaring brass bands shouting, "It's a lie, it's a lie!" nor through politics or sermons or church activities, by argumentation, trying to reason with the world. You cannot reason with a lie. You cannot reason with one who calls darkness light. Political rhetoric is wasted effort.

"'The Lie can only be combated by invisibly and quietly planting seeds of truth. But in our time, even remaining quietly in the background, those who see the truth will be in increasing danger. Truth seed-planters will always be in the crosshairs. As much as we may want to expose the Lie, we must understand that those of the Lie are not just intent upon exposing truth seed-planters as enemies of the Lie—they are bent on destroying them. That is the difference between those of the Lie and those of the Truth. Those of the Truth want to expose the Lie and rescue the deceived and bring them to the Truth. Those of the Lie don't want to convert us—they want to destroy us.'"*

As he listened, what Court had been vaguely thinking gradually coalesced in a definite plan. When the group broke up, he took Timothy aside.

---

* Inspired and adapted from Rod Dreher's *Live Not by Lies: A Manual for Christian Dissidents* (New York: Sentinel-Random House, 2021).

"Timothy," he began with the hint of a smile, "have you ever been to Kentucky?"

Timothy listened for a few moments then glanced at Court in astonishment.

"Just show up," he laughed. "Like you did?"

"These are serious times. God's people need to be united in bonds of mutual brotherhood."

"Why would he want to meet me?"

"Because you are a significant person in all this. If he doesn't know your father's books, he needs to."

Timothy thought a moment. Perhaps this was one of the reasons God had sent Court to them.

"The time for God's men and women standing on the sidelines is over," Court went on. "They are going to face persecution. They may need us, Timothy. You've been at this a long time. They need to know you and your group."

The result of their brief conversation was an afternoon at David's ranch the next day, during which David, Timothy, Court, and Mark discussed serious things, prayed together, and began to formulate a plan.

Jaylene and Grace spent much of the day with Stella Masters, showing her around the Sacramento area, then returned to the Marshall home to prepare dinner for David and the three families, by which time Heather, Ginger, and Craig had also joined them.

92

SPIRITUAL HURRICANE

AUGUST–SEPTEMBER 2048

M ARK FORSTER had been blitzed by a spiritual hurricane swooping into his life from a clear sky. It had swept away half the spiritual comfort zones that had always been foundational to his perspectives as a Christian.

His view of what comprised the church had been turned on its head. His theology of the end times was likewise in the process of being spun inside out.

The nature of what is meant by the "gospel" had shifted on its axis.

The hurricane began blowing toward him almost as if following his family south from Seattle. He'd felt it from the first day he stood in the pulpit of Foothills Gospel Ministries.

In the midst of all these changes had come Stirling Marshall's unsettling, revolutionary, controversial *Benedict Brief*—a document so shocking, so bold, yet so excitingly right, that it could remake the foundations of what was meant by the word *Church*.

His week's study of the New Testament commands, his regular talks with David, his involvement in the GCG group, Charles Reyburn's book, Stirling Marshall's breathtaking vision of the true Church—everything culminating with the courageous Reyburn interviews—the combined impact had unmade him.

And remade him. He was being fitted by God for some new purpose. But for what purpose, he had no idea.

After reading the *Brief* and after watching Charles Reyburn's brave public stand, Mark knew he had to leave his pulpit.

He was both fearful and excited. Stirling Marshall had nailed so many of his misconceptions to the proverbial wall. Perhaps he had needed the years in the church to open his eyes fully to the battle lines now being drawn in the country and in his own life.

Mark Forster had been schooled in the traditional prophetic teaching of evangelicalism, with all its familiar scenarios that had infected conservative Christians of past generations with end-times fervor. As his talks with David deepened and expanded, the subject of prophecy gradually came into it. Some of the ideas David gently intruded into the conversation were so unfamiliar and new that Mark could hardly find a place in his doctrinally trained mind to put them.

A discussion earlier that year, lasting into the early morning hours, took the relationship between the two men—now friends and brothers in an eternal journey—far into previously unexplored realms.

"David, are you saying that you don't believe in the rapture?" Mark had asked. "It is at the core of Second-Coming theology."

"It is indeed—yet its flawed interpretation is based on a mere two verses that are completely misunderstood. To understand prophecy, we have to bring spiritual eyesight to the quest. We can't interpret passages physically and temporally that are intended to be read spiritually."

"What do you mean by spiritual eyesight?"

"I will answer by saying that I do not believe in a physical rapture. Many of the Second Coming passages are to be interpreted spiritually. I say this not to explain them away, but because I believe that is how God intends them to be read. To anticipate Christians flying off the earth into the clouds misses God's deeper intent. Those who are looking for a physical rapture to take them off the earth before the great tribulation are basing such wishful thinking on a false prophetic paradigm."

"You could be tarred and feathered for such a view!" laughed Mark.

"Probably. Christians cling to false teachings because they are comfortable. They would rather believe in a falsehood than dig deeper into God's eternal purposes."

"What about the great tribulation then? If the rapture doesn't take Christians out of the world, are you saying Christians will be on earth during the tribulation?"

"I believe so, yes."

"When will it come? If there is no rapture—"

"Correction, Mark—no *physical* rapture."

"Right. Still . . . then how will the tribulation begin? When will it begin?"

"Soon. Very soon," answered David quietly. "I believe it is imminent."

Mark stared back perplexed.

"How could that be? I mean, where are the wars, the bloodshed, the antichrist, the invasion of Israel, the building of the new temple, and all the rest? Surely there would be evidence of it."

"Your question betrays you," smiled David. "You are still trying to interpret prophetic events through old covenantal eyesight. The prophetic events of the new covenant cannot be understood with old covenant physical eyesight. It is old covenant thinking that has led to all the false teachings of authors of the past. And I fear this includes your friend Ward Hutchins. Remember what I said—prophecy must be read *spiritually*, not physically or literally. Everything you just asked is based on a *physical* great tribulation. But what if, like the rapture, the tribulation will be a spiritual one?"

Again Mark stared back with a blank expression.

"You asked when it would begin," said David. "It may already have begun. We may be in the midst of it."

"Then when did it begin? When will be the end of the seven years?"

"Mark, Mark," smiled David. "You're not listening. The seven-year timetable is based on a literal, temporal reading of certain prophetic passages. I am trying to get you to see that our readings of prophecy cannot be temporal and literal but *spiritual*. We may have been in the tribulation for a long time. It may yet be in the future. I don't know. I am not one who feels compelled to squeeze God's timetable into my limited human capacity to understand his high purposes. I do know enough about how God works toward his eternal ends to realize that his high ways and means cannot be explained by temporal and literal interpretations nor by cartoon prophetic webs spun by spiritual spiders."

"What are the high purposes of prophecy, then?"

"The perfecting of God's sons and daughters," replied David. "That cannot happen if God's immature and foolish people are raptured away and transformed into perfection instantly in the twinkling of an eye. Such is not the way God works."

"You are making my head swim!" said Mark.

"I hope the result will be for your deeper understanding of the way God does work," smiled David.

"Who, then, is the antichrist?" asked Mark. "Or, I should add, if the tribulation has already begun."

"My answer may surprise you. Are you sure you are ready for it?"

"Fire away. You couldn't do much more to blow my preconceptions out of the water!"

"All right—consider yourself warned."

"Noted."

"The antichrist may not originate in the world at all or be a major world figure."

"That would be too literal and temporal, I take it?"

"Good for you. You are getting it! The antichrist may be in league with the world, the world's ally."

"Stirling Marshall's oft-used term. But he calls the church the Ally."

"Exactly."

Mark's expression was now jaw-dropping disbelief.

"You're not saying . . . not the church!" he said after a few seconds.

"Let me be clear—I don't mean the true Church, God's Church, the eternal Church. It is the same distinction Stirling makes in his *Brief*. Many professing Christians are active participants in the worldliness of man's church in its alliance with the world. They are actually helping to further the Ally's complicity with the world against the true purposes of God. In time, as the unseen and invisible tribulation— remember, the *spiritual* tribulation—progresses, the church of man may actually become the enemy—as is everything that is allied with the world against God's purposes—of the true eternal Church of God."

The silence this time was lengthy. The night grew late.

"Let me ask you, Mark," said David at length, "what do you consider to be the essence of what is called the rapture. Put away the preconceptions. What does it mean—what is its essence?"

Mark thought for a minute.

"Christians being taken out of the world," he said.

"Precisely!" said David. "I couldn't agree more. However, the old *Late Great Planet Earth* paradigm is based on a whole range of false assumptions and incomplete scriptural interpretations that have at their foundation old covenantal literal eyesight. Those reading prophecy through old covenantal interpretive glasses will always fail to discern God's high purposes. The end times are imminent. They may have already begun because those times may last a hundred years or more. But those of man's so-called church do not recognize the signs of the times because the new paradigm is so at odds with what they have been taught. The Ally's influence is pervasive within the church of man. Only those with eyes to see God's deep mysteries perceive these things."

He paused. "Let's return to the rapture," David said seriously. "Let's change one word of what you just said. Instead of a taking out of the world, I believe that it is a *coming* out of the world."

Mark waited.

"Again, it is imperative not to be bound by literal interpretations. Flying up into the air is a literal taking out of the world. I believe, however, that God will have his end-times Church *come out of the world* in a spiritual sense.

"A spiritual rapture, as you said before."

"Yes. The rapture, so called, will be invisible, not the comic book version of pilots disappearing from airplanes. It will be a coming out of society, out of culture, perhaps out of man's church. It may have nothing to do with the physical world. It is a *coming out* of all the world represents."

Mark shook his head in wonder of the obvious sense of it. He was at last beginning to see where David had been leading him.

"It will be a true coming out," David went on, "though not in the twinkling of an eye except in a metaphoric sense. It will be a coming out that will proceed in some cases slowly and invisibly. It may be a coming out that lasts a century. The world will not perceive it. Most in man's church will not perceive it.

"This invisible calling out—call it a rapture if you like, though I do not care for the term—has already begun. We are part of it. God is calling his people out of the world and out of all the world's alliances. The very group you and I are part of is evidence that it is already taking place. It is a worldwide coming out. Groups and cells are spontaneously forming the world over as God's true disciples disengage from the Ally and from the world. Not flying up into literal clouds but invisibly choosing to come out, and thus be *taken out*, of the world."

"It is actually amazing when you perceive the magnitude of it," said Mark, at last grasping the distinction between the physical and the spiritual coming out.

"God's true purposes are always amazing," rejoined David. "It is only the small doctrines and interpretations of man that dilute them of their wonder. A second reformation may be at hand, Mark. It will be led by a remnant of bold-thinking-discipleship Christians engaged in an invisible and gradual rapture, if you will, a step by step and increasing coming out as men and women and children are knitted and joined into the true eternal Church, built not by hands but built by the Spirit of God."

93

NEW THREEFOLD CORD

TWO MEN, the larger nearing sixty, the other eight years his senior, approached a modest three-bedroom home in Hillsgrove, Kentucky. Their errand had been born of much prayer, though those who were the object of the visit knew nothing of it.

The larger man rang the doorbell and waited. Footsteps sounded inside. A stately black woman of forty-six opened the door. The expression on her face when she saw the two men registered momentary fear. The door closed an inch or two. Then she hesitated, seemingly deciding to give them the benefit of the doubt.

"Hello, is Professor Reyburn at home?" asked one of the men.

"No," she answered. "He is at school."

"Will he be home later? Would we be able to talk to him?"

"I am Regina Reyburn. My husband is seeing no one. He is giving no interviews."

"That is not why we are here. Believe me, we are loyal supporters. My name is Court Masters. This is Timothy Marshall. We and a group of people in California have been praying for you and your husband."

Mrs. Reyburn listened. She glanced back and forth at the two. Her expression divulged nothing.

"I am a policeman from Washington, DC," Court continued. "Timothy is from California and is the leader of the group I mentioned. He is the son of Stirling Marshall, an author you may have heard of. We believe, as your husband has articulated, that the times are urgent and that true Christians must stand together. We have come to express our support and to offer ourselves in any way we might be able to help."

"You have come all the way from Washington and California?"

Court nodded.

"Help—in what way?"

"That would be up to you and your husband. Help with anything you need. We believe a time is coming when you may be in danger. With my background in law enforcement, I only want to be at your service. Honestly, we have no agenda. We merely felt God leading us to come, to meet you both, and to offer ourselves as two brothers in Christ."

Mrs. Reyburn thought seriously a moment.

"I will talk to Chuck when he returns from school this afternoon," said Mrs. Reyburn, at last with the hint of a smile. "I will tell him what you have said. How may I reach you?"

Court handed her his card on which he had written the number of Hillsgrove Suites as well as his cell. "We are in suite 703."

☆ ☆ ☆

An hour after their return to the hotel, the telephone in their room rang. Court answered it.

"Mr. Masters, I presume—this is Charles Reyburn."

"Mr. Reyburn—it is an honor to speak to you."

"My wife left a message on my phone at the university. I telephoned her immediately. I would very much like to meet you and your friend. Could you come for supper this evening?"

"That is very kind, but your wife seemed hesitant. We wouldn't want to cause her—"

"She is the one who suggested it," said Reyburn. "Her initial hesitancy was merely from wanting to protect me. There have been, shall we say, some difficult issues we have had to face since the book and the television interviews. She is afraid for me. However, we very much want to meet you and hear about the group you mentioned. She was deeply moved to know how far you had come to meet us. And by the way—yes, we do know of Mr. Marshall's books."

"Then we would be honored."

"Six o'clock, then. You know where we live."

By eight o'clock that evening, all reservations were gone. The conversation, as will be the case where all are in earnest, found the right channel before they were halfway through Regina's lovingly prepared meal. Her countenance had so entirely changed in the presence of two mature Christian men who deeply respected, and now loved, her husband that she seemed constantly about to break out in song. It is not often in real life that such conversations occur. But when truth-loving people are set only on uttering what truth they have seen, and gaining more truth from those whose walks with God they respect, then the interaction, whether between two or a hundred, is rich indeed.

Though the evening was still young, Court and Timothy had already heard the entire progression of events leading to the writing of Charles's book. Charles and Regina had heard about the genesis of the GCG, were full of questions about Timothy's parents, and were as intrigued by Court's life as a conservative policeman in the nation's capital as he and Timothy were about Charles's life in the world of academia.

Timothy was reminded throughout the evening of the threefold cord that had resulted from his father's final instructions, realizing that a new such bonding of hearts was in the process of formation that evening. How many thousands more such relational birthings would God bring into being as the remnant of his Church came more vibrantly to life.

"Honestly, Court," Charles was saying, "Regina and I deeply appreciate what you say about wanting to help us with any protection we might need. It means a great deal to us, doesn't it, dear?" he added, glancing toward his wife.

"More than you know," nodded Regina. "I am worried for Chuck. It's all so new to us. We have lived a quiet academic life all these years.

Suddenly there are threats, newspeople hounding us, hate mail. Knowing there are people praying for us makes all the difference in the world."

"We do not want to change how we live," said Charles. "Hopefully the hubbub will subside. But I will certainly do no more television interviews. Not because I am afraid but simply because I have said what I have to say. I will not become the leader of a cause. Like you, Timothy, I am a historian."

"Promise me one thing," said Court. "If anything does arise that you feel may be serious—even if it turns out to be nothing—you call me. Regina," he went on, turning to Mrs. Reyburn, "even should Charles not be concerned, if you are genuinely worried, then you call me. Women, especially wives, can often sense danger. I can be here in five hours. I have to know that you will call. It's what I do. I am a policeman."

"You have my promise, most definitely," replied Regina. "Thank you, Court. I will sleep better knowing you are just a phone call away."

"And you, Charles?" asked Court.

"I will try!" laughed Reyburn.

"Maybe that's all I can ask."

"I have a request I want to add to that," said Timothy. "When our group meets again sometime after the first of the year, will you come to California to join us if possible? We understand that you are busy and have commitments. All I ask is that you try to do so. Our people will be thrilled to meet you. I called my wife, Jaylene, this afternoon to tell her that you had invited us for dinner. She is so jealous! She is looking forward to meeting you."

"We will do our best," replied Regina.

The conversation remained spirited. The two visitors to Kentucky did not return to their hotel until after midnight.

94

Is Jesus Coming Back as Soon as We Think?

SEPTEMBER 2048

THE RESULT of Mark's pivotal discussion with David began a process that led to his own in-depth study of prophecy.

He undertook it exactly as he had his study of the New Testament commands. As much as possible, he went from the beginning and progressed through the Bible chronologically, reading the multiple layers of its diverse prophetic themes as they developed through the centuries.

Mark's entire prophetic outlook was slowly transformed. After reading Stirling Marshall's *Benedict Brief*, he felt that his entire life's progression, too, was coming into a wonderfully new focus. He finally understood. Though he still had much to learn, everything in the Bible fit together into a grand symphony of purpose.

He hoped to lead the congregation of Foothills Gospel Ministries through a similar adventure of discovery. Behind that adventure stood David Gordon, quietly, unobtrusively, patiently, yet persistently encouraging, goading, urging, and driving him continually further up and further in, as he liked to say with a smile on his face, ever higher into the eternal unifying ends of God's High Logos.

What would be the response of the people in the church?

Mark was excited about the truths God was revealing to him. Yet given the widespread enthusiasm for Ward's regurgitation of the traditional prophetic sequences dressed up to fit a new series of world events, he was not optimistic that his perspectives would be well received.

When Mark took the pulpit in the second week of September 2048, he knew that his life was about to change.

Eager to see what new vistas God would open, he was also aware that criticism could accompany what he planned to share. He was about to challenge, if not entirely demolish, many of the long-held sacred cows of evangelical prophecy.

"Good morning," he began from the pulpit. "I announced last week that I would be starting a new series of sermons today at the eleven o'clock hour, both in response to my friend Ward Hutchins's articles, which I know many of you have read, and also as a result of my own study of the Bible for the past several months. The perspectives I will share over the coming weeks may at first be unusual to most of you, even strange and unsettling. However, I hope you will give them an objective hearing. I am convinced that if you are able to do so, you will be richly rewarded with a wonderful new understanding of many of the mysteries of biblical prophecy.

"I will make no attempt to present exciting prophetic scenarios. This will be a thoughtful and in-depth scriptural inquiry. It will be a weighty and intelligent study of an important topic. We need to be seriously minded about these things.

"I will be speaking to those among you who have perhaps felt a quiet longing within your spirits for something deeper, something more personal, something more balanced, something more of the heart, than has until now been offered by most traditional end-times teachings.

"Much of what I share will be controversial and will fall outside the recognized boundaries of prophetic orthodoxy. Much will even diverge from what my dear friend Ward is teaching. But different ideas can be healthy, forcing us to consider alternatives. So I ask you to place our two prophetic visions beside each other, weigh them objectively, and ask God for insight. I can only tell you that I approach this holy and important subject with no motive other than to discover truth. I pray you will carry your own quest in the same spirit, and that we would all pray humbly and diligently to be shown what the Spirit would say to the churches."

Mark paused a moment to collect his thoughts.

"In the time we have remaining for this first Sunday of our study," he resumed after a few seconds, "I want to give you an overview of the ground we will cover together.

"The overarching question that will be the focus of our query is a simple yet to some a shocking one to ask. It is simply this: Is Jesus coming back as soon as we think, as soon as most prophetic teaching of the past three-quarters of a century has promised, even as soon as my friend Ward thinks? To understand biblical prophecy, we have to lay aside our preconceptions and approach this question with open minds.

"To do so, first I believe it is vital that we give thought to how we study the Scriptures to arrive at conclusions regarding truth. Christians interpret the Bible differently. We have to examine the ground rules that determine how we read the Bible before we can get anywhere.

"In order to do so, we will look in some detail at the distinction between general universal truth and specific scriptural details. We will see that in attempting to grasp the high themes of the Bible we must always focus on its universal overarching themes rather than its specifics. In no area of biblical research is this more important than in prophecy.

"With such 'universal truth' of Scripture as our plumb line, we will turn our attention more directly toward the Bible's prophetic themes."

As Mark continued with the body of his message, he was encouraged that people seemed to be listening, even engaged in the progression as he outlined it.

When the service was over, Mark could get no clear read of the prevailing congregational mood. But at least there were no calls for his resignation. He took heart and looked forward to the continuation of the series with a certain degree of optimism.

95

DIFFERENCES
BETWEEN FRIENDS

IT WAS on the Tuesday following the third of Mark's series that his private telephone number sounded.

"Hey, Mark, buddy—it's your old pal Ward."

"Ward! Great to hear from you! What's up? Are you in California?"

"No, home in Seattle—getting set for a week of meetings in Chicago. I'll be releasing my next article in conjunction with the event, building up to the big moment of revelation. Got to keep anticipation high."

"You're still planning to reveal the identity of the antichrist?"

"The *possible* antichrist."

"I think that's a mistake, Ward."

"So I gather. That's why I called. I hear you're preaching a series on prophecy too."

"I have been, yes."

"From what I gather you're preaching against me, undercutting the messages of my articles."

"I'm sorry if it seems that way, Ward. That's not my intent. But I see biblical prophecy from a different perspective. I think it's healthy for people to have alternate views that force them to search the Scriptures on their own."

"You've researched the matter, I take it?"

"I have."

"And you think my prophetic outlook wrong?"

"I'm sorry, Ward—but yes. I think it is flawed at its foundations. It strikes me as little more than a rehash of *Late Great Planet Earth* fast forwarded to our time, with different specifics and characters and nations and circumstances attached to all the same scenarios."

"And you consider that wrong?"

"That's not the word I would use. I simply call it a flawed approach."

"In other words—wrong."

"If you insist, then yes—wrong."

The line was quiet a few seconds.

"I'm disappointed, Mark," said Ward at length. "I thought we were on the same page. This is especially hard given all I've done for you."

"I am sorry, Ward. Yes, you've done a lot for me, and I am grateful. But people grow and change. I'm not the same man I was when you brought me to Seattle as your assistant. God takes people onward and upward. Discipleship isn't static. I am seeing much that I did not see before. My perspectives have deepened."

"That's what I hear."

"What do you mean?"

"The call I got about your prophecy series was from one of your own elders whom I met when I was in Roseville. There is talk in your congregation, Mark."

"What kind of talk?"

"That you've—well, you said it yourself, that you're changing, that your sermons are strange, that you have a one-track mind, that you talk about nothing but obedience, that you never preach salvation or grace or any of the doctrines of the faith. There's concern, Mark, that you're drifting toward liberalism."

Mark could not keep from laughing.

"People think I am becoming a liberal!" he said.

"There is concern, yes."

Mark grew serious.

"I would like to ask who raised these concerns," he said. "But I don't want to put you in the position of divulging a confidence. Besides, I know anyway. I know that Stoddard Holt has kept up a correspondence with you. His wife, Edith, is one of my special challenges. You had your own such experience with Mrs. Barlow in Seattle."

Ward chuckled. "Every pastor is blessed with one or two self-important women who resent not being consulted on every little thing. I even had a call a while back from the Holts' son."

"Lionel?"

"I think that was his name."

"What did he want?"

"He works for someone named Roswell in Sacramento. He over-heard fragments of a conversation about old Viktor Domokos when Roswell was on a private phone call. He only made out half the conversation, so it was disjointed. He probably thought I would gobble it up and be eternally grateful to him for it."

"Could you make sense of what he said?"

"Not much—a document of some kind the old man wrote before his death. But that was years ago. The progressives aren't taking orders from him anymore. I'm more worried about Jeff than I am Domokos."

"Why do you think Lionel told you about it?"

"I think he wants the status of saying he knows me. I got the idea he is of the Mrs. Barlow type—as apparently is his mother, from what you say—a young man who envisions himself a purveyor of information."

"Like mother, like son, I'm afraid," said Mark.

"His kind has to know everyone else's business and then pass it on as it suits them."

"That's Lionel's mother."

"At least he wasn't spreading anything about you," said Ward. "He thought I would jump at the chance to get inside information from the governor's office."

"And probably hoped he could get inside tidbits about you too."

"One definitely has to watch what one says around his type. Their antennae are always up. Leverage in the information game becomes a passion. Their loyalties are constantly shifting. Information is power—that's their motto."

"I think Lionel is harmless," said Mark. "I doubt he's high enough up in Sacramento to do you any harm."

"Be all that as it may," Ward went on, "from what I gather from the boy's father, the talk circulating about you is serious, Mark. You shouldn't take it lightly. I've heard about the mysterious group you mentioned."

"There's nothing so mysterious about it."

"Some think you are trying to start a new church."

"I did not start it, nor am I its leader. As far as I know it's been going for ten years or more."

"What kind of group is it?"

"Just friends getting together. Something like a book club—we often discuss books we're reading or other aspects of faith."

"Some are calling it a cult."

"Ward, that is simply . . ."

Mark stopped, closed his eyes, and said nothing more.

"These things have a way of spreading, Mark, like an unseen cancer. It's how churches are split and reputations destroyed."

"If you are concerned, next time you're in town you can attend with me. You'll see how unfounded the gossip is."

"Maybe I will. But you really need to think about your reputation."

"You cannot imagine how little I care for my reputation, Ward."

"You should care about what people are saying, Mark."

Mark said nothing further. The conversation drifted into somewhat awkward superficialities, ending, however, despite their differences, with mutual expressions of affection that were real and heartfelt. Both men truly loved one another.

"I appreciate your concern, Ward," Mark said. "I know you only want the best for me, as I do you. I value our friendship as one of the precious treasures of my life. I will honestly take what you say to the Lord in prayer and ask the Spirit for wisdom. I hope you will do the same about some of the things I said."

"I will, my friend," said Ward. "I, too, will pray for wisdom."

"May God show us both his will. I will pray for you, Ward, as I know you will for me."

"Amen!"

Mark was thankful as the call ended that the bonds of brotherhood remained strong and that differences of outlook and doctrinal perspective could not destroy the love between them.

96

BREAK-IN

LATE SEPTEMBER 2048

"LORING, IT'S Storm Roswell. There's been a break-in at the compound."

Seventy-six-year-old Loring Bardolf, current heir to Palladium's founding mantle, waited before replying.

"What kind of a break-in?" he asked.

"The safe in the office was opened."

"And?"

"The copy of the Domokos 'Final Declaration' was taken."

"What else?"

"Nothing."

"The charter, membership lists?"

"No."

"The money?"

"Nothing—only the declaration."

"And the vault?"

"Untouched. The original of the declaration with the original charter, all the gold stores—everything undisturbed."

"So whoever it was wanted only the declaration."

"That's what I assume. I ran a record of the copier activity for the past three weeks. No copies of anything inside were made either. The only copies for three weeks are my own."

The elder Bardolf let out a thoughtful sigh. "It makes no sense," he said. "If someone was trying to infiltrate the organization or blackmail any of the members, why take the declaration? What could be the motive? The membership list alone would be worth billions. The gold, the cash, billions more, and without the messiness of blackmail. Besides, no one could have gotten in."

"The vault would have been harder to crack than the safe."

"True, but you keep on hand, what, fifty million in the safe. Who would ignore that? And whoever got into the safe might just as well have discovered how to bypass the vault security. Nobody but you and I have those combinations and codes."

"Gold in any quantity would have been impossible to get out of the compound. But why leave the cash untouched—it's a mystery."

"Were any of the perimeter security systems triggered?"

"Nothing. No one came through any of the gates last night. Though it could have happened some time ago. I wouldn't have discovered it myself for days because the safe was closed. Glancing around the office, I wouldn't have suspected a thing."

"How did you discover it then?" asked Bardolf.

"I needed to check something from the last meeting of the League before my father passed five years ago. Purely personal. I wanted to look over the minutes of that meeting."

"And you noticed something?"

"I have a certain way of replacing the minutes book. A habit I got into—call it superstition. I put it on top of the other documents. The cash, of course, is in the large lower drawer. But the book is always on top of the chest containing the files and documents. I place it face-down on top of the chest, by itself, I suppose just to remind myself of Domokos's old corollary to Alinsky's *Rules*—secrecy. Probably a silly thing, but I want the title and the gold-embossed word to rest upside down and invisible. Just a personal quirk."

"I take it something was different this time?"

"The book was topside up."

"That was enough to alert you that someone had been into it?"

"I always place it facedown. No one but you and I have access to the safe. You haven't been here since the last meeting of the Seven three weeks ago. That was the last time I was in the safe. I remember closing it distinctly—with the book facedown."

"What did you do when you saw it?"

"I pulled out everything—the documents and cash boxes, everything. I've spent the past two hours going through every item in the safe, checking it against the inventory of other contents I keep separately. It's locked in my desk. That's how I discovered it. I even counted the cash down to the last thousand-dollar bill. The copy of the declaration was the only thing missing."

Bardolf drew in a long breath.

"That's a three-week window when it could have happened. It will be hard to trace."

"It has to be an inside job. Someone not only found the combination to the safe, they also managed to disengage the alarms, to the office and the safe, then reset them. No one has those codes but you and me. They're not written down anywhere."

"In other words, you're saying someone got the codes and combination from either you or me?"

"There's no other explanation. Obviously, it wasn't one of us. You haven't been here, and I'm telling you about it. But someone managed to get those codes."

"Well, however it happened, we have to get that document back. In the wrong hands, it could be damaging. We'll need a record of everyone who has been at the compound during the past three weeks."

"There have only been a handful of members, mostly here for two or three days, a few private meetings between some of the finance people. But no organization business. I doubt if there have been more than a dozen members on site during that time."

"Any chance it could be one of the Seven?"

"No one stayed over after the last meeting. All the others left with you on the chopper back to Van Nuys."

"Then it's got to be one of the members or staff who was there since then. Whoever it was, we've got to plug the leak. Permanently."

"Didn't Mike work with Domokos on the original, before the old man died?"

"I don't think so. Mike is guarded in divulging what he did for the old man. But Viktor gave his speech to the membership and presented us with his declaration before Mike became as closely involved as he was later. He may not have seen it."

"I wonder if he would know anything."

"Like what?"

"Perhaps there was someone who showed interest in the thing. Maybe Domokos dropped a name. Didn't Mike say he was losing it toward the end, thought he was your father? I don't know, I'm grasping at straws. But Mike was closer to him than anyone during the final days."

The elder Bardolf didn't need to be reminded of the irritating fact that Domokos had had little use for him but doted on his son.

"I'll look into it," said Loring. "In the meantime, get Lamar up from LA. He needs to handle it personally. For now, no one knows a thing about this but you, me, and Lamar. The first order of business is for Lamar to dust for prints."

97

THE GENERATION OF THE FIG TREE

REACTIONS THROUGHOUT Mark's series of sermons were mixed. Some were excited for a new scriptural method of approaching prophecy. Those wedded to traditional interpretations were not merely skeptical—a vocal minority became increasingly angry toward Mark's non-literal approach. Charges of liberalism continued through the church grapevine. They were based on the obvious fact that Mark was "explaining away" the literal meaning of Scripture.

As the prime mover spreading the accusations, Edith Holt allowed herself to speculate in the hearing of several of her cohorts whose ears always itched for any of Edith's juicy gossip. Without grievances, Edith's life would have been meaningless. Thus she continued to attend the eleven o'clock service rather than one of the others in order to keep her grievance against Mark topped up to the full line. Though of course she, Edith, didn't believe a word of it, she said, there were some who wondered if the ugly rumors about the relationship between their pastor and Ward Hutchins might contain some truth after all.

"Poor Grace," she added, "to have to keep up a brave front when, well . . . you know, with a husband who's . . . that way."

"The poor dear," assented her friends with long faces, as eager to get to their phones as they were to hear what more Edith had to say.

At length Mark wrapped up his four-week series. The final day came in the first week of October as the presidential campaign was reaching its climax.

Mark's final, in his view triumphant, sermon was titled "Genea."

After unpacking the three distinct time sequences of Matthew 24, which taken together prohibited a literal reading of Jesus's predictions and forced a higher and more eternal perspective, Mark turned his attention to the all-important Greek term *genea*—generation. He culminated his series with an explanation of Matthew 24:34—the much-misunderstood timing of the generation of the fig tree.

"The question is not merely the *when* of Jesus's words," Mark said after reading the full passage, "it is also whom he meant by 'this generation.'

"When I realized what Jesus actually said to his disciples, I was shocked that the orthodox prophetic model could have been accepted for so long. I was amazed to discover that the clue to the misreading of this passage had been in the margin of my Bible all along."

As Mark continued, it was doubtful whether Edith Holt was following the sequence of his scriptural progression. There were a handful of those present, however, who were hanging on his every word.

"Jesus was speaking of an era of a people, an entire begotten race, a family of spiritual beings, begotten by the Father into a new covenant. It was a genealogical race of new spiritual standing that was being birthed. Jesus was not saying that he would return within a literal thirty- or forty-year generation after the signs he mentioned. He was speaking of a *spiritual* generation, not a *literal* one. The generation of the fig tree is a genea that will extend down through time to include all obedient sons and daughters of God in a new spiritually begotten *lineage*, the race of eternal Israel."

Mark paused and gazed out at the faces of his congregation, many emotions welling up within him knowing what he was about to do.

"As Jesus sat with his disciples overlooking the temple and talking about things that were to come," he went on, "they were hardly conscious that a new era in the covenant was being born within them even then—a new spiritual era, the era of a new generation not bound by time, a new eon in God's eternal plan.

"Decades later, Peter, perhaps reflecting back to that evening a few days before the crucifixion, spoke of that spiritual process and the nation or race then being begotten:

"'You also, like living stones,' Peter wrote, 'are being built into a spiritual house to be a holy priesthood, offering spiritual sacrifices acceptable to God through Jesus Christ. For in Scripture it says: "See, I lay a stone in Zion, a chosen and precious cornerstone." . . . But you are a chosen people, a royal priesthood, a holy nation, God's special possession. . . . Once you were not a people, but now you are the people of God . . .'

"We, too, are part of that genea, as are all believers through time, including those who will come after us in the noble lineage of the royal priesthood of believers. We are the *genea* of the fig tree—the holy genealogical lineage of the new covenant—as are all who, by faith, believe in Jesus, God's Son, the Messiah of spiritual Israel.

"Father of Jesus, send your Son for his bride in the time that you have ordained for the fulfillment and accomplishment of your high and holy purposes. Keep us from the lure of looking for temporal signs and wonders in world events. Keep us from running after false signs and heeding false prophets who claim to speak for you but are unwitting tools in the enemy's hands. We pray not to know more of that time than you want us to know. We pray only for the strength, the courage, and the faith to be your obedient children, each of us throughout the duration of our own lives, until that time comes. Amen. Come, Lord Jesus."

As Mark's final prayer ended, shuffling could be heard throughout the vast sanctuary in readiness for the final hymn and benediction. Behind the pulpit, however, Mark remained motionless, his eyes still closed. Grace's eyes were riveted on him in prayer for the husband whose courage and wisdom she admired.

Several rows behind her, Stoddard and Edith Holt sat stone faced. What was going through their minds during the words of his final prayer would have been difficult to say. Scattered throughout the congregation were the men and women of the GCG group—numbering by then some fifteen in all—who were members of Foothills, and whom Mark had specifically asked to be present. They included the Wests, Timothy, Jaylene, and Heather Marshall, Faith Silva and her husband, and David Gordon, whose presence among them had caused more than a few heads to turn.

The shuffling continued until everyone realized that Mark was not through. Gradually silence again settled over the ruffled feathers of premature anticipation.

Mark opened his eyes and smiled.

"I would like to ask Stoddard Holt, chairman of our board of elders to join me in front," he said glancing to where the two Holts were seated. "Stoddard, if you would."

Taken by surprise, Holt glanced first at his wife then about the congregation as he slowly rose, inched his way out of the pew, and walked to the front of the church. Mark extended his hand and shook it warmly. He then pulled an envelope out of his coat pocket.

"I want to say how much Grace, Ginger, Craig, and I love you all. It has been a joy and privilege to be among you and for me to serve as your pastor. For reasons that are many, varied, and personal, and which I will be happy to share with any of you in more detail, I have reached the prayerful decision that my time in your pulpit has come to an end."

He turned to Holt at his side.

"Stoddard," he said, handing him the envelope, "this is my official letter of resignation from Foothills Gospel Ministries, effectively immediately."

He turned again to the congregation, now in a subdued uproar of squirming where they sat whispering to one another. "Thank you all again from the bottom of my heart. May God bless you each one and give you wisdom and courage to live as the Lord's disciples."

Grace, Ginger, and Craig rose from where they sat at the edge of the second pew. Mark strode from the platform and down through the center of the congregation. Grace stepped into the aisle to join him, taking his arm, and the four continued toward the rear of the church and outside, with a raucous hubbub erupting behind them.

98

A Soul Looks in the Mirror

SEPTEMBER–OCTOBER 2048

LINDA HUTCHINS Trent set down the copy she had printed of her brother's latest prophecy article. She had started reading them at first almost out of spite—curious to see into what further idiocy Ward's fanatical notions would lead him.

Hardly realizing it at first, she found herself looking forward to them, slowly drawn into the compelling scenarios he outlined as predicted by the biblical writers thousands of years earlier. Not that she believed a word of it. But it made fascinating reading, like a gripping story. She found herself surprised, oddly proud in a way at what a good writer Ward was—even if the whole biblical prophecy thing and Revelation was nonsensical fiction.

Between Ward's articles and the Reyburn book, many things were stirring in her brain. Subtle tremors were shifting things around. Slumbering comfort zones were being roused out of dormancy.

What had prompted her to buy the new bestseller by the history professor from Hillsgrove, she couldn't have said. She had heard about it. Somehow the title—*Roots: America Reclaims Its Heritage*—caused her to pause in front of the bookstore window, then walk in and buy it. She knew of Hillsgrove, of course. Its conservative reputation prejudiced her to be on guard against the usual conservative Christian propaganda.

From the moment she began reading, the tone, so different in every way from Ward's articles, drew her into the balanced historical overview of America's two-and-a-half centuries. Had she not been aware of Reyburn's Hillsgrove connection, she would not even have known at first that the book was written by a conservative.

He gave equal consideration to black, Indian, and white racial contributions to the nation's founding, did not gloss over racism, slavery, or the slaughter of native Americans. Everything was given its due. Reaching page 100, she was so caught up in Reyburn's engaging style and his analysis of the myriad forces contributing to the nation's growth that, if asked, she would still have been hard pressed to say whether the man was liberal or conservative

What he was more than anything was an objective historian. She still had no idea where he was leading her. All she knew was that she had never read such a compelling history of America. If he had an ax to grind, it was invisible. What distinguished his approach was his continual search to discover the deeper themes in the American saga. He did not use isolated events from the past to validate a contemporary, and often historically illegitimate, point of view. Not satisfied with knee jerk explanations, he examined both sides of every issue, every conflict, every point of cultural divide.

As the roots of division went down into the past, he also traced them forward to the present, always looking for the big picture. If the Christian missionary impetus had pitfalls that led to excesses, even racist tendencies and an imperialist view of the world, what were the corresponding benefits to those peoples and races that had been the object of that missionary fervor? If native Africans and native Americans and the Chinese had been cruelly treated by those of European extraction, how had the kindness and underlying goodness of that same largely British culture lifted those native peoples higher in today's world than the native peoples in most lands of the globe? If capitalism had excesses, if the divide between rich and poor was unconscionable, how many of America's so-called poor would trade places with those living in the slums of Mexico City, Shanghai, or Manila? With the bad had come corresponding good. He looked at both sides of every coin.

He drove every issue, every argument, toward its larger context to discover a balanced perspective between the oscillating poles of strident discord that characterized America in the twenty-first century. She did not know whether Reyburn was a Christian. By the time he turned his attention more specifically to the Christian influence inherent in America's roots, he had so established himself as a perceptive historian that his documented research and conclusions fit harmoniously into the larger themes he had been developing.

He approached America's predominantly white and Christian culture not racially but historically, completely absent racial bias and set into the framework and historical flow of humanity's entire global story. While recognizing the flaws and excesses of certain aspects of America's history, he emphasized that it was no different than the historical growing pains undergone by all nations throughout history.

Linda realized that some of his conclusions would anger the Left. But she could not deny that, for the most part, his assessment of the current political and cultural divide in America was correct. The progressive movement of the past decades had been attempting to destroy the foundations that had given all the races and peoples of America the privileges and advantages they now enjoyed.

The changing of her outlook stunned her. How could her perspective shift so dramatically from a book written by a conservative Christian!

Linda had always considered herself unbiased and objective. Along with her fellow liberals on the court, the biases of her conservative colleagues had enraged her. How could they be so blind to their prejudices?

After finishing Reyburn's book, scales fell from her eyes. Within days, the arguments they listened to from the lawyers, the comments and questions posed by her colleagues, the briefs written for the majority and minority opinions—suddenly everything was turned upside down.

It was her far-left colleagues who injected their political bias into their statements and written briefs. For years she had been just the same. Suddenly that terrible obstruction to objectivity by which she had always branded conservatives—bias—had jumped the fence.

Day after day she sat listening to the arguments before the bench, growing more and more silent. Her fellow justices began to wonder if something was wrong. She merely listened, turning toward one or another of her colleagues, hardly able to keep a stunned expression from spreading over her face at what she was hearing.

It was the three conservatives who spoke calmly, quietly, with logic, reason, and common sense, adhering to the law and the Constitution and the intent of the Founders. It was her liberal friends who were bound by their biases, often ignoring the Constitution and dismissing the intent of the Founders to justify points of view bordering on what often crossed ethical and legal bounds.

They always voted in lockstep with the priorities of the Democrat party. They never deviated from that agenda.

The conservatives, on the other hand, were open and objective enough to weigh the pros and cons of both sides. They occasionally did vote with their left-leaning colleagues or were split in their votes. But the six liberals, including herself, invariably voted in lockstep.

The three conservatives were the only open-minded justices on the high court!

It was a shocking admission for a lifelong liberal.

Lying in bed one night, the titanic realization slammed into Linda Trent's brain as if a bomb had exploded in her head:

True objectivity, tolerance, common sense, open-mindedness, even simple kindness existed within conservatism.

Bias, racism, intolerance, subjectivity, and anger toward those who disagreed were all hallmarks of liberalism. What else could the prejudice against whites and the elevation of minorities over whites in the political discourse be called but racism? Liberals, even her fellow justices, condoned breaking the law if it advanced their almighty agenda.

Linda could hardly sleep that night. The underpinnings of her worldview had been undone. The rumbling tremors had become an earthquake!

The changes within her had nothing to do with specific issues. The divide between conservatives and liberals was not about issues—it was about character.

The faces of Ward and Jeff rose in her mind's eye. Ward's prophetic ideas seemed like nonsense to her. On the other hand, she lined up in her political perspectives far more closely with Jeff than with Ward.

But who did she *trust*?

Who possessed the character of manhood she admired?

She did not even have to think twice. Whatever his views, Ward was a man of character. She could not say the same of Jeff.

99

AN INVITATION

THOUGHTS OF the two brought Linda's mind back to the present.

So, she thought nostalgically, Jeff was about to become president. She might have been there with him.

What was she complaining about? She had reached the top sooner than he had. Still, the reminder sent her thoughts back to those Bible studies at Humboldt, forcing the comparison she couldn't help. Mark and Ward were spiritually grounded. They always had been. Jeff was a user, a chameleon. She had been impressionable and hadn't known what she wanted. Maybe the bigger question was that she didn't know what kind of person she wanted to be. No wonder she had been so easily swept into Jeff's orbit.

She smiled pensively. She was at the top of the judicial world—perhaps because of Jeff. She would probably never know that for sure. But had she ever stopped to take stock, not merely of her life but of herself? Had she ever decided what kind of person she wanted to be?

It was a little late to be thinking of it now. She was nearly fifty. If she didn't know now, would she ever?

Thoughts of the old days were pleasant yet somehow bittersweet. She wondered how Mark was doing. He was another man of character. She had seen it back then. Jeff had been dynamic. Mark possessed quiet dignity. Jeff had the charm of a salesman—a born politician. How could she not have seen the difference? Suddenly it was plain as day.

There it was again. She hadn't had the wisdom back then to ask what they were all becoming, what kind of young man Jeff was, what kind of person she wanted to be. She hadn't had the good sense to think about the kind of people she wanted to be around who would help her grow and become better than she was.

Maybe she was finally waking up to the imperative of becoming.

She sighed deeply. Was it possible to change at her age?

A paragraph in Ward's most recent article struck her between the eyes. She knew how he had meant it. But she also knew that Jeff might easily misread it and take it personally. All through the campaign Ward had spoken against the agenda of the Left, condemning the Obama era and Biden's foolhardy policies, which, he said, had paved the way for the more destructive reigns of Pérez and Samara. He rarely mentioned Jeff personally. But his recent apocalyptic language was stronger than what he had written previously. She feared Jeff would take offense. Serious offense.

Eventually Linda drifted into a troubled sleep. Dreams kept her turning over and over, waking, then drifting off again. Dreams of campus dates with Jeff and long talks with Mark and Ward—then crazy things like Jeff storming in carrying a pistol and threatening to shoot them all if they didn't stop talking about Jesus. Then she was walking along a wide sandy beach holding someone's hand though she couldn't see who. A stampede of runners sprinted toward them in the fog, engulfing them, then continued past. She pivoted to watch until they were out of sight. As she turned back again the way she had been going, she was alone on the beach. The frigid water of an incoming tide swallowed her ankles, and she was crying with grief like she had never known—but she did not know why.

The moment she woke the next morning she knew what she had to do. As soon as she hoped he might be awake, and she had a second mug of coffee in her hand, she picked up her phone.

"Ward, it's Linda," she said when her brother answered.

Hearing his sister's voice on his phone rendered the usually loquacious Ward Hutchins momentarily speechless, a fact not helped by a glance at his bedside clock showing 5:45.

"Linda . . . hey. I, uh . . . just woke up. Let me get my brain working."

"Sorry. I thought the early riser of the family would be up."

"I am . . . almost. What's up?"

"I'd like to talk to you. I can come to you, or are you going to be near DC anytime soon?"

"I can be."

"We need to talk. I don't want to do it over the phone."

"I have some meetings in Boston next week. I'll fly out a day or two sooner and stop by."

"Would you? I mean, if you want to—I'd like it if you stayed with us."

"Really! I'd love that. Thank you, Sis."

.

100

SINKING POLLS

OCTOBER 2048

MIKE BARDOLF sat perusing the latest poll figures and news briefings that were delivered to him promptly at six every morning. He was awake by 4:30, showered and with coffee brewing fifteen minutes after that. The first hour was spent reviewing the upcoming day's schedule as agent in charge of the candidate's Secret Service detail and where he would deploy his men through the complex movements every day presented.

The 5:30 to 6:30 hour before he reported to the candidate's hotel room at 6:45 was spent in a more clandestine review of Rhodes's political affairs. Technically he was not a political operative. He worked for the FBI and was assumed to be neutral. In actual fact, he was more important to the Rhodes campaign than its campaign manager.

The same week he had been assigned to the campaign in July—which one call from Rhodes to Erin Parva made sure of—the two had a long and highly confidential talk. Help him get to the Presidential Manor, Rhodes had promised, and he could write his own ticket. Secretly Bardolf was considering asking to be appointed his presidential chief of staff. Keeping out of the limelight was more his style—for now. When he made his move, it would not be on anyone's coattails.

He relished in the power he held over people, including Jefferson Rhodes. For a while longer he was content to wear the public persona of a devoted SS man, while behind the scenes he knew Rhodes depended on him.

He had enough connections to get polling data and national security briefings, along with news bulletins and whatever other information he wanted, delivered to him confidentially every morning. Such went far beyond the boundaries of his SS job description. Even the man who delivered the packet every day had no idea what it contained. As for what he and Rhodes talked about between 6:45 and 7:15, those discussions remained as private as they would continue to be a few months from now when they took place in the Oval Office.

Today's poll numbers were sure to infuriate the senator.

From a twenty-five-point lead after the convention, he had been slipping steadily, down to ten points at the end of August. Now it was five. Rhodes would be incensed, and for good reason. Jansen was a lightweight. Now it looked like he could carry half the south.

He couldn't possibly win. But the momentum was going his way, and there was still a month to go. Who could have foreseen the impact of the Reyburn book? Yet Rhodes would probably blame him for not anticipating it.

It wasn't so much the thought of losing—the very idea was preposterous. For Democrats, presidential politics was no longer about winning—that was taken for granted. It was the margin that mattered—what used to be called the mandate. Ever since the glass ceiling had been smashed and women had joined the club, it had become a spitting contest. Still a little crude, but at least it was an all-gender inclusive metaphor, not the former men-only version.

From Bill Clinton's minority victory to his eight-point reelection, to Obama's seven- and four-point wins, and Biden's four, the goal of all Democrats had been to surpass the icons of former eras. Double digits had been cracked in 2028 and were now commonplace. Jefferson Rhodes's ambition was to be the first president in a hundred years to win by more than twenty points and secure seventy seats in the Senate and four hundred in the House. If he succeeded, it would enable him to push through anything he wanted. Basking in his convention triumph, he was now in danger of slipping into the low single digits. How mortifying it would be to be compared with the hapless Joe Biden. A victory of less than ten points for a man would be a humiliation.

For one intent on his legacy even before he was elected, the numbers he was going to look at this morning would be a bitter pill to swallow.

He would have to face the music, thought Bardolf. He'd better figure out the best way to spin it. He grabbed a pad, jotted down some notes, then began making calls. He didn't care who he woke up. This was no time for lounging in bed.

An hour and a half later, Mike Bardolf sat with his third cup of coffee in the candidate's suite awaiting the senator. He was five minutes late—not like him.

When Rhodes walked in two minutes later, the look on his face made it clear he had seen the latest numbers.

"You've seen the polls, I take it," said Bardolf.

"Dan called me from Minneapolis," replied an agitated Rhodes.

"He suggest anything?"

"Bah, the usual—more speeches in the battleground states, ramp up the rhetoric on Jansen, prime time heart-to-hearts on camera a la Jimmy Carter's sweater speeches. It's the same old routine. Dan's a good guy but a political hack. Doesn't want to get his hands dirty. That's why I have you."

"Do you mind if I get creative, shall we say?"

"We need to. How creative?"

"Very creative. Hands-dirty creative. Ball-game creative."

"Will it get me back into double digits?"

"I guarantee it."

"Sounds good to me—what do we have today that we might use?" said the senator.

"I suggest you stick to your schedule for a day or two. Don't comment. If you're asked about the numbers, smile and congratulate Jansen for his good showing. Give me a couple days to put something together. I think I'm onto the solution. I've been making calls."

"It's Ward's doing!" Rhodes burst out suddenly. "His ridiculous predictions. We've got to silence him!"

"I think the Reyburn book has been more detrimental than Ward Hutchins."

"What about Reyburn, then? Can we get something on him, silence him?"

"He's already silent. Hasn't uttered a peep since his round of interviews and not a word about the election. He's not a political man."

"What can we do? Can we discredit him?"

"Not a good idea. He's squeaky clean. And he's riding so high right now that we need to watch our step. Going after a black man could backfire. The whole racism thing is tricky."

Rhodes shook his head in frustration.

"There's got to be something. Get some young thugs to stage a riot in one of the conservative states with some ugly stuff, white racist types. Show the evil side of the conservative coalition."

"I'm glad we're thinking alike, Senator. I'm already on it. I've got the American Antifa League and the Black Justice Coalition set in Houston, Atlanta, Louisville, Chicago, Baltimore to demonstrate with Jansen posters—using big macho whites, of course, not a black in sight."

"Very cunning! I should have known. You'll have the media following it?"

"Already taken care of. But if anyone finds out, there could be blowback—are you sure you want me to—"

"Of course, dammit. My political future is at stake. Do what you have to do. Concentrate on Texas. We've got to hold Texas."

"Got it."

"Are you still working on busing those Chinese and Russians in from Mexico to vote—it's got to be in the middle of the night. You sure you can get them in?"

"Taken care of. My SS credentials open most doors."

"We'll need more than a few dozen. A hundred thousand minimum. You'll need to bus them in for two weeks—feed and house them somewhere."

"I've got people handling the logistics."

"No chance of leaks?"

"Money in their pockets and a new life in America, they'll go along."

"Just make sure they vote the right way!"

"They will. The instructions we'll give them couldn't be more clear."

"You'll have people at the polling places in the swing states."

"Vote early and often. The new voting laws make multiple voting so effortless, you could get away with casting ten votes in different places."

"I hope that won't be necessary," said Rhodes wryly.

"Don't worry, Senator. I've got everything under control."

Rhodes shook his head.

"D— that Ward! We've got to silence him."

101

SISTERLY CAUTION

MID-OCTOBER 2048

LINDA KNEW she'd probably not be able to keep Ward's visit secret. Given his high profile, she didn't even try. Instead, she let it be known that her brother was stopping by the nation's capital for a brief visit. They hadn't seen each other for some time. She gave no details. No one needed to know what they talked about in the privacy of the Trent home.

She was nervous all week. It was only with the greatest effort that she managed to keep her attention focused on the arguments for the two cases before the Court—yet another attempt from Texas sent up to them from the Fifth Circuit to overturn the nationwide gun ban of 2026 and return the issue to the states. The transgender case from her home state of Washington they would probably refuse to hear. The law designating four legal genders in the US was so well established by now that nothing was likely to threaten it.

Ward was scheduled to arrive late Friday. He would be with them for two nights, catching an early flight Sunday morning for his much-publicized appearance in Boston's largest evangelical mega-church.

Linda met him at the airport. The drive into the city was uneventful, the conversation superficial. Ward probed, but Linda merely said she wanted to wait until they could talk uninterrupted.

"It's nothing serious," she said. "Well, I take that back—I think it is serious. What I mean is that it's nothing for you to worry about.

469

Neither Cameron nor I have cancer or are getting a divorce, and as far as I know Mom and Dad are fine. I just want to wait until tomorrow."

"Sure, Sis—no problem."

The following morning after breakfast, and after Cameron left for a few hours at his office, and with the Saturday free from Court responsibilities, brother and sister sat with coffee in the high-rise condo whose picture window offered a stunning view of the Potomac, with the iconic buildings of the capital spread out in the distance—the black pillar of the Martin Luther King memorial, the multi-colored dome of the Native American Monument, and the Lincoln Memorial, the only one of the three former presidential monuments still with its original name and reflecting the sun from its original white marble.

"It's magnificent," said Ward standing in front of the window gazing upon the panorama. You've reached the top—figuratively and literally. The Supreme Court—who would have thought we'd end up here!"

He paused and turned to face his sister.

"I don't think I've ever told you this," he added, "and I should have. It's long overdue. I know we see things differently. Probably nothing can change that. But I really am proud of you, Sis. You're one of the most respected women in the country. It's an honor to be your brother."

Linda's eyes filled. It was not what she had expected.

"I don't know what to say, Ward," she said, her voice husky. "Thank you. I can't tell you how much that means."

She wiped at her eyes.

"Hey, Sis—nothing to get sentimental about!"

"A girl has a right to cry if she wants," rejoined Linda, trying to laugh.

"A girl, maybe. But a Supreme Court justice! People in the public eye are supposed to wear the mask."

"I'm still a girl inside."

"Your secret's safe with me!"

Ward turned to the window and gestured with his arm. "I will never get used to the ridiculous new names for everything. Couldn't you Supreme Court people get the names of the memorials changed back to Washington and Jefferson?"

"That's hardly in the purview of the Court," replied Linda. "It's the will of the people as embodied in the congress."

"But rewriting our history with Washington and Jefferson and every other white man but Lincoln as villains, it's—"

"I don't entirely disagree with you, but it's the direction the country's been going since Obama. There's nothing I can do to change it."

"Even you must admit that painting the White House—excuse me, the Presidential Manor—in rainbow stripes is hideous. We've become an international laughingstock!"

"I don't want to argue politics, Ward."

"You're right—sorry. But seeing it there—a monstrosity to diversity and inclusion, which America has always stood for anyway—it makes me gag. But," he added, changing the subject, "whatever it's called, it appears that our old friend Jeff will be calling the place home in a few months."

"That's actually what I wanted to talk to you about."

"Jeff?"

Linda nodded.

The two sat again and sipped at their coffee.

"You've been very vocal about the election lately," said Linda at length. "One of the things I wanted to see you in person for is to implore you to back off."

"Look, Linda," rejoined Ward, "I know we don't want to get into our political differences—"

"It's got nothing to do with politics, Ward," interrupted Linda. "I'm worried about you."

"Worried? How do you mean?"

"I'm worried if you persist that Jeff may retaliate."

"I believe his policies are dangerous for the country."

"I understand. But I'm worried about you, Ward."

The urgent, almost pleading tone in his sister's voice momentarily silenced her brother.

"What can he do to me?" he said slowly. "He's already tried to ruin my reputation."

"You think those rumors that have been circulating originated from Jeff?"

"I'm sure they did. But the point is—they didn't ruin me. People recognized them as lies. What more can he do? Sticks and stones, you know."

"I'm afraid it could get more serious than name calling, Ward. I just want you to be careful."

"I will be, Sis. I plan to live a long and healthy life. But I wouldn't be true to my convictions if I didn't speak out."

"All I'm asking is that you keep a low profile. I'm afraid you're courting danger."

"Are you sure you're not making too much of it."

"Just promise me you'll tone down the rhetoric about Jeff. Talk about the issues if you want, but don't get personal."

"I promise to try."

The silence that followed this time was lengthy. Ward could tell serious things were on his sister's mind. He waited patiently.

102

BROTHER AND SISTER

LINDA ROSE and walked to the large picture window and stood for some time gazing out as Ward had done a few minutes earlier.

"Do you remember that day," she said at length, speaking softly still with her back turned, "when you and I were out on the Sound alone in Dad's little rowboat. It was the first day he let us go out by ourselves while he stood on the shore shouting instructions to you about the oars. You were supremely confident. I was terrified you were going to lead us out too far and we'd get hit by the ferry on its way to Bainbridge."

Ward laughed.

"With Sawyer already in high school, I was trying to be the brave older brother taking care of his little sister on a great adventure! I doubt we even ventured fifty yards from shore. I was more intimidated than I let on."

"Finally you turned the boat around," said Linda. "I was so relieved. There was Dad waiting patiently watching us. You gave a couple strokes toward him then stopped. It got quiet. Even though we were so close to shore, the water gently lapping on the sides of the boat, gazing out over the Sound, it was like we were in the middle of the ocean. I was no longer afraid. It was peaceful sitting there gently rocking. I can still see your face as you turned around and looked at the city in the distance, the Space Needle, the skyscrapers. Then you turned back toward me.

"'What do you want to do when you grow up, Linda?' you asked.

"I sat there and stared back at you. We were pretty young to be thinking like that I suppose. But Dad was always talking about goals and plans. Sawyer was halfway to law school by the time he entered high school!" she added, laughing.

"I do remember that day," nodded Ward pensively. "To be honest, I don't remember asking that or what you said. What was your answer?"

"I said I wanted to help people."

"A good answer," said Ward. "You always had a compassionate heart as a girl."

Linda smiled pensively.

"Then I asked you what you wanted to be."

"What did I say?"

"I've never forgotten it, Ward. It was an extraordinary thing for a boy of ten or twelve or however old you were, to say. You said you wanted to be good."

Linda's words hung in the air. Ward said nothing.

"Kind of amazing when you think about it," said Linda after a few seconds. "What a thing for a boy and girl to say. I hope our lives have in some measure fulfilled those childish ambitions."

"Not really so childish," rejoined Ward thoughtfully.

"Yours has been fulfilled, Ward," said Linda. "I may still be a Democrat, and to be honest, Ward, I can't go along with all the prophecy stuff. But Jeff's tactics infuriate me. You are being true to your convictions. Whether I agree or not, I can honor you as a man of principle. I do not believe you would ever attack Jeff's character, only his policies. Jeff, on the other hand, would have no qualms about lying or smearing your character. I guess what I'm trying to say is that you are a good man, Ward. You are a man of character. What you said earlier, I say the same about you—I am proud of the man you are. You set your moral compass early in life—you said you wanted to be a good man and that is what you have become."

"I don't know what to say, Linda. Thank you. That's about the nicest thing anyone's ever said to me."

"I mean it. I am sorry I never expressed it before. I guess people get so caught up in issues they forget that character and integrity are more important than politics. I'm sorry, too, for how the press treats you. You have to know—I hope you know—that in spite of our differences, I love you and think the world of you."

"Thank you. I do know that. The feeling is entirely mutual."

Again it grew quiet.

103

WANTING TO BE GOOD

"I READ REYBURN'S book," said Linda at length.

"Ah," nodded Ward. "It's causing quite a stir. I can't imagine our friend Jeff taking it kindly."

"I'm sure not. Most Democrats dismiss Reyburn as a right-wing clone of the Republican party."

"And you?" asked Ward.

"It's obvious to anyone who's read the book," replied Linda, "that he's got no political agenda. I don't think I've ever read anything so balanced and well researched. Most political writers pretend objectivity, but their bias is glaring. Reyburn is different. Yet most of the liberals I know are lambasting him. They are so biased they can't write objectively or read objectively."

"That's the liberal MO, if you don't mind my saying so," said Ward.

Linda smiled sadly. "I'm sure you're surprised to hear me talk like that. You're right—that is their MO. I've been so immersed in that mindset so long I could never see it. I was the same way. Once I began to see it, the bias was obvious everywhere. Liberals shoot first and ask questions later, or they never ask them at all. If they do, the only questions they ask are versions of have you stopped beating your wife. Even their questions are biased and dishonest. They condemn any idea not in the progressive playbook. It never occurs to them to subject alternate ideas to objective critical analysis."

"I'm shocked to hear you talk like this, Sis."

"Reyburn's book forced me to think about many things. Or I should say it got me thinking in new ways. I'm seeing that the inconsistencies he articulates are endemic to the entire modern cultural outlook. Liberalism's perspective of our country's history is not just based on differing political positions, it is completely inaccurate. For years they have pushed a false version of history that has been taught to an entire generation of children.

"When I think of the things I've heard from otherwise intelligent people," Linda went on, shaking her head. "Justifying destroying political opponents and religious leaders with outright lies—like they did you! Justifying violence and law breaking by activists as long as they're on the Left or carried out by a minority. Blacks get a free pass unless they're Republicans—then they're Uncle Toms. Gays and lesbians get a free pass and can be as judgmental as you please. But if a Christian says anything out of line, they are bigoted, homophobic, and intolerant. From some of the talk you hear at cocktail parties, you would think you are listening to crime thugs talking about a mob hit. It's unbelievable the disregard they have for the law. You hear Democrats gloating that they own the election process now that they have successfully changed the election laws so that foreigners and illegals and criminals can vote.

"They literally laugh at what they call ordinary Americans allowing them to get away with it. That's why they are so frightened of Reyburn. They fear that his book has the power to wake up that sleeping giant of ordinary Americans. They are terrified of a grassroots movement to take back the country they have stolen."

She stopped. Ward sat listening stunned.

"Do you want to know the worst of it?" she asked sadly. "I've been complicit in it. I'm a Supreme Court justice. I'm sworn to uphold the law. Yet I've turned a blind eye to the illegality of much of what the liberals have pushed through. At the same time, I have scrutinized the tiniest violations from the conservative side.

"The country's been hijacked, Ward, and I've been part of it. The progressive legal playbook basically boils down to this: Prosecute conservatives, Republicans, and Christians for jaywalking to the full extent of the law. Dismiss charges of rioting, theft, gang looting, destruction of property, even let murder slide for Democrats, liberals, and minorities. Give criminals the vote but take away the rights of churches. The double standard is monstrous."

She paused. Ward waited.

"Things are changing for me," she went on. "I need to apologize for not being more respectful of your views, Ward. Reyburn's book has jolted me awake. I still consider some of your ideas a little out there. But I realize you are a man of virtue, which is much more important. I am sorry that I have not conveyed that. Dr. Reyburn opened my eyes to the fact that, specific issues and views aside, those on the Right are often people of principles and virtue."

She stopped and began to weep softly.

Ward rose, walked to the couch, sat beside her, and placed a gentle arm around her shoulder.

"I've never felt criticized by you," he said. "We've differed, yes. But you have always treated me kindly."

"That is gracious of you to say, Ward. But I fear when I was in Jeff's circle, I thought you were a bit of a wacko."

She glanced at her brother and forced a tearful smile.

Ward laughed. "You were in good company! Lots of people think I'm crazy. Just read what the media says about my articles!"

"You bring some of it on yourself, Ward," said Linda, though with a kindly expression. "Honestly, naming the antichrist—that is a bit Looney Tunes."

"I'm making no predictions yet."

"That brings me back to what I wanted to say about that day in the rowboat. I've been realizing that as similar as they sound, there's a big difference between wanting to help people and wanting to be good."

"I'm not sure I follow you."

Linda thought a moment. "I'm just thinking about this for the first time myself," she said. "It's new to me since reading Reyburn's book. But what I'm thinking is that helping people exists outside the core of who you are. Bad people can do good. You can help people no matter what kind of person you are. A murderer could walk by a hungry child and give him something to eat. Bad mothers and fathers feed and house their children and probably do some good for them along with whatever bad they also do."

"The shrewd judge bringing her analytical mind to bear on a complex question!"

Linda smiled. "I hope for once it's more personal than just legal analytics," she said. "Reyburn's book helped me see, though he doesn't say it in so many words, that many, if not most, progressives are sincere in their motivation to help people and do good in the world—feed the hungry, help the underprivileged, save the planet, plan for the ice age they're now predicting, raise the plight of the poor, eliminate racism, bring justice and equality throughout the globe. Those are good things that do help people. I want all those things too. I think I have been a progressive because I want to help people, just like I said in the boat.

"But all that can dwell in the mind rather than the heart. You can help people without ever asking what kind of person you want to be. I never stopped to consider what kind of woman I was becoming, what kind of woman I wanted to become. I never thought about wanting to be good."

She stopped. The expression on her face was poignant.

"I know you want all those things I just mentioned, too, don't you, Ward? From feeding people to caring for the planet to helping the poor?"

"Of course. Who doesn't? They comprise not just the liberal agenda, like you say, but the Christian agenda—the agenda of Jesus."

"But you don't only care about them. You also care about being good and being a man of truth."

"Of course. Those things lie even deeper in the agenda of Jesus."

"That's the difference, Ward. Liberals don't set themselves to be men and women of goodness and truth, only to pursue their agenda. If they can do what they want to do but have to break laws and trample on the Constitution to accomplish it, they don't mind breaking laws and hurting conservatives. The agenda is everything. Goodness, truth, right, wrong, and personal virtue are not considerations."

Again she paused.

"But they are to you," she said. "If you were to be shown, just as an example, that your views on biblical prophecy were wrong, I have no doubt that you would change your perspective immediately. The man you are would trump your opinions."

His sister's words probed deep, sending Ward's mind back to his conversation with Mark.

"I hope you are right," he said. "I think I would."

"You care more about truth than your personal agenda. Liberals don't. If they are shown that they are wrong, they don't care. That's why they are so virulent against Reyburn's book. He has exposed the fallacy of the progressive agenda. But they don't care."

Linda drew in a deep breath.

"I thought helping people was enough," she said. "But it's not enough, Ward. It's no longer enough for me. If goodness of character and truth aren't at the foundation, the desire to help people can easily be corrupted.

"You recognized something early in life that I never did. I am now finally seeing it. Without goodness of character, all the good works and good intentions in the world won't benefit mankind in the long run. Appalling as it is to admit, I am just waking up to the shocking reality that, in spite of its desire to help people—progressivism does not nurture the desire to be good. Liberalism does not nurture . . ."

Linda paused and smiled.

"I was going to say goodness," she said. "But without reading too much into the word, I realize that it's more encompassing than mere goodness. What I think I really mean to say is that progressivism does not nurture personal virtue and character. Maybe for the first time I am ready to hear what my brother was saying in the rowboat. I'm asking myself what kind of person I want to be. Who am I becoming? In the words of my brother, do I want to be good? If so, what does that say about my allegiance to an agenda whose core principles are hypocritical and untruthful? I suppose no one can answer those questions but me?"

When they parted the following morning, the embrace between brother and sister was more full of love, and for the first time in their adult lives, mutual admiration, and respect than they had ever known.

Linda watched Ward go with tears in her eyes.

104

MACHINATIONS

OCTOBER 19, 2048

MIKE BARDOLF ended the phone call and nodded thoughtfully.

His people in Texas had everything lined up in preparation for election day. Simultaneous riots were planned for events in LA, Miami, Baltimore, and Denver later this week, staged to look like white supremacists.

But the event in Dallas in two days was the centerpiece of his plan, not only to ensure victory on November 3—in spite of Rhodes's concerns, he wasn't worried about the outcome—but to secure his own position as the future president's most loyal lieutenant. Rhodes's rants about Reyburn and Hutchins and Jansen had been aimed directly at him. It angered him to be blamed for circumstances outside his control.

But he had decided long ago to jump on the Jefferson Rhodes train. His loyalty was about to pay off big time. If it meant occasionally swallowing his annoyance at Rhodes's tirades, that was a price he was willing to pay to reach the pinnacle. Viktor Domokos had influenced the country behind the scenes in the past century far more than Reagan, Bush, and Clinton combined. This was his century to carry his mentor's work forward. If he had to do so in anonymity for a while longer and occasionally eat crow—dished out by pretty-faced lackeys like Clinton, Obama, and even Domokos's granddaughter, the outgoing president, and now Jefferson Rhodes—he was willing to eat it. The objective was the prize.

Along with a transformed America as Alinsky and Marx would have drawn it up had they lived in this century, the personal side of his vision was equally strong—to go down in history as their heir, for the name Michael Bardolf to be spoken on the lips of future generations alongside them, even surpassing his mentor, Viktor Domokos.

All his life he had lived under the shadow of his grandfather's exploits as the great founder and his father's as his heir to the leadership of Palladium. He had heard the story of his grandfather's cunning strategy that had destroyed the reputations of Christians at his university campus so many times he was sick of it.

His aging father, Loring, was still chairman of the League of Seven at seventy-two. He would never step down and give his son his rightful place. His own father didn't think him worthy to carry the Bardolf mantle in Palladium's leadership. But one day he would be greater than his father, greater even than his grandfather.

He would use Palladium's invisible power for a time. He would use the connections his name and even his non-voting membership gave him. But as the president's right-hand man he would have influence beyond any of them. The League of Seven would in time look to *him* to lead them!

He had no intention of being lost to posterity. When the history of the mid-twenty-first century was written, his would be the Bardolf name recognized as the greatest visionary of the times.

Almost as if testing his resolve, the telephone rang. He had been expecting it.

"Mike, have you seen the latest from the Harris group?" barked the senator in his ear.

"I have."

"They've got Jansen now at four points behind, with a point lead in Texas!"

"It's an outlier. Nothing to worry about."

"Nothing to worry about?" Rhodes shot back. "The fool could steal the election!"

"Believe me, within a week Jansen will be through."

"How can you know that?"

"Trust me."

"Trust you! You've been saying that for months. And now this. Four d— points! And what about Hutchins? I can see his hand in this. We've got to eliminate him as a threat. That d— Ward! I know he's angling for something. He probably has his sights set on Jansen's cabinet! Over my dead body!"

"Believe me, Senator," said Bardolf, trying to keep calm though he was weary of Rhodes's small-minded vision. "I have everything in hand."

"How can I believe you? Four points! And Reyburn, for God's sake! Isn't there something you can do to bring him down?"

"Risky, Senator. Let me concentrate on Hutchins and Jansen. Give me till the end of the week. After Dallas, believe me, if you aren't up by over ten, and Jansen destroyed, you can have my resignation."

Rhodes quieted. The confidence in Mike's expression was unmistakable.

"You mean that?"

"I do."

"What about Hutchins?" said Rhodes. "I want him off the table along with Jansen. I don't want to keep dealing with Ward throughout my presidency constantly throwing sand in the machinery."

"I'm working on some ideas."

"Do what you have to. Cut him off at the knees. Jansen will drift back into the Wyoming sunset after the election. But Ward and this fellow Reyburn aren't going away. We've got to undercut them for good."

"I understand. Trust me."

"Okay, okay—you said the end of the week. I'll hold you to that," said Rhodes. "Is everything set for Dallas?"

"I was about to confirm the details with my people when you called. They're in the city and set up in several hotels and planting clues to be found later. Leaks will go out tomorrow that Jansen's people are descending on the city. Nothing will go wrong. I have a special part for you to play that will nail Jansen's coffin shut."

"Which is?"

"I'll tell you later. Believe me, it will be the piece de resistance to our campaign."

"You're not going to tell me?"

"I don't want you getting squeamish."

"Have you ever known me to be squeamish about your schemes?"

"You may be this time."

Bardolf ended the call a minute later, shaking his head in frustration. The man was a nervous Nellie. And was about to be president! The men and women this country had elected since Trump were such wimps.

He sighed and turned again to the notes in front of him then began a series of calls. The first three to his operatives in Dallas.

A few nondescript back-and-forths led to the substance of the call.

"Right—and the printing order for the flyers . . ."

" . . . ready tomorrow morning billed to Jansen campaign . . . didn't bat an eye . . ."

" . . . get them distributed . . ."

" . . . people ready . . . business district . . . anything that burns . . ."

Another call followed to a second hotel.

" . . . sure their faces . . . have to be covered . . ."

" . . . no one will know . . ."

" . . . black face is seen . . ."

" . . . won't be . . . people . . . too scared . . . never notice who's . . ."

" . . . probably right . . . can't be traced?"

"Not a chance . . . usual precautions."

After the third Dallas call, Bardolf glanced at his watch—8:30 in LA. They should be home by now. Though he was not banking his entire personal future on Palladium, two of its members were crucial to the success of his plan.

He entered the first private number.

"It's me," he said. "You still on?"

The answer was brief. Bardolf detected a note of hesitancy in the other's voice.

"Look, Judge," he said, "I don't need to remind you of your oath, do I? Your pledge is, shall we say, more binding than your judicial Code

453 oath. I would not want to have to remind you of the unpleasantness that could result if certain facts should become known."

The response to his unveiled threat was equally brief.

"If I have to, I would not hesitate . . . not my intent . . . hate to see your reputation . . . ."

"Don't worry," said the other, ". . . count on me . . . just that . . ."

Bardolf laughed.

". . . least of your worries, Judge. We own the Central District Court . . . just be certain the warrant . . . needs to be executed quickly . . ."

". . . evidence must be . . ."

"Believe me, it will be solid . . . both addresses I gave you . . . yes, Laramie and LA . . . yes . . . paper trail . . . undeniable . . ."

Bardolf set his phone down.

Nervous Nellies all of them! Didn't they get it? This was the time. This was how things got done—all the great men used the Alinsky tactics just as his grandfather had to oust Christianity from his campus. Now they were using them to oust its influence from the whole country.

Revolutions weren't launched by Milquetoasts! Maybe this wasn't 1917, but the times still required strong measures.

He expected no such nonsense from the next call. He and the chief had come up through the ranks together, first in Oraculous at Georgetown then later into Palladium membership. He was one man he could count on. He reviewed the papers in front of him for several minutes.

"Lamar—it's Mike."

"I was expecting your call. I just got off the phone with Harriman. He's in a snit. Doesn't like you much."

Bardolf laughed. "That's probably good. Keeps him in line if he's afraid of what I might do. Do you think he'll . . . I mean is there any chance he'll cave?"

"He's committed. I should say he's resigned to it. He's got too much to lose. He may not like it, but he'll go along. You could ruin him, and he knows it."

"Just so long as you have that warrant in hand by 8:30 your time on Wednesday. As soon as you hear from me, you telephone Harriman personally. He'll have it prepared. Make sure your people are ready to go."

"You really want me to put him in handcuffs?"

"Absolutely—great theater. Image is everything. But not until the cameras are rolling. I'll have it leaked in time for them to be hounding you. I want you perp-walking him on national TV before midnight on the East Coast so the night programs have it. By the next day, the arrest will be worldwide. That brings me to another point—I'll have Todd Stewart there by morning."

"The kid from NBC?"

"Got him in my pocket. I'll have him on hand at the station. Make sure he's given room. I want you to do the whole Oswald thing—figure out some pretext for moving him with Stewart covering it. We'll get two perp walks for the price of one."

"Can you get him here for the arrest at the Hyatt?"

"Not with a three-hour-plus plane flight from Dallas. By the time the dust settles here, it'll be 10:30 or 11:00—there's just no time. Stewart knows nothing. His emotion will be authentic. He's green behind the ears yet, but the country loves him and I'm bringing him along. With him covering the spectacle at your station Thursday morning, nobody will be talking about anything else."

"His lawyers will go for dismissal immediately, then bail."

"Of course. But Harriman will deny both. Treason's a nasty business. It should keep him long enough for our purposes. We brought charges against Trump with no evidence. I will make sure you have a mountain of evidence."

"Sounds like you've covered every base, Mike," laughed the chief.

"I always do."

Bardolf poured himself a full tumbler of Scotch, downed half of it, and leaned back thinking.

The one angle he hadn't fully resolved was the best solution to the senator's college friend. Whatever it was, Rhodes would not be satisfied with half measures. Nor could it be entrusted to anyone else.

105

Secret Prep

7:00 P.M., OCTOBER 21, 2048

THE STARPLEX Amphitheater in Dallas had originally seated a mere 20,000 but had been continually expanded over the years. Senator Rhodes's campaign organizers were planning on 30,000 for the highly publicized event. Squeezing that many in would require a good number of standees.

Though he hated the comparison with Trump's tactics, Rhodes wanted the feel and flavor of a Trumpian–style "event." He could have boasted a larger crowd at Santa Anna Stadium where the Dallas Native Americans played. But Mike Bardolf had his particular reasons for choosing the largest amphitheater in Texas—namely ease of ingress and egress through the open unfenced 360-degree perimeter. A football stadium would not serve his purpose.

The concert style event was scheduled to kick off at 7:00 with several bands and singing groups who would rev up the crowd before the candidate took the stage an hour later. Prime-time newscasts around the country would televise his final Texas appearance prior to the election.

Tonight would seal the thing and put Rhodes back into a double-digit lead. Or in the best-case scenario—depending on how an emergency session of the Supreme Court decided the thing—invalidate Jansen's candidacy altogether and proclaim Rhodes president by acclamation on November 3.

The door to the candidate's hotel suite opened. Mike Bardolf walked in. Rhodes sent his campaign director and staff out of the room.

"We're all set," said Mike. "I'll be right behind you. When I rush forward, hit the deck. You'll only have a second or two while you're lying there to reach inside and pull off the bandage. Then squeeze hard and rip your shirt sleeve. The blood's got to be fresh. The others will be on you in seconds, so you have to be quick. In the commotion, get the bandage to me. I'll be beside you the whole time. I'll make sure it's never found."

"I've got it," said Rhodes.

Both men looked at each other.

"Okay," said Bardolf. "It's time to do it."

Rhodes removed his coat then rolled up his right shirt sleeve to his shoulder.

"Okay," he said, "do what you have to do."

"This'll hurt. It's got to be deep enough to bleed again."

Rhodes drew in a deep breath and closed his eyes. "Just get it over with."

Bardolf removed a small surgical knife from his pocket and thick gauze bandage. Holding the gauze to the candidate's triceps, he sliced a two-inch slit with the razor-sharp blade. Rhodes winced as his accomplice instantly covered the wound and held the bandage tight then wrapped the arm with a strip of cohesive tape.

"That's it—you survived," said Mike.

Rhodes pulled down his sleeve. Bardolf examined his arm.

"Not a drop showing," he said. "Remember to take off your coat. And you've got to get it flowing freely and the bandage to me. If it's found, the jig's up."

"I'm no moron, Mike. I've got it," said Rhodes. He swiped at his forehead, sweating profusely.

"I'll see you on the podium," said Mike, walking to the outer door. "One more thing. When it's over, make no accusation. Take the high road. Let me be the heavy."

Bardolf disappeared as Rhodes walked to the door of the adjoining suite to let the others back in.

"What was that all about?" asked his campaign manager.

"Mike just had some last-minute details to go over."

"I should be appraised of everything, Senator."

"Relax, Dan. Just details. Mike is more comfortable dealing with me."

"I don't trust him."

"Well I do. And it's my life he's sworn to protect, not yours. So give the guy the space he needs, Dan—is that clear?"

106

CHAOS AT THE STARPLEX
8:00 P.M., OCTOBER 21, 2048

AN HOUR later, to uproarious applause and chants of "We Want Rhodes"—accompanied by thousands of balloons ascending into the darkness of a warm Texas evening and the last of the bands blasting at 120 decibels—Senator Jefferson Rhodes walked on stage, his left arm high and waving, beaming broadly. The raucous welcome lasted more than five minutes, the crowd fully intoxicated by the thrill of cheering the next president, high on the adrenalin that nothing produces like a rock concert.

The band departed. Rhodes continued to wave with his left hand, savoring the moment, attempting to speak into the microphone.

"Thank you—thank you—"

He continued pretending to quiet the throng yet loving every minute of it.

"Thank you—thank you!"

Gradually by degrees, the emotion exhausted itself. At last he was able to make himself heard.

"Thank you very much!"

He waited then spoke loudly into the mic.

"I can't hear you, Texas!"

Again the amphitheater erupted into deafening roar, followed by a resumption of, "We want Rhodes! We want Rhodes!"

The senator laughed and again allowed it to run its course.

"Thank you—" he began again. "It is wonderful to be in the greatest state in the union."

Another wave of cheering shouts and applause.

"And I have no doubt that on November 3, Texas will be celebrating with the rest of country what will be a historic victory for the future of our nation."

He paused.

"Whew," he said, "is anyone else warm?"

He removed his suit jacket, his right arm hanging a little oddly as he wrestled it off, then also loosened his tie with his left hand. He tossed his coat to an agent behind him.

"I hope you won't mind the informality," he said. "This is Texas after all—we're just good ol' boys here, am I right?"

More shouting and applause. As the cheers died down, again Rhodes approached the microphone.

"I want to talk to you this evening," he began, "not as Texans but as my fellow Americans and to all of you watching in your homes around the country. We live in unprecedented times—when a future of true liberty and equality for all races, diverse genders, a great melting pot of beliefs, and those from all national origins wherever they were born is at last in our grasp. It is a future where all will have not mere equality in theory under the law but equality in practice. It is a future where no more divide will exist between rich and poor, where all will have not mere equal opportunity but true equity of lifestyle and income and of every other kind. Our predecessors dreamed of such parity across our society. But the reality of it lies before us. We must not let the forces of outmoded traditions prevent the realization of this sweeping vision, with racist, bigoted, and homophobic policies from centuries past poisoning our national vision. You know who I am talking about. We must eliminate those cancers by whatever means it takes. They must be eradicated because they represent death to liberty and equality for all, death to—"

With uncanny precision, at that very instant, all around the amphitheater shouts echoed above the crowd, drowning out the senator's voice.

"Death to Rhodes! Death to—"

Almost the same instant, explosions of gunfire rang out.

Thirty thousand voices screamed in terror. Pandemonium was instantaneous. Ear-splitting echoes of automatic gunfire reverberated throughout and above the amphitheater.

In full panic, thousands scrambled to find some exit. Pushing and shoving, anyone moving too slow was knocked to the ground, the rest climbing over them, leaping recklessly over the rows of chairs in a headlong stampede.

On the raised platform, at the first eruption of gunfire, Secret Service agents jumped forward. Behind the podium, the senator was instantly on the floor, whisked away seconds later to a waiting ambulance.

In less than two minutes, a motorcade of police and Secret Service vehicles, with the ambulance in the midst of them, was screaming toward Parkland Hospital. It was the same destination to which another Dallas motorcade had sped, to no avail, eighty-five years earlier. The heavy symbolism of the spectacle being played out on national television was lost on no one. It was exactly why this site had been chosen.

Less than a minute after it had begun, the gunfire stopped abruptly. In the mayhem and chaos of 30,000 people scrambling in panic for the wide-open spaces surrounding the unfenced venue, police and the Secret Service could scarcely move.

No one needed be told that the rest of the event was canceled. All anyone wanted to do was get away.

News crews were as frantic to cope with the sudden attack as the police and campaign officials. Half the network vans hurried in the direction of Parkland.

NBC's producers quickly rushed their young star onto the dais.

With men and women running in every direction around him, a microphone was shoved into his hand as the cameras that had been focused on Senator Rhodes seconds earlier zoomed in tight.

Blinking from the sudden lights in his face, Todd Stewart took a deep breath and tried to collect himself. He watched as his producer counted down on his fingers behind the camera—4—3—2—1.

---

* As a point of interest, this was written two years before the 2024 assassination attempt on Trump, which now seems almost eerily prophetic.

107

SKETCHY REPORT

"THIS IS Todd Stewart reporting for NBC News," Todd began. "I am standing on the platform of the Starplex Amphitheater in Dallas where literally just seconds ago shots exploded and pandemonium broke out among the 30,000 on hand for Democrat Jefferson Rhodes's final campaign appearance in Texas.

"If you are just tuning in, this is what we know. Amid terrified screaming and chaos following the gunfire, Senator Rhodes went down onto the platform. We do not know if he was hit or if this was simply the result of swift reaction by the Secret Service. He was immediately whisked away and is en route by ambulance to Parkland Hospital at this moment. The scene is eerily reminiscent of JFK's fatal ride to Parkland in 1963. You can hear the sirens and see the lights in the distance. Reports are sketchy, some that the senator was hit, but we know nothing for certain. There were injuries in the crowd and possibly among the campaign staff, and we think one or two deaths, but that is uncertain at this time.

"To recap, at minutes after eight o'clock in Dallas, as Senator Rhodes began his speech, masked gunmen rushed into the amphitheater, according to witnesses—"

Todd paused a moment as a man walked briskly toward him and handed him a sheet of paper.

"—witnesses who report them shouting . . . uh, and I quote, 'Take America back from the niggers, gays, and perverts!'"

Looking directly into the camera, almost with an apologetic expression for what he had just said, he continued.

"Outside the venue, a pro-Jansen rally had apparently been timed to coordinate with the attack. Gunfire sent the crowd scurrying for cover and stampeding to get out. Though there are reports of injuries, mass fatalities do not appear to have been the intent. It appears that the gunmen have escaped through the crowd. Rioting and looting has broken out elsewhere in the city by Jansen supporters waving Jansen placards and spraying buildings with racist slogans alongside the words 'Vote Jansen.'"

108

HASTY CHANGE OF PLANS

11:10 P.M., OCTOBER 21, 2048

TODD STEWART walked into his hotel room three hours later. It was sometime around eleven. It had been a long day, following Jefferson Rhodes about, half a dozen interviews with key people in his campaign. Then the assassination attempt.

He took off his coat and tie and threw himself on the bed. How could he sleep after all that! He needed something to read to wind down from—

Of course. He'd nearly forgotten.

He climbed back to his feet and walked across the room. From beneath a few socks and shorts and two pressed shirts in his carry-on, he pulled out a copy of *Roots: America Reclaims Its Heritage*. He'd bought the book at Barack Obama International while waiting for his flight from DC. Everyone was talking about it. He figured he ought to see what it was about.

Twenty minutes later he was completely absorbed. The first three chapters set off a chain reaction of utterly unexpected thoughts. He was stunned by his response. He was a liberal. At least so he had always considered himself. Yet everything this conservative traditional Christian historian was saying echoed in his brain with the unmistakable ring of truth.

How could he admit the shocking possibility that all his life, from the moment he could think at all, he had been taught *not* to think, but had been brainwashed into a complex outlook dictated by teachers, the news media, the culture, his friends, then his university professors? How could he admit that he had been indoctrinated into a belief system that—

Suddenly the door of his hotel room opened. He glanced up irritably to see Mike Bardolf walking in. The guy had passkeys to every hotel the Rhodes campaign used! There was no privacy when Mike Bardolf was around.

Todd hurriedly snapped the book shut and stuffed it beneath the blanket. But Bardolf had seen it.

"I hope that's for research on the enemy," he said without benefit of a smile.

"He's not the enemy, Mike," said Todd. "The guy's a respected college professor."

"He's against progress. That makes him the enemy."

"Isn't everyone entitled to their opinion?"

"Not if it's wrong. But I didn't come here to talk about Reyburn. Get your things packed. You're coming with me."

"What—now?"

"Yes, let's go."

"You're kidding! It's going on midnight."

"Didn't you see the news that just broke from LA fifteen minutes ago."

"I saw nothing. I just got here thirty minutes ago."

"I'll explain it to you on the way. You've got a plane to catch. I've got a private jet waiting. I need you in LA before daybreak. You're on the air in front of cameras in four hours."

"Now I know you're kidding!" said Todd. In spite of his disbelief, he climbed off the bed and began stuffing his things into his small suitcase.

"There's going to be fireworks tomorrow," said Bardolf. "I want you covering it."

"How do you know?"

"I get paid to know."

"What kind of fireworks?"

"One never knows. Just think Lee Harvey Oswald. The best news is often unexpected."

"LA—isn't that where Jansen was speaking last night?" asked Todd as they headed for the door.

"It is. His appearances for the rest of the week have been canceled. Let's go. I'll explain everything."

109

THE ARREST

6:56 A.M. PST, OCTOBER 22, 2048

"THIS IS Todd Stewart reporting," began Todd, standing before camera and lights in the glow of a California dawn.

Los Angeles police headquarters behind him was bathed in gold. Injecting whatever energy two hours of sleep and three cups of strong coffee could supply, he continued with the early telecast his producers hoped was not too late for the tail end of the East Coast morning shows.

His plane had touched down at LAX an hour earlier. He had been spirited to a hotel, shoved under a cold shower, given a fresh suit of clothes, had coffee poured into him, and made up in the limo heading downtown to eliminate the bags under his eyes as he groggily reviewed a printout of what he would read from the teleprompter minutes later.

"I am standing in front of Los Angeles police headquarters," Todd continued, "just minutes before 7:00 a.m. For those of you just tuning in this morning, the remarkable series of events of the past twelve hours has thrown our country into what is nothing short of a potential constitutional crisis.

"On the eve of the election two weeks from now, President Samara has ordered Congress to convene for a joint session at 3:00 p.m. today eastern time. She will address the nation from the House chamber. The justices of the Supreme Court will be on hand and have been instructed by executive order to stand by for events that could possibly require an emergency session of the high court.

"To recap, yesterday evening in Dallas at a major campaign event in the thirty-thousand-seat Starplex Amphitheater, an assassination attempt was made on the life of presidential candidate Sen. Jefferson Rhodes. Rhodes received only a minor wound in his right arm from the sniper rifle that was meant to end his life. He was rushed from the scene to Parkland Hospital where he was treated and released two hours later. In the ensuing gunfire, eight injuries were reported and one fatality from Senator Rhodes's campaign staff whose name is being withheld. Two injured women remain in critical condition at Parkland Hospital at this hour.

"Simultaneous to the shooting, riots and looting broke out at several locations in Dallas where pro–Jansen posters and flyers were seen, as well as in Denver, Los Angeles, and Baltimore in what was apparently a nationwide coordinated effort. Though the gunmen eluded authorities in the pandemonium, witnesses report anti-Rhodes and racist chants at a Jansen demonstration outside the amphitheater immediately prior to the shooting.

"Working in conjunction with the FBI and Secret Service, local police in LA and Dallas received an anonymous tip leading them to the campaign headquarters of Republican candidate Harvey Jansen at the Hyatt Hotel in Los Angeles with emergency search warrants in hand. Los Angeles Police Chief Lamar Royce led the raid, entering Jansen's Hyatt suite at 9:05 Pacific time yesterday evening. Evidence was found linking Jansen to the riots in the four cities and the assassination attempt. The nature of the evidence is confidential and has not been released. A search warrant was also issued for Jansen's home in Laramie, Wyoming, which was searched two hours later.

"Shocking television viewers last night in California and across the country, Senator Jansen was placed under arrest by Chief Royce on live camera, read his Miranda rights, then led from his suite in handcuffs. Placed in the back of a white squad car and under heavy guard, he was transported to the Los Angeles County jail. His campaign attorney immediately filed for a dismissal of the charges and, failing that, a writ requesting that the candidate be released on bail. Judge Felix Harriman refused to hear arguments for dismissal and denied bail.

"Jansen remains at this moment behind bars in the building behind me. He will be served breakfast in about twenty minutes, which, in a brief statement issued by the police, will consist of half a grapefruit, coffee, and a bowl of Wheaties. Jansen will be arraigned before Judge Harriman at ten o'clock this morning on multiple counts including murder, attempted murder, inciting a riot under Code 2102, interfering with a federal election under Codes 593, 594, and 610 as well as possible other charges. Those charges may include the most serious, treason."

110

THE PRISONER

9:35 A.M. PST, OCTOBER 22, 2048

"THIS IS Todd Stewart, NBC News, reporting again from the entrance to Los Angeles Police Headquarters where, in a few minutes Sen. Harvey Jansen, who has been held without bail in the building behind me on multiple felony charges, will be brought out of his cell and transported to Federal District Court. There he will be arraigned before Judge Felix Harriman. We will try to get inside the—"

The double doors behind him swung open.

Todd rushed forward and squeezed through, followed by his crew with the camera still running. From inside a dense swarm of police, bodyguards, and lawyers were shoving their way toward the doors.

"Get the press out of here!" someone shouted.

Police Chief Royce waved off the order. "They have a right to be here," he said above the din. "The country needs to see the Bill of Rights at work."

Todd turned toward his cameraman.

"In a scene uncannily reminiscent of the transfer of Lee Harvey Oswald in Dallas in 1963," he resumed, "we are awaiting the appearance of Sen. Harvey Jansen, Republican presidential candidate. Jansen will be taken by armed guard—"

Sudden movement of the crowd bumped Todd away from the camera. Quickly he recovered.

"Here comes the senator . . . now if we . . . I see that he is still in handcuffs . . ."

"Move back, give them room!" shouted Royce.

"Did you order the attempt on Rhodes's life?" Todd called out.

Shouting and commotion drowned out what more he might have said, though his cameraman continued filming the drama for their live audience.

Armed guards shoved their way through, pulling Jansen to the door and outside, where several thousand were gathered. Immediately the crowd burst into shouts.

Jansen demonstrators clearly outnumbered whatever others had come to watch the circus. Most wore hoodies, some sporting white KKK style sheets and waving signs painted with racist slurs. The scene threatened to become violent until Chief Royce ordered tear gas canisters tossed into the Jansen contingent.

Slowly the crowd dispersed as the motorcade bearing the senator sped away.

In spite of the provocation by the Jansen protesters, no arrests were made and the instigators managed to disappear through the crowd, leaving behind several dozen white sheets and hooded sweatshirts strewn in front of police headquarters, along with the placards and posters from the brief demonstration.

111

SEARCH THE SCRIPTURES
WITH AN OPEN MIND

OCTOBER 29, 2048

OUT OF consideration for his sister, Ward Hutchins had promised to scale back whatever political rhetoric might be construed as a personal attack on Jeff. As he did, beginning immediately with his appearance in Boston, Jesus's words, "My kingdom is not of this world," stole into his mind, lodged there, and gradually began its spirit-waking work.

A week later, during his morning prayer time, an altogether ridiculous conundrum crept into Ward's brain. Absurd though it seemed, it grew stronger and eventually probed to the foundations of his entire outlook on his role as a Christian in the world. The query was as simple as its practical implications were profound:

During Jesus's ministry at the height of his public popularity, if Herod Antipas had died and it was decided that the new king of Judea would be determined by popular vote, and furthermore if two candidates had been put forward—one who was favorable to Jesus and his teachings and the other who was determined to persecute his followers and stamp out his teachings—would Jesus have publicly supported the one over the other?

Another question came with it:

Would Jesus have campaigned actively, urging the people of Judea to vote for the candidate most favorable to his teachings?

They were mind-exploding questions.

He had never considered such a common-sense application to the role of Christians in world affairs. He had merely assumed that his duty as a Christian was to actively involve himself in the politics of America.

Suddenly the simple yet titanic question loomed as a piercing query: What would Jesus do?

Had the Lord really meant what he said, "My kingdom is not of this world"?

His talk with his sister, and now these unsought scriptural uncertainties, began the unthinkable—sowing seeds of doubt in his brain.

The next day, when he found himself standing before a crowd of reporters hurling questions at him, the unexpected words came out of his mouth that neither he nor those listening had anticipated:

"I think it would be inappropriate for me to comment on the election at this time."

He left the interview saying no more, leaving the reporters so stunned that he was gone before they could regroup and begin shouting after him.

In the days that followed, his speeches, sermons, and comments to the press were curiously void of any mention of the election, focusing only on spiritual themes. When asked about the election, his only comment was, "Everyone must vote their conscience."

Linda was one of those who noticed the change, and was relieved.

As pulling a loose thread of a sweater can lead to serious unraveling, Ward found that tugging on one uncomfortable strand of evangelical orthodoxy led to an unsettling tugging at others.

Doubts began to nag at him about his last article about Jesus's end times discourse in Matthew 24. If he had missed some of that chapter's subtle and obscure themes, what else might he have missed in his analysis of the end times? He had taken the traditional prophetic orthodoxy as gospel for so long, he had no compartment in his brain for such an enormous question.

Obviously not by coincidence, he simultaneously received a packet from Mark Forster. He opened it and read the cover letter.

Dear Ward,

*I hope you will not take offense or think me presumptuous,
but I felt led to send you this summary of the series of sermons
I completed recently. On the telephone you said you thought
I was speaking against you. I would never do that. But I feel
you deserve to see in more detail what exactly I said to my
congregation, and the scriptural basis for my view of prophecy.*

*I can only ask that you search the Scriptures and try to keep
an open mind. Even if we do not agree on these matters, we will
always remain brothers and friends. I count my friendship with
you as among the closest and dearest of my life, and I thank God
for you.*

*I do not send you this in an attempt to persuade you to my
opinion. God forbid! That tendency is one of the most lethal
of many diseases in the church. I have, however, read all your
articles and feel, in the spirit of us both putting our cards on the
table, that you should see to what conclusions my own research,
and I hope God's Spirit, have led me.*

*May God give us both wisdom as we often prayed together
back in the good old days!*

*If you have not heard, at the conclusion of my series last
month I resigned from the pulpit of Foothills. Grace and I are
praying and weighing our options for the future.*

All the best, my friend. You are dear to my heart.

Mark

Intrigued, Ward began reading the fascinating account of Mark's
personal quest and scriptural study that same day.

112

CHARISMA TRUMPS CHARACTER

NOVEMBER 1–3, 2048

ELECTIONS OFTEN turn on subtleties of reaction to candidates more than policy differences or personal character.

JFK's charming smile and Richard Nixon's five-o'clock shadow and nervous demeanor under the glare of television lights decided the 1960 election. Charisma, neither policy nor character, won the day. The loyal husband lost to the womanizer because of perception. People liked Kennedy and didn't care that he was unfaithful to Jackie.

The high-pitched voices of George Bush and Ross Poirot came across as whiny and strident, thus sending another charming, good-looking womanizer to the White House. Again the electorate chose to ignore defects of personal character because the man was likable on television.

Perception is no respecter of party lines. Subtleties of response buried the hopes of Democrat Michael Dukakis after his disastrous appearance riding a tank looking like a schoolboy on a carnival ride.

Perception was played to no better advantage than in 2020 when legions of Trump haters, in both parties, built upon the false narrative of Russian collusion to characterize the bombastic and self-defeating candidate in ways that were as false as the Russia probe. A man with signs of aging mental weakness was thus put in the White House over a man who, in spite of defects of behavior, had attempted to swing the needle of US culture back toward its core values. Subtleties of perception, neither substance, policy, nor leadership again decided the election.

As the election of 2048 came down to its final hours, once again perception carried the day. In less than twelve hours, a series of deviously clever illegal maneuvers destroyed Sen. Harvey Jansen for good. That the allegations against him were spurious mattered nothing. The damage was done.

Bardolf had learned well from the drawn-out Mueller investigation. Truth was not so important as perception. Legalities had vanished from the liberal political landscape.

The images played over and over for two weeks of Jansen in handcuffs, side by side with command performance telecasts of the chaos at Dallas, produced a domino sequence of events too deeply lodged in the public mind to erase.

Few believed that Jansen was behind it. By all accounts he was an honorable man. But a seed of doubt was worth millions of votes. Could people pull the lever for a man they had seen in handcuffs?

Mike Bardolf was elated. Even he had not quite believed it would go off without the slightest hitch. Pleased but not satisfied. He still had one loose end to tie up to ensure smooth sailing for the Rhodes administration. He wanted no gadflies pushing the new president's temper button. It was time to put that loose end in the rear-view mirror, as Rhodes had said, for good.

No more distractions. Fulfill the dream. Eliminate the problem.

For the moment, however, thought Bardolf, he would enjoy the assurance of victory. Even standing in the suddenly very large shadow cast by the soon-to-be president-elect, he was able to relish in his success. He had not only ensured Rhodes's victory, he had also secured his own place at the pinnacle he had been eying for years. Viktor Domokos would be proud of his protégé.

Though all allegations against Jansen were ultimately discredited, who was behind the conspiracy against him was never discovered. Nor was a single arrest made.

Los Angeles Police Chief Royce and Federal Judge Harriman expressed shock and outrage that they had been used in such a miscarriage of justice. FBI Director Erin Parva joined the shocked chorus of Democrats promising that those behind the affair would be found and swiftly brought to justice. Their public statements were delivered to news outlets the day after the election where they appeared far inside most papers and were not covered by any of the mainstream television newscasts.

Jansen's release from jail after five humiliating days, and the reports exonerating him, were mentioned only briefly on the nightly telecasts adding that the election would go on as scheduled unless further evidence against Jansen was found. This final caveat was enough to keep doubt alive. The most easily manipulated of the country went to the polls thinking that Jansen was still in jail, might have orchestrated the whole thing, and, if so, would spend the rest of his life in prison.

On his own, Todd Stewart eventually uncovered the extent of the lies against the Republican candidate. When presented to his producers, however, they said the network could not sanction the story. His reporting on the election thus continued to be scripted by Mike Bardolf. Todd vowed that after the election he would conduct an interview with Jansen, whom he felt sorry for, whether Bardolf liked it or not.

The polls immediately swung dramatically in Senator Rhodes's favor. By week's end he was again in double digits. He cast his vote in Seattle, amid huge fanfare, with a nineteen-point lead. By 8:30 eastern time it began to be apparent that that estimate was probably low.

The Republican candidate watched the news of his drubbing alone with his wife in their recently ransacked Laramie ranch house. By 7:00 they had had enough. They turned off the election news in favor of two episodes of *Heartland* from their ancient DVD archives. The past two weeks had been so humiliating that Jansen did not even give a concession speech.

113

ELECTION NIGHT

NOVEMBER 3, 2048

THE GRAND ballroom at Seattle's Microsoft Convention Center was already filled to capacity, the mood exuberant—every personality in Seattle's social, business, high-tech, and political worlds, millionaires by the score, even a few billionaires, was on hand. Seattle was, for this night and perhaps for some time to come, the center of gravity of the universe. When the man of the hour, forty-eight-year-old Jefferson Fitzsimmons Rhodes, strode on to the podium to take his place with wife Marcia, son Bradon, and daughter Melissa, his father Harrison would introduce him.

The vote wasn't yet official, and he would not take office for three more months. But there was already talk of a new political dynasty. Whether or not twenty-one-year-old Bradon would get his act together and settle into a career that lent itself to a political future remained the bugaboo in the dynasty scenario.

Standing at the back of the ballroom, Todd Stewart watched the exuberant scene in front of him with a queasy feeling. Something was wrong with this picture. What, he didn't know. But he smelled, if not a rat, something amiss.

Mike Bardolf had been giving him orders for years, disguised at first as suggestions but becoming less thinly veiled over the course of the campaign. It was almost to the point where he wondered if he worked for the network or the Secret Service. All cleverly concealed of course. But Bardolf had a sinister way of making his meaning clear. The consequences of not following his "suggestions" were equally clear. He was as cool and devious a customer as they came.

But for tonight what was there for him to do but finish this thing out? He had been assigned to the Rhodes campaign. This was the climax. He would do his best to convey the upbeat celebratory mood around him, then don a tux for tomorrow night's exclusive victory bash, to which his invitation had been personally signed by the senator:

Todd,

With much appreciation for all you meant to our historic campaign,

Jefferson Rhodes

Then, Todd hoped, he would be able to take some time off, visit his parents and sisters in Tucson, and maybe even hike the Seven Falls Trail.

After that, with any luck, he could find some way to get free of Bardolf's clutches without committing professional suicide.

An hour later he was standing at the front of the ballroom, speaking live and reviewing the day's events using that staple of television journalism, repeating the same things over and over in different ways, waiting for the zero hour.

At last the band behind him burst into "Hail to the Chief," three months premature, it was true, but no one was inclined to stop them.

". . . and here comes the senator now!" said Todd. "We have just learned that he was on the phone with President Samara moments ago, as I'm sure we will—"

Anything further he might have said was drowned out by the thunderous applause, shouts, cheers, and music from the band.

President-Elect Jefferson Rhodes strode onto the platform, spotlights upon him, hands in the air, beaming with effulgent satisfaction, flanked by his father and mother, and followed by his wife, son, and daughter.

114

Mᴀɴ ᴏꜰ Gᴏᴅ

NOVEMBER 4, 2048

THE VICTORY celebration the day after the election was unprecedented. An inaugural ball would be held in January of course. But that would be a DC event featuring the capital's political elite. Harrison Rhodes, the senior, and Jefferson Rhodes, the junior and now the most prominent member of Seattle's first family, had been planning for months to throw a celebration bash Seattle would not soon forget. They would give the northwest an opportunity to participate in the victory of their new president-elect while the exuberant national emotion was at its peak.

With his son's election virtually assured—despite the brief sagging of the polls several weeks earlier—the elder Rhodes had booked the Space Needle and parking area for the day following the election. After an exclusive gathering in the upper-floor restaurant and lounge, the guests completing a revolving 360-degree circle of the iconic Seattle landmark, the president-elect would take the elevator up to the open-air observation deck. There he would address the city, his voice boomed over mega-watt speakers as spotlights illuminating him would be seen up to ten miles away. It would be a spectacle like none other in the city's history.

Thirty miles north of the evening's events, uninterested though certainly not unaware of his former friend's rousing victory, a man of God sat alone in his study in his Everett, Washington, home. For years he had been attempting to sound the warning cry as one of many voices in the wilderness of his nation's decline into the abyss of secularism. His Bible lay on the desk in front of him. It was opened to the sixteenth chapter of the New Testament book of Revelation.

He read the verse a third time.

"The first angel went and poured his bowl on the earth, and foul and evil sores came upon the men who bore the mark of the beast and worshipped its image."

It had been underlined in his own hand long ago, probably during his college years. Back then he had been caught up, not exactly into the air but into the signs and wonders that would lead to the rapturous transport into the clouds many Christians believed to be imminent—the next dramatic event in the prophetic timetable laid out by the guru-prophets of nineteenth-century evangelicalism. An enthusiasm for prophecy, as it did periodically, had swept through his church during the years of his early adulthood, and he had eagerly lapped up every detail.

He sat back in his chair, closed his eyes, and exhaled a long sigh. It had been all too natural back then to read such passages literally. He had been doing so ever since. Now he was seen by many as the heir apparent to the legacies of the Lindseys and LaHayes of those times. All of them were now passed from the scene, dying normal human deaths, not raptured away as they had predicted. All year he had been writing and speaking about the many literal fulfillments taking place in front of them in these times, just as had been done in *Late Great* seventy-eight years before. He had been so caught up in his own predictions that he believed every word with a passion that had swept millions into his wake.

But what if he had had it all wrong?

What if he, too, was destined to grow old and die unraptured for the simple and obvious reason that the rapture theology evangelicalism had been clinging to for so long was wrong?

Had he led those millions down the primrose path of alluring old covenantal prophetic interpretations? He now feared that he had not seen the prophecies of the New Testament with the eyes of God's higher intent. Exactly as Mark had said in his series of sermons, he had fallen into the pitfall of reading New Testament prophecies with old covenant eyesight.

He had not had eyes to see *truly*.

His friend's thorough, well-reasoned, scripturally sound analysis had opened his eyes to many new realms of prophetic interpretation. If Mark was right—and in his heart of hearts, he already knew it—then he had misunderstood everything.

How different it all looked now! He had assumed the beast represented a person. He had been so audacious as to think he could publicly name that person.

The beast wasn't a person at all. It was a way of thinking, a way of seeing. The mark of the beast had been staring him in the face all along. The mark was an outlook, a perspective.

His heart was heavy for what he feared the future portended but now for very different reasons. Until two weeks ago, biblical prophecy was about graphs and charts and timetables. He knew how everything was supposed to play out.

But Revelation 2 and 3 changed everything.

Revelation and its Old Testament counterpart Malachi were not about the world's demise. They were about the church—the worldly Christian church, what Mark called the Ally, and the other Church, God's eternally purified and perfected Church.

If indeed the mark of the beast had come, then the beast had been among them for years, its invisible tentacles subtly infiltrating more and deeper and wider levels of society and culture, politics and education, media and business, entertainment and the church, with every passing year.

Silent.

Unseen.

That was the shocking revelation Mark had opened his eyes to see—the mark of the beast was in the church no less than in culture and politics.

The Great Lie of the enemy had infiltrated his beloved church—its outlook, its doctrines—its entire perspective of the world. Yet most Christians were blind to it. They had allowed the mark into their hearts and minds and families without knowing it.

Undetected.

Masquerading as light, as open-mindedness, as tolerance, as inclusion, as enlightened thinking.

All etched into the brains of unknowing Christians with the same lethal compliance as if the numbers 666 were branded on their foreheads.

An entire outlook and worldview subtly orchestrated by the enemy.

As he made his maiden voyage up the slender pillar inside its glass-enclosed elevator to the top of Seattle's Space Needle, Todd Stewart gazed out on a spectacular view of the city and Puget Sound. The Rhodes compound on Bainbridge Island to the west was well lit. Snow-capped Mount Rainier to the south was visible in the darkness thanks to a squadron of drones circling it, keeping its peak radiant with multicolored spotlights. The entire city was ablaze in light for the celebration. Sailboats and yachts numbering in the thousands cluttered the calm waters of lakes Washington and Union and the many inlets of Puget Sound, crowded so close in Elliott Bay that they floated literally side by side. Spectators with friends on rooftops and penthouses and condo decks might have numbered in the tens of thousands, most already enjoying wine and champagne in anticipation of the show.

Todd reached the top and stepped out into the crowded restaurant, most of whose tables had been removed to maximize floor space. He saw Senator Rhodes across the way making the rounds, beaming, shaking hands, exchanging small talk with the congratulating throng, his newly attentive Secret Service detail of somber agents keeping a close eye on him, Erin Parva keeping watch on them. The president-elect moved freely among the elite crowd. With only one way up—via the elevator Todd had just exited—and the Needle a mile removed from any high rise, which might offer a vantage for a potential sniper, and all the guests thoroughly checked and screened, there were few concerns for Rhodes's safety.

Among the Secret Service contingent Todd did not see Mike Bardolf. He was normally at the senator's side. It was not like him to miss the great moment of triumph. But it would be a relief not having his eagle eye on him.

He noticed the senator coming his way. Rhodes had abandoned the arm sling that, probably wanting to keep the attempt on his life in the public eye, he had worn right up to election day.

"Hello, Todd, good to see you," said Rhodes, shaking Todd's hand as his small retinue circled. "I'm counting on you in the Manor press corps to keep me honest."

"I'll do my best, Sir," replied Todd.

And then he was off to continue greeting the honored few who were his guests for the historic evening.

Half an hour later, explosions of fireworks suddenly lit the night sky. They continued for ten minutes preparatory to the senator's speech.

☆ ☆ ☆

Ward Hutchins's heart wept at the thought of where his beloved country was headed and for the church that was complicit in modernism's lie, if by no other means than going along with it.

How cunningly the deceptions of the times disguised themselves. Christians were no less susceptible than the rest. Frogs in the frying pan of the times. They had helped elect Jeff. What could result in the lives of those who did not perceive the danger but "foul and evil," just as the apostle John foresaw?

In his unbelievable treatise, Mark Forster had seen more eternal themes in Scripture's prophetic sequence than he had ever imagined. He was stunned by Mark's insight.

How foolish he had been all these years, thought Ward, to consider Mark his protégé. The idea now seemed laughable. Quietly behind the scenes, Mark had been plumbing the depths of God's purposes while he had been caught up in the limelight. Mark had passed him long ago.

"God, forgive me!" he whispered. "Forgive my blindness. Thank you for my dear brother Mark and his wisdom into your Word. Now give me courage to right whatever wrong I have done in mistaking the truth."

Ward's prayers fell silent. His thoughts turned to the third of their apartment trio from long ago. *And, heavenly Father, forgive Jeff his blindness. Sting his heart. Pierce his spirit with truth.*

No man was beyond redemption, but he feared Jeff was too far gone in the enemy's deception to find his way back in this life.

"Forgive my lack of faith, Lord!" he cried out. "I do pray for Jeff. My heart aches for him. Help my unbelief!"

Now that his eyes had been opened, what was he to do?

God, give me guidance and wisdom, Ward prayed again.

He had scheduled a major speech a week after the election. It had been his intent to deliver his potential antichrist revelation at that time. "Oh, God, how could I have been so foolish!"

That was now impossible. Instead of canceling, however, might Mark be willing to go onstage with him for the televised event. He would boldly proclaim that he had been shown by his friend that he had misunderstood God's prophetic intent.

That would send shockwaves through the church, Ward thought with a smile.

Then he would turn the podium over to Mark to explain God's true prophetic purposes.

He would call Mark first thing in the morning.

Even as the idea came to him, he knew that Mark would never agree. Mark hated the limelight. In spite of his gift as a biblical teacher, he had never been cut out for the pastorate. Yet henceforth he also realized that Mark needed to be the spokesman for these new perspectives, not him. Mark must increase while Ward Hutchins decreased. Mark was the one to give the clarion call.

Ward smiled. He knew exactly what Mark would say to such a suggestion—that the truth would be revealed one man, one woman at a time, that no televised speeches or rallies would allow the still small Voice to get where God's Spirit needed to live—in the hearts of those men and women, who, in their deepest beings hungered for righteousness and truth.

God, show me what you want me to do and say.

From out of memory, the cryptic message from Lionel Holt about a secret document returned to his mind. The boy had given only vague hints pointing toward revolutionary proposals to transform the fabric of the country. He was under no illusions—the young man was an opportunist. Was he playing both sides? There might be nothing to it. But if there was a possibility that such an agenda existed in writing, did he have a duty as an American, even if no longer a prophetic spokesman, to try to learn more and expose what he could discover?

And Jeff—was he part of it? Or was he but a pawn being manipulated by higher and more invisible forces?

As the fireworks over Seattle spent themselves, President-Elect Jefferson Rhodes took his place atop the observation deck of the Space Needle. Bathed in spotlights from drones flying overhead filming the event, he began. His voice boomed over the city and could be heard from the city center to Microsoft Stadium to upper Queen Anne Hill.

"Good evening, Seattle!" he shouted.

Roars echoed back from the entire city.

"I can hear you! And the whole world will hear us as we embark on an historic quest to take Seattle's groundbreaking innovations in business and leadership, in our culture of inclusion and lifestyle diversity, in the arts and technology, as we take all these to the rest of the nation and throughout the world. We will leave behind the small-mindedness and narrow prejudices of the past. We come together with an historic mandate of a 25-percent victory yesterday, the largest ever in US history. We will mark the half century with giant strides forward into a bright future for all the citizens of the world family. Together we will ride this mandate into the future, and we will change the world."

After several minutes, Ward drew in another breath and bent his face again to the well-worn book in front of him.

He read over the familiar second and third chapters of the Bible's final book that, Mark insisted, along with Malachi contained the key to unlocking what he called the prophetic code. After several minutes, Ward turned ahead to chapter 17:

"I will tell you the mystery of . . . the beast that you saw."

Several blocks away a stealthy figure dressed from head to foot in black knelt on the roof of a twelve-story apartment building adjacent to the exclusive residential complex where the man of God continued his late-night exploration into the high purposes of God.

Far below him, the light still shown in the pastor's study.

Ward Hutchins paused a moment then noted one more phrase:

"This calls for a mind with wisdom."

He leaned back and closed his eyes. *Oh, Lord*, he prayed silently, *I cannot but wonder if enough people are left in your church, as John says, with minds of wisdom. Who will listen when the warning is sounded? Has a believing remnant even survived? Or has the Ally so deadened the hearing, even of your people, who have eyes but do not see and—*

The high-powered rifle was equipped with a deadly accurate scope and silencer. The muffled burst from the rooftop two hundred yards away was scarcely audible. The bullet did not completely shatter the surrounding glass. Only a tiny hole punctured through it—spewing but a small splattering into the room.

The tinkling of glass created but a momentary sound. A handful of tiny shards fell to the floor.

Lethal.

Final.

Heard by no human ear.

Ending in a heartbeat all doubts, plans, and questions, the words of prayer were swallowed into the heart of him to whom they had been spoken.

Blood spurted from the faithful man's head. Deidra Hutchins, asleep downstairs, heard nothing. She found her husband the following morning, stiff and cold, slumped in the chair where death had been instantaneous.

A pool of red—darkening as it dried and seeping onto the pages beneath—spread out across the onion skin of the Bible on the desk. It obscuring the words read only moments before the man of God's unexpected journey to eternity:

"The second angel poured his bowl into the sea, and it became like the blood of a dead man."

THIS ENDS BOOK 2

Tribulation Cult Book 3 follows: *Hidden Jihad*

CHARACTER LIST

THE MARSHALLS—THREE GENERATIONS

Stirling and Larke (Stevens)	1941–2032, 1942–2031
Woodrow (m. Cheryl Burns)	1973
Cateline (m. Clancy Watson)	1974
Graham (m. Lynn Davies)	1976
Jane (m. Wade Durant)	1978
Timothy (m. Jaylene Gray)	1980, 1983
Heather	2014

THE FORSTERS—THREE GENERATIONS

Robert and Laura (Clay)	1973, 1976
Janet (m. Collis Nason)	1998
Mark (m. Grace Thornton)	2000, 2001
Ginger	2028
Craig	2030
Gayle (m. David Dowling)	2005

THE GORDONS—TWO GENERATIONS

Pelham and Isobel (Hamilton)	1939–2014, 1945–2041
David	1971

THE RHODES—THREE GENERATIONS

Harrison and Sandra (Nelson)	1975, 1977
Jefferson (m. Marcia Bergen)	2000
Bradon	2027
Melissa	2029

THE HUTCHINS—TWO GENERATIONS

Truman and Eloise (Warton)	1972, 1973
Sawyer (m. Inga Daven)	1995
Ward (m. Deidra Lindberg)	1999
Linda (m. Cameron Trent)	2000

THE REYBURNS—TWO GENERATIONS

Hank and Valerie (Hart)	1974, 1977
Charles (m. Regina Stone)	2001
Summer	2003
Loni	2005

POLITICAL INDIVIDUALS

Viktor Domokos	1939–2035
Akilah Samara	1993
Slayton Bardolf	1949–2014
Loring	1976
Mike	2001
Amy	2004
Talon Roswell	1950–2043
Storm	1983
Anson	2010
Adriana Carmella Hunt	1989–2033
Harvey and Harriet Jansen	1991, 1992
Elizabeth Wickes Hardy	1996
Todd Stewart	2013

About the Author

MICHAEL PHILLIPS was born (1946) and raised in the small northern California university town of Arcata. After a year at Lincoln University in Pennsylvania, Michael completed his higher education at Humboldt State University (now California State Polytechnic University), where he was a standout miler and half-miler, graduating in 1969 in physics, mathematics, and history. During his final year at Humboldt, he began a small bookstore in his college apartment. He and his wife, Judy, music major and harpist in the university symphony, were married in 1971, the same year  they discovered the life-changing influences of C. S. Lewis and George MacDonald. Moving to nearby Eureka, their One Way Book Shop grew rapidly. For the next thirty-five years, while carrying on their writing and harping pursuits, Michael and Judy's bookstore ministry was a fixture in the life of Humboldt County's Christian community.

MacDonald's profound influence in their lives, coupled with the realization that none of his books were in print and the Victorian author was in danger of being lost to posterity, prompted Michael, amid the busy life of a rapidly expanding business and homeschooling their three sons, to begin the ambitious task of editing and republishing

MacDonald's works. At the same time he began writing seriously in his own right, publishing several books in the 1970s.

Michael's efforts inaugurated a worldwide renaissance of interest in the forgotten nineteenth-century Scotsman. In the years since, Michael has been known as one whose skillful diligence helped rescue George MacDonald from obscurity. Throughout the following forty years, he has published more than eighty studies and new editions of MacDonald's writings in diverse formats and is recognized as a man possessing rare insight into MacDonald's heart and spiritual vision.

Paralleling his work with MacDonald, Michael's own author's reputation in Christian circles expanded quickly. He became one of the premier novelists of the Christian fiction boom of the 1980s and 1990s, his books appearing on numerous CBA bestseller lists with an enthusiastic worldwide following.

In 2021 Michael and Judy celebrated their fiftieth anniversary. Michael continues to write as prolifically as ever. Judy continues the ministry of her harp music, teaching and as a therapeutic musician in several hospitals and medical facilities.

Recognized as one of the most versatile and prolific Christian writers of our time, Michael's wide-reaching corpus and the multiple genres of his work now encompass well over a hundred titles. For many years his books have demonstrated keen insight and uncommon wisdom to probe deeply into issues, relationships, and cultural trends. His writings are personal and challenging. He encourages readers to think in fresh ways about the world and themselves.

The impact of Michael's writing is perhaps best summed up by Paul Young, author of *The Shack*, who said, "When I read . . . Phillips, I walk away wanting to be more than I already am, more consistent and true, a more authentic human being."

A FEW NOTABLE TITLES BY MICHAEL PHILLIPS

FICTION

Rift in Time
Hidden in Time
The Secret of the Rose (4 volumes)
Secrets of the Shetlands (3 volumes)
American Dreams (3 volumes)
Angel Harp
Legend of the Celtic Stone

NON-FICTION

Endangered Virtues and the Coming Ideological War
George MacDonald, Scotland's Beloved Storyteller
George MacDonald, A Writer's Life
The Commands of the Prophets
The Commands of Jesus
The Commands of the Apostles
Make Me Like Jesus
The Eyewitness Bible (5 volumes)

INFORMATION AND BOOK AVAILABILITY CAN BE FOUND AT:

https://michaelphillipsbooks.com
https://fatheroftheinklings.com

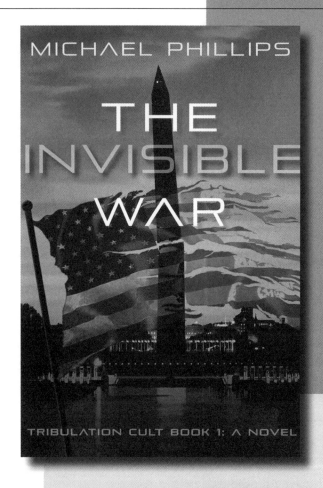

THE INVISIBLE WAR
Tribulation Cult Book 1, A Novel
9781956454321
9781956454338 eBook